Cowgirl Up

Ali Spooner

Affinity
eBook Press
NZ
2014

Cowgirl Up
© 2014 by Ali Spooner

Affinity E-Book Press NZ LLTD
Canterbury, New Zealand

1st Edition

ISBN: 978-1-927328-24-8

Editor: Ruth Stanley
Cover Design: Irish Dragon Designs

Acknowledgments

I would like to thank my readers, for supporting me and providing feedback on my stories.

Thanks to Affinity for continuing to believe, and Irish for the fantastic cover art.

Dedication

To Rhonda, whose encouragement, and patience keep me writing. To Rascal and Shelby, my fur children, thanks for stretching out across my keyboard to remind me to take a deep breath, and smile.

Table of Contents

Also by Ali Spooner

Twisted Lives

The Epitaph

Bailey's Run

Sugarland

Bayou Justice

Chapter One

The heat shimmered in waves off the south Texas asphalt as Coal Bryan drove through the sparse plains, the air-conditioner in her ancient truck struggling to cool the air. She could feel a droplet of sweat slide down the center of her back before it soaked into the green tank top she was wearing. Reflective aviator glasses covered her eyes, protecting them from the glare of the sun as she drove to her destination. It was barely seven in the morning, and the temperature had already risen into the nineties. *Just like being back in Afghanistan.* She focused on the road ahead. Even the large desert hares that would normally dart out in front of traffic were lethargic from the heat, remaining deep in their underground burrows.

†

Melissa Conway, owner of the MC2, fanned herself as she stood on the front porch of her ranch home talking with Stan Watson, her ranch foreman.

"Damn this heat is brutal," she said as she wiped the back of her neck.

"The weatherman claims we'll get some relief later this week when that tropical depression moves inland."

"I just hope we don't melt off the face of the earth before then," she said with a forced smile.

Stan looked up at her and returned her smile. "The only good thing about this heat is it's helping the hay to dry more quickly."

"We have six fields cut, is that correct?"

"Yes, ma'am, we'll start baling and loading later this morning."

Melissa was pleased with his answer. "We are going to need a good supply of hay for this winter, if this heat is indicative of how our weather is going to fluctuate. Hell at this rate, we might even see snow."

Stan shook his head. "I've lived here forty years and haven't seen a flake of snow, but I reckon hell could be freezing over."

A bright flash of sun against chrome pulled their attention down the drive where a beat-up dusty old Chevy was making its way toward them. "I reckon that's our new ranch hand," Stan said. "A fellow named Coal Bryan is joining us today."

"Right now with the hay coming in and a fresh herd of stock to train, we can use all the help we can get," Melissa said.

"This Bryan fellow comes very highly recommended by several top ranchers for his skill with horses. Part Indian, and works some kind of horse charm magic according to a foreman up near Dallas."

"That should be interesting to see."

Melissa was the widow of Mitch Conway and was doing her absolute best at maintaining the MC2 ranch after his untimely death. Mitch was serving in the Texas Reserves when his unit deployed for a tour in Afghanistan. He was two weeks short of rotating back home when he was killed in action. That was nearly a year ago, and she still felt the pain of her loss every day. Mitch had loved the ranch, and she would do anything within her power to keep the ranch profitable and in good repair.

†

Coal pulled the truck up beneath a small tree, which offered the only shade in the yard, and turned off the engine. She rolled down her windows and took a deep breath as she slipped a hat on and stepped out of her truck. She was a friendly sort, but meeting new people, especially new employers always made her feel anxious.

She slipped a work shirt over her shoulders and buttoned it as she walked toward the two figures standing on the porch, watching her carefully.

Stan looked at Melissa when Coal began walking toward them with a look of confusion. "Someone you know?"

Melissa looked at him and shrugged her shoulders. "Your guess is as good as mine."

They both watched in silence as a young woman in her late twenties approached them, her coal-black hair tucked behind her ears.

"Good morning," she said as she stopped at the porch.

"Morning, is there something we can help you with?" Stan asked.

"I'm looking for Mr. Watson, the foreman," she said. "My name is Coal Bryan and I'm here to start to work."

"You're Coal Bryan?"

"Yes, sir."

Stan looked at Melissa with a look of pure terror. They both had assumed their new ranch hand and horse trainer was male. Neither of them expected the woman who stood before them.

Coal had seen that confused look before, and more than once was turned away by prospective employers when they learned she was female. "Are you Mr. Watson?"

"Yes, yes, I am," Stan said as he stepped down off the porch and offered his hand. "This is Mrs. Conway," he said to introduce Melissa. "She owns the MC2."

"I'm pleased to meet you both."

Stan stared at her for what must have seemed an eternity.

"As I said earlier, I'm here to start to work."

He shook his head to clear the cobwebs forming in his mind, looked at her, and then to Melissa, still in disbelief that his new hand was female.

"You have to excuse Stan, we were expecting you to be a man," Melissa said.

"I've my mama to thank for giving me such a name," she said. "I get that reaction often, but I assure you I can pull my weight just like any other hand."

"Well, you've come just in time to help with haying, and in the next few weeks we have twenty head to green break." Stan had finally managed to speak.

"That sounds great to me," Coal said.

"Um, why don't you get your gear and I'll take you to meet the rest of the crew," Stan said.

"Thank you, sir," she said and walked back to her truck.

Stan turned to Melissa with panic in his eyes. "What can I do? I can't put a woman in the bunkhouse with that crew?"

"Relax, she can sleep up here in the house, if that's all you're worried about. Don't discount her just because she's female. There's a feel of toughness with her that I think might just surprise you."

Stan shook his head, totally believing the foreman up in Dallas had duped him. He secretly vowed to exact his revenge the next time he saw him in person.

Coal returned carrying a small suitcase.

"Let me have that and I'll show you the room you will be using later. Have you had breakfast?"

"Yes, ma'am," Coal said as she reluctantly handed Melissa her meager belongings. "I don't need to be housed any differently just because I'm female. I've lived in more than one bunkhouse," she said.

"I'll give you a chance to prove your worth as a ranch hand, but I will not have you living with the likes of these men," Stan said.

"Anything you say then, boss," she said.

"You can cook and eat with the boys, but I prefer you bathe and sleep in the house."

"Very well," she said as she turned to follow him to the bunkhouse.

Melissa watched the graceful movement of the young woman as she followed a suddenly bewildered Stan toward a small building.

✝

Stan opened the door and Coal saw a group of five men seated around a table finishing the last of their breakfast. They were mostly big surly men, ranging in age from early twenties to late forties. "This is Coal Bryan, our new hand," Stan said, turning to her.

"You've got to be kidding, right, boss?" one of the men said. "You expect us to work with a woman?"

The rest of the group broke out in laughter at the prospect. "I just hope and pray you men can keep up with her skills and not embarrass the MC2," Stan said, which immediately brought silence to the group.

"She can sleep in my bunk," the youngest of the bunch said with a grin.

"No, Gene, she will not. I have asked the boss to let her use a back room in the house. I wouldn't expose her to the likes of you at night, even though she insisted she could handle living with you lot."

"Introduce yourselves, and I'll meet you out at the truck in five," Stan said and left the room.

A moment of silence hung in the room until the oldest man stepped forward and offered her his hand. "Harley Boone," he said. "Don't mind this mouthy bunch. They're a good working crew, and they mean well."

"Thanks, Harley, I will work as hard as I can," she said.

The other four men followed Harley's lead and introduced themselves. "I hope you can cook better than the rest of us," Gene said.

"I'm actually a fairly lousy cook, so I'll probably fit right in," she said to a round of laughter.

"Let's go, boys, the daylight's wasting," Harley said.

✝

Melissa took the small bag and carried it into the house into a small bedroom just off the kitchen. She poured herself another cup of coffee and watched as the hands loaded onto the back of a flatbed truck to head out to the hayfields. "Good luck and God bless you," she said aloud as Coal scrambled up behind them on the truck.

5

When they arrived at the first field, Stan assigned each of them to a task. The youngest of the crew, she, Gene, and Lucas, would load and haul the finished bales.

"You wanna stack or load?"

"I'll load," she said. It was the harder of the two jobs, but she needed to prove right away that she could carry her weight.

"Whatever suits you," Lucas said as he hopped back onto the truck.

Harley would run the baler, while another man drove the truck and one more drove the tractor pulling the rake. Stan would be cutting a nearby field, and would leave Harley in charge. "I don't reckon I have to remind you to watch out for rattlers. It's so damned hot they'll curl up in any shade they can find."

They watched as Harley took off behind the rake and the baler began sending out sixty-pound bales of hay. When he was half a row ahead of them, the truck pulled in behind him. Gene and Coal took turns lifting the bales up to Lucas.

Two hours later the first load was full, and they drove back to the barn to lift the bales into the loft for stacking and storing. She and Gene climbed up to the loft and took the bales off the electric winch that lifted them off the truck. The heat was even more stifling inside the loft, so Gene pulled off his shirt to reveal his well-developed and nicely tanned upper body. She pulled off her work shirt revealing an army green tank top. When they finished the load, she tossed the shirt over her shoulder as they rode back out to begin another load.

Harley watched her closely, as did Stan, for any signs of trouble. Both were impressed by her speed and strength. The group worked without complaint until Melissa arrived in her truck to bring them lunch.

She stepped out of the truck and used the tailgate as a table as she laid out a platter of sandwiches, chips, bottles of water, and a pitcher of sweet tea. She had also baked a cake for them, and smiled as each one filed through to make a plate of food. Coal was not shy about her food. She took two sandwiches, a large pile of chips, a bottle of cold water, and sat down on a bale of hay among the crew.

Stan watched as she began to eat then turned with a smile toward Melissa. "So far so good," he said as he fixed his plate.

Melissa sat down with them for lunch and listened to the chatter as they talked about the upcoming weekend, Texas football, and, of course, the weather. She looked beyond Stan as he talked and saw the bare, dark skin of Coal's left shoulder blade as she reached for a drink. Her eyes rested on a familiar tattoo, and she couldn't help but smile.

When all the sandwiches and cake were gone, Melissa packed up the supplies and was about to leave when Stan walked over.

"Did you see her left shoulder?" she asked.

"Yeah, I did, but I don't think the boys recognize what it is just yet."

"I don't think you have to worry much about her," Melissa said before driving away.

Lucas stretched when they reached the truck, ready to return to work.

"We can swap out, and you can stack if you get tired," Lucas said to Coal.

"I'm good, unless you need a rest," she said to him, and then shot him a wink.

"Okay, smartass, load away," he said and hopped back up on the truck.

Gene smiled at her as they began loading the bales onto the truck in the brutal afternoon heat. "You're all right for a girl," he said with a grin.

"I'm so glad you approve," she said to him.

When the sun finally began to sink to the horizon, Harley pulled his tractor to a halt and watched as the last of the bales were loaded onto the truck. Coal and Gene had loaded all day, and he decided to give them a break from the heat. "You two get supper duty while we unload this truck," he instructed them.

Gene felt as if his arms would fall off, but he did not voice a complaint in front of Coal, who still appeared strong enough to go on for hours.

✝

"I hope you know how to cook smothered cubed steak," he said.

"I do, and I can show you how it's done too," she said as they went into the kitchen.

They washed their hands and arms and began preparing the meal.

She prepared the frying pan as Gene coated the meat in seasoned flour as she instructed. They would also have rice and gravy, corn, and fry bread to go with the meal. She began frying the meat and asked Gene to slice and chill several tomatoes for the meal. As she cooked, she walked Gene through mixing corn meal, and demonstrated making fry bread for him. The meal was nearly finished when the rest of the crew entered the bunkhouse.

"Damn, something smells good," Harley said. "Anything I can do to help?"

"Get cleaned up, then you can boil some rice and set the table," she said.

"Yes, ma'am," Harley said with a grin and left the room.

"Is there anything the rest of us can do?" Lucas asked.

"Nope, we don't need too many cooks in the kitchen," Coal said.

"Do we have time to shower then?"

"We should be ready to eat in twenty minutes," she said.

Harley returned and boiled a large pot of rice, then set the table. She handed him a platter of cubed steak and asked him to place it on the table then bring her the carton of milk to make the gravy. The rest of the crew came in and took seats around the table, their mouths watering, as they smelled the meal being prepared.

"Finally, someone who can make gravy," Harley said as she poured up a bowl of the milk gravy to go with the rice and steaks.

Lucas poured them all glasses of tea and they all sat around the table filled with food. "This looks like a real meal," Harley said. "Thank you, Coal and Gene."

"Coal did most of it," Gene said with a bashful smile.

"You'll know how to cook it next time," she said.

"Dig in, boys," Harley said.

They were just about finished with the meal when Melissa knocked on the door and stepped inside carrying another cake she had baked earlier. "Something smells delicious," she said as she walked to the table.

"It was delicious," Lucas said. "May I fix you a plate?"

Melissa fixed her eyes on the food on the table and knew immediately who had cooked the meal. "You know, I wouldn't mind a bite, and all this looks delicious," she said as Gene got up and offered her his seat.

"Coal and Gene cooked us a fabulous meal," Harley said. "We haven't eaten this good since the last time you cooked for us," he told Melissa.

"This is very good," Melissa said as she took a bite.

Coal finished her meal and stood to begin clearing off the table.

"You cooked we clean," Lucas said, "so have a seat and relax for a little bit."

"You have a deal, but I hope one of you guys can cook eggs," she said. "Mine always turn out like rubber."

"Harley is the breakfast wizard around here," Gene said. "He makes one mean killer omelet."

"That sounds really good."

"Breakfast is at seven, so don't be late or these hounds will have eaten it all," Harley said. "Are you a coffee drinker?"

"Unless I can get it straight through an IV," she said.

"It's strong, but it'll get you moving in the mornings."

"In more than one way," Gene said with a chuckle.

Melissa finished her meal and turned to her. "Are you ready to see your room and get a shower?"

"Yes, ma'am, if it's not inconvenient for you."

"No, not at all," Melissa answered.

"I'll see you boys in the morning then."

"Thanks for a great meal, Coal."

"You're most welcome."

They left the men to chatter amongst themselves as they walked up to the farmhouse.

"She's a damned good worker." Coal heard one of the hands say before they closed the door.

✝

"You appear to be fitting in quite well with the boys," Melissa said.

"A good meal goes a long way with hungry men."

"It's not just that. Stan told me that you worked as hard or harder as the rest of them all day in this heat."

"I'm used to the heat and hard work, ma'am."

Melissa waited to see if she would elaborate on her comment, but she remained silent as she gave her a tour of the house. Melissa opened a bedroom door and Coal found her bag sitting at the end of the bed.

"The bathroom is there," she said. "Make yourself at home, and let me know if you need anything."

"Thank you, Mrs. Conway."

"Please just call me Melissa."

"Yes, ma'am."

✝

Coal watched her walk from the room, then picked up her suitcase and laid it open on the bed. She took out the few items of clothing that she had and tucked them away in a small dresser. She left out a pair of shorts and another tank top of army issue and went in search of a hot shower. She showered, dressed, and then slipped on a worn pair of tennis shoes. She reached into the outer pocket of her suitcase, pulled out a small wooden object, and left the house.

Melissa heard the shower start as she walked into the living room to watch some television. She was deep into a program when she heard the back door open and close.

The moon was full and lit the yard as Coal walked over to the corral, where twenty or so horses were milling around, and climbed the fence. She lifted a wooden flute to her mouth and began to play. Several heads popped up from the curious horses to study her when they heard the music, and they slowly began to move closer to her.

Melissa had left a window cracked for some fresh air, and a haunting melody floated across the yard from the corral to soothe her senses. The music was refreshing and relaxing. Melissa found herself pulled toward it. She glanced out the window and saw Coal sitting on the top rail of the corral as the horses crowded around her. She listened for a half hour, and when she could no longer hold her eyes open, she walked to her room and climbed into the bed. She could still hear the faint sound of the flute as she drifted off to sleep.

Coal looked over the stock as she played and was very pleased with the confirmation of the horses. Strongly built, they would make excellent pleasure or working stock. She didn't mind the labor of haying or fence work, but really looked forward to training the young horses. She preferred to use the techniques developed by her ancestors with Apache bloodlines to train horses. She was pleased to see a large lake behind the barn; it would work into her plans perfectly. She was sure the rest of the hands would train the young horses using traditional domination methods to break the spirit of the horse, but hopefully she would be able to train a large portion of them.

A beautiful black stallion caught her attention as he eyed her curiously. He was solid black except for a white star on his forehead, and if not for the star and the bright moonlight, he would have been almost invisible, moving like a shadow in the night.

Her body reminded her that she was exhausted from a long day in the heat, and it didn't appear there was a break in the weather on the horizon. She climbed down and walked to the house, entering the back door and slipping quietly into her room. The cool sheets felt wonderful against her skin, and she was asleep seconds after her head hit the pillow.

Chapter Two

Coal woke up just after sunrise and dressed, then slipped quietly from the house to walk to the bunkhouse. Melissa watched her as she walked quickly across the yard and disappeared.

"Good morning," Harley said when he heard her enter the kitchen. "Grab you some coffee and have a seat." He'd already cooked a large pile of bacon. "How would you like your eggs?"

"Over easy would be great," she said.

"Did you sleep good last night?"

She shot him a smile. "I barely remember lying down."

"This heat can be an ass kicker."

"Yeah, it can, but I've been in worse," she said.

Harley waited to see if she would elaborate, but instead she walked over to the counter and dropped some bread in the toaster. "The rest of the crew still sleeping?" she asked.

"Yeah, I usually get up early, eat and then cook for them as they get up," Harley said.

"That's very nice of you. Have you eaten yet?"

"No, so drop me some toast too. There's homemade apple jelly in the fridge."

Coal took him two plates and put utensils out on the table as she waited for the toast.

"You did a good job yesterday, and I think you even impressed Stan, which isn't easy."

"I try to give a hundred percent to every job. You want butter?" she asked when the toast popped up.

"Yes, please," Harley said as he slid three fried eggs onto her plate and cracked more into the frying pan. "Go ahead before they get cold."

She seasoned her eggs and spread some jelly on her toast. She had just begun to eat when Harley joined her at the table.

"So how did you come about the name Coal?"

"My mother was a full-blooded Apache, and when I was born I had a head full of coal-black hair. When my father remarked on it, she decided that would be a good name for me."

"I bet you have confused quite a few people with that name. I know Stan was expecting you to be male."

"Yeah, I picked up on that pretty quickly yesterday when I arrived," she said with a smirk.

"He's a good man to work for and will treat you fairly as long as you work hard."

"I don't mind the hard work at all," she said and took a bite of bacon. "Thanks for a great breakfast."

"You are very welcome. I took out a pot roast for dinner tonight. Remind me to ask Melissa if she will put it on for us later today."

"Will do. Do you guys like biscuits with your roast?"

"We usually make a few cans."

"How about some homemade ones?" she asked.

"That would be awesome."

"Did I hear someone mention homemade biscuits?" Gene asked as he entered the kitchen.

"Coal is going to make some to go with a pot roast tonight. Grab some coffee and I'll cook you some breakfast in just a minute."

"Take your time; I'm still trying to get my eyes open."

She had finished eating and stood to place her dishes in the dishwasher.

"Did you get enough to eat?"

"Yes, I did, thanks. If you don't need my help I think I'll grab another cup of coffee and go check the stock until the rest of the crew is ready."

"That'll be fine. They should start rolling in now."

"See you in a bit then," she said and left the bunkhouse.

✝

She walked across to the corral and climbed up to the perch she had the previous night. In the daylight, the horses eyed her with more curiosity. The black stallion approached her boldly and sniffed at her worn boots. "You are a handsome devil, and I bet you are as fast as the wind."

His ears pricked forward as if he were listening to her every word.

Her attention was drawn away from the stock as Stan's truck came bouncing down the drive. He saw her sitting on the top rail and smiled as he parked his truck.

"Good morning," she said as he walked toward her.

"Morning, did you rest well last night?"

"Yes, I did, thanks, and you?"

"Slept like a baby. You like what you see here?"

"They're some nice-looking stock. I especially like the young black stallion," she said as the horse danced away from Stan's approach.

"He's a spirited one and is from excellent bloodlines," Stan said. "You have a good eye."

"I've had the good fortune to work with horses all my life."

"I can tell you are ready to get on with the training."

"First things first, we have to finish bringing in the hay," she answered.

"We'll be done soon at this rate. You pushed the boys pretty hard yesterday," he said with a grin.

She was a little surprised at his comment. "I thought it was a productive day, but it didn't seem to be all that hard."

"I bet there wasn't anyone in the bunkhouse that had a hard time getting to sleep last night. Come on, and we can go check while I get some coffee."

"Right behind you, boss," Coal said as she dropped down from the fence.

When they entered, Harley was hollering for the rest of the crew to get a move on so they could get started to work. "This danged heat has everyone feeling lazy," he said to Stan as he and Coal entered the room.

"We could get an earlier start and then lay off during the heat of the day," Stan said. "Don't need anyone dropping from heat stroke."

"Naw, I think we will be fine once we get to moving," Harley said.

She placed her coffee mug in the dishwasher and said, "I'll wait for y'all out at the truck."

"She's a good worker, and a great cook," Harley said to Stan.

"I've been pleased so far," Stan said as he refilled his coffee mug.

†

It took the crew four more days to finish the first cutting of hay and everyone was glad to be finished with that chore. There would be at least one more cutting, but that wouldn't happen for many weeks yet to come.

When they finished unloading the final truck, Stan passed out the weekly paychecks. Coal intended to cash hers and use it to buy some extra clothing for work as her few pairs of jeans were starting to look threadbare. Gene asked for a ride into town so together they piled in her truck and headed off the ranch for town.

Gene gave her the ten-minute tour of downtown, and then directed her to the bank so they could cash their paychecks. "Man, I can taste some cold beers now," Gene said as he tucked the cash into his wallet.

"I need to pick up some jeans, and then we'll head back," Coal said. Earlier in the day, she heard the boys discussing going to town for a few cold beers and knew that they would head back in after supper to kick up their heels. The boys had invited her, but she hadn't made up her mind yet if she was going to join them.

"McCoy's is the best place for jeans," he said, giving her directions.

They walked in together and Gene noticed a few of the customers eyeing her closely as she walked over to a rack of jeans. He smiled to himself as he joined his new friend. "Finding what you need?"

"Yes, my old Levi's are beginning to fall apart," she said as she selected three new pair.

"You should take your old ones into the flea market. People will pay an arm and a leg for worn-out jeans," he joked. "It's beyond me to understand why they would pay good money for jeans with holes and tears, but they do."

She smiled up at him. "You got me on that one. I prefer breaking in my own jeans."

She paid for her purchases and they returned to the truck. "Have you given more thought about coming out with us tonight?" he asked as they drove home.

"I just spent most of my paycheck, but I may drop in and see what you fellows are up to," she answered.

Gene smiled broadly. "You wouldn't have to worry about buying beers. Me and the boys would keep you flowing."

"Actually, I'm not much of a drinker, but I do enjoy a good game of pool."

"Harley is actually pretty good and makes a few extra bucks when we go into town," Gene said, "so don't let him hustle you."

"Thanks for the warning," she said as they turned back down the dusty drive. "I sure hope we get some rain soon, all this dust is making my truck look bad," she teased.

"It's supposed to rain like crazy starting sometime tomorrow," he said. "We have the weekend off so we will probably be stuck inside the whole time."

"At least we don't have to load any more hay for a while."

"Amen to that, I can't wait to start training the stock."

"Me too," she answered. When they arrived at the ranch, she turned to him. "Who's cooking tonight?"

"Lucas is making spaghetti and garlic bread. It's usually not too toxic," he added with a grin.

"I'm going to go shower. I'll be out soon," she said as they went their separate ways.

†

There was no sign of Melissa when she entered the house so Coal went straight for a shower. She felt like she rinsed several pounds of dust from her skin, and when she emerged from the shower she felt renewed and relaxed. She would have dinner with the boys then join them for a few drinks and a game or two of pool. It had been a long week though, so she would not stay out long. She returned to her room and got dressed in a pair of her new jeans, a relatively new shirt, and her better pair of ropers. She walked out of her room to return to the bathroom and saw Melissa coming down the hall.

"Not you too," she said with a voice filled with mock disgust.

"What?" she asked with a genuinely confused look on her face.

"You are one of those folks who can walk in a store and wear new clothes out without alterations. I always have to have my new jeans hemmed after I cut about four inches off them."

Coal laughed softly at her humorous comment. "I'm just lucky like that. Besides if I didn't get some new jeans soon you were going to be seeing a lot more of me than intended."

"I'm sure the boys wouldn't mind. Are you going into town with them tonight?"

"I thought I'd join them for a short while. I'm tired, though, so I won't be out late. Are you going?"

"Heaven's no. I intend to curl up with a good book and pray for some danged rain."

"Just let it hold off until I get home, will ya?" she asked.

"I'll try my best."

She walked through the kitchen to leave the house. "I'll try to be quiet and not disturb you when I get back."

"No worries, when my head hits the pillow these days I'm out for the night."

"See you tomorrow then."

"Have fun, and try to keep the boys out of trouble."

"Yes'm, I'll try, but no guarantees."

She walked across the yard, into the bunkhouse and to the kitchen. Gene had just entered the room also.

"You clean up pretty well," he teased.

"I wish I could say the same for you," she said as she ruffled his hair. The rest of the crew burst out in laughter.

"That was cruel," Lucas said as he took a cookie sheet of garlic bread from the oven.

"Smells good," she said. "Do you need help?"

"Nope, I've got it under control. Pour a drink and have a seat," he answered.

"So you are going to come into town after all?" Harley asked.

"Gene talked me into a few beers, but I won't be out late."

"Would you mind if I rode back with you then? I can't keep up with these wild young'uns."

She laughed softly and said, "Not at all."

The spaghetti dinner was actually tasty and within an hour, the kitchen was clean and the crew of the MC2 was on their way to town. Harley and Gene climbed into her truck while the rest piled into Lucas's truck.

"Where are we going, boys?" she asked as she started the truck.

"Just follow Lucas. He knows the way to the Stockyard," Gene said with an eager grin.

Coal pulled in behind him and they drove to town. They turned past McCoy's and drove to the eastern edge of town to a small bar across from the county stockyards. "I guess the name is pretty self-explanatory."

They walked inside and Lucas paid the small cover charge for her. "Welcome to our hangout," he said as he offered her his arm. She laughed and allowed him to lead her to a table while the others followed.

"What can I get you to drink?" Harley asked.

"What are you having?"

"I stick to Coors Light," he answered.

"That sounds good to me. Bottle please, if they have it."

Harley smiled. "Coming up," and walked to the bar.

The bar was bigger on the inside than it looked, and it was crowded early for a Friday night. Couples were dancing, and there was a small crowd gathered around the three pool tables. "They have a single-elimination doubles tournament every week," Gene said. "You and Harley should enter."

"You are assuming that I can play that good."

"I have no doubt," he said with a devilish grin.

"What's the entry fee?"

"Twenty bucks," Gene said. "I can spot you your half if you need me to," he offered.

"Thanks, but I think I can handle it. What do you think, Harley?" she asked as the big man walked up carrying a round of beers.

"Think about what?" he said.

"Gene says you and I need to enter the tournament, you up for it?"

Harley smiled brightly at her. "Why the hell not." He handed Gene a twenty and said, "Go sign us up."

Gene disappeared like a flash of lightning and returned moments later. "You are next up on table two."

"You do know how to shoot pool, right?" Harley asked.

"That's the game with three strikes and you're out, right?" she teased. "Yeah, I can generally hold my own."

"Figured you could," Harley said with a chuckle. "Is there anything besides cooking eggs you don't do well?"

"I can't sew a stitch," she answered.

"Well, damn, I guess I will have to reconsider my marriage proposal," Harley said. "Let's go take a look at the competition."

She followed Harley and Gene over to the tables. There were only ten teams competing so it wouldn't take long to finish the tournament, especially playing on three tables.

It only took three matches for Coal and Harley to make it to the finals, and when they dropped the final team, they collected the two-hundred-dollar pot, and made their way back to a table. Harley handed her a hundred dollars, and she gave him back ten.

"What's this for?"

"My share of the entry fee," she said.

Harley tucked the money in his pocket as one of the crew showed up with a fresh round of beers. "Thanks, but three's my limit," Coal said.

"I'm gonna pass too and call it an early night," Harley said. "Is your offer of a ride still good?"

"Of course it is," she answered. "You ready?"

"Yes'm, I am."

"I think I will head back too," Gene said.

"See the rest of you guys tomorrow then," she said, just as fireworks began.

Lucas had been dancing with a leggy blonde all during the pool tournament. Her boyfriend, a cowboy from a neighboring ranch, was on the losing team. He received all kinds of ribbing from his crew about losing to a girl, so he already had a chip on his shoulder. When he found Lucas all snuggled up with his girl on the dance floor, Billy Ray lost the remaining hold on his temper.

"It's time to go, Betty Jean," he said as he spun her around on the dance floor.

"Easy man," Lucas said when she cried out in pain from the tight grip he held on her arm.

"Stay out of this or we'll take it outside," Billy Ray snarled.

"Take your hands off her," Lucas said.

"Okay, punk, let's take this outside, and we'll see who gets the next dance," Billy Ray challenged. Several of his buddies with their girls draped over them were watching from a distance.

"Let's do it," Lucas said and started for the door.

Coal, Gene, and Harley followed him out. "You know what you're doing here, son?" Harley asked.

"Standing up for a lady," Lucas said. "We were only dancing."

"I hope she is worth it," Harley said with a lopsided grin.

Billy Ray had a reputation as a brawler. His behavior had caused him to be banned from many a bar in his young life. Harley hoped that Lucas was man enough to hold his own as a small crowd gathered round.

Lucas stepped away from them as Billy Ray, and two of his friends approached. "Let's get him, boys, and mess him up."

"That's not exactly fair odds," Coal said.

"So what you gonna do about it, bitch?" Billy Ray said.

She stepped up beside Lucas. Gene made a move to stop her, but Harley caught him by the shoulder. "Just wait," he said.

Gene looked at Harley, completely bewildered, but stood his ground.

"This is getting better by the minute," Billy Ray said.

Coal looked at Lucas. "I want the big ugly one."

"Take your pick, they are all big and ugly," he said with a grin.

Billy Ray and his boys rushed them, Billy Ray coming in after Lucas while one of his crew took a swing at her. She easily dodged the blow and sent him sailing across the gravel parking lot with a powerful kick to his midsection. The other man looked at his friend sprawled on the ground and tentatively rushed her. This man ended up with a boot to his face, which broke his nose and left him on his knees crying like a baby. The first man got up, decided he didn't want any more of Coal, and pushed his way through the growing crowd.

Lucas wasn't so lucky. A solid right from Billy Ray and a cut lip had blood running down his chin. He landed a few blows, but they had little effect on the more solid Billy Ray. Billy Ray knocked him to the ground and was about to start kicking him when she moved quickly to sweep his legs out from under him.

"Didn't your mama teach you not to kick someone when he's down?" she asked.

"You are really starting to piss me off," Billy Ray said as he picked himself up from the ground.

"So bring what you got," she said, fixing her dark eyes on him.

He hesitated for a moment, intimidated by her challenge, but the goading of the crowd sent him rushing toward her. Coal easily stepped aside and he barreled headfirst into a parked truck. He stumbled and turned back toward her. She landed a powerful blow with her right fist to his jaw. Billy Ray took two steps and dropped to his knees.

"I think it's time we made an exit," she told Lucas. "He's going to wake up even meaner than before."

"You're right. Gene, go get the rest of the crew," Lucas said. "Thanks for your help. I could have taken them, though."

"Sure you could," she said and handed him a rag to wipe his bleeding face.

Gene returned with the rest of the boys. "You were awesome," Gene said from the backseat as they headed for home. "I've never seen anyone take Billy Ray down like that."

"You okay?" Harley asked.

"Yeah, I'm fine. It's not the way I wanted to spend my first Friday night in town, but it couldn't be helped."

"Maybe not, but I doubt you will have any more trouble from Billy Ray, or his boys."

"I hope not, but their kind tends to hold a grudge, and it's obvious they don't fight fair," she said.

They drove back and parked their trucks at the ranch. A light rain began to fall as Coal headed for the house and Gene and the boys took Lucas to the bunkhouse to patch him up.

In the bunkhouse, Harley was tending to Lucas's busted lip. "Man, I have never seen a woman fight like that," Gene said. "Why did you stop me from helping her out?" he asked Harley.

"Have none of you paid any attention to the tattoo on her left shoulder?" he asked.

"No, I guess not," Lucas said. "Why, what is it?"

"Coal wears the ink of an Army Ranger, the toughest of the tough. She could have taken on all three men easily with the training she's had."

"Damn," Gene said, even more impressed with her.

"Well, I'm glad she was there tonight. I was about to get my ass kicked."

"No about to it, Billy Ray was giving you a good pounding. I would give him a wide berth the next time you see him if I were you. That one's as mean as a rattlesnake."

Lucas winced from the cold rag Harley placed on his lip.
The knuckles of Coal's right hand were a bit tender as she undressed in the darkness. The pain would go away soon enough, and she must admit it did feel good to kick some ass. She climbed into the bed and listened as the rain pelted down on the tin roof, falling quickly asleep.

Chapter Three

The next morning Coal woke to the sound of the rain pouring down. She crept from the bed and dressed before washing her face and brushing her teeth. She walked through the house to go check on the boys and get some breakfast. When she stepped outside, she found Melissa sitting on the porch drinking coffee and watching the rain.

"Good morning," she said as Coal approached. "Grab yourself a cup of coffee and join me if you'd like."

"You need a refill?"

"No, I'm good. Thanks."

She poured a cup of coffee, and joined her boss on the porch.

"Y'all came back early last night," she said. "Did you have a good time?"

"Yeah, it was great. Harley and I won the pool tournament, and then Lucas got in a bit of a tussle with a big thug named Billy Ray and two of his buddies."

"Oh, that Billy Ray is a rough character. Was anyone hurt?"

"Lucas has a busted lip, and probably a headache today, but otherwise he's no worse for wear."

Melissa chuckled at her answer. "That's good to hear. I'm sorry it ruined your evening."

"I was already on my way out when the ruckus started so no big deal."

Melissa went silent for a few minutes. "I'm glad we got the rest of the hay in before this rain hit."

"Me too, but I'm glad to see the rain. We needed it, and a break from the heat."

"Amen to that," Melissa said. "Stan is very impressed with your work ethic."

"I believe in a hard day's work for a fair wage," Coal said.

"Do you have plans for today?" Melissa asked.

"I thought I'd go check on the boys and have some breakfast with them. Is there something you need?"

"I was thinking about going to town for some groceries if you'd like to ride along. It doesn't look like there is much else to be done today."

"That sounds good, what time did you want to go?"

"No rush; just whenever you finish with the boys. Make a list of any items they need in the bunkhouse if you would."

"Not a problem," she said with a smile and stepped off the porch to rush across the yard in the rain.

†

She walked into the bunkhouse to find Harley finishing breakfast and sipping on some coffee. It was still relatively early, and there was no sign of the rest of the crew.

"Good morning," Coal said as she walked to the coffeepot.

"Good morning. What would you like for breakfast?"

"That omelet looks tasty," Coal said as she sat down across from him with a pad and pen. "The boss and I are going to do some grocery shopping, and she asked for a list of items we need."

"Let me finish eating and I'll whip you up some breakfast," he said. "Groceries, hmm, let me think. We

24

definitely need eggs, bread, bacon, sausage, and milk. Probably wouldn't hurt to get some butter and syrup too."

"Any ideas for what we will have for suppers next week?"

"I think I'll thaw out some steaks for tonight if this rain will let up some. Let's plan on some pork chops, maybe some fried chicken, some chicken and rice, maybe another roast. Hey, can you cook chicken and dumplings?"

"Yes, I can. Is that a request?"

"That would be great."

"Okay, what else?" she asked.

"I think me and the boys will do some cleaning this afternoon so please pick up some cleaning supplies, oh, and some toilet paper," he added with a grin.

"Cleaning chemicals, sponges, toilet cleaner, paper towels," she said. "Anything else?"

"Not at the moment," Harley said as he moved to the stove to begin cooking her breakfast. "Maybe the others will have some requests as they start coming in. Oh, yeah, coffee, filters, sugar, and creamer."

"This list may take us all morning," she teased. "Do we need tea bags?"

"Probably so," Harley said.

Gene came wandering into the kitchen. "Morning," he said, his eyes still hanging heavy from sleep. "Is it still raining?"

"It's been pouring all night," Harley said. "You want an omelet?"

"Sounds good, Harley," he answered as he sat down with Coal. "Are you making a shopping list?"

"Yes, I am. Do you have any requests?"

"More of your biscuits," he said with a sheepish grin.

She smiled at him and added a few ingredients to the shopping list. "How does Lucas look this morning?"

"He's got one heck of a shiner and his lip's still swollen, but I think he'll live. He should be here any minute."

Coal finished her breakfast and returned to the house to find Melissa ready to go to town. The rain had slacked off to a heavy sprinkle. "Do you want me to go get the truck?"

"Thanks, but I assure you I won't melt."

"Just asking," she said.

"I appreciate that too," Melissa said with a warm smile. "Come on, let's make a run for it."

The closer they got to town, the clearer the skies became. When they pulled into the lot at the grocery store, the sun was peeking through the clouds. "I think we'll need a couple of carts for this list."

Coal walked over to where the carts were stored and grabbed another. "Should we take our lists and split up?"

"That sounds good. I'll join you when I finish my list," Melissa said and headed off down an aisle.

She fished out her list and started her shopping. Thirty minutes later, Melissa joined her and they picked out the last of the items together. "I can't imagine feeding this crew every week," Coal said.

"I can't afford to pay you what you guys are really worth, so the least I can do is feed you, and put a roof over your heads."

"Most ranches wouldn't do that," she said.

"That's true, but we aren't most ranches."

"Point taken," Coal said as she followed Melissa to the checkout.

As they were emerging from the store, a shiny red truck skidded to a halt in front of them. She looked up to find Billy Ray glaring at her.

"Morning, Billy Ray," she said sweetly.

"Fuck you, dyke," he snarled. A large purple bruise covered the left side of his face.

"I really do need to talk to your mama about teaching you some manners," Coal said.

"Billy Ray, you have no need to be nasty," Melissa said.

"I can't believe you take in the likes of her, you stupid bitch."

Coal had heard enough. She stopped pushing her cart and began walking toward Billy Ray. "You are a spineless coward without your boys to back you up. Step out, and I'll give you a better lesson than I did last night, since that didn't seem to make it through your thick, dumb head."

Billy Ray considered her challenge for a minute until he saw the anger flashing in her dark eyes. "You aren't worth the sweat," he said as he spat a stream of tobacco juice toward her.

"You wouldn't be standing long enough to break a sweat," Coal told him.

"Too funny," he said and threw the truck in gear, burning rubber as he left the parking lot.

"He's not one to be messed with," Melissa warned.

"I won't mess with him, but I won't back down from his attempts to bully people. He and two of his buddies were going to pound the stew out of Lucas last night."

"You did that damage to Billy Ray?" she asked with a smirk.

"Yeah, he was about to start kicking the snot outta Lucas while he was down. I couldn't let that happen."

"No wonder he's so pissed off. Billy Ray thinks he rules the Stockyard, and to be taken down by a woman has got to be very demoralizing to him."

"Don't tell me you feel sorry for the jerk," she said.

"Hell no I don't, but you would be wise to watch your back when he's anywhere near. He doesn't forgive and forget very well."

"I'll heed your advice, but if he leaves me no choice I will take him down a few more notches."

"I would expect nothing less from you, Coal. By the way, Gene already worships you, just so you know."

She smiled and chuckled at her comment. "He's a good kid, he just needs growing up."

†

They loaded the groceries in the truck and made it back to the ranch just as the skies were starting to open up again. The crew rushed out, unloaded the groceries, and Gene parked the truck back in the garage. Coal and Melissa put away her groceries in silence.

"I'm going to see if I can find a good movie on the tube if you'd like to join me," Melissa offered.

"Sure, doesn't look like I'm gonna get to do anything outside today."

"Probably not. Grab yourself a drink and I will meet you in the den in just a minute."

Coal took a cold bottle of water and walked to the den. Her eyes took in the room and landed on a grouping of pictures that drew her attention. She walked closer for a better look and gasped as she recognized several of the photos. Melissa walked into the room just as Coal's eyes fluttered and she fainted, her bottle of water spilling across the floor. The love seat broke her fall, but she still slithered in slow motion to the floor.

"Coal," Melissa cried out and ran across the room. She grabbed up the bottle of water, and placed the cool plastic against her skin as she cradled Coal's head in her lap. "Coal, Coal, please wake up," she pleaded.

Coal felt the cool, strong hands on her face as they brushed the hair away from her eyes, and heard the urgency in her voice. It took her several attempts, but she was finally able to open her eyes and stare up at Melissa.

"There you are," Melissa said when she was able to hold her eyes open. "What happened? Are you okay?"

She sat up. Her eyes returned to the pictures on the wall and she burst into tears. Melissa, bewildered by this behavior, pulled Coal into her arms and held her close as the sobs wracked her body. Her hand stroked across her hair as she whispered soothing words to her.

When she could regain her composure, she pulled away from Melissa's embrace. "I'm sorry. I didn't mean to break down like that."

"It's okay, but what happened?"

Coal pointed at the pictures hanging on the wall. "I took those."

"The photographs from Afghanistan?" she asked.

"Yes, the ones of Major Mitch and Tessa," she said.

"That was my husband," Melissa said.

"And my lover," she answered. "I'm sorry, I didn't make the connection of the Conway name."

"There's no need to apologize. Come sit with me and we can talk," Melissa said as she took her hand and guided her around to sit on the love seat.

Coal rubbed her face with her left hand. "I should have known. He talked about Melissa all the time."

"So you served with Mitch?"

"Yes, my unit was assigned to sniper protection for Mitch and his crew. I took that picture of him and Tessa about two months after we arrived."

"Tessa was your lover?"

"Yes," she confirmed. "We had been together for almost two years when we got called back up. She assisted Mitch with defusing the bombs."

"Where is she now?"

Coal took a deep breath. "She's buried at Arlington."

"I'm so sorry," Melissa said.

"She was with Mitch when a terrorist triggered a bomb they were working on, and they died together."

"Can you tell me what happened? I was only told he was killed in action."

Tears threatened to fall again.

"I'm sorry, I have no right to ask you to relive that," she said.

"No, you have every right to know what happened that day," she said. "I need something to drink though."

"Would you like water or something stronger?"

"Something stronger," she answered.

Melissa walked over to the bar, poured two stiff shots of Gentleman Jack, and carried them back to the love seat. She handed Coal a glass and sat beside her.

She took a sip of the strong liquor, and then ran her hand through her hair. "We were only two weeks from cycling out when we got a call. It was one of the hottest days we had, and it was barely eight in the morning."

Melissa shifted on the love seat and watched Coal as she struggled with her memories.

"We geared up and headed for the small neighborhood where a reported car bomb would take out several housing units if it were activated." She remembered the day all too well. How the sweat trickled down her back and face, and how it seemed to sizzle as it hit the dusty pavement. She and Tessa had spent most of the previous night making plans for a vacation once they cycled out, and then made love until late in the night. A smile played on her face for a brief moment, but quickly faded.

Melissa sat and patiently waited for Coal to resume her story. She could see the reflection of happiness, and then pain as she remembered the day over a year ago.

"It seemed like a routine call at first. A late-model sedan parked on the curb in front of a housing unit. The streets were vacant, and not even a breeze disturbed the heat waves as they danced across the pavement."

Melissa shifted, and Coal took another sip.

"It was a Saturday morning and the streets should have been alive with families going to market, children playing soccer in the streets, women hanging out wash, but there was nothing, nothing at all until a small child began crying, and walking down the street."

"Where did he come from?"

"I never knew. He was about four and crying at the top of his lungs as he walked toward the parked car. I yelled at one of the men closest to the child to secure him and find his family. The bomber used the child as a distraction. I looked up to a curtain-covered window in time to see him press a button to activate the bomb Mitch was hovering over."

She took another deep breath. "I pulled the trigger of my rifle a split second too late to stop him. Mitch must have heard the click of the remote detonation because he threw his body across the bomb to dampen its range. Shrapnel exploded into Tessa's body, and the rest of the unit got showered with flying shrapnel fragments. I ran as hard as I could, but Mitch was instantly gone, and Tessa died in my arms waiting on a chopper to airlift her to the hospital."

Coal looked up to Melissa. "Mitch saved the rest of us from being killed or seriously injured when he sacrificed himself." She looked at Melissa and found tears streaming down her face.

"Thank you for giving me that information," Melissa said. "I tried to get more details, but ran up against too much red tape to get a final answer."

"I'm sure it's still classified information, but I don't care. You have a right to know how bravely Mitch died."

"May I share something with you?" Melissa asked.

"Yes, of course."

Melissa stood and walked over to a large rolltop desk and opened a drawer to pull out a stack of envelopes. These were her precious letters written by Mitch. She searched through several of them until she found the one she wanted and carried the back page to Coal. "This is part of the letter that came with that picture," she said.

Coal took the familiar army-issued stationery and held it in her hand while she read.

I'm adding a picture I hope you will enjoy. In the picture is Tessa, a young, bright woman who is also a third-grade teacher in Dallas. She and her lover, another soldier, are so head over heels in love that it makes me smile and think of you when I see them together. Coal took the picture, so I will have to get another and send it soon so you can see Coal and Tessa together.

A tear slid down her cheek as she reread the letter.

"I never realized the Coal he referred to in his letter was a woman, and still didn't make the connection when you showed up this week. The Ranger ink on your shoulder should have jogged my memory, but it didn't."

"I guess it's just a small world," Coal said as she handed the letter back to Melissa.

"Did you have the option of bringing Tessa back to Texas?"

"No, her father is retired military and insisted she be interred at Arlington. I visit as often as I can, but DC is a long way from Texas."

Melissa's heart ached with the pain in her voice. "Tessa will always be with you in your heart, so don't feel like you need to stand vigil over a grave."

Coal nodded her head and took some comfort from Melissa's words but felt mentally exhausted from the conversation. "If you don't mind I'm going to pass on the movie and lay down for a bit."

"I don't mind at all. I'm sorry if I upset you."

Coal stood to walk to her room. "I just wasn't expecting this."

†

Melissa watched her walk from the room and curled her legs beneath her as she sifted through the stack of letters from Mitch. She read several of the letters before the effects of the liquor made her sleepy, and she curled into a ball on the love seat and napped.

✝

Coal had returned to her room, collapsed on the bed, and allowed her tears to flow freely until she cried herself to sleep. She slept for an hour then woke with a start from a dream. She was back in Afghanistan with Tessa and Mitch, reliving the terror of their deaths once more in her dream. Covered with a cold sweat she climbed from the bed and walked out to the back porch. Still frazzled from the dream, she decided to go for a walk to clear her head. The rain had stopped as she started across the yard at a brisk pace. She walked deep into a pasture they would be cutting in a few weeks for hay, and made her way to a grove of red oak trees. There were six trees in a crescent around a small lake and Coal found a bend of a low branch to sit. The quiet crept in around her as her mind relaxed among the ancient trees.

The black stallion had watched as she walked across the pasture. With a burst of speed, he cleared the fence of the corral and followed the strange human until she reached the grove of trees. When she sat down on the branch, he stopped and watched her for several minutes before approaching.

Coal reached into her pocket and pulled out her flute. She was playing it softly, staring across the lake, when she heard soft footprints approaching from behind her. She turned slowly to see the stallion standing five feet from her. "How did you get here?"

He looked at her with his bright eyes and took another tentative step toward her. Coal turned to straddle the limb and watch his approach. She remained frozen as he closed the distance between them and lifted his head to nuzzle her hand. She allowed him to smell her hand then lifted it to stroke his face. "You are a handsome fellow," she said as she stroked him softly.

The young horse lowered his head, enjoying the attention he was receiving. Her grandfather, who was full-blooded Apache, had told her once that a warrior and his horse had a special bond. A successful pairing was one in which the horse and warrior chose each other. At this moment, she felt the young stallion was choosing her. "Will you accept me as your warrior?"

The horse lifted his head several times, as if he was nodding yes in response to her question. She smiled and chuckled softly as she leaned back against the tree limb and resumed her playing. The horse began to graze and then walked down to the lake's edge for a drink of water as her eyes followed his movements.

The emotional exhaustion she had felt slowly slipped away. She found her body and mind relaxing. When her eyes grew heavy, she placed the flute in her breast pocket and allowed them to close. The horse continued to graze on the soft grass until the sun began to set.

†

Coal was purring softly in her sleep as the horse crept up to where she was sleeping and used his head to push her off the limb. She landed with a thud on the rain-softened ground and woke with a start. The horse stepped forward and lifted his head over the limb she had been resting on.

"No, you didn't just push me off that limb," she said in surprise, but wearing a smile as she rubbed her hip.

Coal looked around and saw the sun was quickly dropping from the sky and she could smell the smoke from a grill drifting across a breeze. "I guess you are telling me it's time to start back home." She turned and began the walk back toward the house. The horse fell in beside her. She placed a hand on his neck and walked across the pasture.

†

Melissa looked out at the window and smiled to see Coal and the black stallion walking across the pasture. She thought she had been dreaming when she heard hoofbeats running past the house earlier and now she knew differently. It seemed the horse and woman had bonded together over the afternoon. She smiled and turned away to walk into the kitchen to check the baked potatoes she had in the oven. Harley was cooking some steaks while Gene and Lucas worked on some veggies and a nice crisp salad. She could smell the mesquite chips he had placed on the coals as she pulled the potatoes out and placed them on a large cookie sheet.

As they entered the backyard, the young horse took off at a gallop, easily clearing the corral fence to join the rest of the herd. Coal shook her head at his mischievous behavior, and looked up to see Harley and several of the other men shaking their heads with laughter.

"I guess that answers how he got out to follow me," she said to Harley.

"I've heard of guard dogs, but I've never met anyone who has a guard horse," he teased.

"I was all peaceful, enjoying a nap on this nice afternoon when he pushed me off the branch I was napping on," she said.

Harley closed the lid on the grill. "I guess he kind of likes you then," he said with a grin. "How do you like your steak?"

"Medium rare please, they smell terrific by the way."

"The boys are finishing off the inside stuff, and Melissa is baking potatoes. Would you go see if she needs any help?"

"Sure thing," she said and slipped inside the back door. She walked to the kitchen and found Melissa placing the last of the potatoes on a cookie sheet.

"Just in time to carry these out to the bunkhouse for me," she said when she looked up and saw Coal entering. "I noticed you had some company on your walk," she added.

She grinned up at her. "That young black stallion jumped the corral fence and followed me out to the lake, and that little bugger knocked me off a branch when I was taking a nap."

Melissa broke out in laughter. "You've got to be kidding me."

"Nope, and I swear if a horse could smile, he was smiling at me after he did it."

"That is too funny."

"My grandfather told me when I was a kid that a horse and his warrior had a special bond, and I think today that young stallion and I bonded."

"He sounds like he was a wise man. The rest of the crew has their work horses already." She lifted the potatoes and handed them to her. "I'm sure if you ask, Stan would let you take that stud for yours, if you can train him."

"I would really like that, and I do feel we have a special connection," she said as they walked toward the front door.

"Let's make it happen then," Melissa said as she held the door open for Coal.

Chapter Four

After a filling meal, she and Melissa walked back to the house to retire for the evening. As they stepped onto the porch, Melissa turned to her. "I'm not sure if I told you, but we will be having company join us in the house tomorrow."

"Do I need to move out to the bunkhouse?" she asked.

"No, we have plenty of room in the house. My baby sister is coming for a visit and will be spending a month or two with us."

"That's going to be very nice."

"Just so you know," Melissa said, "Mary Leah is a cancer survivor."

"I'm sorry to hear that she had cancer."

"Me too. She had a double mastectomy and just finished her chemotherapy treatments last month, so her hair is just now starting to come back in."

"Some fresh country air will do her soul good," Coal said.

"It is very therapeutic for healing, isn't it?"

"Yes it is," Coal said with a smile. "I look forward to meeting her."

"There's something else you need to be aware of," Melissa said. "Last week her lover of five years left her. Said she couldn't help but be repulsed by Mary Leah's scars."

"What an asshole," she said without thinking. "I'm sorry, I shouldn't judge."

Melissa broke out in laughter. "I never liked the bitch anyhow," she said as she opened the door for her.

†

The next morning she felt something cold on her hand, and when she chose to ignore it in her slumber, a warm tongue licked across her palm. Her eyes shot open and she found soft brown eyes staring at her.

"Well, hello there," she said as she reached out to scratch behind the dog's ears. "Where did you come from?" she asked the black and gray cattle dog that was wiggling with excitement beside her bed. She propped up on her elbow and continued to stroke the dog.

"Callie, where did you get off to?" a woman asked and then stopped in her tracks outside Coal's bedroom door.

Coal smiled up to the woman from her bed.

"I am so sorry," the woman said, looking away from her.

"No problem, I seem to have animal magnetism," she said with a warm smile. "You must be Mary Leah."

"Yes, I am, so you must be Coal."

"The one and only," she said as she sat up and swung her legs over the side of the bed. "And this adorable creature must be Callie."

Callie's ears perked up when she heard her name and felt it was an invitation to jump into Coal's lap, and cover her face with wet kisses. "Bashful, isn't she?" she asked with a chuckle.

"Callie, down," Mary Leah said. "I'm sorry she's normally not that affectionate with people she's just met."

"She's okay," Coal said. "She's a beautiful heeler."

"You know the breed then?"

"They are the best breed a rancher could ask for," she said. "They are excellent workers, and very loyal animals."

"That they are," Mary Leah said. "May I at least offer you some coffee since she woke you? Melissa isn't awake yet so I let myself in."

"Sure, give me a minute to get dressed, and I'll meet you on the porch. I take a sugar and a little cream, please."

Mary Leah looked back at her and saw that she was wearing a tank top and green shorts. She smiled and blushed when their eyes met, "Come on, Callie," she said and turned away.

Coal dressed quickly and quietly walked through the house to the front porch. "Hello again," she said as she took the cup of coffee Mary Leah offered. "Thanks."

"You're welcome. I couldn't sleep last night so I decided to drive. I just didn't realize how early I would arrive."

"I know Melissa will be glad to see you," Coal said as she took a spot on the swing.

"You must be fairly new. You weren't here the last time I visited."

"I've only arrived last week," she said.

"I hope you are enjoying it here," she said.

Coal smiled. "I feel very at home here."

"I thought I heard voices," Melissa said from the inside of the screened door as she rubbed her sleepy eyes. "You two realize it's only six, yes?"

"It's all my fault, I couldn't sleep last night so I decided to get an early jump, and then when I came in to start the coffeepot Callie went and woke Coal," Mary Leah said.

Melissa looked at Coal and smiled, then said to Mary Leah, "I'm glad you made it, sis."

"Come have a seat and I'll get you some coffee, boss," Coal said.

Melissa pushed the screen door open and stepped out to hug her sister. "It's so good to see you," she heard her say as she stepped inside the house.

"It's great to finally be here," Mary Leah said. Then when Coal was out of sight, she whispered to Melissa. "You failed to tell me how cute she is."

Melissa smiled at her baby sister. "I'm glad you approve."

"A lot has happened since I talked to you earlier this week. I'll have to bring you up to speed later," Melissa said with a wink as they heard Coal's footsteps approaching.

"Here you go, boss," Coal said as she stepped through the door with a steaming cup of coffee.

"Looks like we might get more rain today," Melissa said.

"I don't think a lazy Sunday will hurt anyone," she said.

"I need to make a run into town this morning," Mary Leah said.

Melissa looked at her. "You just got here, what could you need already?"

Mary Leah smiled at her sister. "I was so excited to leave I forgot to pick up my medicine from the pharmacy. I can call and get them to transfer it here after seven then drive in to get it."

"I'll drive you to town," Coal offered.

"Thanks, I would appreciate that."

Melissa smiled over at Coal. "Why don't you stay and have breakfast with us, and you two can go to town later?"

"Okay, boss. I'll be back in a few minutes. I want to check on my buddy," she said as she stood and walked from the porch.

"His name is Shadow, by the way," Melissa said.

She smiled. "Shadow. That suits him."

"Yes, it does," she said. "How do you like your eggs?"

"Anyway you want to cook them," she answered.

Callie jumped off the porch and trotted alongside Coal.

"You have company," Melissa hollered after her.

She turned and smiled at Callie, as Melissa and Mary Leah walked into the house.

†

Shadow saw her approaching and ran to the fence. "Hey there, pretty boy," she said as he lifted his head to her hand and then shied away when he saw Callie. "It's okay," she said, bending down to where Callie was sitting and reached her hand through the fence. Callie stepped forward and she and Shadow stood nose to nose as they inspected one another. "Callie meet Shadow," she said to introduce the two animals.

"Tomorrow's going to be our big day," she told the horse as she stood and patted his neck. "You're going to be my horse and I'm going to be your warrior," she said as her hand smoothed down his back.

Melissa was cooking bacon when she returned to the house. "That smells delicious," Coal said. She reached for a slice and received a prompt slap on her hand.

"You have to wait just like the rest of us," she scolded Coal, who suddenly grinned and motioned for Melissa to turn around.

Mary Leah was chewing on a piece of stolen bacon. "Oh geesh, you're no better than Coal," she said.

"Maybe not, but it is good bacon, and it's all your fault for making it smell so good."

Callie let out a short bark as she sat beside Mary Leah, her nub of a tail wagging as she licked her lips.

"Not you too," Melissa said as she looked at the dog.

"Go, all of you, so I can finish breakfast," she told them.

"We will be on the porch if you need some help," Coal said.

Melissa smiled at her. "It won't be much longer if you will stop all these interruptions."

"Yes, ma'am," she said and led Mary Leah back to the porch. "Has she always been this grumpy in the kitchen?"

"I heard that, Coal," Melissa yelled from the kitchen.

Mary Leah smiled at her. "She's just letting us know she's still the boss, even when she's in the kitchen."

"Ah, I see. It must have been brutal growing up with her then," she teased.

Mary Leah settled down on a rocker and looked at her. "She's the best big sister I could ask for."

"She is a special lady," Coal said.

"That she is. So tell me about you."

"What do you want to know?"

"Anything you feel like sharing."

"Well, I'm twenty-eight. Originally from the Lubbock area, and aside from a six-year stint with Uncle Sam, I have been a ranch hand at various spots across Texas."

"What branch of the military did you serve in?"

"I was an Army Ranger," Coal said proudly.

"Ah, the best of the best, at least according to Mitch," Mary Leah said. "Did you know him?"

Mary Leah saw the look of pain cross Coal's face and knew instantly that she had touched upon a sensitive subject. "I'm sorry if I'm asking too many questions."

"No, not at all. Yes, I had the honor of serving with Mitch. We spent a rotation in Afghanistan together."

Melissa was standing at the screen door listening as Coal and her sister talked. She too saw the pained look on Coal's face, realized how difficult the conversation was for her, and sympathized. Coal too had lost the person she loved on that tragic day.

"Breakfast is ready," she said and saw Coal jump in her seat.

They shared a sumptuous breakfast, and then Coal walked out to the bunkhouse to check on the crew as Mary Leah called the pharmacy.

"Morning, boys," she said as Callie trailed in behind her. The crew was sitting down to breakfast.

"Hey there, Callie," Harley said as the dog trotted over to him and took the slice of bacon he offered. "I take it Mary Leah has arrived."

"Yes, she came in very early this morning."

"Are you ready for some breakfast?" Harley asked.

"No, thanks, I ate with Melissa and Mary Leah already."

Gene smiled up at her from a plate filled with scrambled eggs. "What are you going to do today?"

"I am going to take Mary Leah to town to the pharmacy then I thought I would do some laundry. What about you guys?"

"We have to finish up our cleaning, and then some of us were thinking about going fishing. Would you care to join us?"

"Yeah, I'd like that," she said. "Let me go put a load of clothes in the washer to get a head start. What time do you think you will go?"

Harley looked at the group. "Let's pack some sandwiches and we can have lunch by the lake, and then drown some worms."

"Sounds good to me," Lucas said. Coal smiled at him. His left eye had turned a dark purple. When he smiled back at her, she saw him wince in pain. "By the way, thanks for saving my ass the other night."

"No problem. I can't stand by when it's not a fair fight," she said.

"Where did you learn how to fight like that?" he asked.

"Uncle Sam taught me. I was an Army Ranger for six years."

"Correction, you're still an Army Ranger," Harley said.

"Once a Ranger always a Ranger, yes, I know, but no more service for me," she said. "I will see you guys later then." She walked out of the bunkhouse with Callie at her heels.

†

She walked back into the house to find Melissa and Mary Leah washing up the dishes. "I need to start a load of laundry and I'll be ready to go to town," she told Mary Leah.

"Take your time," she answered.

"The boys are planning a picnic lunch and some fishing at the lake. Would you care to join us?"

Mary Leah looked at Melissa who nodded. "That would be fun. I'll get with Harley while you two are in town and see what I need to make."

"I'll be right back then," she said and left the room.

Coal stopped by her room for a basket of dirty clothes, tossed the new jeans she had bought in as well, and went to the laundry room. She started a load and then walked back to the kitchen. "All set."

"We'll be back soon," Mary Leah told her sister.

"I'll be here."

†

"We can take my truck," Coal said. Callie sat at her feet whimpering. "Yes, you can ride too," she said as she bent down to scratch the dog behind her ears.

"Oh great, someone else to spoil my dog," Mary Leah teased.

"Like she could get any more spoiled," Melissa said.

"Come on then," she said to Callie. Coal followed them out the door.

44

The sun had burned through the rest of the fog as they walked to her truck. "She's not new, but she's reliable," she said, opening the door for Callie and Mary Leah.

"That's what counts," Mary Leah said as she climbed into the truck.

As they drove into town, they listened to country music on the radio. Coal noticed that Mary Leah had been suspiciously silent and turned to look at her to find her ashen white. "Are you okay?"

"Can you pull over?"

She quickly pulled the truck to the side of the road and put it in park as Mary Leah bailed out the door and walked to the end of the truck. She could hear the sound of retching, so she gave Mary Leah her privacy for a few minutes. Coal fished around in the backseat until she found an unopened bottle of water and then climbed from the truck. She walked around the end of the truck to find Mary Leah leaned against it. "Here, this may help some," she said as she offered her the bottle of water. "Sorry it's not cold, but at least it's wet."

Mary Leah accepted the bottle, took a drink to rinse out her mouth, and spit the water into the grass. "Not a way to make a good first impression, I know."

"Don't worry about it," she said. "Are you feeling better?"

"Yes, thank you, Coal. The nausea still hits me sometimes even though I've been done with chemo for a while."

"I can understand that," Coal said as she shuffled her feet. "Your body has been through a lot."

"Yeah, it has," Mary Leah said and took a drink from the bottle. "Thanks for the water."

"You're most welcome. Are you ready to continue?"

"Yes, I am," she said, replacing the lid on the bottle.

Coal walked around, opened the door for her, and got her safely inside the truck. She was relieved to see the color in Mary Leah's face had returned.

When Coal pulled into the lot at the pharmacy she groaned.

"What's wrong?"

"That belongs to a real asshole," Coal said, pointing at Billy Ray's truck.

"Do you want to wait until he leaves?"

"Hell no," Coal said with a grin. She lowered the windows for Callie and walked around to open the door for Mary Leah.

Billy Ray emerged from the pharmacy just as they started across the parking lot. He stopped to glare at her and then turned his attention to Mary Leah. "Another of your freak friends?" he snarled.

"Keep moving, Billy Ray," Coal warned.

"Or what?" he challenged.

"Or, I will have to humiliate you again," she said.

"You got lucky the first time, dyke."

"Luck has nothing to do with it."

Coal took Mary Leah's arm and started for the door. "That's right, run away, bitch."

"Go on inside, and I will be there in a few minutes," she said to Mary Leah.

"Just ignore his ignorant ass," Mary Leah said.

"Ha, isn't that funny coming from a hairless freak," Billy Ray said.

"Okay, Billy Ray, let's do this. I have things to do today," Coal said nonchalantly as she walked toward him. "Right here on the sidewalk or do you prefer to get your ass kicked in the parking lot for anyone passing by to see?"

"We'll see whose ass gets kicked." He charged at her and she easily dodged his approach, using her booted foot to propel him out toward the parking lot.

"Be careful, Coal," Mary Leah said.

"I always am," Coal said as she shot her a smile.

Billy Ray picked himself up from the ground, brushing off the gravel bits covering his front. "One last chance to get in your truck and go," she told him as the pharmacist and several others gathered around.

He took a swing at her. She blocked the blow as she released a kick to his rib cage and he flew into the grille of her truck and doubled over in pain. Pure rage filled his eyes as he straightened up and rushed her. She took him into her midsection, dropped backward flipping him over her body onto the asphalt, and then bounced up quickly to her feet. He regained his feet and approached her more slowly this time. A blow greeted him to his left jaw that dropped him to his knees. She landed a fast kick to the side of his head, which knocked him the rest of the way to the ground.

A sheriff's department cruiser slid to a halt as she started to walk away from Billy Ray. When her back was turned, Billy Ray climbed to his feet and started running toward her. Mary Leah cried out, "Behind you, Coal."

She swung around with a roundhouse kick and dropped him to his knees once more. A huge deputy rushed onto the scene and stood between them. "You need to calm down and go home, Billy Ray, before this lady decides to press charges," he said.

"That ain't no lady," Billy Ray said as he wiped blood from his mouth.

"Lady or no, she's got the best of you, so just go home or I will haul your ass in and throw you in jail."

"All right, Bobby," he said and then moved to see past the deputy to glare at Coal. "This ain't done," he snarled at her.

"Go, now," Bobby said and pointed to Billy Ray's truck.

Billy Ray grabbed up his bag and stumbled over to his truck as the small crowd watched him go. Bobby turned toward her. "He sure doesn't like you."

"The feeling is mutual," she said.

"He's a dangerous enemy to have," Bobby warned. "You can get a restraining order against him."

"Thanks, but I don't need one."

"I see that you can handle yourself pretty well, but try to stay clear of Billy Ray if you can."

"I try to, Deputy," she said.

The small crowd was beginning to disperse as Bobby turned to Mary Leah. "Miss Mary Leah, it's good to see you again."

"Thanks, Bobby; it's good to see you as well. I see some things in this town never change," she said as Billy Ray floored his truck and spun out of the parking lot.

"Boys will be boys," he said with a shrug. "Too bad that one refuses to grow up. Have a good day, ladies," he said and tipped his hat before walking toward his cruiser.

"Sorry about that," Coal said as she rejoined Mary Leah.

"Are you okay?"

"Just some bruised knuckles. I'll be fine," she said as they followed the pharmacist into the store.

"It is good to see you back," the pharmacist said to Mary Leah. "I still have a spot open if you want to join our staff."

"Thanks, Tom, I will keep that in mind," she said as she paid for the purchase.

"Just let me know," he said as they started to walk from the store.

"So you're a drug dealer?" she teased.

Mary Leah laughed heartily. "Yes, I'm a pharmacist."

"Cute and smart," Coal said as she opened the door. "I like that."

"Well, thanks ma'am." Mary Leah smiled as they walked out the door.

The ride back to the ranch turned out to be uneventful. "Thanks for taking me to town."

"My pleasure, ma'am," she said.

"I would like to make an ice pack for your knuckles, if you don't mind."

"I don't mind at all."

They walked up to the porch where Melissa was waiting. "Welcome back."

"Thanks, I'll be right back with that ice pack," Mary Leah said.

"Ice pack?" she asked.

"Billy Ray just can't keep his big mouth shut," she said.

"And, I suppose you helped him out there."

"He said some ugly things to Mary Leah," Coal said when she was sure Mary Leah was out of earshot. "Someone has to teach him how to respect women, especially those he doesn't know."

"And, you are just the person to do that, right?"

"I don't go looking for trouble if that's what you're implying, boss, but I won't tolerate disrespect."

"That's not what I meant at all. Don't forget I witnessed an interaction between you and Billy Ray."

"I'm sorry, boss."

Melissa chuckled. "No need to be. By the way, I put your clothes in the dryer while you were gone."

"Thanks," she said and then smiled as Mary Leah walked back onto the porch.

The brightness of her smile did not escape Melissa's notice. She grinned to herself. Right now, both women needed a close friend. She felt like Coal and Mary Leah would be good for each other.

"Now, let me have that hand," Mary Leah said as she took Coal's hand in hers and pressed an ice pack against bruised knuckles.

"See they aren't bad," she said, but she did enjoy having Mary Leah fuss over her.

"No, but I bet they will still be sore, even after we get the swelling down."

"I've had much worse."

"I'm sure you have, but not from defending my honor," Mary Leah said.

"Yes, ma'am," Coal said as Mary Leah's hand rested on her thigh.

Harley walked up to the porch, and saw Mary Leah tending to Coal's hand. "What happened?"

"Coal had another dancing lesson with Billy Ray," Melissa said.

"Oh yeah? How did that go?" he asked.

"You should have seen her, Harley; she kicked his ass real good."

"Mary Leah! Don't encourage her," Melissa chastised.

"I wouldn't want to make her mad at me," Harley said. "But, damn, that boy sure is hardheaded."

"Yes, he is," she agreed.

"The boys and I are going to head on down to the lake. Is there anything you want me to take?" he asked Melissa.

"You can go ahead and load up the cooler and I'll ride down with you. These two can follow once Mary Leah finishes playing nursemaid."

Mary Leah shot her sister a grin. "We'll be down shortly."

"Y'all can drive the gator down," Harley said. "I'll have Gene drive it up here for you."

"Thanks, Harley," Coal said.

Harley carried the cooler out to the flatbed truck followed by Melissa. Gene hopped down and ran to the barn to drive the gator up to the front porch. He smiled at Mary Leah before rushing back to the truck.

"It's good to see the boys enjoying a nice outing."

"Last week was pretty brutal with the heat and bringing in the hay," Coal said. "A nice break from the heat is well deserved."

"I don't see how you tolerate the heat at all," Mary Leah said as she smiled at her.

She felt her heart flutter at the look of admiration in Mary Leah's smile. She returned her smile and said, "You get used to it after a while, but you learn to live for the cooler weather."

"Are you going to fish?"

"No, I will probably just kick back under the oaks and relax. Do you fish?" she asked.

"I do, but I don't know if I will today."

Coal jumped when a rush of cold water soaked through her pant leg. "Damn, that's cold."

"I guess you have been iced enough for now," Mary Leah said, removing the quickly thawing ice. "Just try not to get into any more fights today and the swelling should stay down."

"Yes, ma'am. Thanks for doctoring me," she said.

"Not a problem. You were a good patient," Mary Leah said with a wink.

"Should we go crash the party?"

"I'll be there in just a minute," Mary Leah said and stepped inside the house.

She climbed inside the four-wheeler and waited for Mary Leah who returned wearing a ball cap to protect her sensitive scalp. She climbed into the vehicle and Callie jumped up between them.

When they were halfway to the lake, Coal turned her head at the sound of galloping hooves to see Shadow rapidly approaching them. She chuckled at the young horse. "Guess who doesn't want to be left out," she said to Mary Leah.

"You really do have animal magnetism," she said with a grin.

She pulled up next to the truck and turned the ignition off as Shadow trotted up to her. "I guess you could say that," she said as the horse nuzzled into her, nearly knocking her over. "Easy, you big brute," she said as she scratched behind his ears.

Harley and the rest of the crew were spread around the lake's edge, fishing, when they approached. They all turned at the sound of Shadow's thundering hooves. Harley shook his head and cast his bait across the water.

"I see you have been followed again," Melissa said, nodding toward Shadow. She turned to Mary Leah. "Harley already has your rod down by the lake."

"I guess I should go and put in an appearance. I'll be back in a little while," she said.

"Don't show them up too bad," Coal said.

Mary Leah smiled at her. "I'll try not to," she said as she turned and walked to the lakeshore.

"Come sit with me, Coal," Melissa said.
She picked up a folding chair and joined Melissa under one of the majestic oaks. A cool breeze greeted them as they lounged in the shade.

Chapter Five

Coal settled down beside Melissa. "You don't fish?"

"Not when I have a crew of men to do it for me," she said with a grin.

She nodded her head. "Good point. Do you think they will catch enough for a fish fry tonight?"

"They should without any problems," Melissa said. "How's the hand?"

She held her right hand up for her to see. "It's as good as new."

"It won't be for long if you keep slamming it against Billy Ray's hard head."

"I know I should do a better job of walking away."

"Yes, you should, but I appreciate you taking up for Mary Leah."

Melissa noticed a sparkle in Coal's eyes when she mentioned her sister's name. "There was no call for that. If he wants to disrespect me it's all fine and good, but I won't allow him to be nasty to Mary Leah, or any other woman," she said as her eyes turned back to the lake in search of Mary Leah.

Coal's lips curled into a smile as her eyes located Mary Leah as she squealed with excitement when she hooked a fish.

"Bring him in," Harley shouted over to her.

"She would be the first to land a fish," Melissa said.

"Why would that be?"

"Mary Leah is good at everything she does," Melissa said.

"That sounds like a proud big sister speaking."

"I have always been proud of her. She was the first in our family to graduate from college. When she became a licensed pharmacist and moved to Dallas, I was certain she had a wonderful future. Then she got involved with Judy."

"I assume that's the asshole ex?"

"Yes, in my opinion, Judy took advantage of Mary Leah's generous heart for five years, and when she needed her most she ran out on her."

"That really sucks," she said. "She seems like a very sweet person."

"She would give you the shirt off her back if you needed it or if she thought you did," Melissa said with a smile. "She deserves to be loved for who she is, not what she can provide."

"That's very true," Coal said as she watched Mary Leah land a large bass.

Mary Leah removed the hook from the mouth of the fish and handed it over to Harley to place on a stringer. "There's my contribution. Now I'm going to relax in the shade," she told him.

"Yes, ma'am," Harley said as he dropped the fish back into the water.

Coal watched her approach and stood to get a chair set up for Mary Leah. "That was a good-sized fish you pulled in."

"Yeah, I got lucky."

"Can I get you something to drink?"

"Yes, a bottle of water would be nice."

"Can I get you anything, boss?" Coal asked.

"I'll take a bottle too, Coal," she answered.

Mary Leah settled into the chair across from her and smiled as she took the bottle of water offered to her. "Thanks."

"You're welcome." Coal returned her smile as their eyes locked briefly.

"I thought we would have a fish fry tonight," Melissa told her sister. "The boys can dress and filet the fish, and I can cook some corn and cheese grits to go along with the fish."

"I can make some hush puppies," she volunteered. "I think we have everything I will need."

"I'll help you," Mary Leah said.

"So, we just need the boys to catch enough fish to make a meal," Melissa said.

"That shouldn't be a problem," Mary Leah said as Gene hollered that he had a big one.

Callie came and sat between Coal and Mary Leah, and Coal found her hand scratching the dog behind the ears as she watched Shadow grazing close to the lake.

"He's a beautiful animal, isn't he?" Mary Leah asked.

"Yeah, he is, and I can't wait to ride him tomorrow," Coal said.

"Will you work with him first?" Melissa asked.

"Yes, I can hardly wait," she answered.

"Would you mind if I watched?"

She smiled at Mary Leah. "No, not at all, but I train very differently from most."

"How so?" she asked.

"You'll have to wait until tomorrow to find out," she said with a grin.

"Oh, that's cruel. Now you will have me up all night wondering about tomorrow."

"Not after you get a belly full of food. You have been up a long time today," Coal said.

"You are right about that. I bet I sleep well tonight."

Melissa smiled at how well the two women were getting along. "I don't know about y'all, but I'm getting hungry," Melissa said. "Will you help me set out the food while Coal gathers the boys?"

"Sure," Mary Leah said.

"I guess that's my cue to get up out of this chair," Coal said. She stood and started to walk toward the lake with Callie on her heels.

"I've noticed a few looks pass between you two," Melissa said.

"What do you mean looks?"

"Oh, the locking of gazes and soft smiles, and I noticed how easily your hand rested on Coal's thigh as you nursed her hand."

Mary Leah blushed. Melissa did not miss much, and she knew her baby sister all too well.

"Normally, I would give this speech to her about not hurting you, but she's pretty fragile right now too," Melissa said. "Her lover died with Mitch, and she was there to witness both."

"Damn, that must be really hard on her. Did she know Mitch was your husband?"

"Not until she saw some of the pictures hanging in the den yesterday. She took them for Mitch to send to me, and when she recognized them I thought she was going to die on me."

"I will treat her gently," Mary Leah said.

"I know you will, little sister," Melissa said. "I think given some time, you two would be very good for each other."

"You wouldn't be playing matchmaker here would you?"

"Who me?" Melissa asked.

"Uh-huh, you," Mary Leah said.

"You could do much worse for a mate," she said.

"I'm not sure I will ever have another," Mary Leah said.

"What makes you say that?"

"My scars are pretty repulsive."

Melissa chuckled, "Don't sell yourself or her short. When the right one comes along, the scars won't matter."

"That's easy for you to say," Mary Leah said, sounding doubtful.

"Trust me," Melissa said.

"I guess time will tell," she said as she placed sandwiches on the bed of the truck.

†

They all gathered around for lunch and then the men fished for another hour before they felt they had enough fish for supper.

"I will set up the fish fryer to cook the fish if you ladies will handle the side dishes," Harley said.

"You have a deal. Let's plan to eat in the bunkhouse since you have more space."

"Sounds good to me, boss," Harley said. "Are we ready to head back?"

The chairs and the fishing gear were returned to the bed of the truck. Coal and Mary Leah followed them in the gator as they made their way back to the house.

"I'll use the stove in the bunkhouse for the hush puppies," she told Melissa.

"Do you need my help, sis?"

"No, I can handle the corn and grits so you can help Coal."

"Great," she said and smiled at her sister.

Coal parked the gator in the barn and met Mary Leah as she walked across the yard. "So you are going to keep me company?"

"Or help you, if there is anything I can do."

"Once we get the ingredients mixed the rest is easy," Coal told her as they entered the bunkhouse kitchen. She washed her hands at the kitchen sink and opened a cabinet to pull out a large ceramic mixing bowl.

Mary Leah watched as she sat the bowl on the kitchen table. "Bring me the bag of cornmeal from the pantry along with two cans of corn and two of diced tomatoes," she said as she rummaged through the refrigerator to find a large onion. "Will you open the cans and drain the liquid off them?"

"Sure," Mary Leah said as she went to work while Coal sliced and diced the onion. Coal also found a large pot and filled it with cooking oil and set it on the burner to heat.

She opened the bag of cornmeal, emptied it into the bowl, and then placed the diced onion in the bowl as well. She poured the whole kernel corn and tomatoes into the bowl and located a large mixing spoon. "Will you bring me two cans of beer from the fridge?"

"Beer," Mary Leah asked.

"Yes, beer, don't worry, you won't be able to taste it." She started to mix the ingredients in the bowl. "Pour it in for me if you would, please."

Mary Leah poured the beer in a large circle around the rim of the bowl as Coal stirred. "This is a very curious mixture," she said as she poured the remaining beer into the mix.

"I hope you'll like the end product," Coal said.

"Something smells good," Gene said as he walked in to the kitchen. "Harley needs a cookie sheet and some paper towels," he said as he searched the cabinet. He took a roll of paper towels from the pantry and disappeared as quickly as he had come.

"Will you bring me a glass of water?"

"Sure," Mary Leah said.

Coal poured the water into the mix and stirred until she felt the texture was right. She carried the bowl to the counter beside the stove and took out a tablespoon. She scooped a spoonful of the mixture and rounded it before dropping it from the spoon into the heated oil. The hush puppy started to sizzle as it cooked. Coal kept dropping small rounded portions into the oil. When the first batch started to brown, she turned to Mary Leah. "Will you place some paper towels on that cookie sheet to drain the oil?"

She watched as Mary Leah covered the surface and then took a slotted spoon and dipped out a crunchy, golden-brown morsel and placed it on the cookie sheet. "Would you dip them out as they get done, and I'll keep adding new?"

Mary Leah took the slotted spoon and stood next to her as they cooked together, their shoulders brushing as they moved.

After several minutes, Coal stopped dropping the batter into the oil and turned back to the cookie sheet to break a hush puppy in half. Mary Leah turned her head to see what she was doing. Coal placed the hush puppy in her mouth and waited.

Mary Leah chewed slowly enjoying the taste and texture. "Those are heavenly. I have never tasted anything like that," she added.

"You approve then?"

"Oh, most definitely," Mary Leah said as Coal offered her another bite. "I'm not sure one batch will be enough though."

"We still have quite a bit of batter to cook yet," Coal said with a grin as she moved back beside Mary Leah and started adding more batter.

Gene slipped back into the kitchen. "Damn, that really smells good now," he said.

"Go ahead and try one," Coal said.

Gene eagerly took a hush puppy from the cookie sheet and took a bite. "That is the best hush puppy I have ever eaten," he raved.

"Thanks. You can take a small bowl to share with the others while we finish up in here and then come in to set the table."

"Okay, Coal, I'll be right back."

Several minutes later Gene and Lucas came in and began setting the table. "Those hush puppies are great," Lucas said.

"Thanks, Lucas."

When they had finished setting the table, she turned to them. "Would you two please go to the house to see if Melissa needs some help?"

"Sure," Lucas said.

When Melissa entered the bunkhouse with the two young men carrying large bowls of cheese grits, and corn, she and Mary Leah had finished making a large mound of hush puppies. "Those smell good," Melissa said.

"They taste really good too," Gene said.

"Have you already been sampling?"

"With permission, boss," Gene said.

Harley walked in carrying a large pile of crispy fried fish followed by the rest of the crew. They took seats around the table and enjoyed the feast until no one could eat another bite. Gene reached for the last hush puppy. He popped it into his mouth as he rose and began clearing the table.

"Save those grits and I'll patty and fry them for breakfast tomorrow," Harley said.

"Is it breakfast yet?" Gene asked.

"You cannot possibly be hungry still," Melissa said.

"No, ma'am, but I love Harley's fried grits," Gene said with a slight blush.

"Thanks for a great day and a fabulous meal," Melissa said to the group. "We'll have to do this again soon."

"I agree," Harley said. "It's been too long."

"If you guys can finish the cleanup without us, I think we ladies will head for the house," Melissa said.

"We got this. Good night, ladies," Gene said.

†

The sun was slowly setting as the three of them walked across the yard. "I think I will walk down to the lake to watch the sun set. Would you care to join me?"

"I would love to," Mary Leah said.

"I'll pass. I need a hot shower and my pajamas," Melissa said.

"See you in a bit then," Coal said as she and Mary Leah walked toward the lake.

"I had forgotten how peaceful it is here," Mary Leah said.

"Beats the hustle and bustle of the city," Coal said.

"You don't miss it at all?"

"Not in the least."

When they reached the scarlet oaks, she and Mary Leah leaned against a low branch and watched the orange ball of the sun sink beneath the horizon as darkness quickly surrounded them. Neither of them made a move to leave, content with the other's company. It wasn't long before Coal started seeing green and yellow flashes down by the lake. She pointed toward the lake and said, "Look, fireflies."

"I see them," Mary Leah said as she leaned closer to her and shivered.

"Are you cold?"

"I just got a chill," Mary Leah said.

Coal wrapped an arm around her shoulder and pulled her close to her body. "I've got plenty of heat for two, but we can start back if you'd like."

"Not yet," Mary Leah said as she snuggled into her warm body. She rested her chin on the top of Mary Leah's head as they embraced.

61

A few minutes later, a breeze began to stir and the temperature dropped further. Despite the closeness of Coal's body, Mary Leah shivered again.

"I think we better start back," she said and they began walking toward the house. Their hands brushed together as they walked and Mary Leah surprised Coal by lacing her fingers between hers.

They walked back to the house in silence and when they entered the house, Mary Leah went in search of Melissa while Coal went to shower. "Good night," she said and disappeared into her room.

The hot water pulsed over her body completely relaxing her. When she dried off and slipped into shorts and a T-shirt, she walked back to her room. She climbed between the sheets and closed her eyes with thoughts drifting back to the lake with Mary Leah. She surprised herself by admitting how much she enjoyed the physical contact with Mary Leah. She drifted off to sleep to dream of Tessa.

Chapter Six

Coal woke up breathless from her dream kiss with Tessa. The sun was peeking through her window as she wiped the sleep from her eyes and sat up in bed. The dream had been so vivid. Coal licked her lips and found the taste of Tessa on her lips. A tear slid down her cheek as Tessa's last words came to her from the dream. Tessa had told her that she would always love her, but it was time for Coal to move on with her life and give the love Coal had blessed her with to another. She wasn't sure she was ready for another relationship, but Tessa's consent had set her guilt free.

What she was ready for was to begin training Shadow. She climbed out of the bed, slipped her feet into a pair of hiking sandals, and went to wash her face and brush her teeth. She returned to her room to dress in shorts, a sports bra, and tank top before leaving the house in search of breakfast.

"You're up mighty early," Harley said from the stove where he was frying bacon.

"I wanted to get an early start," she said as she moved to the coffeepot.

"How about some soft scrambled this morning?" he asked.

"That sounds good. I'm also looking forward to trying your fried grits," she said.

"I've got some cooking. Pour us some juice and drop some toast, and I'll have eggs ready in a jiff."

Coal dropped four slices of bread into the toaster and poured two large glasses of orange juice to place on the table. Harley placed a platter of bacon and fried grits on the table and went back to stir the eggs. When they were finished, he carried the frying pan to the table and divided the eggs between their plates while she buttered their toast.

"Will you be starting with Shadow?"

"Yes, I want to make him my cow pony," she said.

"He'll make a good one."

"Yes, I think so too," she said, taking a bite.

"I'll clear out the corral for you after we eat if you want to get started."

"I won't need the corral," she said, "I use a different method to train."

"Okay, you have my interest."

"I use the Native American technique of water training," Coal said. "Shadow and I will swim until he is exhausted and he becomes used to my weight on his back. When he is ready, I'll introduce a saddle and we will go from there."

"I've never seen that in all my years of ranching. Would you mind if I watch?"

"No, not at all," she said. "Besides, hitting the water is much easier on the body than hitting the hard ground."

Harley chuckled. "That makes perfect sense. My old body groans from memories of breaking horses when I was younger. These days I gladly allow Gene and Lucas to eat that dust."

✝

Coal finished eating and took another cup of coffee with her as she left the bunkhouse. She walked to the corral and clipped a double-ended lead onto Shadow's halter and led him out the gate. They were walking past the porch when Mary Leah spoke.

"You are starting mighty early."

"Take your time with breakfast and come down to the lake at your leisure. This process takes some time," she said.

"I will be there shortly then," Mary Leah said.

Harley was eager to watch Coal and quickly fried up a platter of eggs for the rest of the crew and sent Gene to wake them up. "I'm going down to the lake to watch Coal with Shadow," he announced before leaving.

Gene grunted something indistinguishable and went in search of the rest of the crew.

Harley emerged from the bunkhouse and walked around the back of the house when he saw Mary Leah. "Are you okay to walk or do you want me to get the gator?"

"I think the walk will do me some good."

As they started across the pasture, they saw Coal and Shadow entering the water.

Coal stopped at the edge of the lake to slip off her sandals then led Shadow into the water. When they reached a depth that neither of them could touch the bottom, Shadow instinctively began swimming. Coal allowed his movement to pull her along beside him across the cool water.

Harley and Mary Leah walked over to the closest oak and sat on a low branch as they watched horse and trainer swim through the water. After roughly forty-five minutes, she climbed on Shadow's back and floated above him until his progress brought him close enough to shore for his hooves to gain firm footing. When he felt her weight on his back he attempted to lurch forward and buck his back legs in the air, but the resistance of the water prevented the movement. Coal allowed him to continue toward the shore, but as soon as he started bucking, she turned his head and forced his forward motion to take him back out into deeper water.

They continued this routine for almost an hour until Shadow was exhausted and breathing hard.

"It looks like he is finally submitting control to her," Mary Leah said, watching as they started toward shore. Just as she finished speaking, Shadow bucked and Coal flew off his side. She was able to maintain her grasp of the lead and pulled his head to the left taking him back to deeper waters.

"Okay, so maybe I spoke too soon," she said to Harley.

"She's getting there," he answered.

The silence of the morning was broken when they heard hollering from the corral where Gene and Lucas had begun training of their own. "Sounds like the excitement has begun in earnest," Mary Leah said.

"More like someone just hit the ground," Harley said.

"Ouch, I bet that hurts."

"It's no fun, that's for sure," Harley said as his eyes wandered back to Coal. "I think she's got the right idea."

"It has to be less painful for both horse and rider," she said.

"Without a doubt," he said. "I'm going to walk back up and see how things are going at the corral. Can I bring you anything when I come back?"

"A bottle of water would be good."

"I'll see you in a little while then," he said.

Melissa was sitting on the top rail of the corral watching the two young cowboys as they both struggled to stay on bucking steeds. Just as Harley climbed up to join her, he heard Melissa groan. "That had to hurt," she said as Gene gingerly climbed to his feet. "How's it going with Shadow?"

"Much less painful than this," Harley said. "She has a much different method, and it seems to be working."

"Good, I'll go down and check on them in a bit," Melissa said as her body leaned hard to the left, mimicking Lucas who was barely hanging on in the saddle.

At the lake, Coal climbed back onto Shadow and started for the shore. This time he failed to buck and she turned him to the left to walk in two feet of water while he adjusted to the weight of her on his back. After several minutes of walking calmly, she turned Shadow and they headed toward shore, and left the lake to walk to where Mary Leah was sitting. Shadow adjusted to her weight and walked toward the trees.

When they arrived, she slid down his back and allowed Shadow to drift off to graze while she walked over to Mary Leah.

Mary Leah smiled as she approached. The wet clothing plastered to Coal's body left little to her imagination. Her eyes slowly wandered from the broad shoulders down to Coal's slim waist and powerful legs. She felt a warmth flow through her as her eyes caressed Coal.

"I'm glad you came," Coal said, returning her smile.

"Me too, it looks like you are making good progress."

"After a short break, I think we'll both be ready for a bridle and saddle."

"He's a beautiful animal and you two will make a handsome pair," Mary Leah said.

"Thank you, ma'am," she said as she sat next to Mary Leah, the water still dripping from her body.

Mary Leah blushed when Coal caught her staring at her.

"What are you blushing for?"

"The wet T-shirt look is nice on you," Mary Leah said.

It was Coal's turn to blush when she realized her nipples were rock hard and visible through the dark shirt.

Mary Leah chuckled softly when she attempted to cover them. "Don't bother, the look is very enticing."

Coal blushed furiously. "If I didn't know better I'd say you were flirting with me, Mary Leah."

"That's because I am," Mary Leah said as they locked eyes. She watched the smile grow on Coal's face as she watched the tip of her tongue snake out across her lips in anticipation of a kiss. Coal accepted the invitation and was moving slowly toward Mary Leah's lips when the jarring sound of the gator broke the silence of the moment.

She glanced up to see Harley and Melissa flying across the pasture, coming in their direction. "Damn," she said.

Mary Leah chuckled. "No worries, I won't let you forget what you were about to do."

"Is that a promise?" she challenged.

"Oh, most definitely," she said with a devilish grin.

"We thought you two would like something to drink," Melissa said as she walked up to them and handed out bottles of water. The look she got from her sister made it obvious her arrival interrupted a special moment. She shrugged when she realized what the look meant.

"How's it going?"

"I think he is ready for some tack," she said. "In a few minutes I'll go change into riding clothes and grab my tack from the barn, and we'll see."

"How are things going up at the corral?"

Harley smiled. "I think Gene and Lucas are going to be very bruised and sore by the end of the day."

"I bet," she said with a grin.

"Drink up, and I'll give you a ride back up to the house," he said.

"Let's go, I'll finish this later," Coal said and put the lid back on the bottle. "Are you going back to the house?"

"No, I think I'll stay and watch if that's okay."

"Most definitely," Coal said. She looked at Melissa.

"I'll stay until you get back and then have Harley take me back to start on some lunch."

"Okay, boss," she said as she followed Harley to the gator.

"You go change clothes. I'll grab your tack and meet you at the corral," Harley said as he slowed the gator at the back of the house.

"Thanks, Harley," she said as she stepped out of the vehicle.

†

"You have horrible timing, sister," Mary Leah said.

"Yeah, I got the impression from your glare that I had interrupted something. I'm sorry."

"I was about to be kissed," Mary Leah said with a pout.

"I'm sure Coal will forgive me," Melissa said.

"I might not," Mary Leah said as she nudged Melissa's shoulder.

"It's just a matter of time," Melissa said.

"You think?" Mary Leah asked.

"Oh yeah, you can feel the chemistry building between you two."

Mary Leah smiled as she allowed her sister's words to sink in.

†

Coal slipped out of her damp clothes and rinsed off with a quick shower then dressed in jeans, shirt, and her well-worn ropers. She ran a brush through her hair, and walked out to the corral. She arrived just as Gene flew off the back of a large mare.

"Ouch," she said as he landed.

The blow knocked the wind out of Gene.

"I think these two may need to take a break before lunch," Harley said. "I'll drive you back out and get you set up, and then come back to check on them again."

Coal followed him to the gator and saw her tack loaded in the back. "Thanks for loading my tack."

"No problem," Harley said with a grin.

They drove back to the lake and she walked over to Shadow and led him over to the gator where she slipped a bridle over his head and removed the halter and lead. Harley held the reins as Coal stroked Shadow's neck. Next, she introduced the blanket to him, laying it gently across his

69

back. Then she picked up her saddle and draped it across his back. He stomped his feet, but allowed her to continue to cinch the girth around his belly. She draped the reins over his neck, secured them on the saddle horn, and then slapped Shadow's back haunches to spook him. He lurched back away from her and when the stirrups hit his side, he began bucking trying to dislodge the saddle. He ran several hundred yards, bucking and jumping from side to side.

"Unless you need us, Harley can take me back, and I'll start lunch," Melissa said.

"No problem, I'm going to let him get used to the saddle for a while, and then I'll mount him."

"I'll drive the gator back when lunch is ready and give you both a ride in," Melissa said.

"Okay, boss," she said as Melissa and Harley pulled away.

✝

She walked over to sit beside Mary Leah and picked up her water bottle, took a drink and then turned toward her. "Now, where were we?" she asked with a grin.

"I do believe you were about to kiss me when we were interrupted," Mary Leah said.

"I thought you were about to kiss me," Coal teased as she leaned forward.

"Does it really matter?"

"No, it doesn't," she said as she reached up to stroke the side of Mary Leah's face while she leaned forward to brush her lips softly across hers. The merging of their lips was tender at first then surged electric when Coal penetrated Mary Leah's lips with her tongue. Tongues swirled together in a dance of dominance as her hand found the back of Mary Leah's neck to pull her closer.

Mary Leah's hands sought out Coal's waist and held her close as they kissed. They were oblivious to the approach of hooves and were startled from their kiss by the sound of Shadow blowing air through his nostrils in an impatient gesture as he stood three feet away from them.

Coal looked over to Shadow and then turned back to Mary Leah. "It looks like I'm going to have to take you away somewhere to get an uninterrupted kiss."

"Just let me know when," Mary Leah said.

"Maybe we can go for a ride in my truck later tonight."

"Find a place to park like a pair of teenagers," Mary Leah said.

"That's not a bad idea," Coal said and quickly kissed her. "Now, I need to get back to work," she said as she turned away from Mary Leah.

"Be careful."

"Always," she said with a grin.

She walked over to Shadow and ran her hand down his neck. "Are we ready to ride?" she whispered.

The young horse shivered under her touch. She continued to talk quietly with him as her left foot slipped into a stirrup. She took the reins in her left hand as she pulled her body onto his back. She quickly located the other stirrup with her right foot and squeezed her knees into his sides. She had to duck a low branch as Shadow took off in a dead run deeper into the pasture.

Coal gave him his head, allowing him to run as far as he wanted to run. He quickly worked up a lather of sweat and began to slow his speed. Suddenly he stopped dead in his tracks. Prepared for this move, she managed to keep her body from flying over his head. When he failed to dislodge her from his back, Shadow bucked wildly for several seconds, but Coal's knees locked tight against him. When he stopped bucking, she leaned over to pat his neck and speak to him with her soothing voice. She used the reins to turn him back toward the lake and found that it was no longer in sight.

Mary Leah watched them quickly disappear into the horizon. The speed at which Shadow and Coal departed took Mary Leah's breath and she worried for Coal's safety when they were out of sight, but had to trust in her skills as a horse trainer to know what she was doing. Still, her heart raced when she finally saw the dust that was being kicked up by Shadow's hooves as they came thundering back toward her.

Coal slowed him to a canter and maneuvered him through figure-eight patterns until he grew accustomed to the pressure of the reins against his neck to follow her instructions. She pulled back on the reins, pressing her knees into his sides, and he backed up quickly in a straight line. She dismounted and walked forward to turn and face Shadow. She dropped the reins and waited to see if he would run off. She smiled as he dropped his head to look at her and stood his ground. She stepped forward and placed her hand on his forehead. "Good boy," she said as she stroked his face. Coal picked up the reins and walked to his side, and mounted him again. There was no resistance as she sat squarely upon his back.

A flicker of bright light caught her attention and she looked up to see the gator approaching the lake. *Lunch must be ready.* She urged Shadow forward into an easy canter.

"Would you look at that?" Harley said aloud. Mary Leah looked up when they heard them approach. "Lunch is ready so Melissa sent me after the two of you. Are you sure you didn't trade out horses with someone?" he teased.

"No, sir. Shadow is turning out to be a right good cow pony," Coal teased back. She smiled brightly at Harley. "Take Mary Leah in the gator and we'll ride along beside you."

Mary Leah stood up and stretched. Callie, who had been dozing in the shade, rushed up when her master stood to leave and ran to her side. She jumped into the gator, and sat on the seat between Harley and Mary Leah.

$\dagger$

After lunch, Coal unsaddled Shadow and returned him to the corral so she could begin training another of the young horses. She returned to the house to change back into shorts and a tank top for another round of swimming with the horse. When she returned to the corral Harley had placed a halter and lead on a big, strong filly. "I thought she would do nicely for your next big adventure," he said as he handed her the lead.

"Thanks," she said and led the horse from the corral as Gene and Lucas attempted to stretch out sore muscles. "I really feel for you guys," she said.

"I'm almost tempted to try your method," Lucas said. "My ass is killing me," he added with a grin.

"Come down to the lake and watch if you'd like," she offered.

"That's not a bad idea," Stan said. "I'm getting tired of picking y'all up off the ground."

"I'll wait if you want to go change into something more appropriate for swimming," she told them.

"Go ahead, and we will find two easy ones for y'all," Harley teased.

Gene and Lucas disappeared into the bunkhouse and returned a few minutes later in cut-off shorts, T-shirts, and their dusty boots.

Harley and the crew whistled at the boys as they strode across the yard to the corral. "Have them legs ever seen sunshine before?" one of the men called out.

Lucas looked at Gene. "Just ignore the old farts, they're just jealous."

"I really don't care about showing off my white legs, if it will save the pain in my backside," Gene said.

"This really is a Kodak moment," Melissa said as she walked up to the corral.

"Okay, guys, let's make hay while the sun's still shining," Coal said.

Melissa and Mary Leah took the gator, while Stan and the rest of the crew loaded up on the flatbed and drove to the lake.

"When we get to the lake you two need to ditch those boots. Then we will lead the horses into the lake and let them swim until they are good and tired." Coal looked up at the sound of thundering hooves to see Shadow running toward them.

"I don't think he was named Shadow for nothing," Lucas said. "I think you have got a new best friend."

"It sure looks that way," she said. "Anyhow, when they are tired from swimming we will bring them closer to shore until they can get their footing, and we will mount up bareback to let them get used to having a rider on their backs." She looked at Gene and smiled. "Then we will walk them parallel with the shore in shoulder deep water so they can get accustomed to our full weight. If they start to buck turn them toward deeper water and tire them out swimming."

They had reached the shore of the lake and Coal had kicked her sandals off while Gene and Lucas took off their boots. Gene looked nervous. "Are you okay, Gene?" she asked.

"I'm not the best of swimmers," he admitted.

"Let the horse do the work, and hold onto his mane down on his withers so he can pull you along, but don't hesitate to holler for help if you need to," she added. "Are we ready?"

Both Lucas and Gene nodded their heads. "We have the whole lake, so spread out some. Let's hit the water."

The small crowd watched as the three ranch hands led the horses into the lake. Gene was very tense at first. When he relaxed, he allowed his body to get accustomed to the water. They allowed the horses to swim for a half hour, and then she told them to mount.

The sorrel stallion Lucas was training immediately started trying to buck when he mounted, and he turned him back into deeper water just as Coal had instructed. She smiled as she watched them take control of their mounts. An hour later, all three had their mounts walking calmly in the shallow water.

She slipped off the filly and led her out of the lake followed by Lucas and Gene. They tied the horses to a low branch and walked to the group. "Y'all hop on, and we'll drive back to the house so you can change clothes and we'll pick up your tack," Harley said.

"You have a deal," Coal said as she slipped back into her sandals and they loaded onto the back of the truck. "We have time to rinse off quickly," she told them as they bounced across the pasture.

"That part went surprisingly well," Stan said as they watched the truck roll toward the house.

"It's amazing what Coal had Shadow doing in such a short time," Mary Leah said.

"She definitely has a way with the horses," Stan said.

"With the guys too, I think they are already appreciating the fact they aren't hitting the hard ground every few minutes," Melissa said.

"Heck, I think even us old farts could help out with training like this," Stan said.

Melissa chuckled and he looked at her with a raised brow. "You don't think we could handle it?"

"I'm not sure we could handle seeing a bunch of old farts in shorts," Melissa teased.

"You're probably right. Mine are just as white and covered with more hair than Gene's or Lucas's," he said.

"That is a visual I can do without." Mary Leah chuckled.

When the ranch hands returned with tack and fresh clothes, they saddled the three horses, and Coal took them through the steps she had taken with Shadow. Gene hit the ground once when his horse crow hopped and he wasn't expecting the move. He climbed right up, and minutes later had his mount cantering in a figure eight behind Coal and Lucas.

After another hour of maneuvers, she led them back to the crowd at the tree. "That is so much less painful," Lucas said.

"Yes, it is, for both rider and horse." Shadow trotted up to her and nudged her knee.

"I think someone wants to be ridden," Stan said.

"I'm thinking you're right," Coal said. "Have you two had enough for today?"

"I think we all can call it a day," Stan said. "Good work, everyone."

"Would you like to go for a ride?" Coal asked Mary Leah.

"I can saddle my mare for you at the barn," Harley offered.

"Yes, I would like that," Mary Leah said with a smile.

Coal dismounted and took the tack off the filly and placed it on Shadow. She put a halter and lead line back on the filly. "I'll meet you at the barn," she told Mary Leah.

Harley drove ahead of the gator, then he and the boys quickly got Mary Leah situated on the mare and ready for her ride, while Coal took the filly back to the corral.

"Thanks for helping us out today," Lucas said. "That ground was killing me."

"My pleasure," Coal said as she handed him the lead to the filly. "We'll go at it again in the morning."

"Sounds great," he said as she turned Shadow toward the barn in search of Mary Leah.

The late afternoon sun made everything glow about them as Coal and Mary Leah rode through the pastures. "Have you seen the bluffs yet?" Mary Leah asked.

"No, I haven't. We've been busy bringing in the hay, and now training the yearlings so I really haven't taken time to explore."

"You have a treat awaiting you then. I think it is the prettiest view on the property."

"Show me," Coal said.

Chapter Seven

Coal questioned Mary Leah as they rode and learned that originally her family was from Oklahoma and moved to Texas when both she and Melissa were in high school. After she finished school, she went to Austin to pharmacy school then moved to Dallas to begin her career. That was where she met Judy and their relationship began.

"We had been through so much with the trauma of surgery and the cancer treatments," Mary Leah said. "I thought after that we could survive anything, but Judy taught me differently. I quickly learned that she was repulsed by my body, and she stepped out of our relationship to meet her needs."

"I am very sorry to hear she treated you like that."

"Thanks, that is very sweet of you, but her behavior opened my eyes to her shallowness, and made me begin to question my future." She looked over at Coal as they rode. "I came here for some solace and to help me decide where I'm going."

"Judy must be a fool to let you go like that."

Mary Leah chuckled. "I never realized appearance was so important to her. She was embarrassed for me to be seen without my prosthetics, said I was less of a woman without breasts."

Infuriated by the comment, she pulled Shadow to a stop. When Mary Leah realized she was no longer beside her she pulled the mare to a halt and turned to Coal. "What's wrong?"

"I hope you don't believe that crap. Having breasts does not make a woman whole or perfect, it's what is in her heart."

Mary Leah smiled. "I don't believe it for a second, but I was devastated when Judy used it as a veiled excuse to end our relationship."

"Like I said, she must be a fool," Coal said as she brought Shadow up beside the mare.

There were tears in her eyes when Coal looked into them, and she sensed it was time to end the conversation. Mary Leah turned away, and wiped her face and then said, "We are almost there."

They topped a small hill and Coal discovered why Mary Leah enjoyed the view. The bluffs looked out across a verdant valley of lush grasses, grazed by a herd of cattle. A river wound its way through the valley. The setting sun cast gold and orange hues across the landscape.

"This is breathtaking." She dismounted and took hold of the mare's bridle.

Mary Leah dismounted and Coal released the horses to graze as they walked to a boulder at the edge of the bluffs and took a seat. "I thought you might like the view."

She smiled at her and their eyes locked. "It's a perfect spot for that kiss."

"What are you waiting on then?" Mary Leah asked.

Coal leaned forward, brushing her lips softly across Mary Leah's. The parting of Mary Leah's lips invited her tongue inside, and they shared a long, slow, kiss with no interruption. Her fingertips caressed Mary Leah's face as they kissed, and she could feel the heat building between them.

Mary Leah was slightly breathless when Coal pulled away to break the kiss. Her eyes were sparkling with excitement as she smiled at her. "That was so worth the wait."

Coal blushed and returned her smile. "Yes, it was and much better here than the cab of my truck," she teased. She slipped a protective arm around Mary Leah's shoulder and they watched the sun disappear into the horizon.

As the darkness grew around them, Coal turned to Mary Leah and said, "I reckon we should head back before Melissa sends out a search party."

Mary Leah laughed. "She knows I'm safe with you, but I do hear that stomach of yours rumbling with hunger."

Coal took Mary Leah in her arms and kissed her deeply once more before they walked to the horses to return home. The fireflies emerged from the darkness as they walked back through the pastures, and the stars glimmered in the sky. This is a perfect spot, she thought as they rode in silence.

Gene was waiting for them on the front porch of the bunkhouse and walked out to take the mare's reins as Mary Leah dismounted. "Dinner is almost ready," he told Coal.

"Great, I'm starving," she said as she turned to Mary Leah. "Thanks for sharing that with me. I'll see you later in the house."

"No," Gene said. "Melissa and Mary Leah are joining us for dinner," he said with a grin growing on his face.

"Let's get these horses taken care of so we can eat then," she said.

She and Gene removed the tack from the horses as Mary Leah made her way to the bunkhouse. She entered to find Melissa and Harley arguing at the stove. The smell of barbeque ribs wafted across the room as they debated whether to add more sauce or not. As expected, Melissa won the argument and Harley spread more of the deep red sauce across the meaty ribs.

"Dinner smells wonderful. Can I help?" Mary Leah said as she walked into the kitchen.

"You can help me set the table," Melissa said. "Did you have a good ride?"

"Yes, it was very nice," she said with a light blush rising to her cheeks.

Melissa spotted the glow on her sister's face and smiled.

After dinner, Coal excused herself to take a shower. As she was dressing, she heard Melissa and Mary Leah return to the house. She slipped on an old pair of tennis shoes and headed out the back door.

Melissa heard the back door close as she and Mary Leah entered the kitchen. "You want to shower first?" she asked.

"If you don't mind, I still smell like a horse."

"No, not at all, take your time," Melissa answered. She watched Mary Leah head off to her room, and then walked back to the front door and looked out into the darkness. The moon had risen and she could see Coal sitting on the top rail of the corral about to lift her flute to her mouth. *Must be her way of thinking through life.* She turned back into the house.

†

Coal climbed the fence and took up her perch on the top rail as the horses gathered around her. They had become accustomed to her presence and the music that floated from her flute. Her mind got lost in the music as she replayed the scene at the bluffs over and over. She had enjoyed the kiss, but wondered if she was ready for a relationship? Coal thought about how kissing Mary Leah had felt so right and she knew the answer to her question. But how should she proceed? She pondered this thought as the music floated over the night air.

Harley sat out on the porch of the bunkhouse listening to the music she was playing as he smoked a cigar. The bright red end of the cigar glowed as he took a drag and the brief puff of smoke was the only evidence he was sitting in the darkness of the porch.

Mary Leah finished showering and dressed for bed. She found her sister sipping a cup of coffee. She was disappointed that Coal wasn't in the kitchen and assumed she had retired for the evening. "I think I'm going to call it a night," she said.

"Sleep well, and I'll see you in the morning. Love you," Melissa said.

"I love you too, sis," Mary Leah said and turned away.

Melissa watched her go then took her coffee and walked out the front door.

Harley saw Melissa step onto the porch and watched as she walked across the yard to the corral where Coal was sitting.

"Mind if I join you for a few?"

"Not at all, boss, come on up."

"I enjoy the sound of your music," Melissa said as she climbed up the fence. "It is very beautiful."

"Thanks, it has a way of soothing my soul."

"The animals too apparently," Melissa said as she looked out at the stock crowding around.

Coal smiled. "I think the sound touches on some primal instinct for them."

Melissa wanted to talk to her about Mary Leah but was unsure how to start the conversation. Coal sensed her hesitancy and asked, "Is there something we need to talk about?"

She chuckled as she turned to Coal. "I was wondering if you enjoyed your ride this afternoon half as much as Mary Leah."

"I enjoy being with her if that is what you are asking," she said, trying to hide a grin.

"That is exactly what I'm asking," Melissa answered. "I can tell she is getting quite smitten with you."

Coal hiked an eyebrow in surprise at Melissa's statement. "I don't know about being smitten, but there is a building chemistry between us."

"So it's mutual?"

"I would say very much so."

"Good," Melissa said and remained quiet for several minutes, then said, "I'll be heading to Amarillo for a couple of days to look over some stock. I asked Mary Leah if she wanted to join me, but she decided to stay here near you."

"Is that going to be a problem?"

"No, not at all, Coal, but—" She hesitated.

"But what, Melissa?" she asked.

Melissa looked her directly in the eyes. "Back in Oklahoma we have an expression."

Coal looked at her curiously and waited.

"Cowgirl up or sell the horse," Melissa said. "It's kind of an Okie version of shit or get off the pot. It's time for you to cowgirl up, Coal, if you are truly interested in Mary Leah. Just keep in mind she doesn't need another heartache after what Judy put her through."

She nodded as she let Melissa's words sink in.

"I will be gone for two nights," Melissa said as she climbed down from the fence. "Make good use of them," she said and left Coal sitting on the fence to ponder her words.

Harley stubbed out his cigar as he watched Melissa walk back to the house. He stood and stretched and walked inside to drop into his bunk for the night. Coal lifted the flute back to her lips and began to play.

She couldn't help but smile at the comments Melissa had shared with her. Yes, it was time, and Melissa's absence would give them some privacy to get to know each other better. There was a heightened lightness to her music as she played for another half hour before climbing down to head to her bed.

Both Melissa and Mary Leah had opened their windows to listen to the music Coal was playing. Mary Leah felt her face smiling as she heard the back door open and Coal's soft steps as she crept down the hall to her bedroom. Callie whimpered softly and jumped down from the bed and trotted from the room.

Coal kicked off her shoes and climbed into the bed, the weariness sinking deep into her bones. She heard the clicking of claws on the hardwood floors then felt Callie's cold nose in the palm of her hand.

"Hey, girl," Coal said as she leaned over to pet the dog.

Callie licked her hand and then turned to leave the room.

"Thanks for checking in on me," she said with a chuckle and pulled the covers over her body.

†

The next morning Melissa and Mary Leah were finishing their coffee on the front porch when they saw a sheriff's department cruiser coming down the drive. "I wonder what this is about," Melissa said as she turned to look at Mary Leah.

Bobby Poole, the deputy who had sent Billy Ray home after his second altercation with Coal, pulled his cruiser to a stop. He slipped on his hat as he stepped out of his car and walked toward the porch. "Morning, ladies," he said with a warm smile.

"Good morning, Bobby, what brings you out this way so early?" Melissa asked.

"I wish it was a social call for a cup of coffee, but I'm afraid I'm on official business."

"No reason not to have that cup of coffee," Mary Leah said. "How do you take it?"

"Just black please, Mary Leah."

Mary Leah slipped inside the house to get a cup of coffee for the deputy. As the screen door closed behind her she heard Bobby clear his throat. "Do you still have a woman by the name of Coal Bryan working for you?"

Mary Leah's heart stopped at the mention of Coal's name. What could Bobby possibly want of her?

"Yes, as a matter of fact I do. Why?"

"I need to talk to her as soon as possible," Bobby said. "Official business," he added.

"I'll go get her from the bunkhouse while Mary Leah gets your coffee. I'll be right back."

"Thanks, Mrs. Conway," Bobby said.

"Please just call me Melissa like everyone else. I'm not that much older than you."

Bobby blushed furiously. "Yes, ma'am," he said as he took a seat in one of the porch chairs and pulled out a pen and writing tablet from his pocket.

Mary Leah rushed to the kitchen to get the coffee as Melissa walked across the yard.

Inside the bunkhouse, the crew was just finishing breakfast as Melissa stepped inside. Coal saw her enter and noted the serious look on her face.

"Morning, boss," Harley said.

"Morning, boys," she answered. "Coal, can I see you outside for a minute?"

"Sure, boss," she said and picked up her cup of coffee before following her outside. Coal saw the sheriff's cruiser and looked at Melissa. "What's up?"

"Bobby Poole is here and he asked to speak to you. Other than that I have no idea."

"Well, let's go find out what this is all about."

Mary Leah walked from the house and handed Bobby the cup of coffee.

"Thanks, Mary Leah."

"You're welcome," she said then smiled when she saw Coal and Melissa walking across the yard.

Melissa stepped onto the porch followed by Coal. "Good morning, Deputy."

"I hate to bother you all so early, but I have some questions for you," he said.

"Would you like us to leave and give you some privacy?" Melissa asked.

"No, boss, I have nothing to hide," she said as she sat down on the top step and took a sip of coffee.

Bobby set down his cup of coffee and flipped open his notepad. "Ms. Bryan, can you tell me where you were between the hours of ten and two this morning?"

"I was right here all night," she answered.

"I assume you have someone who can corroborate that for you?"

"I can," Melissa said. "I was talking with her until almost eleven out at the corral. Then I heard her come inside and go to bed close to midnight."

"So you can alibi her until midnight, but not after?"

"No, I can alibi her up until three," Melissa said. "I'm leaving for a trip later today, and I was up packing until about one, and then I couldn't sleep until almost three."

"Is there any way she could have left the house without you knowing?"

"Not with these creaky old wooden floors," Melissa said.

"What is all this about? Am I being accused of something?" Coal asked.

"I think everyone in town knows that you and Billy Ray have had a few altercations by now," Bobby said.

"That's true, but what happened last night?"

Bobby took a deep breath and looked at Coal. "Billy Ray was shot and killed last night."

Her face blanched white. "You think I killed him?"

"Honestly no, I don't, but with the history between you two, I had to verify your whereabouts last night."

"I never left here last night and I don't own a gun," she said. "Where was he killed?"

"Just outside his home," Bobby said.

"I don't have a clue where he lives," she said, "although I don't think it would be hard to find that big truck of his."

Bobby nearly choked on the sip of coffee he had just taken.

"It wasn't me," Coal reiterated.

"With his reputation, I would think Billy Ray had many enemies," Melissa said.

"Well, one thing's for certain, one of them did him in last night, filled his body with three rounds from a large caliber gun."

Bobby placed his cup back on a small table and stood to leave. "Thank you for the coffee," he told Mary Leah.

"You are very welcome."

When he approached where Coal was sitting, she stood. "Don't make any plans to leave town anytime soon," he told her.

"I have no intentions of going anywhere," she replied, "unless Melissa plans to can me."

"Not a chance of that," Melissa said.

"Thanks, and have a great day, ladies," Bobby said. He tipped his hat and walked back to his cruiser.

Coal leaned against the support post on the porch steps. "Well, that was interesting. Thanks for backing me up, boss."

Harley walked out of the bunkhouse in time to see Bobby pulling away and rushed over to the porch. "Is everything okay?"

"For us it is, but Billy Ray got himself shot and killed last night," Melissa said.

"And they thought you did it?" he asked.

"Well, we didn't have a very good relationship," Coal said.

"But still, you wouldn't have needed a gun to take him out," Harley said.

"No, I wouldn't have, but no matter how much I didn't like him, I had no desire to kill Billy Ray."

Coal looked over at Mary Leah who had remained deathly silent. "I'm going to get more coffee," Mary Leah said, rushing into the house.

Coal looked at Melissa who looked just as confused. "I'll go check on her," Melissa said as the rest of the crew came wandering out of the bunkhouse.

Harley looked at Coal. "You ready to get to work?"

"Daylight's a wasting," she said as she followed him off the porch.

They met the rest of the crew at the corral, and she couldn't help but whistle at Gene's white legs. "You really do need to get some sun, my friend," she said as she slapped him on the back.

"You know you love my sexy legs, Coal," he teased back.

"Not in your wildest dreams, Gene."

"Oh, that hurts my heart," he cried, clutching at his chest.

"Let's get to work, you goofballs," Harley said. He was anxious to get her mind off Bobby's visit and he knew once she was on a horse she was all business.

"Good morning, Shadow," she said as they opened the gate and he trotted up to her.

✝

"Are you okay?" Melissa said when she walked into the kitchen to find Mary Leah leaning against the counter.

"I guess her casual attitude about killing someone just threw me for a loop," Mary Leah said.

"Whether you like it or not, Coal will always be an Army Ranger. She has killed for this country. But that doesn't mean she liked doing it or would kill again unless it was totally necessary," Melissa said.

"How do you know she's killed before?"

"Because she killed the man that was responsible for Mitch's and Tessa's deaths," Melissa said.

Mary Leah hung her head, hearing that news. "I'm sorry, I know you're right. I just wasn't expecting all of this today."

"Well, I'm sure it was no picnic for her either. If memory serves me correct she was defending Lucas, and then you with Billy Ray."

The reminder embarrassed her. "Yes, she was," she said with a shy smile.

"Don't discount Coal for what she's done in the past in the service of her country. Just appreciate her for the woman she is."

She lifted an eyebrow.

"Remember, older sisters are wiser. I can see what is developing between the two of you, so don't try to deny you are attracted to Coal."

With no self-defense readily on her lips, Mary Leah chose to remain silent. As usual, Melissa's insight was right on target. She should know by now she couldn't hide anything from her, least of all her feelings.

To change the subject, she asked, "Are you all set for your trip?"

"Yes, I am. I thought I'd head out after a shower, but I'll call later to let you know I made it safely."

"I'll wait for you to leave and then go down to watch the training."

"Go now if you want. I'll be okay," Melissa said.

"That's okay. I think it will be another full-day event, besides I need another cup of coffee."

"Suit yourself. I'll be back in a few minutes," Melissa said.

Mary Leah sipped her coffee and opened the refrigerator. In Melissa's absence, someone would need to make lunch for the crew and she wanted to see what her options were.

"I've got a large bowl of egg salad prepared, so all you will need to do is make sandwiches," Melissa said as she entered the kitchen, towel drying her hair.

Mary Leah jumped, startled by her sister's silent approach. "Damn, you startled me," she said as she closed the door.

"Sorry, but I wanted to make sure you were all set for lunch today. There are plenty of cold cuts out in the bunkhouse for sandwiches tomorrow."

"I thought I might make some lasagna tomorrow for dinner," Mary Leah said.

"Damn, I hate I'm going to miss that. You'll have to go to the grocery store, though, for ingredients."

"I'll go later today, and I'll put you some lasagna back for when you return."

"Good luck with that. Those guys can really eat."

"I'll make a separate dish for you and cook it for your return then."

"Now we are talking," Melissa said and returned to her room for a small bag. "Is there anything you need?"

"No, I think I'm good. Do you need some help?"

"Nope, I can handle this. You can walk out with me though."

Mary Leah walked out to the barn with Melissa and watched her load her bag in the backseat. Melissa turned and gave her a hug. "Have some fun while I'm gone."

"I will," Mary Leah said as she returned the hug. "You be careful and hurry back."

"See you sometime Friday," Melissa said and climbed into the truck.

Mary Leah watched her drive off and then got into the gator to drive down to the lake. Harley and several of the other men were mounting up when she arrived. "We're going to ride out and check the herd."

"Will you be back in time for lunch?" she asked.

"We wouldn't dream of missing a meal," he said with a smile.

"See you at lunch then," Mary Leah said and walked over to sit beside Stan, who was watching the riders in the lake.

"Good morning, Stan."

"Morning, Mary Leah, how are you today?"

"I'm great thanks, and you?"

"I'm fine. Just trying to wrap my head around this new-fangled training," he said.

"It may be new to you, but the Native Americans have used the method of training for a century or more," she reminded him.

"That's true, but it's just not the cowboy way."

"Maybe the cowboy way needs to change then," she said, nudging him with her shoulder.

"I reckon you're right. The boys sure seem to be enjoying it," he said with a nod to the lake.

"Yes, they do," she answered, but she couldn't take her eyes off Coal. The way the wet clothing clung to her body accentuated her fluid curves and strong legs. Mary Leah felt a tingling in her body she hadn't felt for months and couldn't begin to suppress her smile.

The morning passed quickly and when Mary Leah saw Harley and the men riding back toward the lake she turned to Stan. "I'm going to head back and get lunch ready in the bunkhouse. You can bring the crew in whenever you're ready."

"We'll see you in about fifteen minutes, if that gives you time enough," Stan said.

"That should be plenty of time."

Chapter Eight

After lunch was finished and the table cleared, Mary Leah told Coal she was going to drive in to town for some supplies.

"Do you need any help?"

"No, I think I can handle this. Do you need anything while I'm in town?"

She smiled at her sweetly. "I'm good, thanks. Be careful and I'll see you at dinner. We're going to grill some burgers tonight."

"That sounds yummy. Y'all don't make plans for dinner tomorrow because I'm going to cook some lasagna."

"Homemade?"

"But of course," Mary Leah said.

"I can't wait for that."

"Well, you are going to have to wait until tomorrow night," Mary Leah teased.

"My mouth is watering already."

"I'll see you later," she said and walked back to the house to get her keys and shopping list.

Coal and the boys loaded their tack on the truck and drove back to where they had tethered the horses they were training. By the afternoon, their steeds were performing maneuvers and had become accustomed to having a rider's weight on their backs.

She watched as Mary Leah's truck came bouncing down the drive and a smile grew on her face.

She was glad when Stan told them to head back to the corral to call it a day. Shadow had followed her patiently all day and she decided while there was still daylight she would take him for a quick run. His flanks quivered as she placed the saddle on his withers and then mounted. Shadow walked across the yard and she increased him to a smooth canter as they left the yard.

Mary Leah was disappointed to see her ride off, but walked out to the bunkhouse to find Harley. "Is there anything I can do for supper tonight?"

"No, ma'am, we will get cleaned up and start cooking soon. You can relax, and I'll send one of the boys to fetch you when we get close."

"Very well, but don't hesitate to ask if there is something I can do."

"You know what," Harley reconsidered. "We could use a dessert."

"I can handle that," Mary Leah said and walked back to the house and entered the kitchen. She opened the pantry and found a yellow cake mix and a container of chocolate icing. She whipped up the batter and placed the cake in the oven to bake while she waited for Coal to return.

Out in the pasture, Coal was very pleased with the smoothness of Shadow's gait, urging him faster until he was galloping at full speed. She gave him his head, allowing him to run hard for several minutes then slowed him to begin cooling down his muscles. She started back toward the corral when he had cooled down. She could see smoke rising and smell the grill as Harley was preparing to cook.

She removed the tack from Shadow and took him back to the corral, then walked into the house to shower before dinner would be ready. The smell of a cake baking greeted her at the front door and she walked in to find Mary Leah sitting at the kitchen table.

"Something smells terrific."

"I agreed to make a dessert and I thought a cake would be nice."

"If it tastes half as good as it smells it will be great."

"Are you going to shower before dinner?"

"Yes, I am heading that way now. Why, do I smell like horse?"

"As a matter of fact you do, but it's not an unpleasant smell," Mary Leah said.

"I'll be back soon," she said as she grinned and turned to leave the room.

"Coal," she said to stop her.

"Yes?"

"I wanted to apologize for this morning. I wasn't expecting any of that to happen."

"You aren't the only one shocked by the visit, but I understand, and there's no need to apologize."

"Yes, I should have said something to support you instead of waiting for Melissa to confirm you were here all night."

She stepped back toward her. "Really, it's okay, Mary Leah."

Mary Leah looked at her shyly. "Will you watch a movie with me tonight?"

"That depends," she answered.

"Depends on what?" she asked, puzzled.

"Is there going to be popcorn?"

Mary Leah relaxed and returned Coal's smile. "Of course there will be popcorn. Extra butter?" she asked.

"Yes, ma'am," she said and walked to her room.

She showered and dressed then walked to the kitchen to find Mary Leah finishing the icing on the cake. "That looks really good," she said as she dipped her finger in the container of icing.

"Stop that," Mary Leah chided.

She grinned and was about to say something when Gene came bouncing in. "Supper is ready," he announced. He saw the cake sitting in front of Mary Leah. "All right, we are having cake," he said with a huge smile.

"Can I trust you to carry it out to the bunkhouse?" Mary Leah asked.

"Yes, ma'am, I promise to be very careful," he said, taking the cake from her and heading toward the door.

"Hang on, and I'll get that for you," Coal said. She opened the door for Gene, waited for Mary Leah to walk through the door, and then followed them across the yard.

Coal ate two burgers, chips, and baked beans, but made sure to save room for a large slice of the cake. She helped Mary Leah serve the cake then settled down with a piece for herself. She took a bite and moaned. "My lord, this is heavenly," she said.

"I am glad you approve," Mary Leah said with a smile.

"It is fantastic," Harley said. "Does anyone else need a big glass of cold milk?"

"Sit tight old-timer and I'll get it," Lucas teased.

"I got your old-timer," Harley shot back with a grin. "Add some ice too, then, whippersnapper."

Coal chuckled at the two men and was amazed with how well the entire group got along. She had worked at other spreads that didn't come close to the harmony she felt here. The men, Melissa, and Mary Leah were beginning to feel like family. Her eyes fell to rest on Mary Leah, and she felt the smile growing on her face.

With nothing but crumbs left on the cake plate, they walked back to the house. Coal rinsed the plate and placed it in the dishwasher while Mary Leah got their movie set. "Do you want popcorn now?" she called from the den.

"No, ma'am, I'm still stuffed from dinner," she answered as she walked into the den.

"All set then?"

"Yes'm, I am," Coal said as she sat next to Mary Leah on the love seat.

Mary Leah turned the player on and started the movie. Then she reached up to turn the lamp off. She tried to concentrate on the movie, but all she could think about was the warmth seeping into her from Mary Leah's body as their thighs touched. She could feel her eyes drawing away from the movie to look at Mary Leah. When Mary Leah caught her looking, her eyes filled with passion.

"Do you not like the movie?" she asked innocently.

"I guess I am a bit distracted," she answered, happy the darkness of the room hid her blush.

"What has you distracted, Ms. Bryan?" Mary Leah asked coyly.

"It could be the beautiful woman next to me that I am dying to kiss, but I'm not sure."

"So why not kiss her and find out."

Coal leaned over to brush her lips softly across hers. "Yep, that's definitely the distraction," she whispered against Mary Leah's cheek.

Mary Leah's hand found the remote and turned the movie off, leaving the room in complete darkness. "There, now the movie isn't a distraction anymore," she said as she pulled closer for another kiss.

They deepened the kiss as Mary Leah's hands roamed over Coal's back. She was breathless when she broke the kiss and felt Mary Leah's body trembling. "I want to make love to you," Coal breathed against her skin.

"Yes, please, Coal," Mary Leah whispered, her voice full of need.

She stood and lifted Mary Leah from the love seat and began to walk down the hall to her bedroom.

"Coal."

"Yes?"

"My bed is bigger," she said and led her into the bedroom.

Coal kissed her sweetly as they stood next to the bed. She broke the kiss and her hands were shaking as she pulled the shirt over Coal's head. She removed the sports bra and her fingers marveled at the smooth skin as her eyes devoured Coal.

Coal's hands wandered down to the hem of her blouse and Mary Leah gasped with shock and grabbed Coal's hands.

"What's wrong?"

"I'm not sure if you'll want to see me," she said, tears glistening in her eyes as the painful reminder of Judy's harsh words came flooding back to her.

She lifted Mary Leah's chin until their eyes met. "In my eyes you are perfect the way you are."

Mary Leah relaxed and allowed Coal to continue undressing her, but waited for the rejection that was sure to come when Coal removed her bra and prosthesis, and saw the scars reminding her where her breasts once were.

Coal could feel the tension in Mary Leah's body as she slipped her hands behind her back, unclasped her bra, and let it fall to the floor. She guided her gently onto the bed, and lay down next to her as her fingers tenderly caressed the trail of scars on Mary Leah's body, causing her to shiver.

"Does this hurt?" she asked softly.

"No, Coal, it feels fantastic," she managed to say. She was surprised how aroused she was becoming as Coal's fingers softly explored her body and her lips planted silky kisses along the damaged flesh.

Mary Leah pulled Coal on top of her and they kissed passionately as her hands roamed across Coal's back. She whispered to Coal. "I want to be naked with you."

Coal smiled and climbed off the bed to remove her jeans while Mary Leah slipped out of hers. Mary Leah took Coal in her arms and pulled her atop her naked body.

Coal snuggled into Mary Leah's body and remained propped on her elbows as their bodies slowly melted together in a passionate embrace.

Mary Leah pulled Coal's face to hers for a deep kiss as their bodies moved together in a sensual dance. The rest of the night they explored one another's body until both lovers were completely sated.

"That was so beautiful," Mary Leah whispered as her fingers played across Coal's stomach, her head resting on Coal's shoulder.

"It's just the beginning," Coal whispered back to her as she felt the first tears fall from Mary Leah's face.

✝

When Melissa returned from her trip, her first point of business was to track Coal down. Bobby had called while she was driving home. He informed her that a man had turned himself in and confessed to shooting Billy Ray. He was the husband of a local woman that Billy Ray had been involved with, and when he learned about the affair he flew into a killing rage. Bobby asked that she apologize to Coal for him, but Melissa assured him that Coal was aware that he was just doing his job.

Coal and the crew were walking from the bunkhouse when she pulled into the yard.

"Someone got on the road mighty early this morning," Harley said as Melissa parked the truck. "I hope everything is okay."

"Welcome home, boss," Coal said as she removed Melissa's bag from the backseat and tossed it to Gene.

"Thanks, it's great to be home. I couldn't wait to get here to tell you about a phone call I got this morning," she said to Coal.

"Good news, I take it."

"Nothing we didn't already know, but Bobby called to officially clear you from the investigation of Billy Ray's death. Apparently, an enraged husband discovered an affair his wife was having with Billy Ray and snapped. Bobby said he turned himself in and gave a full confession." She grinned at Coal. "He also asked me to send his apologies for the accusation."

"He was just doing his job. It wasn't like Billy Ray and I had the best of relationships, and I'm a newcomer to town to boot."

"I assured him you would understand and there was never any question you had anything to do with his death."

"Thanks, boss," Coal said. "Did you stop for breakfast?"

"Yeah, I had something at the hotel before checking out. What are you all up to this morning?"

"Finishing breaking in the new stock," Stan answered.

"Will you be finished early today?"

"We can be. What do you want us to do?" he asked.

"We need to cook some steaks and celebrate. My trip went well, and we'll have a new herd of steers arriving in a few weeks."

"That's great news," Harley said. "I'll get the steaks ready and the grill set up while these young'uns finish with the stock."

†

Melissa pulled Coal to the side as the rest of the crew walked to the barn to gear up. "How'd things go with Mary Leah?"

"Fantastic," she said with a blush. "She's decided to take the job at the pharmacy, so I reckon you'll be stuck with the two of us, at least until we can figure out where we're headed."

"That's great to hear, and I'm in no hurry for either of you to leave. It's been great having you both in the house. It feels like home again."

Chapter Nine

The storm raged on the Texas plain, and inside the bedroom of the log cabin that Coal and Mary Leah had called home for almost two years. Lightning flashes burst through the clouds to spread fiery fingers across the horizon and booming thunder echoed into the night, rattling the windows of the house. Mary Leah looked on helpless as Coal writhed on the bed deep inside horrific dreams.

Coal's body glistened with sweat as her features contorted with unspoken terror, curling into a fetal ball as she fought against the convulsions. She ached to pull Coal into her arms to comfort her, but every time she touched her, Coal recoiled with a loud groan. The torment she was experiencing terrified Mary Leah and tears ran down her face. She looked on powerless to do anything to bring her lover back to her.

The wind howled around the house as it brought the rain pummeling down on the tin roof, mixed with a pelting of hail as the temperatures clashed in the clouds bringing the threat of a tornado. A flash of brilliant lightning lit up the room and the house sounded like it was tearing apart as a peal of thunder crashed down upon them.

"Incoming!" Coal yelled out and thrust her body across Mary Leah's to protect her. The solid contact with Mary Leah's body woke her from the nightmare.

"Oh, my God, what did I do?" she cried out when she saw the terrified look on her lover's face and the tears flowing down her cheeks. "Are you okay? Did I hurt you?" she implored. Coal's dark eyes filled with fear.

"No, Coal, I'm fine sweetheart. You were having another nightmare."

She rolled over and sat up on the bed, her hands covering her face as she burst out in tears. "What is wrong with me?"

The distraught tone in her voice terrified Mary Leah worse than the dream itself. Coal was the epitome of strength and to see her in such a fragile state was heartrending.

Her eyes were wide with a look of panic as she looked at her lover, "I need to check on Shadow," she said and rushed from the room.

Coal stepped outside, the pouring rain pelting her skin as she rushed to the small barn where her horse, Shadow, would be secured in a stall protected from the elements. She stopped at the door and looked up at the clouds rushing by, catching a glimpse of a full moon now and then as the rain cooled her body. Pulling the door open, she stepped inside and waited a moment as the motion sensor activated lights lit up the barn. The white star on Shadow's forehead was the only color to separate his body from the pitch-black until the light strengthened and lit up his stall.

He could sense his warrior's distress as she stood at the opening to the stall and pressed his face into her shoulder to nuzzle his rider.

"Hey there, boy." She wrapped her arms around his neck. "I know this weather's got you on edge tonight too," she whispered as her hands stroked his neck. Coal leaned into his solid form, thankful for the horse's strength as tears rushed down her cheeks and her body trembled with anxiety.

A flash of lightning lit up the stall and a clash of thunder arrived. Coal jerked at the sound and her movement spooked Shadow who flinched away from her. He stepped forward again after the shock of the thunder disappeared and she lifted her arm to his neck again as his soft muzzle filled her hand.

"Thank goodness this storm is moving through fast," she spoke to him as she wiped away her tears. "I'm not sure I can take much more of this tonight."

Shadow took a step back and fixed her with his dark eyes before lifting his muzzle to caress her cheek in an effort to comfort Coal.

"Yeah, I love you too, big guy," she said with a grin and walked to a fresh bale of hay to gather an armful for his bin. She checked his water, and after a final hug to his neck, she left the barn to return to the house.

Mary Leah was sitting against the headboard, her arms wrapped around her knees as she waited for Coal to return. Coal's dreams had gotten worse and were coming more frequently. She worried about her lover's physical and mental health and decided it was time they talked about getting her some treatment. Her years of experience as a pharmacist, and her medical training, led Mary Leah to believe that Coal was suffering from post-traumatic stress disorder from the events that occurred during her time in the Afghanistan desert.

Mary Leah knew Coal blamed herself for the death of Tessa, her lover, and Mitch Conway, Melissa's husband, when her concentration was broken during a mission to disarm a car bomb. She never talked about it much, but the memories from that terrifying event and her overall service were obviously impacting her. Mary Leah looked up when she heard Coal returning to the house. She watched as her lover stripped out of the wet clothes and crept back into the bed. She saw the strain on Coal's face and the dark circles that were beginning to appear under her eyes from the lack of sleep. She took Coal in her arms and could still feel the trembling of her muscles.

"It's time we get you some help," Mary Leah said, stroking Coal's damp hair.

"I won't argue with you this time. I can't go on like this," Coal answered.

"Do you want to talk about it?" Mary Leah asked.

"I can't right now," she said through a veil of tears.

"Okay, baby," Mary Leah said, pulling her close. "I'll make an appointment for you tomorrow."

Coal cried herself to sleep in her lover's arms. Mary Leah held her the remainder of the night and when they woke the next morning, it was hard to tell which one of them looked worse for wear. Both had eyes red-rimmed from tears and a lack of sleep.

Mary Leah's eyes had roamed over Coal's body as she slept. The scars that covered her left side were horrible reminders of the trauma she had experienced in her young life, but the mental scars worried her the most. *Will you ever be free of those?*

✝

"Come with me and I'll prepare some breakfast while you brew the coffee," Mary Leah said, taking Coal's hand as they walked to the kitchen.

Coal started the coffeepot and leaned back against the counter as Mary Leah fried bacon and prepared to scramble eggs.

"Do you have a busy day today?" Mary Leah asked.

"We're bringing some of the steers in from the back pastures to send to market and then we're practicing for next month's rodeo in Dallas."

Mary Leah smiled when she heard this news. The boys had talked Coal into participating in the amateur rodeo held each year in Dallas when she arrived at the MC2 two years earlier and they enjoyed going into Dallas for a long weekend for the rodeo. It was the closest thing to a vacation for most of the ranch hands and Melissa treated them to a grand time.

Coal had initially entered the barrel race the first year, and even though Shadow was still learning to run the barrels, they had taken second place. The following year they took first and Gene had convinced her to enter the team roping competition. They placed third but had worked hard to get their times and teamwork down to perfection. They had started with Coal doing the heading and Gene the much harder job of heeling, but they found her to be the better heeler, so this year they were swapping assignments. Gene hated to admit she was better with a rope, but he would gladly give up the position to improve their chances of winning.

"What time do you think you will be practicing?"

"We hope to be done loading the steers by two," she answered.

"Good, I'll be home by three thirty, so I can watch," Mary Leah said as she took bacon from the frying plan. "Will you drop some toast?"

"Sure," Coal said and poured them both cups of hot coffee. She handed one to Mary Leah and said, "I'm sorry about last night."

"You have nothing to be sorry for, my love. You have no control over the nightmares."

"I know, but I'm so afraid I will hurt you one night. Will you call your friend today and see when I can get an appointment?"

Mary Leah knew this was a big step for Coal to admit she needed help. She smiled at her and answered, "I will call her on my way in this morning."

"Thanks," she said, her cheeks flushing with embarrassment. The toast popped up and she turned back to butter it and carry it to the table with the bacon.

"Grab some plates, these eggs are almost ready."

After breakfast, they enjoyed a leisurely shower together then dressed for work. Mary Leah pulled her car from the garage as Coal saddled Shadow and led him from the barn. She walked over to kiss Mary Leah and then swung up into the saddle.

"We'll see you later," she said and nudged Shadow into a canter as she rode across the pasture to join up with the rest of the crew.

Mary Leah pulled out her cell phone, scrolled down to the number of an old friend, and started down the drive as she hit Send and the phone began to ring.

†

A sultry voice answered the call. "Well, this is a pleasant surprise to hear from you this morning."

"Good morning, Del, I'm glad I caught you," Mary Leah said.

Del could hear the strain in Mary Leah's voice and knew something was wrong. "What's happened Mary Leah?" her old friend asked. "Are you okay?"

"I'm fine, but Coal is having some problems. I thought you might be able to help."

"What is happening?" Del asked.

"Are you still contracted for the VA?"

"Yes, I am."

Mary Leah's voice trembled as she spoke. "I think she's suffering from PTSD from her time in the desert. She has started having horrific nightmares and they are becoming more frequent."

"Does she talk to you at all about them?"

"No, not really, I mean, I know some of her story, but I don't know what she is dreaming. What I do know is how terrified she becomes and the physical toll it's taking on her body. She's lost weight and her sleep is very erratic. She had a bad episode last night during the storm and has conceded to getting your help.”

“Well, that is a good sign. Just admitting she needs help must have felt like defeat to her. Give me her personal data and I’ll retrieve her records.”

Mary Leah provided the information she needed to access Coal’s medical and psychological records.

“When can you bring her in so I can evaluate her?”

“As soon as you can see her,” Mary Leah answered.

“Bring her in tomorrow night at six, then. That will give me time to review her records.”

“I can’t thank you enough,” Mary Leah said.

Del chuckled softly. “You know I have been dying to meet her for a while now. I just wish it weren’t under these circumstances.”

“I know, but time just seems to always slip away from us,” Mary Leah said.

Del chuckled. “You are still newly in love, so that’s normal. I’ll do everything I can to help Coal,” she said.

“Thanks, Del, I know you can help her,” Mary Leah said. “We’ll see you tomorrow night.”

“Drive safely,” Del said and hung up the phone. “I hope I can help,” she said to herself as she booted up her computer and entered the VA medical records site to request Coal’s records.

†

Coal pulled Shadow up just outside the bunkhouse and tied the reins to a hitching post before walking inside. Harley was at the stove cooking breakfast when she entered and he turned at her approach.

“Have you eaten yet?”

“Yes, thanks Harley, I’ll just have some coffee while you boys get ready.”

Harley slid a healthy portion of scrambled eggs onto his plate and joined her at the table. He studied her face, noticing the dark circles under her eyes. He was truly worried about his young friend. Harley was also a veteran and knew what horrors Coal endured in the desert. "Are you feeling okay?"

She struggled to manage a smile for him. "Yeah, that danged storm played havoc with my sleep last night."

"It stormed last night?" he said with a grin. "I just thought that was Gene snoring, but I guess it could have been thunder."

Coal chuckled. "It was rattling our windows."

"Well, yeah, Gene can do that too."

"What can I do?" Gene said as he walked into the kitchen rubbing sleep from his eyes.

"Rattle the windows with your snoring," Harley teased.

"Ha, ha, very funny," Gene answered, but he didn't deny Harley's claim.

"Do you want me to scramble some eggs for you while Harley finishes eating?"

It was Gene's turn for a smart comeback. "No offense, Coal, but I'll wait for Harley. Your eggs are too rubbery for me," he teased.

"Yeah, I still haven't learned to cook them." She grinned.

"Speaking of cooking, we decided to grill some steaks Friday night and wondered if you and Mary Leah would join us," Harley said.

"We would love that. What can we bring?"

"Will you make some of your macaroni salad and some baked beans?" Gene asked.

Coal smiled at the young man and his abundant enthusiasm. "I'll ask Mary Leah to stop by the store for supplies on her way home," she answered. "I'll go call her while you guys get in gear."

"We shouldn't be much longer," Harley said as he finished his meal and the rest of the crew was walking into the kitchen.

"See you in a bit then," she said and carried her coffee across the yard to the main house.

"Good morning, Coal," Melissa said from one of the rocking chairs on the porch.

"Morning, boss, can I use your phone for a minute?"

"Sure, help yourself and then join me on the porch."

She went inside, dialed Mary Leah's cell number, and waited for her to answer.

"Hey, baby, it's me," Coal said when she answered. "The boys have invited us to a cookout Friday night and I want you to stop by the grocery store on your way home tonight."

She could hear Mary Leah's soft chuckle across the line. "Let me guess, they want macaroni salad and baked beans."

"Yes, ma'am, you guessed it. Can you pick up supplies for me?"

"Sure, no problem. By the way, you have an appointment with Del tomorrow night at six."

Mary Leah listened as Coal hesitated for a few seconds. "She got me in pretty fast," she finally said.

"Well, you know she's been dying to meet you," Mary Leah said.

"You realize this isn't going to be the best first impression I could give her."

"Oh honey, Del is just pleased to finally meet you. I really think she can help us."

"I sure hope so. I need to run. I'll see you tonight, okay?"

"I love you," Mary Leah said.

"Love you too, sweetheart," she said and hung up the phone.

She wasted no time in setting up the appointment with her shrink friend. Coal shook her head at the thought and refilled her cup with fresh coffee then joined Melissa on the porch.

"How are you this morning?" Melissa asked.

"I'm all right, boss, and you?"

"I was glad that storm moved through quickly last night. When I heard the hail coming down I was worried we'd get a tornado."

She stretched her legs out in front of her. "Yeah, it was pretty wicked for a while."

She could feel Melissa studying her closely as they sat together. Coal knew that Melissa could see the physical signs of her distress and waited for her to ask the questions others were afraid to ask.

"You can tell me to mind my own business if you want, but I'm worried about you, Coal. You're losing weight and those dark circles tell me you're not sleeping well. Are you all right?"

She took in a deep breath. There was no use denying her struggles to Melissa. She had been a great friend to her since she arrived two years ago. She was also quite certain that Mary Leah had mentioned something to her sister. "I've been having bad dreams."

"Are you dreaming of your time in the desert?" Melissa asked.

"Yeah, I just can't shake the memories."

"Is there anything I can do to help?"

Coal smiled at Melissa. "You have been so good to me, but I don't think there is anything you can do. I do appreciate your concern. Mary Leah has made an appointment for me with a shrink friend of hers for tomorrow night."

"Del Carson?" she asked.

"Yes, do you know her?"

Melissa smiled at her. "She and Mary Leah went to college together. After Mitch died I saw her for a couple of months, and she really helped me put life into perspective again. I was really floundering without her help."

"That's good to know. I really haven't dealt well with this, and I worry about hurting Mary Leah. Last night I pounced on her when I thought I was covering another soldier from incoming fire."

Melissa chuckled. "Mary Leah isn't as fragile as you think, Coal. I think I can speak for my sister when I tell you she is more worried about your health than you possibly hurting her."

"I just pray this shrink can help me get past this," she said as she drained her cup and stood to join the rest of the crew as they exited the bunkhouse. "Thanks, boss, for all your support."

"You're family to all of us," Melissa said, nodding toward the group of men who were walking to the barn to saddle up their horses. "There isn't one of them that wouldn't fight to protect you."

"I know," Coal said as tears came to her eyes. "I just hope it never comes to that."

"Are y'all practicing for the rodeo tonight?" Melissa asked to change the topic.

"Yeah, after we finish rounding up the steers and loading them for market."

"I think I'll cook up a hearty late lunch for y'all then," she said as Coal stepped off the porch.

"See you at lunch, boss," she said and joined her crew.

†

Coal mounted Shadow and rode to the front of the barn to wait for the rest of the men. Gene, who was already mounted, joined her in the yard. "You ready to do some roping today?"

"I was born ready," she said with a grin.

Gene idolized Coal for many reasons and grinned back at her. "I think we are going to win it all this year."

"Even Austin?"

"Yes, even Austin."

The top two winners from each event at Dallas would receive invitations to compete in the annual amateur rodeo championships in Austin. The event was seen as one of the major platforms for contestants to earn a shot at going professional, and while neither of them was interested in a full-time rodeo career, to win events there was a prestigious honor.

"That would be something, huh?"

"It would be nice to bring Top Cowboy honors back to the MC2," Gene added.

"We have to win more than the team roping to do that," Coal said.

"Well, in my book, you and Shadow are a sure bet for the barrel racing. We're going to take the team roping too. Lucas and I will also be entering the bronco riding and steer wrestling. If we can take three titles, we can win Top Cowboy."

"Good lord, the energy of youth," Harley said as he rode over to join them, catching the end of Gene's rambling.

"Are you entering any events this year, Harley?" she asked.

"Heaven's no, that's a young man's sport. I've had all my share of eating dirt, but we'll all be there to cheer you on."

The rest of the crew arrived, and Stan, the ranch foreman, said, "Let's get a move on so we can get those steers off to market. The truck will be here by noon."

Gene kept up a steady stream of conversation as they rode to the pasture where the steers were located. Even with the rains the previous night, the grounds were dry and the hooves of the horses kicked up plenty of dust, coating each of them with a fine layer. Once they started moving the herd, it would only get worse so Coal pulled a bandana over her mouth.

✝

Dr. Del Carson shook her head as she reviewed the military service records of Coal Bryan. "It's no wonder you are having nightmares," she said aloud as she read the debriefing reports on the incident that claimed the lives of two soldiers in her unit, mere days before they were due to return from duty in Afghanistan.

Coal had an appointment at six tomorrow, and Dr. Del wanted her case notes to be fresh in her mind. All too often these days she was treating vets returning from the desert for PTSD. Warfare was difficult at all times, but the horrors troops serving in the Middle East were forced to witness, and were subjected to on a routine basis, were more than a great deal of their psyches could handle.

Del noticed Coal left the service with an honorable discharge nearly three years earlier and wondered if she had been suffering with nightmares for that long or if another event had occurred to trigger the anxiety. An Army Ranger, she would be a tough cookie and Del worried that she had been suffering all this time for fear of showing a weakness. She looked at her watch and knew the time would come to get those answers the next evening. Del looked one last time at the smiling young soldier staring back at her from the case file photo and once more shook her head.

"She's a looker, I have to give you that, Mary Leah," she spoke aloud. She and Mary Leah had become close friends in college, and their friendship continued to grow in the years since. Mary Leah had come to her professionally after her long-term partner abandoned her when diagnosed with breast cancer. She had also brought her sister to her when her husband Mitch died in Afghanistan.

She let out a deep sigh. "Way too many of America's youngest and brightest are being burnt out like this," she said as she laid the file on her desk. She had treated hundreds of cases in the last few years alone. She felt it was such a travesty when so many came home with the multitude of physical injuries, amputations, and closed head injuries, and then the added burden of PTSD on top of that.

Del hoped that Coal would be a candidate for a relatively new virtual reality program called "Virtual Iraq," that had proven helpful in the treatment of PTSD, using video simulation to re-enact and desensitize the affected soldiers to the event or events that elicited their trauma.

"We can do this," she said as her secretary buzzed her intercom to let her know her next appointment had arrived.

✝

"Go get him, Gene!" Harley shouted as a steer broke away from the group. Gene took off in pursuit of the stray.

They were finally in sight of the holding pens where they would herd the steers. When the truck backed the trailer up to the chute, they would be loaded and on the way to market. The morning had taken a toll on Coal who felt exhaustion creeping into her bones. Stan had also noticed her weariness and rode up beside her. "When we get them in the pen, I want you to go get a shower and a quick nap in while we get the steers loaded."

"I can handle my share of the work," she argued.

"I know you can, and I watch you do more than your share day after day, but today I want you rested before it's time to practice. Grab a shower and nap. We'll wake you for a late lunch after the steers are on the way."

The look Stan gave her made her choke back any further argument, so she nodded her head. "Yes, boss."

"Gene can look after Shadow for you, so get some rest."

She nodded and took off to run down a steer trying to break away from the herd.

When they reached the pens the steers moved in quickly. Gene rode over to her. "Stan says for me to follow you to the barn and take care of Shadow while you go help Melissa with lunch."

Coal was grateful that Stan had told Gene a little white lie about sending her off to rest, but she knew that the crew would understand Stan's decision. They rode to the barn, and she dismounted and handed her reins to Gene. "Take good care of him," she said.

"You know I will," Gene said with a grin.

She walked across the yard and entered the back door to the house. She could smell lunch cooking in the kitchen and walked in to find Melissa toiling away. Melissa looked up at her and smiled.

"Stan told me to take a shower and catch a nap before lunch," Coal said with a flush of embarrassment.

"I think that was a wise decision. You're covered in dust," she teased. "Leave those clothes in your old bedroom and I'll wash them for you while you shower. I'll bring in a T-shirt and shorts for you to nap in."

"Thanks," she said and walked to the bedroom. She stripped out of her clothes, and climbed into the shower to allow the cool water to rinse the dirt and dust from her body. Her arms felt like lead as she washed her hair. She took a mouthful of the water to rinse the grit from her mouth. Weary, she stepped out of the shower and dried her body before slipping into a pair of army green shorts and a tank top. The cool sheets of the bed felt like heaven as she climbed between them and allowed the exhaustion to overtake her.

✝

Melissa placed her clothes into the washer then continued working on lunch. When she heard the shower stop, she waited a few more minutes then walked down the hall to check on her. She leaned against the doorframe as she watched Coal in a deep sleep. "Rest well, my friend," she said and closed the door behind her.

Chapter Ten

The rest of the crew finished loading the steers and took their horses to the barn. They were preparing to wash up for a much-deserved lunch when Melissa walked into the barn. She pulled Harley to the side.

"I think it's best to let Coal sleep through lunch. If you and Gene will help, we can carry the food to the bunkhouse and not disturb her rest."

"That's a great idea. I was really worried about the way she looked this morning."

"The desert has come back to haunt her," Melissa said.

"I was afraid of that," Harley admitted. "Has she talked to you about it?"

"Not much, but Mary Leah has gotten her an appointment with Del Carson for tomorrow night."

Harley smiled. "If anyone can fix Coal, she would be the one to do it."

"I pray you're right, Harley. Grab Gene and let's go."

Harley and Gene met her on the front porch. "Be quiet now, Gene, Coal is sleeping."

Melissa watched the blood drain from his face. "Is she sick?"

She smiled as she placed a hand on his shoulder. "She just had a rough night with the storm and needed some sleep."

"Okay," he whispered and followed them quietly into the kitchen.

Two trips later they had carried the food to the bunkhouse table. "Where's Coal?" Lucas asked.

"She's going to eat a bit later, so you lot save her some food," Melissa said.

"Should I go ahead and fix her a plate and keep it warm for her?" Gene asked sweetly.

Melissa smiled at the young ranch hand. "That would be great, Gene. Good idea."

He beamed with pride as he speared a large fried chicken breast and placed it on a plate, with a large portion of mashed potatoes, gravy, and corn, then covered it with aluminum foil and placed it in the oven, which he turned on low. He returned to the table and realized he had forgotten biscuits. He jumped up to wrap three in foil to add to the plate in the oven.

✝

Coal slept for another half hour and woke to a quiet house. She climbed out of the bed and got dressed in the fresh clothes Melissa had placed on the dresser for her. The nap was exactly what she needed and she left the room in search of food. She was starving and knew Melissa had cooked a huge lunch for them. When she found she was alone in the house, she stepped out into the late afternoon sun and walked to the bunkhouse.

All heads turned her way when she stepped inside. The men had finished eating and had moved on to dessert.

Gene nearly toppled his chair when he jumped up and rushed to the oven.

"Gene's been keeping a plate warm for you," Melissa said as Coal approached the table.

"Thanks, Gene," she said as he placed the plate in front of her and poured a glass of tea. She winked at him. "Save me some of that strawberry shortcake too."

"I will, Coal." He placed a huge mound of the crushed strawberries on top of a slice of pound cake.

Coal started on the plate of food. "Damn, this is good, Melissa."

"I'm glad you approve." Melissa smiled. "The boys have decided to give their food some time to settle before practice tonight," she added.

"After eating like this, that's not a bad idea," she agreed.

"Besides, it will give us time to shower and get some of this dust off us," Gene said.

"Stan and I have already set up the barrels for you," Harley said.

"Thanks, Harley," she said between bites.

"No problem," he said as he reached for another portion of dessert. "You outdid yourself on this meal, Melissa."

"You all have been working really hard, so I thought something heavier than sandwiches was in order for today."

"It was a great treat," Lucas said. "It's hard to get a good meal around here since Coal abandoned us," he teased.

"Good grief, I'm only a quarter of a mile from here," she said.

"Do not invite these lugheads to come over or they will be there every night," Harley said.

"Well, maybe I could be convinced to come and cook once in a while," she said.

"Oh, Coal, I'd loved to have some of your cube steak or chicken and dumplings," Gene said.

"I think that can be arranged," she said between bites.

"Cool," he said. He began placing the dishes in the dishwasher, too excited to sit still any longer.

"Will you have a cup of coffee with me?" Melissa asked as she finished the meal and reached for the dessert.

"Yeah, that sounds good," Coal answered.

"Would you care for a cup, Harley?"

"Sure, boss," he answered.

Melissa poured them cups of coffee and carried them to the table. Gene and the rest of the crew had left to go take showers and Stan was on his way home. "I think I'll go ahead and make our reservations for Dallas tonight," she said.

"According to Gene, you might as well make reservations in Austin too," Harley said with a chuckle.

"You have to appreciate his optimism," she said.

"He's not too far off the mark either, they do have a very good chance of making it to Austin this year."

"Well, maybe I'll go ahead and make those reservations too," she said. "What do you think, Coal?"

She smiled at Melissa and Harley. "We have improved this year. Our times are down on the barrels and since we switched roles, our roping time has improved. We could do it."

Melissa liked the excitement in her eyes when she talked of winning. It was a relief to see that sparkle in her eyes, given what she had been experiencing lately.

"Speaking of winning, I think I'll get a few runs in while the boys are getting ready. Will you come and time me after you finish your coffee?" she asked Harley.

"Go saddle Shadow and I'll meet you at the corral."

†

Coal crossed the yard to the barn. Shadow stood patiently in a stall waiting for her return. When he saw her enter, his head lifted and his ears perked forward.

"Are you ready to run, big boy?" she asked him as she opened the door to the stall and led him out to saddle. "We've got some work to do to get ready for the rodeo."

Shadow tossed his head in agreement with her. When she finished cinching the girth strap, they walked outside and she climbed into the saddle. She rode into the corral and urged Shadow into a gentle canter to warm his muscles. They made the circuit of the cloverleaf pattern used in barrel racing twice before she felt they were ready.

Harley and Melissa followed them out and climbed onto the top rail to watch. Harley pulled out a stopwatch to time her when she was ready for a run. She was still warming up when she saw Mary Leah's car approach down the drive. The smile grew on her face as she positioned Shadow just outside the entrance of the corral and gave Harley a nod. He nodded back, her heels nudged Shadow's side and he flew into action. Coal guided the strong horse to the first barrel and they took a wide turn around it before heading across the ring to circle the left-hand barrel and then flew to the top of the ring to finish out the cloverleaf and then race to the finish line.

Harley clicked the stopwatch to a stop. "Not bad, but you can do better. That first barrel turn was too wide. You've got to bring him in closer."

Coal watched as Mary Leah climbed up beside Melissa. Gene and Lucas were saddling their horses and would warm up in the ring, and Tom and Roy positioned steers in the chute. "Let's make two more runs, and then Shadow can rest as we watch them bulldog for a bit."

"Tighter turns," he reminded her.

She nodded and turned back to the entrance of the ring. "Okay, let's show them how it's done," she said. She gave Shadow his head as her heels prompted him into action. Shadow cut the turn around the barrel so tight, she worried her boot would get caught on it and tip it over, but Shadow brought them safely through the first turn, escaping what would be a five-second penalty if they knocked a barrel over. They finished the cloverleaf two full seconds faster than the first run.

She pulled Shadow to a stop outside the ring and they walked over to Harley. Shadow's nostrils were flaring with excitement, he was ready for another run. "Better?" she asked.

"Two seconds faster, but you can do better."

"Hey, baby," she said to Mary Leah.

"You two are looking good," Mary Leah said.

"This will be better," she said. They spun around to trot back outside the ring. She felt Shadow was eager to go faster, and this time she would give him complete control over the speed of the run. "It's all on you, big boy," she said as she lowered the reins to his neck and gently pressed her heels in his sides.

Shadow took her instruction and raced to the first barrel, turning so close that dirt flew up in Coal's face from the tight turn of his hooves. His speed picked up as he made the second turn and raced for the final barrel and when he turned for the homestretch, Coal was grinning from ear to ear, knowing this was one of their fastest times ever.

Harley clicked the stopwatch and hollered, "Hot damn, that was fast. You would win Austin with that kind of run," he added.

"I hope we can do that in Dallas in a couple of weeks."

"That was really incredible," Mary Leah said.

Coal walked Shadow over to the railing and took her rope from around the top of a fence post and tied it to her saddle, then took a pair of thin leather gloves from her back pocket. One of the tasks to team roping was to wrap the rope around the saddle horn or "dallying" the rope to secure the animal that had been roped. Ropers learned early on that a finger caught between the rope and the saddle horn became mangled beyond repair. She turned Shadow toward the far end of the corral where steers moved into the chutes.

Lucas and Gene had mounted their horses and moved inside the corral to begin practicing bulldogging. Gene galloped down to the entrance of the corral and closed the gate to secure the steers inside the ring. They would use the same steers to practice roping after he and Lucas had finished wrestling with them.

Roy and Tom, two of the other ranch hands, worked the first steer into the chute as Lucas backed his horse in beside the chute, into a position called the box. In competition, there would be a rope barrier across the entry point where the cowboy would start. Horse and rider could legally break the barrier only after the steer had left the chute, giving the steer a head start. If the rider breached the barrier too early, he would be assessed a ten-second penalty, effectively eliminating them from competitive times.

Lucas nodded that he was ready and the first steer was released from the chute. Lucas broke the barrier and raced after the steer coming along his left side as Lucas leaned across his horse and launched his body reaching for the steer's neck and horns. His task was to turn the steer's head back toward his body and wrestle him to the ground. Lucas launched and dug his boot heels into the dirt, slowing the steer's progress as he wrestled him to the ground. His first attempt was almost perfect as he brought the steer to the ground, and then climbed back to his feet, dusting his pants off.

"Great job, Lucas," Harley yelled out.

Gene was eager to get into the action, and backed his horse into the box as the next steer ran into the chute. Gene nodded his head and the steer released, rushing from the chute. Gene's timing on the barrier was good, but the run went downhill from there. Gene launched his body toward the steer, just as the animal decided to put on the brakes. Gene's momentum carried him beyond the steer's neck and he somersaulted across the dirt.

"Whoa," Harley shouted. Coal stifled a laugh.

"You okay, man?" Lucas asked with a grin.

Red-faced, he looked up at Lucas as he approached with Gene's horse. "I definitely wasn't expecting that."

"Mount up and try again," Lucas said.

Gene's second attempt went off without a hitch. They each made two attempts that were more successful before Gene looked over at her. "Are you ready to do some roping?"

"Are you done eating dirt?" she teased.

"For today," he hollered back.

"Let's do it then," she said as she helped Lucas herd the steers back into the catch pen.

Gene entered the box on the left-hand side of the chute as Coal took up the right. He looked at her and she nodded her readiness. Gene nodded to Roy, and the first steer released from the chute. Gene raced toward the steer, swinging the rope above his head and launched his loop at the steer's head. He pulled the rope tightly around his saddle horn and turned the steer back toward him as Coal moved in to rope the steer's back legs. She threw her loop, but the steer kicked out one leg before she could tighten her loop. She wound her rope around the horn to dally her rope and backed Shadow to stretch the steer out until he was immobile.

"Damn," she said. Catching only one leg would be a ten-second penalty. She urged Shadow forward and loosened the tension on her rope allowing the steer to kick out and rid himself of the rope.

Gene also retrieved his rope and coiled it back into his hands. "Let's go again."

They took up their positions and the next three runs were perfect. On the last steer, Gene missed his first throw and had to pull out a backup rope. By the time he had the steer headed and Coal could heel it nearly twenty seconds had elapsed.

"We can't stop with that," she said and rounded up two more steers.

The next run finished with perfection and they decided to call it a night. "Not bad, but we definitely need more practice," Coal said.

"Tomorrow night?" Gene asked.

"Nope, it will have to wait until Friday. We can practice before the cookout. I have an appointment tomorrow night."

"Friday night it is then," Gene said.

They released the steers back into a small pasture to graze and then she rode over to where the sisters were talking. "I'm going to head home so I can get Shadow taken care of," she told Mary Leah. "See you tomorrow, boss."

"We are cutting hay tomorrow," Melissa reminded her.

"Right," Coal answered. "See you then."

She rode Shadow home and unsaddled him, brushing him down before placing him in the stall for the night. "You did good today, big boy," she said as she stroked the brush across his back. She was very pleased with how much progress he had made from last year. Shadow had turned into a great cow pony. She was lost in thought as she tended to her mount and did not hear Mary Leah arrive home.

"Are you just about finished here?" Mary Leah asked from the barn entrance.

Coal started as she spun toward the sound of her lover's voice. "Yeah, I won't be long."

"I didn't mean to startle you," Mary Leah apologized.

"That's all right, honey; I was just enjoying my time with Shadow."

"What would you like for dinner?"

"Something light, I'm still stuffed from that huge lunch Melissa cooked for us."

Mary Leah thought for a second. "I could make us a salad," she offered.

"That would be perfect," she answered.

Chapter Eleven

Coal was thankful for a restful night without dreams disrupting her sleep. She woke up refreshed the following morning and snuggled into Mary Leah. "Good morning," she whispered.

"Hey, baby, did you sleep well?"

"Thankfully yes, I feel good this morning."

"Toast and cereal okay for you?" she asked. "I want to get on the road early so I can get home sooner tonight for our drive. Can you be ready by four if I promise to treat you to a nice dinner?"

"Can we have beef brisket?" Coal asked with a grin.

"You can have anything you want," Mary Leah said as she rolled over and kissed her.

"That sounds promising," she said as she wrapped her arms around Mary Leah.

"Do you want a ride this morning since you are cutting hay today, or do you plan to ride Shadow?"

"I might as well ride him. If I don't he'll just jump the fence and follow me anyhow."

Mary Leah burst out laughing. "Good point. You can ride him home after work and get ready then."

"I'll be all shiny clean by the time you get here to pick me up," Coal said as she climbed out of the bed. "If you'll pour us a cup of coffee I'll start the toast and get some cereal ready."

"Deal," Mary Leah said as she climbed from the bed and put on a robe before following Coal to the kitchen.

†

Coal finished breakfast and then saddled Shadow as Mary Leah left for work. She rode to the MC2 and unsaddled Shadow, leaving him in the corral before walking into the bunkhouse. Stan and Harley were discussing the morning's assignments.

"We have equipment to cut and rake three fields," Stan was saying as she poured a cup of coffee. "I'd also like to have the older hay brought down into the barn so the fresh cut can be placed in the loft."

"How many bales are still in the loft?" Coal asked.

"Two hundred or so," Harley said.

"Why don't Gene and I take care of that while the rest of you start cutting? Then we can ride out to help when we're done," she suggested.

"I have a better idea. You two move the hay and then you can help Melissa bring out lunch. It's going to still be smoking hot up in the loft. If we have everything in hand by lunchtime then you two can have the afternoon off."

"That sounds fine with me," Gene said.

"Eat up, big boy, and let's get started then," she teased Gene. "I'm going to check on Melissa and will meet you in the loft."

†

"Morning, boss lady," Coal said as she stepped onto the porch of the main house and found Melissa drinking coffee.

"Good morning, Coal, it looks like it's going to be a beautiful day."

"Yes, it does." She brought Melissa up to date on the plans for the day.

127

"You and Gene will have a good workout this morning," she said.

"We should be able to knock it out in a few hours and work up a good appetite."

"How about I prepare some egg salad sandwiches for lunch then?" Melissa asked, knowing they were Coal's favorite.

"I will never complain about egg salad," she answered. "Gene and I are supposed to help you bring lunch out when we're done, and then we'll have the rest of the afternoon off."

"Maybe you can get a nap in before Mary Leah gets home."

"She promised to take me for beef brisket before my appointment with the shrink." Coal grinned at the thought. "I guess I better get busy then," she said and walked off the porch.

"I will bring y'all something cold to drink in an hour or so," Melissa said.

"Thanks, boss," Coal said as she started across the yard.

Her boots kicked up dust as she walked and the sun shone brightly in the cloudless sky. She reached the barn and climbed the ladder to wait for Gene. She opened the doors at both ends to allow a cool breeze to enter the loft, which gently lifted stray strands of hay sending them floating down to the barn floor. She sat in the open door, her feet dangling outside as she waited for Gene. In the distance, she could hear the cry of a red-tailed hawk, and her eyes scanned the air in search of the predator. She spotted the bird as it flew toward one of the oaks near the lake and landed near its mate. The pair would have a successful morning hunt as field mice and small animals fled the sound of the tractors and mowers in the hayfields.

The sound of laughter brought her attention back to the yard as the crew exited the bunkhouse and walked toward a flatbed truck. The tractors had been driven to the fields the day before allowing them to make an early start.

Gene looked up to see her sitting in the loft opening and smiled. "You ready to rock and roll?" he asked as he stepped into the barn.

"Just waiting on you," she teased. "Roll that slide over and I'll start shooting bales down to you," she said as she put her gloves on.

Moving the bales down from the loft would be much easier than lifting the bales with a winch into the loft. A metal slide, similar to a playground slide, would be propped against the edge of the loft. She would place bales on them and Gene would catch them and stack them in the rear of the lower level of the barn.

"Remind me to load a dozen or so onto the back of the truck to take to my place for Shadow," she said to Gene as she placed the first bale on the slide.

"You want me to get the truck and we can load yours first?"

"Sure, go ahead. I'll send a dozen down and come help you load them."

"Just drop them and I'll get them loaded," Gene said and jogged out of the barn.

She began carrying bales to the slide and had four down when Gene raced back into the barn and picked up two bales. "Showoff," she yelled at him as he disappeared with a smile growing on his face.

After Gene loaded her hay, they got into a rhythm and moved fifty bales before Melissa entered the barn carrying a pitcher of lemonade and glasses. "Come on down and take a break," she hollered up to Coal.

She took the easy route and slid down the slide.

"That looks like too much fun," Melissa said, grinning as Coal stood and brushed the hay from her jeans.

"It sure beats taking the steps," she said.

Melissa poured glasses of lemonade and handed them to Coal and Gene. "How is it going?"

"We've got fifty or so moved and restacked. Gene loaded a dozen bales for me on the truck too. When we finish here, I'll take them over to my barn and unload them."

"Do you have room for more?"

"I could probably store another dozen bales. Why?"

"Well, you might as well take more if you can store it," Melissa said. "By midweek next week there will be a few thousand more to be loaded and stacked."

"All right, we'll load another dozen on the truck then," Coal agreed. "You doing okay down here or do you want to swap up and I'll stack for a while?" she asked Gene.

"Nope, I'm good," he said. "Besides, I can carry two at a time, so it should go quicker."

"Showoff," she repeated with a grin.

Gene flexed his arms and struck a pose for the two laughing women. "I got guns," he said with a grin.

"You have started filling out nicely," Coal said, making him blush. "I know a few young ladies in town who can't keep their eyes off you."

"Oh please, Coal," he groaned.

"I'm serious, Gene, if you'd pay attention you would see it too, but don't go getting the big head on us," she warned.

Blushing furiously now, Gene could only nod his head in agreement. He downed the rest of his drink and started carrying bales to the truck.

"Now I know how to make him go quiet," Coal said to Melissa, who chuckled at her comment.

"Are you nervous about your appointment?"

"I'm trying to stay busy, and not think about it," she said.

"Enough said then," Melissa answered, placing the pitcher and empty glasses on a workbench. "Just give me a holler if you need anything else."

"Thanks, boss," Coal said and watched her exit the barn before she climbed back up to the loft.

✝

It took two more hours to finish moving the hay, and after downing another glass of lemonade, she turned to Gene. "I'll carry this back to the house, and if you'll meet me there with the truck we can deliver the bales to my barn."

"Let me make a pit stop at the bunkhouse, and I'll meet you there," Gene answered.

Coal gathered the glasses and the now empty pitcher and carried them across the yard to Melissa's house. As she stepped onto the front porch, she could hear Melissa singing as she toiled in the kitchen preparing lunch, and wearing a smile she entered the house.

"You should go to town with us one Friday night and do karaoke," she said as Melissa turned at the sound of her approach, the song lyrics dying on her lips.

"I could definitely clear out the place with my crooning," Melissa said.

"No way, you sounded very good," she said.

Melissa tossed a kitchen towel over her shoulder as she resumed working. "You better have Del check your hearing tonight too," she teased.

"There's nothing wrong with my hearing. You have a nice voice, boss."

Melissa didn't look up from the bowl of salad she was mixing. "Are you and Gene done moving the hay?"

"Yes, ma'am, we are going to take the truckload over to my barn, and then we will be back to help you deliver lunch."

Melissa looked up at Coal. "That should be about perfect timing then. I'll have the coolers filled and ready to go."

"See you soon then," she said and left the house as Gene pulled the truck to a stop.

"I am so ready for some of Melissa's egg salad," he admitted. "I'm starving."

"Let's get to it then so you can feed that beast of yours," Coal teased.

Shadow eyed the truck as they drove by the small pasture where he was grazing. She was surprised when he lowered his head and continued eating. She had fully expected him to jump the fence and follow her home.

Gene backed the truck up to the barn door and they made quick work of unloading and stacking the bales of hay in her barn. Coal figured she could hold another six bales if they found they needed more room once they began baling the fresh hay.

"Are we ready to eat?" she asked Gene.

Gene grinned back at her. "My stomach's been growling for a half hour now."

"Let's go get the boss and some food in our bellies. I don't know about you, but I'm looking forward to a full stomach, a hot shower, and maybe a nap."

"Lucas and I are going to practice bulldogging later tonight once it cools down some," Gene said.

"A long weekend in Dallas is exactly what we are going to need after we finish cutting this round of hay," she said.

Gene was a young man, but his excitement over the rodeo was like a child at Christmas. Coal was excited too about the competition, but nothing compared to Gene. The prize money for the winners wasn't that spectacular, but the bragging rights and the pride of winning the events is what made the rodeo so popular with ranch hands.

"Just two more weeks after this one," she said, making Gene's smile grow even wider.

†

As she had predicted, Melissa was finished preparing lunch and had coolers filled with the egg salad, bottles of cold water, and a couple pitchers of iced tea. Gene carried those out to the flatbed while she and Melissa carried baskets with paper plates, utensils, plastic cups, napkins, and a huge batch of warm chocolate chip cookies she had baked for them. Gene climbed in behind the wheel as Coal and Melissa took a seat on the back of the truck.

Coal watched as dust stirred in the wake of the truck as Gene drove toward the fields being cut and raked by the rest of the crew. The summer was a typical Texas summer. The lack of rain caused dust to swirl behind any source of movement and there had been some brutally hot days over the past weeks. While rain was needed Coal hoped any rain would hold off until they could get this round of hay into the barns.

Gene pulled the truck under two large trees that provided the only shade for thousands of acres as the men began moving toward them. He took the cooler of drinks and placed it near one of them as she and Melissa began making sandwiches for the crew. Gene opened several bags of chips and removed the plastic from the large tray of cookies, filling the air with their sweetness. When he reached to grab one, Melissa's glare stopped him in his tracks.

"You can wait two more minutes until the others get here," she chastised.

"Yes, ma'am," he said and began opening the plates, handing one to each of the men as they arrived.

"How's the cutting going?" Melissa asked Stan as she placed two sandwiches on his plate.

"Good. This is going to be a great summer for hay if it stays this hot and dry," he answered.

"I don't think we have to worry about the heat going away anytime soon," Melissa said.

"Me either, boss," he said, taking a seat on the ground to eat his lunch.

The rest of the crew began eating while Coal and Melissa made a plate of food and joined them under the shade.

"These are great sandwiches," Harley said to Melissa.

"There is plenty, so eat all you can," she said.

"No problem," Lucas said as he stood to get more sandwiches.

"Since Coal and I have the afternoon off, I thought I'd cook dinner," Gene announced. "What would y'all like to eat?"

"I have some chicken thawed out that I think would be nice for you to grill," Melissa said. "I'll make some potato salad and you can boil some corn and toss a salad."

"You have my mouth watering already," Harley said.

Coal passed around the tray of cookies and the men finished off their meal, eager to get the afternoon's work done so they could rinse the dust from their bodies and relax until dinner. When everyone had finished and returned to the equipment, Coal, Gene, and Melissa packed up the remnants of lunch and drove back to the house.

"If you'll help Melissa carry everything inside, I'll saddle up Shadow for you," Gene volunteered.

"You have a deal," Coal said as she carried the coolers into the kitchen and helped Melissa tend to the scarce leftovers.

"I hope tonight goes well for you," Melissa said as they worked together.

"Me too," she answered. "I've got to get relief from this somehow."

"Del is a great doctor. I have faith she will be able to help you through this, Coal."

"I hope so," she answered. She looked up to see Gene leading Shadow across the yard. "My ride has arrived," she said with a grin.

"See you tomorrow. Give my regards to Del."

"I will, boss," she said and left the kitchen.

She stepped out onto the porch and Gene stood holding Shadow's reins. He scuffed his boots in the dry grass kicking up dust then looked up at Coal. "I'm no doctor, but if you ever just need someone to talk to, I'm your man," he said sweetly.

She stepped off the porch and wrapped her arms around the young man and kissed him on the cheek. "That means a lot to me, Gene. Thank you for being my friend."

Blushing furiously when she let him go, he said, "You mean a lot to me, and you have been a good friend to all of us."

"You're my family now," Coal said and smiled when she saw tears fill his eyes.

"Be careful tonight, and I'll see you tomorrow," he said as he handed her the reins.

"Don't eat too much dirt tonight," she said as she swung up into the saddle.

"I'll save you plenty," he yelled back as she and Shadow cantered away.

She raised her hand in a wave as she headed for home and a hot shower.

†

Shadow pranced, eager for a hard run and Coal gave him his head as they raced back home. Her adrenaline pumping through her veins, she urged the willing horse past the turn to their home and they ran for another mile, Shadow barely breathing hard when she brought him to a halt. She reached down and patted his neck. "We both needed that, didn't we boy?"

She and Shadow trotted back to the barn. After removing his tack and rubbing him down, Coal fed her faithful steed and walked to the house for a shower and a nap. Her mind was racing with anxiety over the appointment

135

with Del as she climbed between the cool sheets and she feared she wouldn't be able to nap, but her full stomach and the hot shower worked its magic.

†

Mary Leah finished her work at the pharmacy and arrived home just as Coal was waking from her nap. She walked into their bedroom to find Coal sitting on the side of the bed, stretching.

"Did you nap well?" Mary Leah asked.

"Yes, I actually feel refreshed," she answered as Mary Leah slipped into her lap. She kissed her lover deeply as she held her close. "I missed you today," she whispered when the kiss ended.

"I can tell," Mary Leah said, nearly breathless from the kiss. "We could skip dinner."

Coal chuckled. "No way, you promised me brisket, but I'll save plenty of room for dessert when we get home."

"I'll look forward to that," Mary Leah said. "I'm going to take a quick shower while you get dressed."

Coal watched with pride as Mary Leah undressed in front of her. It had taken several months for Mary Leah to become comfortable undressing in front of her in the light because of the scarring from the surgery to remove her breasts. Her ex had used the disfiguration as the excuse for abandoning Mary Leah when she needed a lover's support the most, and the emotional trauma had devastated her self-esteem.

Mary Leah sensed Coal's eyes watching her and turned to find Coal smiling at her. "What?" she asked.

"I was giving a second thought to skipping dinner," she confessed.

Chuckling, Mary Leah said, "You better eat a hearty meal, because you're going to need the energy tonight," she

136

said. She sashayed into the bathroom, leaving Coal grinning on the bed.

Coal climbed from the bed, pulled on fresh Levi's and a short-sleeved shirt before slipping on socks and her best pair of ropers. She passed Mary Leah in the hallway as she returned to the bathroom to brush her teeth and hair. Time for a cut, she thought as she brushed through her shoulder-length hair. Finished, she grinned and followed the scent of Mary Leah's perfume back into the bedroom where her lover had just pulled a shirt over her head. Coal hugged her from behind and buried her face into the base of her neck, breathing deeply of the alluring scent. Mary Leah's light brown curls were soft against Coal's face, smelling sweetly of the shampoo she had used.

"You smell delicious," she said.

"Thanks, I know this is your favorite."

"Yes, ma'am, it is. That scent suits you perfectly." Her hands slipped down to her lover's waist. "It makes me hungry for dessert."

"You can have all you want when we get home," Mary Leah answered, turning in Coal's arms to kiss her before slipping into a pair of boat shoes. "Are you ready?"

Coal took in a deep breath, filling her lungs with the perfume. "I am now," she answered. "Are you driving or do you want me to?"

"I'll drive and you can relax," Mary Leah said.

Mary Leah cranked the car and cold air blasted from the air-conditioning, bathing Coal in coolness. She smiled thinking of the lack of air-conditioning in her old truck. Her only relief was commonly called 460—four windows down and sixty miles an hour. Still, the truck was a fixture in her life and even though she could afford to buy a newer one, she couldn't part with her old friend, at least not yet. She hoped to get another few years before it breathed its last.

Coal reached inside the glove compartment for a pair of sunglasses to shade her eyes from the setting sun. She froze for a second when her hand landed on a pair of aviator glasses. They had been standard issue in the desert as protection from the intense sunlight and had become a part of her uniform. She hesitated for a moment to shake the memory of the desert from her mind and then pulled the glasses out and put them on. "Ah, that's better," she said as she relaxed back in the seat.

Mary Leah glanced over to see Coal's left knee bouncing up and down, a symptom of her anxiety over the impending appointment. She reached over, took her hand, and brought it to her mouth for a soft kiss and then entwined their fingers. "Are you still planning to get the brisket?"

"It's a toss-up between that and the baby back ribs," she answered.

"Why don't we get one of each and split them," Mary Leah suggested.

Coal smiled at her lover. "I love the way you think."

†

Dinner was finished with little conversation. Mary Leah watched as Coal picked through her food, eating half of what was normal for her and she knew Coal was thinking about her appointment. "Do you want to get a doggy bag for later?" Mary Leah asked.

"Sure, if you want. Sorry, my eyes were bigger than my stomach."

"No worries. These are even better as leftovers," she said. "I'll ask the server to box them up for us and pay the bill so we can get out of here."

"Okay. I'll be right back," she said as she left the table to visit the restroom. She washed the barbecue sauce from her hands and stared back at her image in the mirror. "I hope this works," she spoke aloud, tearing a paper towel from the holder to dry her hands.

"Ready?" Mary Leah asked when she returned to the table.

She nodded. "Let's do this," she said and took the carryout bag from Mary Leah.

She followed Mary Leah to the car. Despite the cold air-conditioning, Coal felt her hands begin to grow clammy.

Chapter Twelve

Mary Leah weaved through traffic and made it to Del's office with ten minutes to spare. The parking lot was empty so she parked in front of the entrance, turned the car off, and looked at Coal. "You are going to be just fine," she said to reassure her lover.

"Yes, I am," she said and climbed out of the car.

†

Del was reviewing the file on Coal when she heard the chime on the front door sound. She had already sent Linda, her receptionist, home, so she walked out to meet Mary Leah and Coal. She smiled when her eyes met Coal's. "Hi, I'm Del," she said, offering her hand.

Coal reached out and gave her a firm handshake. "Pleased to meet you, Del."

Turning to Mary Leah, she said, "Make yourself comfortable and we will see you soon. We are the only ones here so I'm going to lock us in," she said as she flipped a lock on the front door. "There are cold drinks in the kitchen if you get thirsty."

"I'm good for now, thanks," Mary Leah said as she took a seat on a comfortable-looking couch.

"Are you ready to get started?"

"Yes, ma'am," Coal answered. With a final smile to Mary Leah, she followed Del into her office.

Del closed the door behind them and turned to Coal. "Where would you be more comfortable sitting?" she asked.

"The couch is fine with me," she answered.

"Make yourself comfortable then while I get my notepad. I usually tape our sessions to refer back to later. Are you all right with that?"

Del looked up to see a smirk on her face. "Did I say something funny?"

Coal realized Del had caught her expression. "I'm sorry, I was just thinking, apparently too loudly."

"Would you care to share what you find so humorous?"

She felt heat rise to her cheeks. "I thought you would have been taller the way Melissa and Mary Leah talk about you."

Her smile comforted Coal. "Just remember dynamite comes in small packages."

"Yes, ma'am," she said as she sat on the couch. Coal watched Del closely, taking in her blond curls and the sparkle in her blue eyes when she looked at her. Her warm smile revealed a grin and a dimple in her left cheek.

Del walked slowly to her desk to give Coal a few moments to get comfortable. When she returned and sat in a deeply cushioned chair beside the couch, she smiled warmly at Coal. "It's a pleasure to finally meet you. I've heard so much about you from Melissa and Mary Leah."

"I'm sorry it's under these circumstances," Coal said shyly.

"There is no need to apologize. There is no shame in realizing you need some help to sort through what you endured in the desert. I've had a chance to read over your file and know a little about your service, but I want you to feel comfortable with our sessions. If you begin to feel too anxious, I want you to be honest with me. There is no timeframe to complete your therapy, so we will move at the pace you feel comfortable with."

"Thanks, Doc."

"Can we start by you telling me what has been going on lately?"

Coal took a deep breath and let it out slowly before beginning to speak.

†

An hour later, Del knew the full extent of the trauma Coal had experienced in the desert and the memories that were haunting her life. She was even more surprised to find that Mitch had been one of the soldiers killed on that terrible day. She moved next to her on the couch and took a sobbing Coal into her arms for a warm embrace. "I think we have done enough for tonight," she whispered.

Coal nodded her head in agreement and wiped the tears from her cheeks. Her shirt was soaked with perspiration from her anxiety.

"You did remarkably well tonight. There is a relatively new program that I would like you to participate in," Del said. "It is a virtual reality program called Virtual Iraq and it will help to desensitize you to the traumatic memories you have and allow you to finally cope with the events that terrorize you. Are you interested in participating?"

"If you think that is best for me, then yes."

"It will take me a week or longer to program the series to meet your specific criteria, but I would like to meet with you three days a week to continue our sessions. Is that acceptable to you?"

"Yes, Doc, that would be fine," she said. Coal looked into Del's warm brown eyes. "Do you really think you can fix me?"

"No, I can't," she replied. "Together we can, but it has to be you. You are the only one who can fix you."

Coal smiled for the first time since entering the office. "We can do this."

"Yes, we can, and we will," Del answered.

"Do I need medications?" she asked.

"No, I don't think you do. If anything, I would suggest using melatonin to help you get better sleep. It is a natural supplement and over the counter. I'm sure Mary Leah can get you set up."

"Thanks, Doc."

"One other thing, don't worry about hurting her. Mary Leah is not as fragile as you think. I would also recommend talking with her about your episodes. The more you discuss what happened, the easier it will become to let it go." She smiled at Coal. "No more holding it in. If you don't feel good talking to her about it, find someone else close to you. Do you have any other questions tonight?"

"How much do I owe you?" Coal asked as she pulled out her checkbook.

"Your service to our country is paying for your treatment. You have paid enough."

With that, Del stood and offered her hand to Coal. "Let's plan to meet Monday, Wednesday, and Friday next week. Is this time good for you?"

"Yes, it is. Thanks again," she said as she stood and followed Del to the door.

Del opened the door and Mary Leah stood from her seat. "Get some rest tonight and have a good weekend, and I will see you Monday."

"Thanks, Del," Mary Leah said and hugged her friend.

"Stop and get her some melatonin and make sure she takes the maximum dosage before going to bed each night."

"I will," Mary Leah said.

Mary Leah reached for Coal's hand as they left the building. Once back inside the car, she turned to her and asked, "How are you feeling?"

"Exhausted," she said honestly.

"Kick back and relax then and I will get us home."

"You'll get no argument from me," Coal said and reclined her seat back.

They hadn't made it out of the city before Coal was sleeping peacefully in her seat. Mary Leah made a stop at a chain pharmacy and bought the melatonin. When she climbed back into the car, Coal still slept and did not stir.

Mary Leah gently woke Coal as they neared the ranch. "There is a bottle of water and a container of pills. Go ahead and take three before we get home," she instructed.

Coal took the pills and drained the bottle of water as she relaxed into the seat. "I don't think I'm going to be able to take you up on your offer of dessert tonight. I'm whipped physically and emotionally."

"Baby, don't worry about that. As long as your warm body is next to mine I am perfectly content."

Coal reached over to entwine her fingers with Mary Leah's. "Thank you, my love."

When they reached home, they entered the house hand in hand. They walked to the bedroom and stripped out of their clothes before entwining in one another's arms to sleep peacefully through the night.

†

Coal woke before sunrise to find her lover spooned up next to her. Her hand softly stroked down Mary Leah's arm and hip as her lips softly caressed her neck. She could feel her begin to stir, and Mary Leah was wearing a smile when she rolled onto her back and looked up at her. Coal lowered her face to kiss her sweetly as her hand continued to play across Mary Leah's skin, and when she felt her shiver, she moved on top of her lover.

Her hips rocked slowly between Mary Leah's thighs as they continued to kiss. She ended the kiss and opened her eyes to see desire building in Mary Leah's eyes. She kissed down Mary Leah's neck, her soft lips caressing the scars on her chest left bare from the cancer. Mary Leah groaned in pleasure. Coal had never complained about her lack of breasts or the ugly scars the surgery had left behind, but Mary Leah longed for the feeling of a lover suckling her breasts.

Her hands played in Coal's dark hair as Coal's lips brushed the sensitive skin down the front of her body and her tongue entered the wetness nestled in the center of her being. Mary Leah moaned as Coal's tongue and lips explored her body, and when she slid a finger into the silky wetness, stars began to erupt behind her eyelids as her passion reached its climax and she ground her body into Coal's mouth.

Coal felt the trembling deep within her lover's body as her tongue and finger glided through wetness and her soft moans encouraged her to continue until she felt Mary Leah's body release in waves of convulsions. She continued her ministrations until she felt Mary Leah relax and then removed her finger and kissed her way back into her lover's arms.

"Good morning," she whispered.

"It has definitely started off well for me," Mary Leah said with a purr in her voice.

She grinned back at her. "I didn't want you to think I had forgotten your offer of dessert."

Mary Leah wrapped her arms tightly around Coal's shoulders. "Do you need some attention?"

"I have what I need right here," she said as she moved to lie next to her lover, placing her head on her shoulder.

"Did you sleep well?"

"Like a rock, for a change, and I woke up feeling refreshed."

"I can definitely tell the difference," she teased. "That felt terrific."

Coal looked over at the clock. "Do you want to snooze a little longer before we have to get up?"

"As long as you promise not to move from this spot," Mary Leah answered.

"Only long enough to do this," Coal said as she raised her face to kiss Mary Leah. "I love you," she said and snuggled back into Mary Leah's arms.

"I love you too."

†

When the alarm sounded two hours later, Mary Leah reached over to turn it off. "What time do we need to be ready for the cookout tonight?"

"The guys usually have dinner ready by seven, why do you ask?"

"I thought I would come home and help you with the beans and macaroni salad."

"That would be great," she said as she heard the beep of the coffeepot, notifying them the coffee had finished brewing. "Sit tight and I'll grab us a cup," she said.

Mary Leah snuggled under the covers, still enjoying the glow of their lovemaking as she waited for her to return.

Coal returned with steaming mugs of coffee and handed one to Mary Leah before sitting on the edge of the bed.

"What does your day look like?"

"I'm not real sure. I'll probably be helping with the haying. I'm not sure if we are ready to start baling yet or not, but you can guarantee it will be another hot day for us," she answered.

"Do you think y'all will be working this weekend?"

"Probably Saturday if we start baling, why do you ask?"

"I thought I might take my best girl to the movies on Sunday," Mary Leah said.

"Find us a movie and it's a date," she said with a smile.

Chapter Thirteen

Coal tied Shadow's reins to the rail of the hitching post outside the bunkhouse and walked inside to find the crew finishing breakfast. "Morning," she said as she walked to the counter and poured a cup of coffee.

"Good morning," Harley answered. "We were just discussing the work for today."

She joined them at the table. "What's on tap for today?"

"Stan wants to give the hay we cut yesterday the morning to dry, so we are going to work on the next field. He wants you and Gene to ride up to the north pasture and check the boundary fence. Some of the neighbor's herd made it into our pasture and may have done some damage."

"That sounds like a good way to eat the morning up," she said.

"If you see any more of their herd, move them back on their side of the fence and try to be back for lunch. If everything works out well we will start baling after lunch and you two will get a workout then," Harley said with a grin.

"Speaking of Gene, where is he?"

"He's already gone to the barn to saddle up and put some tools together," Lucas said.

Coal grinned and drained her cup. "I guess I'd better get a move on then."

"We'll see you at lunch," Harley said as she placed her cup in the dishwasher and headed for the door.

"See you soon," she answered and opened the door to find Gene already mounted and waiting for her. She swung her body into the saddle and they started walking across the yard.

"Looks like we lucked up with fence mending duty," he said.

"We better enjoy this morning. By the time we start loading those bales it will be nice and hot," she said.

"Nothing like working up a good sweat," he teased.

"I'll remind you of that about two o'clock," she teased back.

They rode in silence for a few minutes, and when Gene straightened in his saddle after closing a gate behind them, he turned to look at Coal. "You look refreshed and relaxed this morning."

"I had a good night's sleep for a change."

"Did your appointment go well?"

Coal really didn't want to talk about it, but remembered Del's advice about talking about her experience in the desert. "Yeah, it did. I think she can help me get over the past."

"You know I almost joined up after high school," he said.

"Be glad you didn't. In hindsight, I wouldn't wish that on anyone."

"How did you get in the army?" he asked.

"I joined after college and went through Army Ranger School and served four years before I had enough and transitioned to the reserves."

"Is that where you learned to fight so well?"

"Yeah, I learned how to be a killing machine." Coal seemed thoughtful for a few seconds. "My first experience in the desert was easy, pretty much mop-up duty. The major conflict had been over for months and our unit deployed to assist with transitioning troops back home. There was no fight left by then, but we had to remain vigilant for snipers and bombs."

"Did you have to kill anyone while you were there?"

"Not while I was active duty. When I rotated out and joined the reserves, I went to work at a ranch in Dallas for a while. That's when I met my girlfriend, Tessa, and Mitch. They were both part of my reserve unit."

"I had just started working at the MC2 when he got called up," Gene said. "He seemed to be a really great guy."

"He was," she said. "I really enjoyed serving with him."

Gene bent over in the saddle to open another gate and they rode through. "How long were you with Tessa?"

Coal smiled at him. "You are full of questions this morning."

Gene frowned. "I'm sorry, I didn't mean to pry."

"That's okay, Gene. Tessa was a teacher in Dallas. We lived together for two years before our unit got recalled and we were sent to Afghanistan."

"What was she like?" He noticed a dreamy look in her eyes as she thought of the words to describe Tessa.

"She was beautiful and had the kindest heart of anyone I have ever met. She worked at an elementary school in a low-income section of Dallas. I used to tease her that she spent most of her salary providing for the kids in her class. She always made sure her students had what they needed, whether it was a coat or notebooks, she was always first to act for their benefit."

"She sounds like a good woman. What happened to her?"

She felt tears welling in her eyes and when she looked at Gene, he swallowed hard, realizing he had struck a painful memory in his friend. "Damn, I'm sorry, I should shut my big mouth," he said, hanging his head.

"No, Gene, the doctor actually encouraged me to talk about it to help me with my therapy, so you are actually doing me a big favor. What I'm telling you Mary Leah doesn't even know yet, so this is like a rehearsal."

Gene smiled in relief at her comment. "That doesn't make it easy though, I'm sure."

Coal shook her head. "No, it doesn't." She took a deep breath. "We were two weeks shy of rotating back to the States when we were sent on a mission. It was a blistering Saturday morning and there was eeriness in the air. Normally, the streets on a Saturday morning would have been bustling with activity, families rushing to market and running errands, but that morning the only movement was the heat waves dancing on the streets."

They had reached the final gate, so she waited until they passed through to continue. "We were called out on a report of a car bomb in a residential area. Mitch and Tessa were the bomb experts on our team and I was part of the sniper protection for them. As they approached to begin disarming the bomb, a crying child walked out to the street, headed directly toward the car. I turned my head for a fraction of a second to bark out an order for one of the soldiers to move the child to safety and my moment of distraction allowed the terrorist to activate the bomb. Mitch heard the click of the ignition and dove on the bomb to protect the rest of us and was killed instantly."

Coal hesitated for a second as her eyes rested on a stray steer that did not wear the brand of the MC2. "Let's get him back home and then I'll continue," she said. "Might as well find out where he breached the fence first," she added.

"You check the fence and I'll round him up," he said and rode toward the stray.

She rode forward along the fence line and found the area the steer had pressed his way through and whistled to Gene who was already moving the steer in her direction. She backed Shadow away from the gap to allow plenty of room for the steer to enter his home pasture and waited for Gene to run him through.

Gene stopped beside her and said, "I'll fix this section if you want to keep riding the fence line to make sure this is the only breach. I'll catch up with you when I'm finished."

"You sure you don't need help?"

"Naw, I've got this."

Coal nodded and turned Shadow to continue riding the fence line. She reached out and checked posts as she passed them to ensure they were solid and the wire was intact. The cry of a hawk overhead broke her concentration, and she looked up to see him flying toward the pasture the crew was cutting for hay. He soared in the soft winds high above, his sharp eyes searching the ground for any signs of movement. She watched for several more seconds until his cry rang in her ears again and he dove swiftly after his prey, becoming lost to her vision as he descended beneath the tree line. She waited for several seconds to see if he would reappear with his prey caught in sharp talons, but he remained invisible to her eyes.

She resumed her investigation and Gene joined her ten minutes later. "Welcome back."

"Thanks, did you see that hawk?"

"Yeah, I did. I wonder what he caught?" she said.

"I couldn't tell either," he said as he settled in beside Shadow.

They walked in silence for a few minutes before she resumed her story. "When Mitch dove on top of the bomb, it killed him instantly but protected several others from major damage. Tessa, however, was closest to him and took a major hit from the flying shrapnel. I took out the terrorist with my rifle, but I was a second too late. I rushed to Tessa as another team member called for a medical evacuation unit, but it was too late for her too. She died in my arms and there was nothing I could do to save her."

"Damn, that sucks," Gene said. "I'm sorry, Coal."

"Thanks, Gene."

"Were you injured?"

"I took some shrapnel to my side, but my injuries were not serious. I didn't even realize I was bleeding until the chopper arrived. A few dozen stitches and I was good to go, physically at least."

"Is that when you came to the MC2?"

"I resigned my commission when I returned to Dallas and tried to live in the home Tessa and I made, but I couldn't live there without her. I heard from my ranch foreman that the MC2 was hiring, so I applied, not knowing that it was Mitch's ranch or that Melissa was his wife. I guess fate just brought me home."

"When did you make the connection?"

She chuckled. "Melissa and I were going to watch a movie after we had finished the hay in my first week here. When I walked into the den I saw pictures of Mitch and Tessa I had taken hanging on the wall and I passed out in shock."

"I bet that was a shock to your system."

"Neither Melissa or I had made the connection until that night."

"Thank you for sharing that with me. I promise I won't tell anyone else what happened, but I really hope you don't blame yourself for what happened."

"I did for a long time," she admitted.

"What is happening with you now?"

"I don't know. Mary Leah and the doctor think I may have post-traumatic stress. I don't understand why it is coming out now, but I've been having nightmares and losing sleep."

"I hope therapy will work quickly for you, Coal," he said, blushing.

"Thanks, Gene, I hope so too."

They had checked the remainder of the fence line and found no further breaches. "You ready to throw some hay?" she asked.

"Sooner we start, the sooner we finish. Are you going to feel like practicing some tonight after dinner?"

"I think that could be arranged. I know Shadow is ready for some exercise."

"Let's give them a short run then," Gene said and urged his horse into a gallop as they raced across the open field.

†

Melissa had just driven up with lunch when Coal and Gene arrived at the hayfields. "Well you two sure have perfect timing today," she teased.

"Gene smelled food," Coal answered and Gene laughed.

"You know I can smell it from a mile away."

"Tend to your horses and join us. I'll fix your plates," Melissa said.

Coal and Gene tied their reins on tree branches and then unsaddled their horses in the shade. "Should we let them loose to graze?" he asked.

"Might as well. We're going to be here a while," she answered and took Shadow's bridle and hung it on the limb.

They walked over to the group resting in the shade, enjoying lunch. Melissa brought plates and drinks and then sat with the group. "You know, I can drive the truck to allow two to load and two to stack," she said.

"That would speed things up some. Are you sure you wouldn't mind?" Stan asked.

"Not at all, you guys are cooking dinner, so I'm free for the afternoon."

"You have a deal then," he said with a grin.

"Let me finish lunch, and I'll get going with the baler to get a head start on you. Roy can drive the rake. That way you can finish cutting the next field," Harley said.

153

"Sounds like a plan in motion," Stan said as he dusted off his clothes and walked back to the mower.

Gene and Coal dove into the stack of sandwiches on their plates, eager to get back to work. "You two need to slow down and chew," Harley said as he walked to the baler. "Give me a good half hour head start."

"Yes, boss," they said in unison and slowed down to enjoy their food.

Melissa shook her head as she grinned at the pair. "I swear you are two peas in a pod."

"Yeah, but I'm the better looking one," Coal said as she punched Gene's shoulder.

"I guess that leaves me the strong one," he said, flexing his arms, making the rest of the crew laugh.

"I hope you can still do that when we get done today," Melissa said.

"I'll be ready to throw some rope after supper," Gene said.

"Are you two practicing tonight?" she asked.

"Yeah, at least for a little while," she said. "I'm sure Stan will want to get an early start tomorrow to beat the heat, so we won't be long."

"Well, the reservations are all set for Dallas, and I went ahead and booked rooms for Austin too," Melissa said. "So don't disappoint me."

"We're going to do our best, boss," Coal promised.

"I have no doubt of that," Melissa said. "Do you need more to drink?"

"No, I'm good, thanks," she said as she handed her the empty plate and cup.

Coal watched as Harley drove down the second row of raked hay, the baler dropping the sixty-pound bales about every thirty seconds. She was about to ask if they were ready to go when for the second time that day they heard the hawk's cry and looked up to see his body streaking to the ground a hundred yards behind Harley, then taking flight with a large rattlesnake dangling from his talons. She looked over at Gene. "Our guardian angel has arrived."

"I'm glad he got that one. I'd hate to pick up a bale with a snake curled up inside it," he said.

"I hear that. We better keep our eyes open, though, for the rest of the family."

"Damn straight, Coal," he said. He stood and offered her a hand to pull her to her feet. "Let's roll."

They both looked at Melissa. "Ready, boss?" They pulled her up from the ground.

Tom and Lucas jumped on the back of the truck ready to stack the bales that she and Gene would toss onto the bed of the truck while Melissa drove.

The truck started to roll slowly forward and Coal lifted the first bale onto the truck bed, Gene following close behind her from the opposite side of the truck. As they reached the end of the first rows, Melissa turned the truck down the next rows and Gene took advantage of the short break to pull off his work shirt leaving him wearing a white tank top undershirt.

"That's not a bad idea," Coal said and unbuttoned her shirt and tossed it to Gene, who rushed to the window of the truck and pitched them inside.

"Is everything all right?" Melissa asked.

"Yes, ma'am, just stripping down a bit," Gene answered with a cute grin.

"Don't you two forget to take a break and get some fluids back into y'all."

"Yes, ma'am," Gene repeated and turned to collect the first bale on his side of the truck.

Halfway through the next row they had the truck filled to capacity. Lucas jumped down and walked to the cab of the truck followed by Tom. "You two catch something cool to drink and some shade and we'll get this up to the loft," Lucas said.

"You'll get no arguments from me," Coal said.

"The coolers are filled with water, tea, and lemonade," Melissa said. "Drink plenty; you two are soaked to the bone."

"Yes, boss," Coal, said as she tipped her hat. She and Gene walked toward the shade.

"What can I buy you to drink?" Gene asked.

"I think I'll have some lemonade," she answered.

"Me too," he answered with a boyish grin.

She sat on top of one of the coolers and enjoyed the respite of the shade as she turned to look at Harley. They were making good time on this field and, with some luck they would finish it today and be ready to work on the next in the morning. Her eyes moved over two fields and Stan was barely visible through a cloud of dust as he cut the next field. "I bet he's eaten plenty of dust today," she said to Gene, nodding toward Stan.

"Yeah, it's been crazy dry this summer. Worse than last year I think."

"I agree, hotter too," Coal said as she took off her straw work hat and wiped her brow.

Gene looked at her with concern. "Do you need to take a break from loading to stack a while?"

"Heck no," she answered. "I'd much rather be moving around on the ground."

"I hear ya," Gene said. "Looks like we are about to get some company."

Harley and Roy had also decided to take a break and were walking toward them for a cool drink. "Hey, boss, what would you like to drink?"

"That lemonade looks good," he answered.

"Me too, please," Roy said.

She poured two more glasses of lemonade and refilled Gene's and her own before sitting down with them.

Harley took a long drink and sighed. "Damn, that hits the spot. You two doing okay in this heat?"

"Yes, sir, I think we are good for now," she answered.

"One more load and Stan says we will be done for the day. I don't know about y'all, but I'm ready for a nice juicy steak."

"You're singing my tune, boss." Gene grinned. "I feel like I could eat a whole steer about now."

"Melissa's got chocolate chip cookies in the basket if you need a snack," he told Gene.

Gene did not need a second invitation to respond and quickly moved to the picnic basket. Coal watched him as he opened it like a kid at Christmas. She saw bananas in the basket too. "Hey, bring me a couple of those bananas, please."

"Smart woman," Harley said.

"I can't do too much sugar in this heat and my muscles need the potassium."

"You two want anything?" Gene asked before closing the basket.

"No, I'm good," Harley said.

"I'll take a banana," Roy said with a grin to Coal.

Thirty minutes later they could see the dust the truck stirred up as Melissa drove back toward them. "I guess break time is over," Harley said. "Pace yourselves and don't overdo it," he said. He and Roy walked back to the tractors.

When Melissa, Lucas, and Tom returned, Coal poured them drinks.

"Y'all doing okay?" Melissa asked. She looked at the army green tank top Coal was wearing and could see the dried salt stains forming. She looked at the banana peels at Coal's feet and smiled.

"Yes'm, we're good," she answered.

"Harley said one more load today and we were done for the day," Gene said.

"That's good. This sun is brutal and all I'm doing is driving," Melissa said.

"A nice cool shower is going to feel good tonight," Lucas chimed in.

"I'll second that," Gene said.

"Let's do it then, so we can all get cleaned up," she said.

They resumed loading the bales and had made it to the end of a row when she felt a stinging on her left side, like a wasp had stung her. She didn't think anything more of it until Gene cried out.

"Coal, what's wrong," he said, pointing down at her side with panic in his eyes.

Melissa heard him cry out, and slammed on the brakes, tossing Lucas and Tom into the stack of bales and flew from the cab of the truck.

Coal cocked her head at Gene whose face was rapidly turning white as the color drained from it, and then looked down at her side. There was a growing red stain on her shirt and a shard of metal poking through.

Melissa stopped in her tracks and stared as Coal gently lifted her shirt to find a piece of shrapnel had finally worked its way out of her body. She guessed the strain of lifting the bales onto the bed of the truck had finally forced it out of her body. She placed the tip of a gloved finger in her mouth, and pulled off the leather glove, spitting it to the ground before painfully pulling the inch long metal shard from between her ribs. Melissa turned back for the medical kit in the truck.

"Oh, dear God," she heard Gene cry out, and turned in time to see him crumple to the ground.

Lucas and Tom jumped down from the bed of the truck and Lucas rushed to her side as Tom checked on Gene.

"What happened?" Lucas asked.

"I had one piece of shrapnel left inside me and it decided to make an appearance today," she calmly explained to him as Melissa approached.

"That's been inside you for three years?" Lucas asked incredulously as he looked at the metal shard she was still holding.

"Yeah, they couldn't find it at the time."

"You're damned lucky it didn't puncture a lung or go to your heart," Melissa said as she pressed sterile pads against the wound to stop the bleeding.

"I'll be all right, boss," Coal said. "I'm not too sure about Gene though."

Harley saw the truck stop and the flurry of activity so he shut off the baler and drove for the truck. He surveyed the scene—Gene flat out on the ground and Melissa tending to Coal— trying to understand what was going on.

"What happened?" he asked, skidding to a halt after running over to them.

She looked up at him. "My last shrapnel shard made its appearance today," she said. She opened her palm to show him the wicked-looking metal.

"I've heard of that happening," he said calmly. "Are you okay? Do we need to take you for stitches?"

Melissa lifted the blood-soaked bandage to inspect the wound. "It looks like a fairly clean slice, but I'd feel better if you had it looked at."

"I've had much worse," she said.

Melissa glanced at the long scars down Coal's side and knew she was being honest. "Maybe you have, but I'm taking you to town to get it checked out," she commanded. "Lucas, get the truck for me, please."

"Yes, ma'am," he said and took off running across the field.

"How's Gene?" she asked.

Melissa turned to look toward Gene who was now in a sitting position. "He looks fine. I think he just passed out when he saw the blood on his hero," she teased with a grin.

She started to chuckle and then grimaced with pain. "Dear God, please don't make me laugh."

"Sorry," Melissa said as she took out clean gauze pads and held them next to the wound while Harley placed several strips of tape across it tightly to keep the pressure firm. "Hold onto that and let's get you to town," she said as Lucas arrived with the truck.

Gene had finally made it back onto his feet and he walked shakily over to Coal. "Are you all right?" he asked, the color yet to return to his face.

"Yeah, I'm okay, Gene. How are you?"

"Feeling stupid for passing out at the sight of blood," he said with shame.

"There is nothing wrong with that, son," Harley said with a pat on his back. "Especially when it's something you weren't expecting."

"I still feel like an idiot," Gene said, hanging his head. "Do you need help with her?" he asked Melissa.

She didn't, but she looked at Harley who nodded.

"Sure, Gene, will you sit in back with her and make sure she doesn't take her hand off that bandage?"

"Yes, ma'am," he answered, and opened the door for Coal.

"He wouldn't be any good to us the rest of the day anyhow, worrying about her," Harley told Melissa. "We'll finish out this load and head for the barn. I'll let Stan know what's going on. You take care of her and let us know if you need anything."

"Thanks, Harley," Melissa said and walked to the driver's side as Gene slipped in beside Coal.

"Let's get her done, boys," Harley barked, and the crew snapped to attention as he went to the driver's side of the truck.

†

"Do you want me to call Mary Leah?" Melissa asked as she carefully drove across the rough pasture.

Coal didn't hesitate to answer her. "No, it's nothing serious and I don't want her to worry."

"Fine, but you take the rap tonight when she flies off the handle that we didn't call her."

She grinned. "I will, I promise."

"Will you look at that?" Gene said as he looked out the side window.

Shadow was trotting beside the truck, his sensitive nostrils flaring from the scent of blood. "Stop at the barn if you would and I'll put him in a stall so he doesn't follow us to town," Gene said.

"He probably would too," Melissa said. "He loves you too," she said with a wink to Coal in the rearview mirror.

†

When the truck reached the hard road, Melissa picked up speed and within ten minutes, they arrived at the small walk-in clinic. Gene jumped out of the truck and rushed around to open her door and help Coal from the truck.

Melissa opened the clinic door to usher them inside and then went to the triage nurse to explain what had happened. The nurse took Coal directly to an exam room and left Melissa and a pacing Gene in the waiting room.

"Let's see what we have here," she said as she helped her to sit on the exam table. She lifted Coal's shirt over her head to inspect her for other injuries. "My name is Terry, Ms. Bryan, and I will get you cleaned up for the doctor's examination."

"Nice to meet you, Terry," she said.

Terry pulled the tape off Coal's skin as gently as she could and removed the gauze to look at the wound. "You said this was done by a piece of shrapnel?"

"Yeah," she said as she held out her hand. "My last souvenir from Afghanistan." Terry took the metal shard in her gloved hand.

"This looks wicked," she said as she turned the shard in her hand.

"They used everything metal they could salvage for shrapnel in their bomb making," she said. "The doctors told me they got all of it out, but a later exam revealed a piece still floating around inside."

"How long ago was this?"

"A little over three years," she answered.

"You're lucky this didn't puncture a lung or pierce your heart."

"That's twice in the last hour I've heard that," she said with a grin.

The exam room door opened and a young male doctor walked into the room. "I'm Dr. Thomas," he said. "What do we have here, Terry?" he asked, looking at the shrapnel in the nurse's hand.

"Shrapnel leftover from Afghanistan," she answered.

"It finally worked its way out today while I was loading hay," Coal said.

"Have you had a tetanus shot recently?" he asked as he cleaned the wound with Betadine.

"Three years ago," she answered.

"That's good, but I want to give you a fresh one. That's one wicked piece of metal. A good clean exit though."

"Will she need stitches?" Terry asked.

"No, I think some surgical glue would work better," he answered. "Less of a scar too," he said with a warm smile to her. "Are these from the rest of the shrapnel?" he said, examining the other scars on her side.

"Yeah, I had two dozen or so stitches to close it up once the docs finished digging out the metal."

"Damn," he said.

The doctor pulled out a tube that did look suspiciously like superglue and used it to seal the wound. He placed a clean bandage over the wound as Terry gave her the tetanus shot in her right arm. "Try to take it easy for a few days and this should heal with little problem. I want to give you some antibiotics too just as a precaution," he added.

"Thanks, Doc," she said as he exited the room.

Terry helped her back into her tank top and walked out with her to the waiting room where she repeated the doc's instructions for Melissa's benefit. "No heavy lifting for three days and take all of these antibiotics." She handed Melissa a bottle of pills. She smiled at them and handed Coal a small plastic bag with the shard covered in gauze. "Your souvenir," she said.

"Thanks. Will you send me a bill? I didn't bring my wallet."

"Uncle Sam's got this one," Terry said. "Thank you."

She let Gene usher her back to the truck and he closed the door behind her then ran around to open Melissa's door. "Are we taking her home?"

"Yes. I'll stay with her and wrap her in some plastic wrap so she can shower. I'll drop you at the barn so you can ride Shadow home and ride back with me."

Gene chuckled at her comment.

"What's so funny?" she asked, confused.

"No one rides him except for Coal. I tried once and ate more dirt than I cared to. I'll walk him over, it's not that far."

Melissa smiled at her young cowboy. "Thanks, Gene."

"Anything for Coal," he said as he closed the door behind her.

✝

Melissa dropped Gene back at the barn and drove Coal home. The rest of the men were returning when he led Shadow from the barn.

"You want me to take him?" Lucas asked.

"Naw, I've got this," Gene said as he led Shadow across the yard.

The rest of the crew watched as Gene proudly led Shadow from the yard.

"He's like a puppy when it concerns Coal," Harley said, shaking his head with a laugh. "Let's get cleaned up and ready to start dinner."

†

"Let's get you out of these clothes and into the shower," Melissa said to her. "Do you have some plastic wrap?"

"Yeah, in the pantry," Coal said as she slipped her shirt and bra from her body.

When Melissa entered the kitchen, she saw Stan standing at the front door. She walked over and let him in.

"How's Coal?" he asked.

"She's going to be fine. I'm going to wrap her in some plastic, so she can take a shower."

"Oh," Stan said. "I won't keep you then. I just wanted to know she's okay."

"I'll let her know you stopped by to check on her. Are you coming back for the cookout?"

"Not tonight, but I'll see you in the morning, boss."

"Thanks, Stan," she said and watched him leave the house before turning back to Coal.

Melissa returned to the bedroom and wrapped the plastic around Coal's body. "Leave this on until you finish the shower and then you can remove it and wash around the wound gently. Okay? Yell if you need help. By the way, Stan stopped by to check on you."

"That was very sweet of him. I hope you told him I was fine."

164

"I did. You know, all the crew thinks of you as a sister, except Gene, of course. You hung the moon for him." She chuckled.

"Thanks, Melissa," she said.

When Melissa returned the plastic to the pantry, she saw the ingredients for the macaroni salad and baked beans sitting out on the counter and decided she would give Coal a head start on her dishes. She placed a pot of water on the stove to boil and had just placed the dish in the oven to bake the beans, when Coal entered the kitchen.

"I thought I heard someone in the kitchen," she said as Melissa turned toward her.

"I've got your beans on and water on to boil. Is there anything else I can help with?"

"Put another pot of water on please, I want to surprise the crew with some deviled eggs," Coal said.

"Oh, yummy," Melissa said. "How do you feel?"

"A little sore, but much better now that I'm clean again," she answered.

"It wouldn't hurt to take some ibuprofen and don't forget the antibiotics tonight when you get some food in your belly."

"I won't," Coal said. She heard Gene's boots on the front porch and waved him inside.

"Shadow is all set for the night," he said.

"Thanks, Gene, did you ride him over?"

"Hell no, we walked." He grinned. "I've already hit the ground once today."

"That you have, my friend," she said and surprised him by taking him into an embrace.

Gene carefully encircled her with his arms and hugged her gently. "Is there anything else I can help with?"

"Thanks, but Mary Leah will be home soon to help. Go get cleaned up and ready for grub," she said as she released him.

"Okay, I'll see you tonight," Gene said and walked out to the truck.

"You sure you're okay?"

"Yes. Mary Leah will be home in ten or fifteen minutes, so there isn't much trouble I can get into before then."

Melissa chuckled. "There will be plenty once she arrives home, so let me make my escape now." She hugged her. "I think I'll bake a cake," she said aloud.

"Yellow cake with chocolate icing?" Coal asked.

"What else?" Melissa said with a wink and left the house.

✝

She turned back to the kitchen and walked to the refrigerator to take out the two dozen eggs Mary Leah had brought home and placed them in the pot to boil. She poured a large box of elbow macaroni in the pot now boiling and took a seat at the counter.

Ten minutes later, she heard the sound of Mary Leah's car coming down the drive and then her lover coming through the front door.

"Hey, baby," Coal said as Mary Leah placed her purse on the table.

"I'm surprised to see you home this early," she said, hugging Coal tightly and causing her to yelp in pain. "What's wrong?"

She stirred the macaroni on the stove and told Mary Leah about the events of the afternoon.

"So neither of you thought it was important for me to know?" Mary Leah said her anger evident in her words. "Just wait until I see her tonight."

"I made Melissa promise not to call you. If it had been something serious, I would have called you." She grimaced at the look her lover shot her. "Please. Melissa is not to

166

blame for this. I'm just relieved that piece is finally out and will cause me no more pain."

"Dammit, Coal, that could have killed you," Mary Leah said.

"But, it didn't," she said as she wrapped her arms around Mary Leah's waist and kissed her face softly and then her lips.

Mary Leah's tension melted in her arms. Her kisses always had that effect on her. When the kisses ended, she looked into Coal's eyes. "Every time you kiss my face like that you plant a kiss on my heart."

Coal saw tears filling Mary Leah's eyes. "Where did that come from, my love?"

"I don't know," Mary Leah said, wiping her tears, "it just came out."

"Those are the most romantic words I have ever heard," Coal said as she held her close.

The timer on the stove sounded to bring them back to reality. Her eggs had finished boiling. "Will you do something for me?"

"Sure, what can I do?"

"Lift the pot with the eggs into the sink for me? The doc doesn't want me to bust the seam on the superglue he used on me," she said with a grin.

"No problem," Mary Leah said as she chuckled and placed the heavy pot in the sink and turned on the cold water.

"Thanks. I can handle things from here if you want to shower and get ready for dinner."

"I'll be right back then," Mary Leah said, kissing her before leaving the room.

†

Coal prepared the macaroni salad and placed it in the refrigerator to chill, and was working on the deviled eggs when a pair of warm arms circled her waist. "Welcome back," she said as Mary Leah's body pressed into her back.

Mary Leah stood on her tiptoes to look over her shoulder. "Those look good," she said as she watched Coal fill a halved egg white with the mixture she had concocted.

She carefully turned in Mary Leah's grasp and offered her a bite. Mary Leah opened her mouth and bit half of the egg, and Coal popped the remainder into her mouth.

"They taste even better than they look," Mary Leah announced after a loud moan.

"How are we doing on time?" she asked.

"It's a little after five."

"Care to join me for a cold one before we head over to the cookout?"

"I'd love too. The doctor didn't put you on any pain medicine did he?"

"No, ma'am, only antibiotics which I will take after dinner, besides I'll only have the one with you," she answered. "Go have a seat on the deck and I'll bring our beers out in just a second when I put these eggs in to chill."

"All right, my love," Mary Leah said and walked out to the deck.

She placed the eggs inside and took out two beers before closing the door behind her and walking to the deck. Mary Leah was reclined on a lounger, relaxing as a cool breeze blew softly. The brilliant orange of the setting sun glowed on her face as Coal approached. "You look beautiful," she said as she sat next to her lover.

"Why thank you, Coal." She accepted the beer she offered.

"The sunset is going to be beautiful tonight if this is any indication," she said as she nodded to the glowing horizon.

"Another glorious weekend ahead for us," Mary Leah said. "Do you still want to go to the movies on Sunday?"

"Of course I do," Coal answered. "I'd go anywhere with you."

Mary Leah chuckled. "You are such a smooth talker, Coal Bryan."

"Tell me you don't love it."

"I love you."

"I love you too," she answered and took a long drink from her beer. "We could probably go tomorrow if you wanted. I doubt Melissa will let me do anything tomorrow. Well, I would hope not."

"We can prepare lunch for the crew if that will make you feel any better," Mary Leah said.

"Yes, I'd like that."

Together they watched as the sun continued to creep toward the horizon and then Mary Leah announced it was time to go to the ranch. "I'll carry a tray with the beans and macaroni salad if you can grab the deviled eggs," she said as she took her hand and they walked inside.

Chapter Fourteen

Gene ran up to the car as they pulled in front of the bunkhouse and opened Coal's door. "How are you feeling?" he asked with a worried expression.

"I'm fine," she said as she stepped out of the car.

"Here let me get that for you," he said as he took the tray with the baked beans and macaroni salad.

Coal reached onto the floorboard and took out another dish.

"What's that?"

"Deviled eggs," she answered.

"Oh hell yes," he said with a whoop of excitement.

Mary Leah looked over at her and smiled. "I think you made his night."

"It would appear so."

She and Mary Leah walked to the group of men sitting in lawn chairs surrounding the grill. When Gene returned from the bunkhouse, she gave him the dish of deviled eggs and sent him back inside.

"What can I get you ladies to drink?" Lucas asked.

"Just a glass of tea for me please," Coal answered.

"I'll take a beer," Mary Leah said and winked at Coal.

"How are you feeling?" Harley asked.

"I'm a little sore, but I'll be good to go in a day or so."

"Melissa says the doc said no lifting for at least three days, so we decided next week you can drive the rake, if you feel up to it," Harley said.

She grinned, happy to be able to help. "I'm good with that," she answered. "Mary Leah and I have already decided to cook a nice lunch for you all tomorrow."

"What's it going to be?" Lucas asked.

"It will be a surprise, but I guarantee you won't go away hungry," she promised.

"We'll only work until lunchtime tomorrow and then have Sunday off," Melissa said.

"We're going to practice tomorrow afternoon instead of tonight, so you can come and watch," Gene said as he settled down beside her.

"That sounds like a good plan," she said.

"If we can finish up the hay next week, Stan says we can spend the afternoons the following week practicing before we leave for Dallas on Thursday," Lucas said.

It was obvious to her that Gene's excitement was growing contagious and Lucas had caught the bug.

Harley busied himself cooking the steaks while the others relaxed and talked together. Lucas and Gene pulled several folding tables out of the barn and set them up so they could eat outside and enjoy the evening that had finally begun to cool down.

Coal stood to go inside and bring the food outside. Gene quickly redirected her. "You ladies sit tight and let us guys do the work tonight."

"All right, guys serve away," Melissa said and gestured for her to return to her seat. "Let them enjoy this tonight," she said to Coal.

✝

Coal enjoyed the nice break and allowed the men to take control over the meal. She was eyeing seconds of macaroni salad when Melissa reminded her of the cake she had baked. She quickly dropped the spoon back into the salad bowl.

"Cake, oh hell, we forgot to bring the cake out," Gene said and dashed back inside the bunkhouse.

"I can't believe Gene would forget about dessert." Melissa chuckled as he raced back to the table. "Put it down here, and I'll cut everyone a slice."

"Would anyone besides me like a big glass of milk?" Harley asked.

"That sounds great," Coal answered.

"I'm going to nix that," Mary Leah said. "You need to take those antibiotics and they don't mix well with dairy products."

"You heard the lady," she said and passed her tea glass to Lucas for a refill. "Fill 'er up, please."

Lucas laughed and filled her glass as Melissa passed slices of cake around the table. "This looks fantastic," he said as he handed Coal's glass back to her and took a slice of cake.

Gene returned with a gallon of milk and poured for those that wanted a glass. "You know, I was thinking today, Coal."

"Now that's a scary thought," Lucas teased.

The crowd around the table roared with laughter and the goodhearted Gene shook his head at Lucas.

"What were you thinking?" she asked.

"I was thinking that you and Shadow should also sign up for the pole bending event. As fast as he is, I bet you would win."

"That's not a bad idea," Melissa said. "It could be another notch made toward Top Cowboy honors," she added with a wink to Gene, who wiggled in his seat.

"Exactly," Gene said. "I'd be more than happy to pay your entrance fee."

"I'm paying all the fees this year," Melissa said, surprising the crew.

"That's not necessary," Coal said, "I can handle the fees."

"I know you can, but you all have worked hard and we've had a great year, so it's my treat. No more arguing."

"Yes, ma'am," Coal said and took a bite of her cake.

"So, what do you think, Coal?" Gene asked.

"Where do I sign up?" she said with a smile. "Do we have the materials to make a course?"

Harley grinned as he came up with an idea. "We have some of those orange traffic cones and we can get some broomsticks to use for poles."

"Just let me know how many and I'll go to town tomorrow," Melissa said.

"Why don't you let us do that since Coal is on house restrictions tomorrow," Mary Leah said.

"I need to make a grocery store run in the morning for some lunch ingredients anyhow," Coal said.

"I reckon that's decided then," Harley said. He looked over at Gene, who was about to bounce out of his seat. "You and Lucas go saddle up while Tom and Roy pen the steers. Melissa and I will clean up here and meet you at the corral."

Melissa looked at Coal and Mary Leah. "You two can carry a few of these chairs over to the corral for us."

"Yes, boss," she said and picked up two chairs and carried them over to the corral.

"Flip the switch on those lights too, please, it will be full dark soon," Melissa added.

Coal and Mary Leah carried the chairs and put them in place, and turned on the lights to illuminate the corral. She settled back into the chair and propped her boots on the railing as they waited for the show to begin.

She heard the sound of thundering hoofbeats and turned in her seat to see Shadow galloping across the field. "I guess someone was feeling left out." She chuckled.

"That is one smart horse," Harley said as Shadow slowed his approach and stood beside her, his head leaning over the top rail to see what was going on.

†

The group watched Gene and Lucas practice for over an hour until Mary Leah noticed Coal's head starting to nod.

"I think it's time for us to head home," she said to Melissa as she nodded toward a dozing Coal. "We will see you in the morning." She gently shook her awake. "Time to go," she whispered.

"I guess I can't argue since I can't keep my eyes open."

"Let's go home, big boy," she said to Shadow, who raced ahead of them and cleared the fence. He was halfway across the pasture before they made it to the car.

"He's such a showoff," Melissa said with a chuckle.

"Yeah, he is," she said with a grin. "Thanks for a great dinner."

"Thank you, you made a lot of it," Melissa reminded her. "Oh, wait a second," she said and walked inside her house. She returned a moment later carrying a plate covered with foil. "A slice of cake for later, if you wake up hungry."

"Thanks, boss, see you tomorrow," she said as she climbed in beside Mary Leah.

"Let's get you home and to bed," Mary Leah said as she pulled out onto the drive.

†

Coal barely remembered taking her medicine and climbing into bed. When the alarm sounded the next morning, she sat up and, without thinking, raised her arms above her head to stretch. "Damn," she said, quickly lowering them.

"A bit sore this morning," Mary Leah asked.

174

"Yeah, my side is a bit tight."

"Lay back and relax and I'll get our coffee," she said.

She fluffed up their pillows and waited for her lover to return.

"What did you have in mind to cook for lunch?" she asked.

"I thought I'd make a big pot of chicken and dumplings for the crew. Maybe some corn on the cob and biscuits," she answered.

"Why don't you let me use Melissa's bread machine to make a loaf of fresh bread?"

"That does sound good," she admitted. "Makes me hungry just thinking about it."

"Let me treat you to breakfast in town. Then we can run by the hardware store for the broomsticks and the grocery store. Do you need to shower?"

"No, I think I'm good."

"Well, let's drink our coffee and then dress for town," Mary Leah said.

†

After purchasing the broomsticks, they went to the grocery then drove back to the ranch. She could see the dust trailing the machinery as the crew worked in the fields. She couldn't be out there with them today, but she could make sure they had a great meal in their stomachs.

Together they carried the groceries into Melissa's kitchen, and Melissa took the broomsticks and placed them on the porch. Coal would carry them out to the barn later. She was sure Harley, or more likely Gene, would jump on the task of making the poles for her training. She smiled as she entered the kitchen and went to work preparing the chicken breasts for cooking while the water on the burner came to a boil.

Mary Leah pulled out Melissa's bread machine and mixed the ingredients for a loaf of sourdough bread. "Will you preheat the oven for me?" she asked her.

"Sure, darling," she said and reached down to turn on the oven. She finished placing the breasts in the water and walked to the table to take the bag of flour from the grocery bag to begin mixing dough for her dumplings. She also took out tubes of chocolate chip dough and placed them on the counter. They had decided on cookies to add a sweet treat for the crew.

They worked quietly side by side until Coal looked over to see Mary Leah watching her. "What?" she asked.

"I was just thinking how good you look in the kitchen, up to your wrists in flour and dough," she said.

Coal smiled at her lover. "I really enjoy cooking for the guys. They appreciate the effort so much."

"It's nice to have someone to cook for isn't it?"

"Yeah, it is. It never seems to matter what is cooked. They always seem to enjoy the food."

"You are a good cook, my love," Mary Leah said and leaned over to kiss her lips. "Do you want me to start brewing some tea?"

"That would be great. I thought we could make a gallon of lemonade too."

Mary Leah put a pot of water on to boil, mixed the lemonade, and put it in the refrigerator to chill. Coal poured some flour on the counter and took out the first dough ball to begin rolling it out to cut the dumplings.

"Do you want me to shuck the corn?"

"Yes, that would help me out here," she answered. "Will you also check to see if Melissa has more black pepper in the pantry?"

Mary Leah walked over and opened the pantry door with a chuckle. "Would you like the industrial size or regular?"

"I've emptied out her shaker, so refill it with the industrial size, if it's open."

"Yes, ma'am," Mary Leah said.

They toiled together in the kitchen until the dumplings were cooking slowly and the corn was on to boil. "Let's take a break," Coal said as she washed the flour from her hands.

"That sounds good to me," Mary Leah said.

They walked onto the porch and watched a truck full of hay pull in front of the barn. Gene, Lucas, Roy, and Tom stepped out of the truck Melissa drove and began unloading the hay. She and Mary Leah walked across the yard.

"Do you need drinks?" she asked Melissa. "We made some lemonade."

"Yes, that would be good."

"Hang tight and I'll get it," Mary Leah said.

"How's it going this morning?" she asked.

Gene and Lucas were placing bales of hay on the lift to raise it to the loft. "It's going well, but we miss having you out there with us," Gene said.

"I'll be back in the field Monday," she answered.

"How's lunch coming along?" Melissa asked.

"Very well, we were just taking a break when we saw you pull up. What time do you want to eat?"

"Right about now," Gene said with a grin.

Melissa smiled back at him. "We are going to put in another hour and then call it a day."

"Should we set up for lunch in the bunkhouse then?" she asked as Mary Leah returned.

"That would be great. I think these guys have had enough sun for today."

"We will be all ready to go in an hour then," she promised.

Mary Leah passed around glasses of lemonade as the crew took a short break.

†

Lunch for the crew was a great success and after cleaning up the mess in the kitchen and storing the leftovers for the crew's dinner, Coal and Mary Leah started for home.

"I think a nap is in order," Mary Leah announced as they arrived home.

"That's not a bad idea at all. Later would you mind if Shadow and I go for a ride?"

Mary Leah turned to face her lover. "Of course not, but remember to take it easy so you don't open up that wound."

"Yes, ma'am," she answered.

Mary Leah flipped the switch on the bedroom wall to turn on the ceiling fan as she and Coal began to undress. When they climbed into the bed, Coal spooned next to her lover and held her until she drifted off to sleep. Unable to follow her lover in a nap, Coal rolled onto her back and stared up at the ceiling. She closed her eyes willing herself to sleep to no avail.

The soft whirring sound of the ceiling fan grew louder and reminded her of the distant thrumming of helicopter blades. She felt her heartbeat begin to race as her skin broke out in a cold sweat. She squeezed her eyes tightly together in an effort to exorcise the visions from her memory, but the images remained. The thrumming grew louder as the helicopter approached, dust swirling through the scorching air, coating everything with a rust-colored film. The evacuation chopper had arrived, skids settling on the dirt with a groan as the metal door slung open with a loud bang and the medics rushed from within.

Coal ripped her eyes from the approaching medics to look down. Tessa's lifeless face stared up at her, her brilliant blue eyes fading with the pallor of death.

"Move away, soldier, and let us tend to her," she remembered a medic saying, but she refused to move.

Her arms cradled Tessa's body to her. "It's too late for her, you're too late for her," she remembered saying.

The medic's fingertips reached down to Tessa's neck, searching for signs of a pulse. Finding none, he looked into Coal's eyes. "I'm sorry," he said as tears flowed down her cheeks.

Cries for help from one of his team made him tear his eyes away from hers as he ran to help some of the wounded soldiers in the unit, leaving her cradling Tessa's lifeless body in her arms as her body rocked back and forth in complete anguish.

The co-pilot and another soldier placed Mitch's torn body into a body bag as the medics prepared the injured for transport, leaving she and Tessa the last to be loaded. When they were ready to depart, the medic returned to Coal.

"It's time to take her home," he gently said. "You have to let her go." He carefully removed Tessa's body from her arms and she watched in horror as they placed her in a black body bag, her still beautiful face disappearing from view as the zipper slowly closed.

The medic helped her to her feet, pain ripping through her side as her wounds became evident. "Come, let's get you tended to," he said, offering a hand and her feet moved mechanically as she was led to the chopper.

Coal bolted up in the bed, gasping for a breath. Mary Leah lay unmoving beside her. She crept from the bed, hoping to leave without disturbing her slumber. She needed air and space, so she left the cabin and walked quickly to the barn to saddle Shadow.

Mary Leah rolled onto her back, her hand instinctively resting on the spot just vacated by Coal. She had awoken when she felt Coal's body grow stiff from the tension of her memories. She desperately wanted to talk with her, but she remained frozen with no idea of what she would tell her or ask of her. She silently prayed she would come to her one day to speak of the horrors she had experienced in the desert.

Shadow stamped his hoof in excitement as she walked into the barn. "It's time to go, isn't it, big boy?" Coal opened his stall and walked him over to the tack, slipping a saddle blanket onto his back. She gingerly lifted her saddle, wincing at the pain in her side as she placed it on his strong back. Ignoring the pain, she continued to saddle her steed and after slipping the bridle over his head, she placed her foot in the stirrup to mount Shadow.

They left the barn and walked deep into the pastures, beyond the haying fields toward the herd grazing in the furthermost section of the ranch.

From the front porch of her home, Melissa saw Coal and Shadow as they entered the pasture. She sensed Coal's distress and her heart reached out to her. Gene stepped from the bunkhouse at that moment and she hollered out to him. "Gene, will you saddle a horse for me?"

"Yes, ma'am," he answered and rushed to the barn as Melissa entered the house in search of her boots.

Gene saddled Melissa's palomino mare and led her to the front porch. When Melissa emerged from the house, she found Gene waiting for her. "Is everything all right, boss?"

"Yes, I'm just going out for a ride," she said as she took the mare's reins and mounted her. "Thank you for bringing her to me."

"You're welcome. Be safe and enjoy your ride," he said as he watched her ride from the yard. In the distance, he saw the fading view of a black horse and rider, knowing instantly Melissa was following Coal.

Coal allowed the soft thuds of Shadow's hooves relax her as they crossed the open expanse. She could see nothing but fields for miles, ringed by thin strips of gnarled trees, scorching in the summer heat. The memory of Tessa lying in her arms weighed heavily on her heart as she slumped in her saddle. She knew she had to find a way to purge the guilt of her death before it drove her mad. Tears flowed down her cheeks, Shadow, sensing her distress, plodded aimlessly, no purpose but to serve his master.

The cry of a hawk circling above drew her attention to the sky. It had been some time since she had seen the pair flying together and she wondered if it too had lost its mate. Her eyes followed the flight of the bird as he dove and then emerged, carrying a squirming rabbit in his talons. A cry from the distance solved her riddle as the predator's mate called to him. A slow smile grew on her face as she watched the bird fly swiftly to the tree, dropping to a branch to share the bounty of the kill with its mate.

Approaching hoofbeats made her turn in the saddle. She shielded her eyes from the sun to see a golden horse and rider approaching through the haze of heat waves. "Melissa," she spoke softly.

She pulled Shadow to a halt and waited for Melissa and the mare to catch up. "I saw you out riding. Mind if I join you?"

"Not at all," Coal said, managing a smile.

Melissa saw the tearstains on Coal's cheeks. "You can tell me to mind my own business if you want," she said.

"I would never do that," she said.

"You look like you're having a rough time."

Coal sighed deeply. "Mary Leah and I laid down for a nap, but I couldn't sleep. I closed my eyes and the whirring of the ceiling fan sounded like copter rotors and my head was filled with memories of that last day."

"When Tessa…and Mitch died?" Melissa asked.

She nodded her head.

"Share them with me," Melissa said.

"I was holding Tessa in my arms when the chopper landed. She whispered, 'I love you' and then died in my arms. Mitch was lying several feet away, the pooling of their blood running together as the dust kicked up by the chopper filled the air." She choked back her tears. "They took her away from me and she disappeared behind the zipper of a body bag. I let them die," she said and broke down in tears.

"You are not responsible," Melissa said. "For Tessa's death or Mitch's."

"My hesitation got them killed."

"No, it didn't. The bomb killed them. Coal, no matter what you think, you couldn't have stopped that."

"But, I could have if I hadn't been distracted."

"His death grip on the detonation device would have triggered the explosion and more would have died if Mitch hadn't buffered the bomb."

A part deep inside her knew that Melissa's words rang true.

"How long has it been since you have visited her grave?"

"Too long," she admitted. "It's just so far away."

"You can have whatever time you need off, if you want to visit."

"There is too much to do, and we have the rodeo coming up," she said. "Maybe afterward," she said. But even to her own ears, the words didn't sound sincere.

"Have you talked to Mary Leah about what you experienced?"

"No, besides you and Del, Gene is the only one I have talked to about my time in the desert. I'm not sure how to talk to her about Tessa."

"Just open your heart to her and the words will come," Melissa said.

They rode in silence until they reached the boundary of the MC2, and Melissa reached for Coal's hand. She smiled at Melissa's gesture and they turned to stare at the setting sun.

"Are you ready to head home?" she asked Melissa.

"Yes, let's go home, Coal."

✝

Mary Leah watched as she rode back into the barn and unsaddled Shadow. She was washing vegetables in the sink for a fresh salad when the door opened and she walked into the kitchen. Coal strode across the floor and took Mary Leah in her arms for a fiery kiss. "We need to talk," she said.

"Over dinner?" she asked.

"Now. I can't eat until I get this off my conscious," she answered.

"Grab some beer and I'll meet you on the deck. Maybe we could have a fire in the pit?" Mary Leah said.

"I will start one," Coal answered with a smile.

Mary Leah placed the salad and the rest of the vegetables back into the refrigerator then joined her on the deck.

Coal had a fire blazing in the pit and handed Mary Leah a beer as she took the seat next to her. "I need to tell you about Tessa and my time in the desert," she said.

✝

Mary Leah had broken down in tears, wrapped in Coal's arms she finally understood the trauma her lover had experienced in the desert and the haunting memories she was struggling to resolve. When she regained control of her emotions, she turned to look in her dark eyes. "Thank you for sharing that part of your life with me."

"It was selfish of me to keep that to myself," Coal said. "I didn't want you to think of me as damaged goods."

183

“I love every ounce of you, Coal Bryan,” Mary Leah
said and kissed her softly.

Chapter Fifteen

The next week passed in a blur. They finished bringing in the hay and Coal survived three sessions with Del. They were painful, but Del assured her the pain was necessary for her to move on and she was beginning to believe Del could fix her.

"I am very pleased with the progress you are making," Del said when they ended her Friday night session. "Do you think you are ready for Virtual Iraq?"

"Next week will be a short week. We leave for the rodeo on Friday morning," Coal answered.

"Would you rather wait until the following week to begin then?"

"It will be pretty intense, won't it?"

"Yes, it will. Let's take next week off then, and you can return Monday after the rodeo. Good luck, by the way."

"Thanks," Coal answered.

"Have a great weekend and I will see you soon," Del said as she walked with her back to the reception area.

"Did you remember to ask her about Thursday?" Mary Leah said when they stepped into the room.

"No, thanks for reminding me," she told Mary Leah. "We're having a cookout Thursday night and we would like you to join us."

"Thursday is a short day for me," Del answered. "What time?"

"We'll be having a last practice run for our events starting at three and will eat at six," Coal said.

Del grinned. "I'd love to watch y'all practice."

"So come out as soon as you close up shop," Mary Leah said.

"I will," Del said. "I'll see you Thursday then. Have a great weekend."

†

Gene and Lucas rushed to clear the table after Thursday's lunch. "Are you riding today?" he asked her.

"Yes, I thought you and Lucas could practice a while first, and then we could do some roping. I think, Shadow is set on the barrels, but I'd like a few more runs at the pole bending before we leave tomorrow."

"You're on, my friend. We'll chill until three and then get to it while Harley gets the grill ready for the cookout. Man, I can't wait to dig into some of his ribs," Gene said, bursting at the seams.

"I swear you are a bottomless pit," Coal told him with a chuckle.

She helped Melissa carry the last of the food into the house and stretched. "Would you mind if I crashed in my old room for a nap?"

"Absolutely not, what time do you want to be up?"

"By two thirty so I can get the baked beans cooking. Mary Leah will bring the macaroni salad when she comes after work."

"Hit the sack then," Melissa said. "I'll wake you when it's time."

"Thanks, boss," she said and walked to the bedroom and pulled off her boots.

†

186

Melissa poured a cup of coffee and walked back to the tables they had set up for lunch. A cool breeze left the shade of the trees very enjoyable, and she relaxed as she watched the rest of the crew puttering around.

"Mind if I join you, boss?" Harley asked.

"Grab a cup of coffee if you want, the pot is still hot."

"You need a refill?"

"Sure," Melissa said, handing him her cup.

Lucas and Gene were loading bales of hay and feed for the horses into the horse trailer. They would head out for Dallas early the next morning and she would bet her last dollar that Gene would not sleep a wink tonight. She smiled as she watched their youthful energy.

Harley returned with their coffee and followed her gaze as she watched the young men. "Oh, to be young again," he said with a sigh.

"It would grand to go back to that age, wouldn't it?" Melissa said with a grin.

"What and give up the aches and pains of these old bones?" he teased.

"Are you ready to cook?" she asked.

He smiled at her. "As soon as they finish loading the trailer, I'll have them drag the grill out. I've got the ribs ready to go and some sausage to munch on while they cook."

"Sounds yummy, is there anything I can help with?"

"As a matter of fact, yes, you can be the official timer when the youngsters start practice," he said. "Other than that, I think we are covered."

"I guess I'll just kick back and relax then."

"Well, it looks like you'll have company to relax with," Harley said, nodding at the car stirring up dust on the drive.

"Del's here," she said.

"She seems to be working wonders with Coal. It's good to see her relaxed again."

"Yes, it is," Melissa said as she stood to greet her arriving guest.

Del opened the car door and climbed out of the car. "Am I too early?"

"Heaven's no, we are taking a short break after lunch. The practice session will begin at three. Did you have lunch?"

"Yes, I had a salad before leaving the office. I heard there are ribs tonight so I opted for a light lunch," Del said with a grin.

They walked over to the table and Melissa introduced Harley to Del. "May I get you something cool to drink or some coffee?"

"Some tea would be great."

"I will be right back. You okay, boss?" he asked.

"Yes, I'm good, Harley, thanks."

Del took a seat next to Melissa. "It feels really peaceful out here. How have you been?"

"I'm doing great thanks. I appreciate what you're doing with Coal too," she added.

"Where is she?"

"Catching a quick nap," Melissa said.

"Is everything all right?" Del asked.

"Yes, she's just resting before practice."

"Good," Del said.

Harley returned with her tea. "I heard her stirring, so don't be surprised if she joins you soon."

"So much for a nap," Melissa said.

"Don't let her fool you, she's just as excited about the rodeo as the boys," Harley said with a chuckle.

"What events is she entering?" Del asked.

"She'll do barrel racing and pole bending on her own, and then team up with Gene for team roping," Melissa said.

"What about the boys?"

"They will compete in steer wrestling and bronco riding."

"That's going to make for a busy weekend," Del said.

"Most of the competition will be held Saturday," Harley said. "You should drive up for the day."

"I just might," Del said.

✝

Coal climbed from the bed and walked to the bathroom to wash her face. She went to the kitchen and prehcated the oven as she prepared the beans for baking. She glimpsed out the window to see that Del had arrived and was sitting with Melissa and Harley. Lucas and Gene were setting up the grills. When she slid the pan of beans in the oven, she poured a glass of tea and went out to join her friends.

"Glad you made it, Doc," she said as she took a seat.

"I'm not one to miss out on good ribs," she said with a wink to Harley. "How are you feeling?"

"Good, thanks. The beans are in the oven, so remind me to keep an eye on them," she said to Melissa.

"A rodeo star and she cooks too?" Del teased.

"No star, but I can hold my own in a kitchen," Coal said with a chuckle.

Del smiled at her patient. It was comforting to see a smile on her face after all the anxiety she had experienced inside her office.

Harley walked over to light the coals on the grills as the boys saddled up and moved the practice stock into the holding pens.

"Should we move this party to the corral?" Melissa asked.

Harley took a stopwatch from his pocket and handed it to Melissa. "Push them hard, boss."

The small group of women watched Gene and Lucas wrestle steers. When they were down to the last two steers, Coal stood and stretched. "I'm going to saddle Shadow and get ready to throw some rope."

"Have fun," Melissa said. She and Del watched her walk to the barn.

"She's a good woman," Del said.

"Yes, she is," Melissa, agreed. "We all lucked up when she came into our lives."

They turned at the sound of a car approaching. Melissa smiled at Del. "Mary Leah most of all."

"She and Coal make a nice couple," Del agreed.

†

"Damn, she's good," Del said as they watched her heel yet another steer.

"Yes, she is," Mary Leah said with pride. "You should see them run the barrels or poles. They are really fast."

"I think I will take a ride Saturday. This is exciting stuff."

Melissa looked at Mary Leah and winked. "Another rodeo junkie has been born."

"Maybe so," Del said with a grin.

Lucas and Gene herded the steers back into the small pasture and set up the course for Coal while she rode over to chat with the women.

"Very impressive," Del said as she rode up to the fence.

"Thanks, Doc, one of the things I do well." She grinned.

"Among many other things," Mary Leah said.

"Would you care to share more of those," Del teased her college friend with a wiggle of her eyebrows.

Mary Leah blushed furiously and Coal chuckled.

"Wow, I haven't seen you in that shade of red for a long time," Melissa tossed in.

"Okay, y'all can stop anytime now."

She decided to rescue her lover from further embarrassment. "You have your stopwatch ready, boss?"

"I sure do," Melissa said, digging it out of her pocket.

"Let's roll then," Coal said. After winking to Mary Leah, she rode to the entrance of the corral. She looked over to Melissa, who nodded she was ready, and Coal made the first run of the course. Shadow learned the new route quickly and it took minimal reining to weave him through the course. When they cleared the last pole and turned for the homestretch, she gave him his full head and he galloped past the poles to the finish line.

"Woohoo!" Melissa yelled out. "Your fastest run yet!"

"Good, but we can do better," she said to Shadow, leaning down to pat his neck. "Two more runs and we will call it a day."

When they two runs were over and they had trimmed nearly a full second from their time, Harley called out, "Dinner's ready."

Mary Leah, Melissa, and Del walked toward the tables to help set food out while Coal and the boys cared for their horses. When the tables were set and everyone gathered around, Harley blessed the meal. "Let's eat," he announced.

Two hours later, their bellies full, the group dispersed for the evening. Mary Leah and Coal walked Del to her car.

"Thanks for coming out tonight, Doc," Coal said and hugged her.

"Thanks for the invite. I had a blast," Del said. "I will see y'all in Dallas on Saturday."

"I'll save you a seat," Mary Leah said.

"See you then," Del said.

"Are we ready to head out too?" Mary Leah asked.

"Yeah, let me get Shadow and we can race him home."

Coal walked to the barn and opened the stall door for Shadow. "Let's go home, big boy," she said and he trotted ahead of her and when she reached the car, he took off at a full gallop.

"We will never beat him, you know," Coal said with a chuckle.

"I know, but it's still fun," Mary Leah said as she gunned the engine.

Chapter Sixteen

The big day arrived, and when everyone was packed and the horses were loaded into the trailer, the crew of the MC2 left for Dallas. Coal, Mary Leah, and Melissa would get them settled into their hotel while Harley, Gene, and Lucas arranged for the horses at the rodeo arena. Gene had volunteered to sleep in the small camper housed in the front of the trailer to keep a close eye on the horses while the rest stayed at the hotel.

Coal was certain Gene had not slept the night before, being so excited about the rodeo, and she hoped he would get a nap in on the two-hour ride to Dallas. She drove Melissa's truck, following the trailer, and Melissa and Mary Leah kept up a friendly banter.

"What time is your first event tomorrow?" Mary Leah asked.

"The barrel racing begins at ten and then team roping at four," she answered. "The finals for the bulldogging and bronco riding are all on Sunday morning."

Melissa chuckled. "That means Gene will bouncing off the walls all weekend."

"He is a bit excited," she agreed.

"I thought once we all got settled we could go out for a nice meal and get a good night's rest," Melissa suggested.

"That sounds really good to me. I'm starving all of a sudden," Mary Leah said.

"I know just the place to take care of that," Melissa said as the Dallas city limits came into view.

"What do you have in mind?" Mary Leah asked.

"I was thinking the Saltgrass," Melissa answered.

"That's a great choice."

"I hope they have good-sized portions," Coal said.

"I guarantee you won't leave there hungry," Melissa promised.

When Harley exited the interstate to drive to the rodeo grounds, Melissa directed Coal to the next exit for the hotel. Melissa walked inside to start checking them in as Coal and Mary Leah got a luggage cart and began unloading the bags. When they pushed the cart inside, Melissa met them at the front desk.

"All set," she said as she handed Mary Leah a packet of keys. "We can take this upstairs, if you will park the truck and meet us on the third floor."

"I'll be right back then," Coal said.

Melissa and Mary Leah pushed the cart toward the elevator. "How has she been sleeping?" Melissa asked.

"Much better since she began her sessions with Del. I really hope she can relax and have some fun this weekend," Mary Leah answered.

"I hope you both can," Melissa said with a grin.

They stopped in front of room 322. "This is your room and I'm two doors down," she said as she prompted her sister to open the door with one of the electronic keys. "I'll meet the boys downstairs to give them their keys and then we should plan to meet at six for dinner. I'll call for a reservation so we should be all set."

Coal arrived just as Mary Leah was taking off the first bag. She picked up the remaining two bags and looked at Melissa. "Hang on a second and I'll take your bags for you."

"Don't be silly, Coal, I can handle this. Go on in and relax. We're going to meet at six for dinner."

"Okay, boss," she said and followed Mary Leah into the room with a huge king-sized bed.

"Would you look at that," Mary Leah said and let out a low whistle.

Coal set the bags on the bed and turned to see what her lover was admiring. A large whirlpool tub was the centerpiece to the bathroom and a bucket of chilled champagne sat beside the marble tub.

"Wow, should we take advantage of this now or later? We have three hours before we meet the others for dinner," she said.

"Let's wait until we get back from dinner. Then we can completely relax and enjoy the evening together," Mary Leah suggested.

She unzipped the first bag. "That's fine with me. I want to unpack these bags and make sure everything is ready for tomorrow. Then maybe we can catch a quick nap before we shower and dress for dinner."

"As usual, you must be reading my mind," Mary Leah answered. "Is there anything I need to iron for you?"

"An outfit for tonight if you don't mind, and I'll put the rest of our clothing away and get the bathroom set up."

"Deal, but it's going to cost you," Mary Leah teased, approaching her.

"What's the price?"

"One of your kisses," she teased.

She dropped the jeans in her hands back on the bed and turned to take Mary Leah in her arms for a deep passionate kiss. When she ended the kiss, she smiled at her lover and said, "I will gladly pay that price any time."

"I will definitely keep that in mind," Mary Leah said, and with a swat to Coal's backside, she walked to the closet to take out the ironing board and iron. "Starch?" she asked.

"Will it cost more?" she teased.

"Of course," she teased back.

"Starch then, please." She smiled.

 †

After a great meal, the women drove back to the hotel while Harley and Lucas dropped Gene off at the arena for the night.

They had agreed to meet at seven in the hotel for breakfast, so when they arrived at the arena, Harley looked at Gene and said, "Be ready at six thirty and I'll come get you for breakfast. Get some sleep tonight too, so you'll be well rested for the competition."

"Yes, Harley," he said as he stepped out of the truck.

†

Mary Leah started the bath and opened the bottle of champagne as Coal set out her clothes for the next day and set the alarm on her phone. Mary Leah poured glasses of the sparkling champagne and placed them on the edge of the tub.

They stripped out of the remainder of their clothing and slipped into the warm water. "This is heavenly," Mary Leah said, positioning herself in front of Coal.

"Thanks for a great night," she said and offered her glass to Mary Leah.

"The first of many more to come," Mary Leah said and touched her glass to Coal's.

†

They made love slowly for several hours and feeling beautifully content, Coal fell asleep in Mary Leah's arms.

When the alarm sounded the next morning, she stretched next to Mary Leah and kissed her lover awake. "Will you shower with me?"

"I'd love that," Mary Leah said as she sat up on the edge of the bed.

196

Coal followed her into the large shower and kissed Mary Leah deeply, hands roaming over her lover's body.

Mary Leah chuckled. "You keep that up and we will be late for breakfast."

"We could skip breakfast," she said as she caressed Mary Leah's back with a soapy cloth.

"You have a big day today, so no skipping breakfast."

"Yes, ma'am," Coal said.

†

"I forgot how handsome you look all dressed up," Mary Leah said from the bed as she watched Coal fasten the pearl snaps on the green paisley western shirt.

"That is very sweet of you to say," Coal said, tucking the shirt inside her jeans and fastening her belt. "Will you grab my hat for me?"

Mary Leah climbed from the bed and walked to the closet to retrieve the new gray felt Stetson she had bought for her. She handed her the hat and asked, "All set?"

"Yes, ma'am," she said. She walked to the door and held it open for Mary Leah. "After you, ma'am."

Coal's two racing events were first on tap for the day. The barrel racing would be first, followed closely by the pole bending. Then the bull riding would begin, and late afternoon the steer wrestling would occur. The roping competition and bronco riding would conclude on Sunday.

After breakfast, they rode to the rodeo grounds and Gene raced ahead of the group to get Shadow from his stall as she pulled her tack from the trailer. "Good luck," Mary Leah said with a hug and then she and Melissa walked to the bleachers. They met Del at the entrance to the bleachers.

"Good morning, have I missed anything?"

"No, Del, you're just in time to help us find good seats," Melissa said as she led them up the steps.

197

Lucas held her saddle and bridle as Coal leaned down to fasten the brown leather chaps to her legs. She was all set, and as she walked to where Gene was holding Shadow, she heard the overhead announcement that the barrel race event would be starting in ten minutes. Harley pinned the paper competitor number on the back of her shirt as her heart began to race. She had pulled the fifth run so she mounted Shadow and rode him into a practice ring to warm up.

Once she settled onto his back, Coal's nerves calmed. Riding him was as natural as breathing to her, and she was confident that he would give her his best runs today. A grin formed on her face as they cantered easily in the ring.

"She looks ready to go," Harley said as he slapped Gene on the back. "I hope you are that confident when your events start."

"I will be, boss," Gene said with a grin and they took up seats on the railing of the arena to watch.

†

Coal watched as the sun gleamed off a beautiful palomino mare that cantered in front of them. The horse and rider, a feisty woman named Shelly Brewster, would more than likely be their top competition in both events. The horse was quick, and if ridden properly, they would give them a run for their money. But Coal knew the weakness in the team was the rider. Shelly was a spoiled, rich daddy's girl. Her dad could buy the best horse money could buy, but her lack of practice showed in her performance. She had drawn second run so Coal would know her run time before her turn.

†

"You look more nervous than Coal," Melissa told her sister as they waited for the competition to begin. "Relax, she will do fine."

"I know, I just want her to kick Shelly's ass this year," Mary Leah said.

"Who is Shelly?" Del asked.

Venom flowed through Mary Leah's voice as she answered Del. "A spoiled rich kid who thinks daddy's money can buy her anything."

"You like her that much, huh?" Del teased.

"Uh-hmm," Mary Leah said.

Del was about to speak again when the first competitor was announced. They sat back and watched as the competition began. The first run was clean but not an incredibly fast run. Shadow shouldn't have problems beating that time.

The next competitor stepped to the starting line and was introduced to the crowd. She waved like a beauty queen in a parade. Del turned to Mary Leah. "A bit cheesy isn't she?"

"That was actually pretty mild for Shelly," Melissa said.

Shelly took off from the starting line and made it through the right-hand barrel fairly well, but her boot caught the second barrel. It didn't topple over, which would have meant a time penalty, but it threw her horse off stride. The crowd watched as her horse raced for the final barrel, and after rounding it, Shelly used her reins to whip the horse's flanks urging more speed.

Watching Shelly's run from outside the ring, Coal growled, "Damn, I hate when she does that."

"If she'd give the horse her head it would run faster," Harley said. "Whipping it is totally uncalled for."

She watched as the horse broke the plane of the finish line and she looked up at the time. Faster than the first run, but still not a blazing time. "We can beat that," she said into Shadow's ear as she reached down to pat his neck.

The next rider dumped a barrel and Coal moved into the rotation with a rider ahead of her. The dirt around the barrels was becoming soft from all the turns ahead of her so she would need to be careful not to slip in too close. She watched as a cowboy lifted the barrel back into place and listened as the announcer introduced the next rider.

Coal could feel Shadow's muscles tensing beneath her. He was ready to run. He danced in place as the rider finished her run and she walked him to the starting line. She barely heard the announcer calling her name as her eyes focused on the course ahead of her. She looked to the left at the timer. When he nodded to her, she pressed her heels into Shadow's sides and they blasted into the ring. She lowered her hand holding the reins and Shadow took the first turn perfectly. She glanced down and saw her boot an inch from the barrel. She held her breath until they cleared it and galloped toward the next barrel.

The wind whipped through her hair and she could feel a grin growing on her face as Shadow's turn was just as sharp on the next barrel and they were racing to the end of the arena and the final barrel. Coal again lowered her hand and Shadow turned so tightly his hooves threw dirt into her face as he cleared the final barrel and then opened his stride as he raced to the finish. Dirt and all, she grinned wildly as they galloped to the finish.

They flew past the finish line and Coal leaned down to pat his neck. "Great run, big boy," she said as she waited to hear their time.

"Ladies and gentlemen we now have a new leader," the loudspeaker blared as the announcer gave their time.

"That's going to be hard to beat," Gene said as he raced over to them.

"I hope so," she said with a huge grin.

"Damn, that was fast," Melissa said in awe from her spot in the bleachers.

"Good enough to win?" Del asked.

"Oh yeah," Melissa said. The trio of women all let out a whoop of celebration.

Coal turned at the sound and saw Melissa, Del, and Mary Leah cheering for her. She waved to them and turned back to Gene. "I'm going back to the ring to walk Shadow and keep him warm."

Coal started back to the warm-up ring and passed Shelly talking with her brother Bubba. "Nice run," she said with a glare.

"Thanks," she said and kept moving.

There were six riders scheduled to compete after her so Coal took Shadow to the trough for a drink of water. Then they walked the circuit of the ring until the loudspeaker announced them as winners. She and Shadow finished a full half-second ahead of the closest competition.

"One down and one to go," she said to Shadow.

They had drawn the tenth run of twelve for the pole bending, so they would have to wait for the course to be set up and nine riders to complete runs before they would make their run. Shadow was ready to run again so she let him canter around the ring for several minutes before she slowed him back to a walk.

When the third rider started her run, Coal rode back to where the crew was sitting on the rails to watch the next few riders. Lucas turned at their approach and grinned. "They got nothing on y'all," he said.

Gene tossed her a bottle of water and she took a long drink and handed it back to him. "Thanks."

"Would you look at that," Harley said.

They all turned to see the bulls for the bull riding competition emerging from a large trailer. "Damn, they look like an ornery bunch," Lucas said.

"Makes me glad neither of you signed up for that event," Harley said.

"Me too," Gene said as he turned back to the arena. "There's no way I want to be tied to the back of one of those monsters."

"I don't know it looks kind of fun," Coal said as the entire crew turned to stare at her. "Psyche," she said and broke out laughing.

"Damn girl, I thought you were serious for a second," Harley said, holding a hand to his chest.

"No way, man," she answered, still laughing.

When it was time for their run, she positioned Shadow at the starting line and waited for the signal. The timer nodded to her and she and Shadow took off at a dead run until they reached the first pole. They quickly fell into rhythm, weaving tightly through each turn until they reached the end and raced for home, dirt flying from his hooves as he powerfully raced to the finish line.

Their time put them in first place, but Shelly and her mare still had to run. With only two riders left, Coal rode Shadow back to the crew to watch the remainder of the competition. The next rider came in with a slower time and Coal found herself holding her breath as Shelly came to the starting line, flashing her beauty queen routine as she the announcer called her name.

"Come on, just get it over with," Gene groaned.

They watched as the mare performed nearly flawlessly, but once again, Shelly's poor horsemanship held her reins back instead of giving the horse freedom to run her fastest. Her time was short of Coal's first-place time. For the second event in a row, Shelly finished behind Coal and Shadow.

Coal's eyes stared at the scoreboard as the lights flashed announcing their time as the winning time. "Yes," she yelled and pumped her fist in the air just as Shelly rode past. "Nice run," she said but Shelly ignored her compliment and rode past them.

"I'm going to unsaddle Shadow and then cool him down," she said and turned to walk into the stables.

Gene and Lucas jumped down to walk with them as Harley and the rest of the crew waited for the women to join them from the stands.

Coal draped the reins over the top rail of Shadow's stall and dismounted. She took her saddle from his back and handed it to Lucas to store then bent down to take off his leg braces. The air filled with loud blasts. The noise startled Shadow, who had lowered his head to watch her, and as he flinched toward the noise, his head crashed into Coal's face, busting her lip, the metal edge of his bit slicing a gash in her chin before knocking her to the ground as he fled out of the stables. Lucas dropped the saddle and jumped into an open stall to prevent being run down by the frightened horse. Gene took off at a full run after the stampeding horse.

Laughter exploded behind her. Coal looked up to see Shelly and her brother Bubba laughing as the last of a string of firecrackers ignited on the ground.

"Oh shit," Melissa said as Shadow raced past them and she saw the look on Coal's face. She took off at a run as Coal returned to her feet.

Coal stood and her right foot lashed out, her boot heel catching Bubba square in the mouth, breaking his four front teeth and she bounced on her feet in an offensive position. Lucas rushed to grab her from behind in a bear hug as he yelled out to Shelly.

"Get him the hell out of here, before I let her go."

Shelly looked at the blood pouring from her brother's mouth. "You crazy bitch," she snarled as she rushed Coal, still held in Lucas's grasp.

Melissa stepped between them and caught Shelly by her shoulders, spun her around and pushed her toward Bubba who had the good sense to move away. "Go," she shouted.

Lucas saw them moving away and released his grip on Coal. She raised her hand to wipe the dirt from her face and when she looked at her hand, she saw the fresh blood smeared across her palm. When she turned back toward her friends, Del saw the feral look in Coal's eyes. The sound of the firecrackers exploding had triggered a trauma reaction from her, and she needed to get her somewhere to settle her down and tend to her wounds.

"Where is the first-aid kit?" she asked Melissa.

"In the trailer," Melissa answered.

"Let's go," Del said, and gently took Coal's arm.

"Where's Shadow? If he's hurt, I'll kick in more than his teeth," she growled.

"He'll be okay. Gene is chasing him down. I'll help him and bring him to you," Lucas said.

She nodded and allowed Del and Mary Leah to lead her from the stables.

A crowd had gathered in the stables to investigate all the commotion. They parted like the Red Sea when Coal left the stables.

"How do you feel?" Del asked as they walked.

"I've got a massive headache," Coal said.

"Go get your truck," Del said to Melissa as they reached the trailer. "We need to take her to be checked out."

Harley was standing at the trailer. When he saw her moving toward him with her face bloodied, he reached inside for the first-aid kit.

Mary Leah rushed ahead and took the kit from Harley, pulling out gauze to hold against Coal's chin.

"What the hell happened?" he asked.

"Those stupid Brewster brats set off fireworks and spooked Shadow."

"Damn kids, I ought to kick their asses," Harley growled.

"Don't worry, Harley, she got Bubba good," Mary Leah said.

"He's going to need some serious dental work," Del said as she cleaned Coal's busted lip, while Mary Leah held pressure over the gash on her chin.

Melissa arrived with the truck and Del urged her to climb inside, but Coal balked. "I'm not going anywhere until I know Shadow is safe."

Harley looked around and saw Gene and Lucas walking the horse toward them. "There he is," he said, pointing behind Coal.

She turned to see her horse being led back to her by Gene and Lucas. She sighed with relief and hugged Shadow's neck as her tears began to fall.

"See, he's fine. Now we need to go take care of you," Melissa said.

"Take care of my boy, Gene," she said.

"I will, Coal, you take care of you," he said as he too started crying.

"Good grief. You better get her out of here before we all start bawling," Harley said and walked her to the back door of the truck. "Call me if you need anything."

"Just take care of Shadow," Coal repeated and climbed inside the truck.

†

Melissa located a nearby emergency room and they were surprised to find it wasn't overflowing with patients. Mary Leah and Del led her inside while Melissa parked the truck.

"What happened here?" a nurse asked as they entered the triage area.

Mary Leah quickly explained the accident as the nurse peeled the blood-soaked gauze away from Coal's chin.

"Do you have a headache?" she asked.

"Yes, my head is pounding."

"Let's get you into an exam room, so we can get you cleaned up and examined by Dr. Tully," she said with a warm smile. She looked at the three women surrounding Coal. "I can probably sneak one of you back, but not all three."

"Go with Coal," Melissa said to Mary Leah.

Mary Leah nodded and helped support Coal as they were led to an exam room. The triage nurse got Coal settled on the exam table and said, "Cindy will be in to get you cleaned up in a few minutes," and left the room.

Mary Leah sat in a chair next to Coal and held her hand while they waited.

"Knock, knock," a voice said and then the curtain opened. The small woman took one look at Coal in her boots and chaps. "All right, a cowgirl," she crowed with a cute smile. "You in town for the rodeo?"

"Yes, ma'am," she said as the woman reviewed her chart.

"I can tell you one thing right off the bat," she said.

Coal cocked her head at her comment.

"Your horse's head is definitely harder than yours," she said with a chuckle.

"That's debatable," Mary Leah teased, and all three broke out in laughter.

"Hey now, I resemble that remark." Coal fell into the humor. She smiled and then grimaced as pain shot through her chin.

"Ouch, sorry about that, no more humor. My name is Cindy, by the way. I get the pleasure of cleaning your wounds before Dr. Tully comes for a visit. Any pain in your jaw?" she asked.

"No, just my chin and I've got a killer headache," she answered.

"No broken jaw or you wouldn't be talking this good," Cindy said as she cleansed her chin with Betadine. "Is superglue okay or do you want a few stitches?"

"Superglue is fine with me," she said.

"We need to buy stock in that stuff," Mary Leah said.

"Oh yeah? Do you frequently head-butt horses?" Cindy asked.

"No, I had a piece of leftover shrapnel make an appearance a few weeks ago," she explained.

"Did you heal well with the glue?"

"Yes, I did," she answered.

"I'll let Dr. Tully know you prefer the glue then," she said.

"Can I get something for a headache?" she asked.

"Unfortunately no, not until Dr. Tully examines you. She will probably order a CT scan of your head to make sure you don't have a concussion. Once we get your picture, I will give you something."

"Did I hear my name called?" a woman said as she entered the room. "Hi, I'm Dr. Tully. I hear you've been head-butting a horse."

"He definitely got the better of me," she said.

The doctor pulled out a penlight and completed a routine exam. "Your neurological check looks fine, but I'd like a CT scan just to rule out a concussion. Is that good with you?"

"Yeah, that's fine, Doc," she answered.

"I'll key in the order if you want to hit that chin with some glue and then take her upstairs to the lab," the doctor told Cindy.

"What can she have for a headache?"

"Any allergies to medications?" she asked Coal.

"No, ma'am."

"Take some Tylenol 3 up with you and she can have them once we have films on her."

"Yes, Dr. Tully," Cindy said.

"I'll see you when you get back," the doctor said and left the room.

Cindy sealed the gash with the surgical glue. "Do you want a bandage? You really don't need one."

"I'm good then," she said.

Cindy stepped into the hall and returned with a wheelchair. "Let's roll, cowgirl," she said and helped her into the chair. "Are you joining us for a stroll?" she asked Mary Leah.

"Yes, if I can," she answered.

"Not a problem. I'll even let you push the buttons in the elevator," Cindy said as she rolled Coal from the room. "Two please," she said with a chuckle when they entered the elevator.

"Are you always this chipper?" Coal asked.

Cindy chuckled. "My wife calls me her little ray of sunshine."

"She's a lucky woman," Mary Leah said.

"Yeah, I tell her that all the time," Cindy said with a wink as the elevator doors opened. "Let's go get your Kodak moment done and you can be on your way. Are you finished at the rodeo?"

"No, ma'am. I've got another event in the morning."

"Well, it's been lovely meeting you, but please don't come for another visit tomorrow."

"Trust me, I don't plan to," she said with a grin.

"Okay, Suzy, she's all yours," Cindy said as she rolled Coal into the x-ray lab. "Watch her close, she's a cowgirl," she teased.

"She's in good hands. I'll bring her back in just a few," Suzy said and closed the door.

†

Twenty minutes later, she rolled back into the emergency room exam room to wait the results of her CT scan.

When Dr. Tully entered the room, she looked at Coal. "How is the headache?"

"Easing off some, thankfully," she answered.

"That's good news. Your scan looks good and there's no sign of a concussion. I'd recommend wearing sunglasses as

208

much as possible while you're outside and by all means no more head-butting."

"Not a problem," Coal said.

"If that headache continues, feel free to come back and we'll take another look at you," she said and offered Coal her hand. "Good luck at the rodeo."

"Thanks, Doc," Coal said as she shook her hand.

"Have a great rest of the weekend," Cindy said as she took them back to the waiting room.

Melissa and Del stood when they approached. "Let's get out of here," Melissa said.

"Let me make arrangements for the bill," Coal said.

"It's handled. Let's go," Melissa said. "The boys will be competing soon."

They walked out to the truck and made it back to the rodeo arena in record time.

"Here, put these on," Mary Leah said, pulling out a pair of Ray-Ban's

Coal slipped them onto her head and sighed. "That's better already."

"Good, let's go check on the boys, and then we'll find a seat in the stands," Melissa said.

†

"Are you all set?" Coal asked Gene.

"Oh yeah, I can hardly wait."

"It won't be long now."

"This should be interesting," Mary Leah nodded toward a bear of a man approaching them.

Melissa turned to see what her sister was referring to and smiled at the man as he stopped near them.

"Melissa, Miss Mary Leah, it's been a long time, how're you?" he asked.

"Doing well, Big Bob, and you? How's Bubba feeling?"

209

Coal realized then that Big Bob was Bob Brewster, father to Shelly and Bubba. She winced.

"He needs some dental work, but from what I heard, he's lucky that's all he needs." He turned to Coal. "Are you Ms. Bryan?"

"Yes, sir," she answered.

"I'd like to apologize to you for the behavior of my children," he said. "What they did was unforgivable, but I hope you will accept my apologies."

"Thank you, sir."

"Is there anything I can offer to make this right?" he asked.

"You can reimburse me for this," Melissa said as she pulled out the bill for Coal's medical attention.

Big Bob looked at the total. Without flinching, he pulled out his wallet, and took out twelve, one-hundred-dollar bills and handed them to Melissa. "I hope you will allow me to pay for a nice dinner for you ladies as well," he offered.

"This will cover it nicely," Melissa said.

"Thank you and I hope you have a great rest of the weekend," he said and started to turn away.

"Mr. Brewster," Coal called to him.

He stopped and turned back toward her. "Yes, ma'am?"

"There is one other thing you can do."

He looked at her with steel-gray eyes. "What would that be?"

"Teach your daughter to ride properly. Her mare is wicked fast and she shouldn't receive punishment for the failure of her rider. If Shelly will lower her hands and give the mare her head, she will run much faster than being whipped with her reins."

"I agree, and will see to it," he said.

"Thank you, sir," Coal said and offered him her hand.

Bob shook her hand and nodded, then turned and walked away.

"You handled that well," Melissa said.

"So, where you taking us to dinner?"

"Are you sick of the Saltgrass yet?"

"I would love to try out their ribs," Coal said.

"That was easy enough," Melissa said. "Let's go find a seat."

"Good luck, boys," Coal said and followed the others out of the stables.

†

She stopped at the trailer to remove her chaps and then joined the others in the stands. Her headache was finally beginning to ease off, but she kept the sunglasses on to shade her eyes from the bright sunlight. As she walked past a trailer, a sultry voice called out to her.

"Nice riding this morning, cowgirl. That wasn't a bad kick either, from what I've heard. I'm glad someone has finally found out how to shut Bubba's mouth."

Coal turned at the sound of the voice and stepped toward the woman coiling a rope. "Thanks. I'm not proud of kicking Bubba's teeth out, though," she answered.

"That's been coming for years," the woman said. She stepped forward and reached out her hand. "Stormy Braxton, I have worked for Big Bob for a year now, so I've seen how the dynamic duo behaves."

"Coal Bryan, I ride for the MC2," she said, taking the woman's hand. She took a good look at her well-muscled physique and charming smile. Her close-cropped dark hair and dark skin made her wonder if she had some Native American blood in her.

"Yes, I know. Very impressively too, I might add. Your horse is gorgeous and his rider's not too bad either," the woman said obviously flirting.

She blushed and smiled. "Thanks." Not knowing what else to say, she smiled again and said, "Have a great one."

"You too, Coal," she answered and returned her smile with a wink of her deep blue eyes.

Coal found the crew in the stands and began to climb toward them as the event was about to begin.

✝

"There you are. We were just contemplating a burger for a late lunch," Mary Leah said.

"That actually sounds good," she said.

"Sit tight and watch the competition. Del and I will grab some burgers and drinks."

"Thanks, sweetie," Coal said as she sat beside Melissa.

"How're you feeling?"

"Like I was hit by a bus, but I'll live," she said with a cockeyed grin.

"You don't have to compete tomorrow if you don't feel up to it."

"Are you kidding, nothing will keep me from roping with Gene tomorrow."

"Okay, okay, I was just making a comment," Melissa said, throwing her hands up in surrender.

Coal relaxed. "I'm sorry, boss. This competition means so much to Gene. I wouldn't dream of letting him down."

"You wouldn't be letting him down. You know he worships you, Coal."

"I know, and that's more the reason I won't back out on him."

"We will make it an early night so you can get some rest for tomorrow then," Melissa said.

"That sounds good to me. What draws did the boys get, do you know?"

"Lucas is fourth and Gene is seventh," she answered.

"He's going to be a bundle of nerves." Coal grinned.

She was surprised when the announcer introduced Stormy as the third contestant in the steer wrestling competition. "I didn't know women could compete in the steer wrestling," she said.

"Title Nine made a difference in all sports, even rodeo. Women cannot be banned from competition in any event," Melissa explained.

"Interesting," Coal said.

"Just don't get any ideas of entering the bull riding competition," Melissa warned.

"No way, boss, I'm content riding and roping."

"Good. I've seen many great cowboys ruined by bulls; young men crippled and maimed for life," she added.

"I hear you. I'm glad Lucas and Gene are staying away from that event."

As Del and Mary Leah climbed back toward them, Coal leaned forward to watch Stormy's run. The steer released from the chute at a dead run and her horse burst through the barrier in hot pursuit. She held her breath as Stormy launched her body from her horse, grabbing the steer by the horns as her boots dug into the dirt. Her raw power turned the steer's head back toward his hindquarters and she pulled him to the ground. "Damn, that was quick," she said, letting out a low whistle.

"Great run," Melissa agreed.

They both looked up at the scoreboard to see that Stormy had moved into first place.

"Here you go," Mary Leah said, handing out burgers as Del passed around drinks.

"Thanks," Coal said, placing the burger and drink next to her. Lucas was up next and she leaned forward in her seat as he backed his horse next to the chute. "Here we go," she said as Lucas nodded his readiness to the cowboy working the chute.

The steer barreled out of the chute and Lucas's horse exploded through the barrier in pursuit. Lucas launched his body after the fleeing animal and the force of his momentum and perfect timing drove the steer to the ground. Lucas jumped up and pumped his fist in the air realizing he made a great run. He looked up at the scoreboard to see his name flash into first place, bumping Stormy to second.

"Woohoo! Way to go Lucas," Coal yelled and immediately regretted her actions. The flare of pain in her chin reminded her of her injury and she grabbed at her face.

"Are you all right?" Mary Leah asked when she saw her wincing in pain.

"Remind me to not holler," she said with a grin. "It hurts like hell."

"Better put that mouth to better use," Mary Leah said with a smirk and handed Coal her burger.

Coal chewed on her burger until it was Gene's turn for a run, then she wisely placed it in the seat beside her. "Come on, Gene, give it a go," she said and crossed her fingers as he backed his horse beside the chute.

Gene nodded. The steer burst from the chute and immediately took a right turn, but Gene was prepared and launched himself at the steer. His improved strength allowed him to wrestle the steer to the ground easily. He bounced to his feet and looked up at the time, disappointed to see his was a tenth of a second behind Lucas's, but still in second place. The right-hand turn by the steer had cost him additional time.

She watched as Gene jogged over to his horse and mounted, before riding to the end of the arena to exit. "Damn," she said. "I'll be right back." She climbed from the stands to go in search of Gene.

Coal kept an eye on the arena for the last three contestants to compete as she made her way to the end of the arena. The next cowboy overshot the steer and ended up with a mouthful of dust. "That had to hurt," she spoke aloud as she reached Gene and Lucas.

"Great run, boys," she said. "Let's hope they hold up." She stood next to Gene and watched as the next steer took four strides from the chute and then reversed directions. Several seconds elapsed before the cowboy could turn him back into position, virtually eliminating him from the competition. "Only one more to go," she said.

Gene dismounted and stood next to her as the cowboy backed next to the chute.

She reached down and held his hand as she held her breath. He squeezed back with his hand and she knew he was also holding his breath.

The steer blasted out of the chute and the cowboy took off in hot pursuit. He worked fast and had the steer on the ground extremely fast. He had the time to beat both Gene and Lucas until they looked back at the chute to see the cowboy was being assessed a time penalty for breaking the barrier prematurely.

When they saw the yellow flag flying, Coal grabbed Gene in a hug. "You two did it," she said. "You took first and second."

"Not bad for a day's work," Harley said as he slapped Lucas on the back, nearly sending him flying off his horse.

Gene looked up at Lucas and smiled. "We really did it."

"Congratulations, boys," Stormy said as she walked up to them.

"You had a great run too," Gene said as he shook her hand.

Lucas finally dismounted and looked at her. "Are you competing in the bronco riding tomorrow?"

"Don't you know it," she said with a lopsided grin.

"Me too," he said. "You'll have another shot at an invite to Austin."

She flashed him another grin. "I've already got an invite. I went to Amarillo a few weeks ago and placed second in both events, so I will see you there."

"Awesome," Gene said.

"The boss is taking us to dinner if you boys want to get your horses settled for the evening," Harley said.

Gene and Lucas walked their horse to the trailer to remove and store their tack. "Good luck tomorrow, if I don't see you in the morning," she told Stormy.

"You too. I understand you and Gene are team roping," she said.

"Yes, we are," she answered with a grin.

"Have a great dinner and get some rest," Stormy said then tipped her hat and walked away.

"Thanks, you too," Coal answered and went in search of Mary Leah.

†

Mary Leah, Del, and Melissa were walking toward her as she turned around. "Who is that with Coal?" Del asked.

"Stormy Braxton, she rides for Big Bob," Melissa said.

"Oh," Del said.

"Hey, ladies," Coal said as she met them. "The boys are getting their horses settled."

"Do you all want to go get cleaned up before dinner or go ahead and eat and call it an early night?" Melissa asked.

"My vote is to eat," Coal said. "I forgot the rest of my burger."

"Yes, you did," Mary Leah said with a scowl.

Coal did not miss the look Mary Leah shot her, but turned back to Melissa. "Are we presentable enough to go to dinner with you?"

"If you were covered in mud, I'd still be honored to go to dinner with you," Melissa said, looping her arm through hers. They started to walk to the stables. "How are you feeling?"

"Sore, but good, and hungry too," she answered.

"Well, let's go get some grub," Melissa said as they walked to the truck to wait on the others.

Del took Mary Leah's arm and held her back. "I saw that look you gave Coal. Trust me when I say you have no need to be jealous. That woman is completely in love with you," she told her friend.

Mary Leah smiled weakly at Del. "I know, but I wonder sometimes if I'm enough for her."

"You and Coal are perfect together, so don't let your imagined jealousy screw it up," Del said. "Trust is a very important thing."

"Yes, of course you're right," Mary Leah said.

They walked over to the group. "Hey, Coal, would you ride with me?" Del asked.

"Sure, Doc," she said and walked with Del to her car.

When they fell into place behind Melissa, Del turned to Coal. "How are you feeling?"

"Sore and embarrassed as hell for losing control," she answered.

"The wounds will heal, and we will get you back in control. My opinion, though, is the asshole got what he deserved for his behavior. A lot of people could have been injured."

"Is that your personal opinion or a professional one?" Coal teased.

"Both," Del said with a grin.

†

Coal pushed back her plate. "Those ribs were good, but they don't hold a candle to yours, Harley."

Harley smiled at her compliment. "Thanks, Coal, but you're jaded."

"Maybe so, but I'm not and I agree with her completely," Del said.

"We will have to cook out again soon then, Doc," he said.

"Count me in," Del said with a grin.

"Will you be coming back tomorrow to watch?" Gene asked her.

"I've decided to stay over and booked a room at the hotel," Del answered.

"Even better then," Gene answered.

"Do you want to swap out and sleep at the hotel tonight and I'll stay with the stock?" Lucas asked him.

Gene grinned at him. "No, I'm having way too much fun talking with the other riders."

"Is there anyone in particular?" Coal asked.

"Maybe," Gene said but didn't elaborate.

"Well, don't say I didn't offer," Lucas said.

"Oh, I won't," Gene said with a grin.

"Are you ladies ready to go?" Melissa asked after paying the bill.

"Yes, ma'am. I'm ready for a hot bath and a comfortable bed," she said.

Chapter Seventeen

After soaking in the bathtub until her skin pruned, she climbed from the tub and dried before slipping into shorts and a tank top. "Can I get another Tylenol?"

"Is your head still hurting?"

"Yeah, but it's a dull ache, nothing like before."

Mary Leah walked to her purse and pulled out the pill bottle Cindy had given her at the hospital. She took out a pill and poured Coal a glass of water. "Here you go, sweetheart."

"Thanks," Coal said. She took the pill and downed it with a long drink of water. "Are you all right, love? You've been really quiet tonight."

"Yes, I'm fine," she said as she lay down on the bed. "I have to confess I had a moment of jealousy today when I saw you with Stormy, but Del's threat to kick my ass brought me out of it."

She climbed in beside her lover and chuckled. "There is no need to be jealous. I am completely in love with you."

"That's good to hear, but you have to admit she is handsome in a very androgynous sort of way."

"If you say so, I wasn't looking at her in that way. We were just talking about the competition and the Brewster brats, as she calls them."

"She definitely nailed that one." Mary Leah chuckled and Coal relaxed.

"Yes, she did. Now are you going to snuggle with me or not?" she teased.

"Of course I am, silly. Turn out the light," Mary Leah answered.

†

After meeting for breakfast the following morning, the crew packed their bags and drove out to the rodeo grounds. The bronco riding was the first event scheduled, and it normally took several hours or longer to complete the two events, so Coal decided to check on Shadow while Melissa, Del, and Mary Leah took their seats in the stands.

She walked into the stables and opened the gate to Shadow's stall. "Hey there, big boy," she said as she stroked his neck. "One more event today and we can head for home."

Shadow nuzzled her neck with his soft nose. "Let's get you some fresh water and some feed," she said as she picked up the water bucket and left the stall. She was walking down the aisle to the water station when she heard someone call her name.

"Hey, Coal," Stormy said. "How're you feeling today?"

Coal turned to see her approaching, decked out in her chaps, carrying a bronco competition saddle. "I'm hanging in there, thanks. Are you ready to ride?"

"I'm always ready to ride," she answered. "Are you still roping today?"

"Oh yeah, I wouldn't miss it for anything."

"You're going to be competing against Bubba, and another of our cowboys," she said.

"How is Bubba?"

"He will look pretty goofy until he gets his teeth fixed, but he'll survive his own stupidity," she said with a chuckle.

"Is he any good?"

"It's one of the few things Bubba can do fairly well, but he can only head. His heeler is pretty good though."

"I guess we'll find out soon enough," she said as she filled the water bucket.

"I need to go get stretched out. Good luck," she said.

"You too," Coal said and walked back to Shadow's stall, placing the fresh water inside then pouring a small portion of feed into the trough. "I'll be back for you in a little while."

She was walking out of the stable when she heard her name called again, this time by a male voice. Coal turned and saw Bubba approaching.

"Hey, Bubba," she said.

"Hey, Coal. I wanted to apologize for yesterday. What I did was stupid and dangerous."

"Yeah, it was Bubba, but I shouldn't have kicked your teeth out."

"I got what I deserved. No hard feelings," he said as he held his hand out to her.

"No hard feelings," she said as she took the big paw he offered and shook it. "Good luck today."

"You too, Coal," he said and walked away.

She stepped out into the bright sunlight and was thankful for the sunglasses she pulled down to cover her eyes. She walked to the trailer where Gene and Lucas were stretching as they prepared for the competition. "Knock 'em dead, boys," she said and walked to the bleachers to find the rest of the crew.

"Welcome back," Mary Leah said. "Is everything all right?"

"Yep, I gave Shadow some food and fresh water and wished the boys good luck."

"How nervous is Gene?" Melissa asked.

"He's definitely pumped up," she answered. "I hope he pulled an early draw."

"He's third and Lucas is fifth," Harley said as he joined them in the stands.

The competition began and Coal sat forward in her seat, eager to watch her crew compete. The first two riders scored poorly, and she hoped the judges would ease up on their scoring. Gene climbed the chute rails and prepared to settle into the saddle, then took the lead rope from the chute staff.

He climbed into the saddle and nodded quickly to have the horse released from the chute. The big bay horse he drew was monstrous in size and she hoped Gene could hang on for the required eight seconds and get his scoring actions complete. The horse jumped from the chute, crow hopped and began bucking, his powerful thrusts lifting him completely from the ground. Gene rode him hard, spurring and staying intact in the saddle as the horse tried his best to dislodge him. When the buzzer sounded to mark the end of the ride, a cowboy rode up beside the bucking horse. Gene lunged toward the rider, dismounting the gelding, which continued to buck until he reached the end of the arena, and escaped to a holding pen.

"Damn, what a beautiful ride," Harley said, letting out a low whistle. "Are you sure that was our Gene?"

"That was definitely our Gene," Coal said, restraining from hollering, having already learned that lesson. "I think loading all those hay bales has finally paid off."

Their eyes stared at the scoreboard as they waited for Gene's score. He was walking to the end of the arena to retrieve his saddle and lifted his hat in salute when the score was announced taking him to first place. "Way to go, Gene!" she said, excited for her young friend.

The next cowboy to ride came out of the chute off balance and ended up with a face full of dirt after three seconds. It was Lucas's turn and everyone held their breath as the horse in the chute threw himself against the metal chute walls. He calmed just long enough for Lucas to climb into the saddle and the chute to open. The horse began bucking violently, twisting his body, causing Lucas to lose his tight grip on the lead rope controlling the horse's head. Feeling the rope go slack, the horse reversed directions and dislodged Lucas from the saddle. He flew through the air in front of the rampaging horse. The support rider barely managed to turn the horse, protecting Lucas from a collision with the raging animal.

The crowd let out a loud groan followed by a sigh of relief when they saw him safely shielded from the horse. It was a disqualifying ride, but they gave him a round of applause for his effort. Lucas raised his hat in appreciation, but Coal knew he was disappointed. His shoulders slumped as he trotted to the end of the arena. "I think someone needs picking up," she said to Harley. "We'll be back," Coal said and trailed Harley down the stands.

Lucas had just arrived back at the trailer with his saddle when she and Harley walked up. "Tough ride, man," Harley said.

"Dammit, I thought I had him," Lucas growled.

"Just a bad break, Lucas. I'm glad you got out of there without getting injured," she said.

"I was scared shitless for a second when he was barreling toward me," Lucas admitted with a grin.

"Hell, I was scared shitless too, and I wasn't eye to eye with him," Coal said.

She took a cold bottle of water from the cooler and tossed it to him. "Shake it off. You still have bareback to ride."

Lucas caught the bottle and twisted off the cap. "I know, I just hate losing," he growled.

"So don't lose the next one," she said and slapped him on the back as she turned to Gene. "That was a great ride you had."

"Yeah, it felt good too. Now if Stormy doesn't bump me, I'll be set."

On cue, a male voice announced Stormy as the final rider for the event. Coal stepped forward to peer out across the arena to watch her ride.

"Oh hell, she's pulled Diablo," Gene said. "He's a wicked ride."

The gate swung open and the huge black horse exploded from the chute. Stormy sat well balanced in the saddle as her spurs raked his shoulders sending him into a fury of bucking and twisting his body as he tried to dislodge the rider. Coal held her breath and counted down the seconds internally, releasing her breath when the buzzer sounded and the escort rider rushed toward Stormy. She kicked her feet from the stirrups, went flying through the air, lucky to land on her feet to the roar of applause.

"Damn," Gene said as he watched the score flash up on the scoreboard. She had scored one point higher, dropping his score into second place.

"You still qualified," Coal said.

"You have to admit that was a fantastic ride, especially for that horse," Harley said.

"Yeah, it was." Gene grinned. "I'm glad she got that monster instead of me."

"What draws did you get for bareback?" Coal asked.

"I'm second and Lucas is tenth," Gene said.

"I'll watch you ride and then go saddle Shadow," Coal said. She reached inside the trailer to pull out her chaps. She bent over to fasten her chaps when Stormy walked up to the group.

"Nice view," she said to Coal.

"Thanks. That was a great ride."

"I got lucky today."

"That was a beautiful ride," Harley said and reached out to shake her hand.

"Thanks, Harley, a few more rides like that and I can afford to leave Big Bob behind."

Her comment surprised Coal. "Are you planning to rodeo full time?"

"No way, I'm not good enough yet, but I hope to get signed on with another crew. Do you think I could get on at the MC2?"

Coal looked at Harley, who shrugged. "You won't know until you ask the boss lady," he answered.

"The worst she can say is no, right?" Stormy said.

"That would be cool," Gene said. "We could really kick some ass then."

Coal chuckled at Gene's excitement. He looked over his shoulder to see Melissa, Del, and Mary Leah approaching. "No time like the present," she said, nodding toward the group.

Stormy looked up and smiled nervously. "Now?" she asked.

"You could ask to come out and talk to her about it this week," Harley suggested.

"That's exactly what I will do. Thanks Harley."

"Great ride, Stormy," Melissa said as they arrived.

"Thanks, Mrs. Conway," she answered.

"Call me Melissa, please," she said. She looked at Gene and Lucas. "Are you boys ready for your last ride?"

"Yes, ma'am," Lucas said.

"Are you riding bareback as well?" she asked Stormy.

"Yes, ma'am, I ride sixth," she answered.

"Good luck to you then," Melissa said.

Harley nodded to her, and Stormy shuffled her feet. "Mrs. Conway, could I have a minute in private with you?"

"Sure, but you must call me Melissa," she said as they walked away from the group.

"What's that all about?" Mary Leah asked.

"She wants to ask Melissa about hiring her for the MC2," she said.

"That's interesting," Mary Leah said.

"Why is that?" Coal asked.

Mary Leah leaned forward to whisper in her ear. "She and Del have been talking about her quite a bit."

"That is interesting," she said and turned to look at them talking. "I think she would make a good addition to our team."

"I better get going," Gene said.

"Come on, I'll walk with you," Lucas said.

"Good luck, boys," Harley said as Melissa and Stormy returned.

Coal noticed Stormy wearing a smile, so she assumed their talk was positive. "Hang on guys," she said and rushed to catch up with them.

"What do you think about her coming to work with us?" Melissa asked Coal and Harley.

"I think she would be a good addition," Coal answered.

Harley smiled. "If she works like Coal does, I agree."

"She's coming out tomorrow night to talk. I want to talk about her with Stan too."

"You ready to share your house again?" she teased.

"You turned out well, so yeah, I think it would be nice to have another woman in the house again."

"Point taken," Coal said as she moved to the railing to watch for Gene.

"When will you get ready to rope?" Mary Leah asked.

"I'll go saddle him up after Gene's ride."

"Are you nervous?"

"No, not really, I'm ready to be done and headed for home," she answered.

They watched as Gene put in a good ride. Not as exceptional as his first, but good enough to put him in the top position. Coal hoped the score would stand up through the rest of the riders. "That's my cue to get a move on, "I'll be back in a few."

"Do you want some help?" Harley asked.

"Sure," Coal said as she picked up her tack.

They both knew she didn't need help, but she wasn't going to turn down his offer. "Do you miss competing?" she asked.

"I miss the excitement, but I know these old bones couldn't take that kind of abuse any longer, so I will enjoy watching you young ones compete," he said, opening the stall gate for her.

She led Shadow from the stall and saddled him while Harley placed the bridle over the horse's head. "Will you fasten my rope, while I finish?"

"No problem," Harley said. "You got your gloves?"

"In my back pocket," she answered.

"There, you're all set," he said, handing the reins to her and they emerged from the barn.

She looked up at the scoreboard to find Gene still in first place and Stormy about to ride. She tied Shadow's reins to the trailer and walked over to stand beside Mary Leah. They watched as the chute gate opened and the horse burst out of the gate. Coal could tell immediately that she was in trouble. Her body was too far forward on the horse and she struggled to regain her balance on the horse without success. The horse turned violently to the left and Stormy's body shifted in an awkward position, wrenching her shoulder. The pain must have been intense as she lost her grip and flew from the horse's back, further jarring her damaged shoulder. She cringed as the crowd erupted in painful moans.

Stormy regained her feet and the way she held her right shoulder as she walked made it evident that her shoulder had been injured, possibly dislocated. One of the rodeo clowns rushed to her aid and ushered her out a small side gate.

†

Harley rushed off to assist, having experienced the trauma of a dislocation before. He knew all too painfully well what would have to be done to put the shoulder back in

227

place. When he reached the small medical station under the grandstand the staff were already busy preparing an ice pack and locating a large ace bandage. Stormy looked up from the chair she was seated in when Harley arrived, her faced soaked with the perspiration of intense pain.

"Just hang on, it will feel better in a few minutes," he said.

"That shoulder has to be put back in place," the medic said.

"Yeah, we know," he answered. Harley took her hand. "It's going to hurt like hell for a few seconds, but it's got to be done."

The medic took her right hand in his and lifted it to a ninety-degree angle to her body, and placed a hand on her shoulder to feel when the joint slipped back into place. He looked at Stormy, who nodded she was ready, and he slowly lifted her arm and the joint slipped back into place.

"Fuck," she ground out between gritted teeth. She felt a *clunk* as her shoulder slipped back into place and tears filled her eyes.

"All done," Harley said as he continued to hold her hand. He was fuming mad that Big Bob hadn't even sent anyone to check on her condition.

"Let's get her iced and wrapped," the medic said. "I want to get some ibuprofen in her and you can take her home." The medic placed her arm in a sling and turned back to Harley. "Keep her in a sling and if you have a pillow, it may provide some additional comfort if you slip it between her arm and the side of her body."

Harley waited until the staff wrapped the ace bandage around a large ice bag draped over her injured shoulder, and then walked her back to her truck. "You sit here and relax. I will load your horse and get you home," he told her as Coal helped her into the passenger's seat.

"Take her to the MC2," Melissa said. "Get her set up in Coal's old room."

"Do you still have some Tylenol left?" she asked Mary Leah.

"Yes, there are four left," she answered.

"How about giving her one of them to help ease the pain," Coal said.

"Hold up a second, she's already had a dose of ibuprofen," Harley said.

"Take them with you and give her a dose if the ibuprofen doesn't kick in soon," Del said.

Mary Leah rummaged in her purse to get the pill while Del retrieved a bottle of water. Coal gave her the bottle of pills and water while Gene and Harley loaded her horse and gear into the trailer.

"Do you need me to go with you?" Gene asked.

"No, you stay for the festivities and pick up your winnings. I can handle this," Harley answered. "Is your pillow in the trailer?"

"Yes, do you need it?" Gene asked.

"Yes, please." He waited for Gene to return with the pillow and tucked it beneath her arm.

"Thanks," she told Gene and Harley.

The announcer called Lucas as the next rider. "Go watch him, and I'll see you all later tonight," Harley said.

"Take care, Stormy," Coal said.

"Thanks," she answered as Coal closed the door behind her.

Coal watched Harley pull the small trailer from the grounds and then walked to the arena to watch Lucas ride.

Fueled by his earlier disappointing ride, Lucas completed the ride of his life and moved into first place with Gene several points behind him. Their scores held on through the rest of the riders and they captured the top two spots.

"Top Cowboy, here we come," Gene said as he gave Lucas a high five.

"We have one more piece of business to handle and then we can all celebrate," she reminded him.

"I'll be right back," Gene said as he ran to the stables to prepare his horse.

"I'll load up the rest of the gear and my horse while you two warm up. When you're done, we can load the rest and be ready to roll after the ceremony," Lucas said.

"Good idea," Melissa agreed. "Ladies, shall we take our seats?"

"Good luck, Coal," Mary Leah said and followed them to the stands.

Coal slipped on her roping gloves and turned Shadow toward the warm-up ring. They entered and started to canter around the ring to stretch Shadow's muscles. Gene joined them a few minutes later and they both threw a few times at a fixed target to loosen up their shoulders.

"Let's do this," she said when they were ready to go. They rode to the opposite end of the arena and stood in line until it was their turn to rope.

They watched as Bubba headed the steer cleanly, but his partner allowed the steer to kick out a hind leg. The penalty took them out of a competitive time, and Coal knew she couldn't make the same mistake.

When it was finally their turn, she and Gene entered the arena together. They backed into position and when she nodded she was set, Gene nodded to the chute to release the steer. Gene shot out after the steer like a cannon as Shadow lunged into action. Coal heard the whirring of her lasso over her head, and when Gene turned the steer, she focused on the hind feet and threw her rope. It landed in perfect position. She dallied her rope, guiding Shadow back, stretching the steer into position.

She looked over at Gene who was grinning broadly. They both knew it was a near-perfect run. When the judge lifted the flag, she moved Shadow forward to loosen the rope to allow the steer to kick out and Gene retrieved his rope.

They cantered together to the end of the arena to exit. They walked over to the watering trough to give the horses a drink, and then rode back to the trailer to unsaddle and load their horses and gear.

"You did good, big boy," she said to Shadow as she slipped a halter over his head and took the lead to load him into the trailer.

After the final team competed, Gene and Coal remained in first place. She, Gene, and Lucas joined the others in the stands to await the final ceremony.

"Great job you two," Melissa crowed when they arrived.

"Thanks, boss," Coal said, taking a seat beside Mary Leah.

†

After the awards ceremony, the crew departed with handsome paychecks and the Top Cowboy trophy. Melissa also accepted Stormy's winnings in her absence, much to the chagrin of Big Bob. Melissa was determined to prevent him from getting his hands on her earnings when he couldn't be bothered to leave the shade of the stands to check on his injured rider. She decided then that the MC2 just added another rider.

"Would you mind if I ride back with Del?" Mary Leah asked her.

"Of course not," Coal answered with a smile. "Are you coming out to the ranch?" she asked Del.

"I thought I might. To check to make sure Stormy is getting along," Del said with a light flush to her cheeks.

"We'll see you there then," Melissa said as she climbed in behind the wheel as Coal removed her chaps and climbed inside the truck.

†

"Give Harley a call and see if we need to bring anything home. Check on Stormy too, please," Melissa said.

Harley answered on the third ring. "Hey Coal, what's up?"

"The boss wants to know if we need to bring anything home, and to check on Stormy," Coal explained.

"I've kept her on ice, and she refuses to lie down and rest, so she's watching me destroy the boss lady's kitchen."

"Oh dear Lord, what are you doing?"

"Cooking dinner," he chuckled.

"What are you cooking?"

"Fried chicken, mashed potatoes, gravy, corn, and green beans," he answered.

"You've got my mouth watering already. Is there anything either of you need?"

"Hang on a sec."

She could hear him talking to Stormy in the background. "No, ma'am. We appear to be good. How much longer before ya'll make it home?"

"About forty-five minutes."

"I'll be ready to serve by then," he answered. "Be safe and I'll see you soon."

Coal ended the call and turned to Melissa. "He's cooking dinner, and apologizes in advance for destroying your kitchen. Stormy is sitting in the kitchen, so he's keeping an eye on her."

"That's good. He can make a mess, but the man can really cook."

"I will gladly clean up after one of his fried chicken dinners," she said.

"Oh my, yes. Call the boys and tell them to drop Shadow off first and then come to dinner."

"Should I also let Del and Mary Leah in on the dinner plans?"

"Yes, let them know I'm going to stop off at the bakery for something sweet for dessert."

"I'm all over it," she said and started making calls.

Chapter Eighteen

The kitchen filled with a flurry of activity when Melissa and Coal arrived at the house. The crew was busy carrying the meal out to the bunkhouse to a larger table, and Mary Leah and Del were fussing over Stormy.

"How are you feeling?" Coal asked.

"It's painful, but Del just gave me some of the Tylenol."

"I plan to take her to see a doctor first thing in the morning, unless you feel you need to go tonight," Melissa said.

"I'll be fine, Mrs. Conway. You don't need to go out of your way for me."

"I make sure all of my hands are taken care of," Melissa told her.

"That's right, Stormy, and we don't argue with the boss," Coal told her.

"Yes, ma'am," she said.

"Come on. Mary Leah and I will help you out to the bunkhouse," Del said.

"Is there anything else that needs to go out?" Coal asked Harley.

"Just that delicious cake you brought in," he answered. "I think we have some ice cream to pair with it," he added.

"Let's eat then," Melissa said.

✝

After enjoying the wonderful meal, the team pulled together to clean up as Melissa and Del took Stormy back to the house. They sat her on the edge of the bed and Melissa leaned over to remove Stormy's boots.

"Where have you been living?" she asked.

"I rent a room at the boarding house in town," she answered.

"After we finish at the hospital tomorrow we'll go by and get your stuff. Do you want something to sleep in tonight?"

"No, ma'am, I'm okay in my T-shirt and boxers. If you'll help me get out of this sling I can manage from there."

"I don't mind helping you," Melissa said.

"I appreciate that, ma'am, but I can undress myself," she said with a bashful smile.

"Okay, just holler out if you change your mind and want help," Melissa said as she eased Stormy's arm out of the sling. "Do you want more Tylenol?"

"That would be great."

"Hang on and I'll go get them with some water," Del said.

"I'm only a few doors down the hall, so if you need me tonight just holler out," Melissa said.

"Thank you, ma'am."

Del brought her the bottle with two pills remaining and a fresh bottle of water. She poured a pill into Stormy's hand and opened the water for her.

"Thanks," she said and took the pill.

†

Melissa and Del left the room. "Will you call me tomorrow and let me know what the doctor says?"

"Of course I will," Melissa said. "Coal starts back to therapy with you tomorrow night doesn't she?"

235

"Yes, we start phase two this week. The first few sessions may be really tough for her."

Mary Leah and Coal walked in as they reached the kitchen. "Come on, we'll walk you out," Mary Leah said.

"See you tomorrow, boss," Coal said as they left the house.

As they walked across the yard, Del looked at her. "I will see you tomorrow night. It's going to be a hard session, but you're going to do great."

"Thanks, Doc," she said as she opened the car door. "See you then."

"Goodnight, Mary Leah," Del said and hugged them both.

"Drive safe," Mary Leah said when she released Del.

Del nodded and climbed into her car. Coal closed the door behind her and they watched as she backed into the drive. She slipped her arm around Mary Leah's shoulder and said, "Let's go home."

✝

They drove Melissa's truck to their home and parked in the drive. Coal walked around to open the door and offered Mary Leah her hand. "I want to check on Shadow. Would you like to join me?"

Mary Leah slipped her hand inside Coal's. "Yes, I'd like that," she said.

They walked hand in hand to the barn to check on Shadow. The boys had given him fresh water and a block of hay. She hugged the horse around his neck and patted his shoulder. "You were great this weekend, big boy."

"You were both great," Mary Leah said.

"Yeah, we were, weren't we?" Coal said with a grin.

"Come with me, cowgirl, it's time for bed," Mary Leah said with a devilish grin.

Coal drove Melissa's truck back the next morning and walked into the house to find Melissa and Stormy sitting at the kitchen table drinking coffee. "Good morning, ladies."

"Someone is bright and chipper this morning," Melissa said as Coal walked to the coffeepot.

"It's good to be home. How are you feeling Stormy?"

"I'll live," she answered with a grin.

"Were you able to sleep last night?"

"Until about five when the throbbing in my shoulder woke me and I took the last of the Tylenol."

"I'm taking her to the hospital this morning," Melissa said.

"Good, better to be checked out to make sure there isn't any permanent damage."

"Are you two going to team up against me?" Stormy teased.

"Nope, when the boss speaks, we listen," she said with a wink to Melissa.

"Is the crew heading back to the hayfields today?" Melissa asked.

"Yes, ma'am. Tom and Roy got a couple of fields cut over the weekend, so they are taking the day off while we continue cutting and baling, if the hay's ready."

"When we get done at the hospital I'm taking Stormy to pick up her gear and if we're running late, I'll bring some lunch from town," Melissa said.

"I can come back and make sandwiches, if you get hung up," Coal volunteered.

"Keep your phone handy, and I'll text you if we're running late," Melissa said.

"I don't have much at the boarding house, so we can come back here and I'll go back to town and get my stuff," Stormy said.

"Don't be silly. We can get it while we're in town. These guys won't starve."

Coal finished her coffee and rinsed her cup, placing it in the dishwasher. "You won't win an argument with the boss, so you might as well get used to it," she teased.

"Yes, boss," Stormy said.

"See y'all later," Coal said and walked out to the bunkhouse.

"Let's roll," Melissa said.

Stormy followed Melissa from the house and they headed for town.

✝

The rest of the crew was sitting around the breakfast table. Stan had joined them and they were discussing the day's work. "I hear we have a new hand," he said as she sat beside him.

"Yeah, Big Bob treated her terribly when she got hurt," Harley said. "He didn't even check on her or anything."

Stan just shook his head. "How is she?" he asked Coal.

"The boss is taking her to get checked out, but Stormy is pretty tough, and will be fine," she answered.

"She can do some of the driving this week until she's cleared for lifting," Stan said.

"What are the assignments this morning?" Harley asked.

"I'll drive the rake if you want the baler. Coal can drive the truck and Lucas and Gene can load and stack. If she's up to driving when she returns, Stormy can drive the truck and Coal can rake while I start cutting again," Stan said. "We also have a surprise coming this week."

"What's that?" Gene asked.

"The boss has agreed to green break two dozen colts for a ranch out of Austin and they will be delivered Wednesday.

If we finish the hay this week, you young'uns can start on the horses this weekend."

"Good deal," Gene said.

"I thought that might give you some extra incentive," Stan told the young man.

"I'll go get the truck," Gene said, leaving the bunkhouse.

†

The x-rays and tests cleared her from any serious damage. She left with instructions to use the sling for two more days and prescription strength ibuprofen to help reduce the swelling and pain. When they left the hospital, she gave Melissa directions to the boarding house.

Melissa parked and walked inside with her. "Hey, Stormy," the owner Sue Thompson said as they entered the kitchen. She smiled when she saw Melissa. "Melissa Conway, I haven't seen you in ages. How have you been?"

"Good, thanks, Sue, and you?"

"Hanging in there, thanks. What brings you two in together this morning?"

"I'm stealing your boarder," Melissa said.

"Are you finally giving Big Bob the boot? Damn, I didn't see your arm. What happened?" she asked all in one breath.

"I dislocated my shoulder at the rodeo yesterday. Mrs. Conway is letting me join her crew."

"Well, you've got yourself a hard worker, Melissa," Sue said.

"We're glad to have her join us," Melissa said.

Stormy shuffled her feet with embarrassment. It was clear to Melissa that she wasn't used to receiving compliments or praise. She wondered what the young woman's history was.

"Can I get two big garbage bags from you?" she asked Sue.

239

"I've got luggage you can borrow," Sue offered.

"Thanks, but I don't have much."

Sue walked to the pantry and returned with three plastic bags. "Do you need some help?"

"No, ma'am, I've got this, but thanks," Stormy said and left the kitchen.

"She's a good person, but she's had some bad luck in her young life. I hope working for you will help her to continue moving forward," Sue said.

"I'm sure she will be fine," Melissa said and left to go help Stormy.

†

Stormy had emptied the closet and placed six pairs of jeans and work shirts on the bed on their hangers. "I'll take these out to the truck if you want to empty the dresser," Melissa said.

"Yes, ma'am," she said and opened the top drawer.

Melissa picked up the hangers and carried them to the truck. She checked her watch and smiled. They were in good shape for time. She would stop off for sandwiches from a deli before leaving town. She walked back inside to find Stormy struggling to open a bag with one hand and she was about to remove the sling when Melissa walked in.

"Hold on and I'll help you. You need to keep that sling in place," she reminded her.

"Yes, ma'am," she said as Melissa took the bag from her and opened it.

"You hand me the clothes and I'll bag them."

She nodded and emptied the three drawers, which easily fit in two bags. "I've got a few things in the bathroom and I'll be ready."

"I'll take these out to the truck then and wait for you," Melissa said. "Are you squared up with Sue?"

"I'll pay up on my way out," she said.

Melissa carried the bags to the truck and placed a call to the deli to order sandwiches while she waited for Stormy. The heat was already soaring, so she cranked the AC on high to cool off the truck.

A few minutes later, Stormy emerged from the boarding house carrying a final small bag, which she placed in the backseat, and climbed in beside Melissa.

"All set?"

"Yes, ma'am," she answered.

"Let's drop by and pick up sandwiches and then go home."

"That sounds good to me. Thanks for taking such good care of me, Mrs. Conway."

Melissa smiled at her as she put the truck in gear. "You're part of our family now, and we take care of each other."

"Yes, ma'am," she said and laid her head back against the seat.

"It's time for some ibuprofen, isn't it?" Melissa saw Stormy nod. "I'll get a bottle of water when we stop for sandwiches and you can take a dose."

When they reached the deli, Melissa told her to sit tight and went in to grab a bottle of water. While they finished the sandwiches she brought it to her then returned inside. Five minutes later, they were on their way home.

✝

Coal looked up from the tractor to see Melissa's truck kicking up dust as she drove toward them. She turned and motioned for Harley to break for lunch and as she finished the row, she hollered for Gene to hop on the truck and then drove to where Melissa had parked.

"Hey there, what did the doc say?" she asked Stormy.

"He says I'll live. I have to stay in this sling for a couple more days, but otherwise I'm good. No permanent damage done."

"That's great news," Harley said. He introduced her to Stan.

"I've heard a lot of good things about you," he said.

"Thank you, sir, I will work my best for you," she promised.

"Why don't you take the afternoon to get your stuff settled. We can put you to work driving the truck tomorrow, if you're up to it," he suggested.

"I'm good to go now, sir," she said.

"Maybe so, but we're going to make it an early day anyhow, so get settled in and rest up. Can you cook?" he asked.

"Some, but I'm no gourmet." She grinned.

"Well, I believe it's Gene's night to cook and he's laid out cubed steak to smother. I'm sure he would appreciate some help with dinner."

"I'll take all the help I can get," Gene said. "Coal has taught me some things, but I'll always welcome learning something new. Can you make biscuits?"

"Yeah, but not out of a can," Stormy said.

"We will get along just fine then." Gene smiled.

✝

Melissa and Coal spread out the sandwiches, chips, and drinks on the truck tailgate and the crew shared lunch together. After the meal, they walked back to their equipment to return to work. "Are you sure I can't help today?" Stormy asked Stan.

"Don't worry. There will be plenty for you to do tomorrow, and we have two dozen colts being delivered

242

Wednesday that we need to green break next week," he said. "So, get all the rest you can."

"Yes, sir," she said and climbed into the truck beside Melissa.

✝

Melissa helped her carry her belongings into the house and settle into her room. "The crew will be done in an hour or so, if you want you can catch a quick nap."

"Could I ask one more favor of you?"

"Certainly, what can I do?"

"Could you make me an ice pack and wrap me?" Stormy asked shyly.

"No problem, get ready to lie down and I'll be right back," she said and left the room.

Stormy pulled off her boots and jeans then slipped into a pair of shorts. She had just finished sliding her arm back into the sling when Melissa returned with an ice pack and a bottle of water.

"It probably wouldn't hurt to take some more ibuprofen," she said as she gently placed the ice pack on Stormy's shoulder and wrapped the bandage around to secure the pack.

"That feels so good, thanks," she said.

Melissa walked to the bathroom, poured a pill into her hand, and took it to Stormy. "Try to get some rest if you can."

"Will you wake me when Gene is ready to start dinner?"

"Yes, ma'am," Melissa said and closed the door behind her as she left the room.

✝

When Stan called work to a halt for the day, Coal drove the partially loaded truck to the barn and helped Gene and

243

Lucas store the bales in the loft. Then Gene drove her home so she could shower and dress for her appointment with Del.

†

Mary Leah was just pulling into the drive when Coal finished dressing and walked to the refrigerator for a bottle of water.

"Hey, baby," Mary Leah said as she walked into the kitchen and hugged her. "You smell nice."

"Thanks. Did you have a good day?"

"Yes, not bad at all and you?"

"We got a couple loads of hay done," she said.

"What did the doctor say about Stormy's shoulder?"

"No permanent damage, but she's got to wear the sling for a couple more days."

"That's great news. Have you decided what we are having for dinner?"

"I was thinking I would buy you a steak," Coal said with a grin.

"That sounds delicious. Are you ready to go?"

"Just waiting on you, ma'am," she said as she kissed Mary Leah softly.

†

Coal's heart began to race when they pulled into the lot at Del's office. Del had warned her that this week's sessions would be difficult for her and anxiety threatened to overwhelm her.

Mary Leah sensed her anguish. "You will be fine. Del won't push you any further than you're willing to go," she said.

"I know," she answered. "I guess the sooner we start, the sooner I'll be done."

"I'll be waiting for you," Mary Leah said and reached over to squeeze her hand.

"Thanks for being here for me," she said.

"You're welcome," she answered.

†

The first thing Coal noticed when she entered Del's office was the lighting had been dimmed.

"I want you to sit in the recliner and relax. Feel free to close your eyes, while I talk for a few minutes," Del said.

She sat back on the recliner and leaned her head against the cool leather.

"Pull the footrest up and get comfortable," Del said as she walked to the chair across from her carrying two bottles of water. "Are you thirsty?"

Coal's mouth was dry, she felt like she'd been sucking on cotton balls. "Yes, I'm parched."

Del handed her the bottle. She took a long drink and placed it on the table beside her.

"There is plenty, so if you need more, just let me know."

"Thanks, Doc," she answered and relaxed back in the chair.

"Tonight we are going to begin working with the Virtual Iraq software. It has been programmed with several of the scenarios you have described to me during our sessions."

Coal felt her heart lurch in her chest as a bead of sweat broke out on her forehead.

"In just a few minutes, I will place a helmet on your head. Similar to your standard-issue helmet, modified specifically for use in therapy. It has built-in headphones and video goggles. I won't lie to you and say it's cool to wear, because it will be hot, but that will also help with the simulation of the heat in the desert."

Coal listened to Del's soft voice and tried to calm her racing heart.

"There is no timeline for your therapy, so if you become too uncomfortable and feel you need to stop, we will. I do want to encourage you to push your limits as far as you feel comfortable with."

The leather that had been cool against her skin just minutes before was reacting to the increase in her body temperature, and she felt perspiration soaking through her T-shirt. She felt her fingers digging into the arm of the chair and opened her hands to flex her fingers.

"How are you feeling?" Del asked.

"I'm anxious as hell," she stated without opening her eyes.

"Do you need a few minutes or can we get started?"

"I'm ready as I'm going to be, Doc," she said.

"Okay then." Del stood and walked to the cabinet beside her and opened the door. She took out a helmet and told Coal, "Open your eyes."

She opened her eyes and they landed on the black helmet Del held in her hands. Del offered her the helmet.

Coal took the helmet with unsteady hands. "It's heavier than I thought it would be."

"It's still a prototype; hopefully they will fabricate a lighter version soon," Del said.

She turned the helmet in her hands inspecting it closely, and then bent her head forward to place it on her head. She positioned it comfortably then attached the chinstrap, slowly releasing the breath she had been holding.

"Good so far?" Del asked.

Coal nodded. "Yes, Doc."

"When you're ready, position the goggles over your eyes," she instructed.

Coal waited a few seconds to adjust to the weight of the helmet. She pulled the goggles over her eyes and was panic-stricken when she could see nothing through them.

"I should have warned you that you wouldn't be able to see through them," Del apologized.

"That's okay, Doc," she said as calmly as she could.

"I'm going to turn some music on when you're ready so we can test the sound," she said.

"Ready when you are, I just hope it's country," Coal teased.

"Only the best for you," Del said. The music started playing. "How's the volume?"

"It can come down a notch," she said.

Del used a remote to lower the volume. "How's that?"

"Much better, thanks."

"Have you played many video games, Coal?"

"No, not really," she answered.

"In just a minute, I'm going to place a joystick in your hands. You will need to use this to move the soldier forward, backward and from side to side. This is one way you will have control over the simulation. The video will not move forward without your command."

"That sounds easy enough."

"Are you ready to move forward?"

"Yes, Doc, I think I am."

"Very well then." Del walked to the cabinet and retrieved the wireless joystick that she placed in her hands. "On top of the joystick is a button, when you push it the video pauses. I am going to start the video. I want you to practice pausing and moving for a few minutes before we attempt the first scenario. Is this okay with you?"

"Yes, Doc," she said as her heart hammered against her chest.

Del sat close to her to monitor her visible signs of distress as she used the remote to turn the video to play.

Coal waited in the virtual darkness for several long seconds, then she began to hear a faint sound as the screen began to glow and slowly brightened to a scene of a deserted street. Heat waves danced across the broken asphalt and the sound grew louder.

"That sounds like the blades of a chopper approaching," she said.

"That's good, Coal. That is exactly what the sound is. Can you move forward?"

Coal's hands were sweating as she used her fingers to move the joystick forward. She sensed the movement inside the goggles. "That feels really strange, like I am actually moving."

"Are you comfortable with it?"

"Yes." She moved the joystick forward and then side to side.

"Will you walk down to the end of the street and stop there?" Del asked.

Coal moved the joystick and the soldier walked forward, instinctively scanning from side to side watching for the enemy. She could hear the crunching of rocks under the soldier's feet, and when she moved her head down, she saw the soldier carrying a rifle identical to the one she had used. The thumping of helicopter rotors grew louder and she looked up and to the left to see a large Huey passing overhead. The copter's gunner was sitting inside the open door, his legs dangling through the air. He waved as they passed over, causing her to smile and lift her hand.

Del watched the movement in Coal, and realized she was submerging into the video well.

She continued forward and watched as the other soldiers in the unit, returning from their assignments as they made their patrol rounds, surrounded her soldier. She could hear the gentle bantering of the other soldiers, but could not make out their words.

"Let's fall into place, soldiers, and for God's sake keep your eyes open," the squad leader barked out in her ears as he turned and led them forward.

As the squad began moving forward, the auditory atmosphere began to change. Coal could hear the barking of a dog somewhere off to her right, and she remembered the huge black dog they had passed on so many occasions chained to a tree in the backyard of one of the homes. Her mouth went dry and her heart rate soared with the memory.

Del could see Coal licking her lips. "Are you thirsty?"

"Yes, my throat is parched," she answered.

"Hit the pause button, and I will hand you the water."

Coal did as instructed and depressed the button. The goggles flickered, and then went dark.

Del twisted the lid from the bottle and placed it in her hand. "How are you feeling so far?"

"I'm doing okay, Doc. It's surprising how real this feels."

She took a long drink of the water. "I can feel the heat and taste the dust in the air," she remarked. "I never could get enough to drink to wash that taste out of my mouth."

Del smiled. It was good she was remembering other facts than just the trauma she experienced. "Let me know when you've had enough to drink and are ready to move on."

Coal took another drink and blindly handed Del the bottle.

"Push the button when you are ready."

She took a breath and pressed the button to activate the video. The goggles glowed for several seconds as the scene came back to life. The unit froze in place until she realized she had to use the joystick to move them forward.

She pressed the joystick forward and the group moved together in unison down a wide alley until they reached another broad street. This one was not deserted. Cars lined along the curb. Children were playing in the street, kicking a soccer ball between them until they spied her group's approach, then they came running toward the soldiers. Coal gasped for breath. She remembered how beautiful the children were, but also that in some areas children occasionally were bombs, their tiny little bodies strapped with explosives as they rushed into a unit of soldiers in hopes of candy or money. Several American soldiers died from the explosions as the child, sacrificed in the name of war, brought great honor to his family. She felt her arms rise lifting her rifle as the children approached and a dark-eyed child stopped in front of her. She felt her lips curling into a smile as her hand disappeared and then returned with a chocolate bar she handed to the child, who rushed quickly away to enjoy her gift.

The smile left her face when the children, like ghosts, disappeared and angry voices were shouting down at the children and the soldiers who had begun walking down the street, their ever-vigilant eyes scanning for threats. She raised her head as her eyes scanned the windows for any signs of a sniper. She heard the droning of approaching helicopters once more and looked up to see three flying quickly overhead on their way back to base. Her nerves were tense as the additional sounds threatened to paralyze her movements and she felt her breathing becoming more rapid. She felt her skin breaking out in a cold sweat, and she pressed the button to pause the video.

Del watched her carefully for several seconds to see if she would continue, and then spoke softly to her, "I think that's enough for tonight."

Coal certainly wasn't going to argue with her. She was relieved to be able to escape the stimulation of the video.

"Pull the goggles up and then you can take the helmet off," Del said as she took the joystick from Coal's tight grip. She placed the joystick and then the helmet on the table beside her. "I think you did remarkably well for a first time. How do you feel?"

Coal made a motion to stand up from the recliner, but Del held her in place. "You need to sit and relax for a few minutes," she instructed, handing her a fresh bottle of water.

"You may feel a bit nauseated, like you're getting motion sickness, but that is quite common for virtual reality therapy."

"I feel fine, Doc," she said, as she took the bottle of water from Del. She opened it and took a long drink.

Del could see the obvious signs of the stress to Coal's system. Her shirt and hair were soaked with perspiration and there was still a look of panic in her eyes. It was obvious she was ready to escape the room for the outdoors and some fresh air.

"Are you feeling comfortable with this form of therapy?" Del asked.

"Comfortable, no, but if you're asking if I can handle it, then yes," Coal answered a bit sharply.

"What about it makes you uncomfortable, Coal?"

"It's so realistic, it's almost like being back in the desert, but I assume that's the way it should feel."

"Exactly, but remember we will take this on at your pace, so you can adjust all you need before we move on."

She nodded her head and stood up to leave the room.

Del followed her out to the waiting area and smiled at Mary Leah. They watched as Coal quickly disappeared out the front door. Mary Leah turned and looked at Del with concern.

"She's okay. She just needs some fresh air."

"She looks like she's been through the wringer," Mary Leah said.

"It wasn't easy for her, but she did great for the first session. Make sure she gets plenty to drink she worked up a good sweat in there. Also, don't be surprised if she gets nauseated on the road home, it's a type of motion sickness sometimes associated with virtual reality, but nothing to be worried about."

She walked Mary Leah to the door and locked it behind her. She returned to the office to review the videotape of Coal's session.

Mary Leah walked out to find her leaning against the back of the car. "Are we ready to head for home or do you need a few minutes?"

"I'm ready, sweetheart," she answered, and climbed inside the car.

Mary Leah turned the key and Coal asked, "Would you mind if I roll the window down? I need some fresh air."

"No problem at all, do we need to stop for something to drink?"

"That would be great. I'll even treat you to an ice cream cone if you'll stop."

"You have so got a deal," Mary Leah said as she pulled from the parking lot.

When they arrived home, she looked much more relaxed and announced, "I'm going to take a shower."

"Okay, baby," she said. "I'm going to get the coffeepot ready for in the morning and then get my clothes ready for work."

Coal stripped out of her still damp clothes and quickly rinsed the sweat from her body. She was bone weary, and after drying and taking her medicine, she slipped into the bed. Mary Leah walked into the room to get her clothes to iron and said, "I won't be much longer and then I'll join you."

"All right, honey," she answered.

Ten minutes later when Mary Leah returned with freshly ironed clothes, she found her fast asleep. She put her clothes away and finished her nightly routine before climbing into bed beside a softly snoring Coal. She watched her lover sleep for several minutes, glad to see her relaxed

and that the tension left over from the intense session had left
her body.

Chapter Nineteen

"I did it again, didn't I?" she said as Mary Leah walked back into the bedroom.

"Did what, honey?"

"Fell asleep on you again."

Mary Leah handed her a cup of coffee. "You were worn out last night."

"Yeah, I was, but I feel like I'm neglecting you."

"Oh, baby, you are not neglecting me," Mary Leah said.

Coal sipped on her coffee as she listened to her lover. She knew Mary Leah would never complain, but it didn't make her feel any less guilty. "Tonight I should be able to stay awake."

"Really, Coal, it's not a big deal. I'm more concerned with you getting plenty of sleep right now."

Deciding to change the subject, she asked, "What would you like for supper?"

"Do you think you will feel up to grilling us some chicken breasts?"

"I think I can handle that. Would you like them barbecued?"

"I will make us a salad and some corn if you will handle the chicken."

She smiled at her warmly. "You have a deal, my love."

✝

Coal fed Shadow before leaving for work. "We will go for a ride soon, I promise, big boy," she said as she placed fresh hay in his bin. He looked at her with big brown eyes. "Okay, I get the message," she said and opened the stall to lead him out into the aisle. She saddled Shadow and rode him to work.

Melissa and Stormy were sipping coffee on the front porch when she rode into the yard. "Good morning, ladies," she said.

"You look well rested," Melissa said.

"I should be. I slept like a rock, and fell asleep on your sister, yet again," she answered. "How are you feeling, Stormy?"

"Still a bit sore, but nothing like before. I'm ready to get to work."

"Stan plans to have you drive the truck today while the boys load and I'll take over the rake."

"I wish I could do more," she said.

"Don't worry there will be plenty of haying to be done before this summer is over," she reassured her. "Plus we have horses to green break."

Stormy's eyes glittered with excitement.

"Can you swim?" Melissa asked.

"Yes, ma'am."

"Good, we do things a little differently around here," she said.

"How's that, ma'am?"

"You'll find out this weekend," Melissa said mysteriously.

Coal chuckled and dismounted Shadow. She unsaddled him and draped the saddle and blanket over the porch railing and removed his bridle.

"Aren't you going to put him in the corral?"

"It wouldn't do any good," Melissa said. "Shadow would just jump the fence and chase after her once they leave for the hayfields. I swear he follows her around like a puppy."

"That's my boy," she said as she stroked down his back.

"You want some coffee?" Melissa asked.

"I'm good, thanks. I've had half a pot already." Coal climbed the steps and sat on the porch swing. "Are the boys in gear yet?"

"They were finishing up breakfast when I left," Stormy said. "We had biscuits and gravy left over from last night that Harley used. He cooked fresh eggs too."

"I hope you made the gravy. There's not one among that lot that can make good gravy."

She smiled at her. "I did and the biscuits as well. Gene did really well with the cubed steak though. It appears you taught him well."

The morning was getting warm quickly, and there was no sign of a breeze. "Looks like it's going to be another hot one," Coal said.

"Triple digits again today," Melissa said. "Are you ready for egg salad sandwiches?"

"I can never get enough of them," she said.

"I think I'll do some baking too," Melissa said.

"Do you need me to do anything before we head out?"

"No, Gene has already filled the coolers and I'll bring more tea and lemonade when I bring lunch."

The door to the bunkhouse swung open and the crew began to filter out. "I guess that's our cue to get a move on," she said to Stormy.

"Let's load up and get to it, boys," Stan said. "And girls," he added as Coal and Stormy settled on the bed of the truck.

Coal shot him a grin then he slipped behind the wheel of the truck.

✝

When they reached the fields, Stan dropped Coal and Harley off at their tractors. He and Roy would continue cutting the next fields while Tom, Lucas, and Gene loaded the bales. Coal pulled the rake in front of Harley. They started to work as Stormy pulled the truck up to the bales they had left the previous day and the boys started to load. Coal pulled her hat down over her eyes and smiled as she watched a hawk circle the fields. *Our guardian angel,* she thought.

She finished raking and watched as Stormy drove the first load back to the barn. Harley was a few hundred yards behind her so she drove over to the next field and began to rake the hay to prepare for his arrival. She could see Stan and Roy stirring up dust as they cut the field next to the one she had just entered. Coal broke out in a smile when she saw Shadow grazing the field they had just finished baling. She hadn't seen him arrive at the field. He lifted his head to watch her drive toward the next field. A few minutes later, he trotted beside the tractor and when she lowered the rake, he dashed off to find a spot to graze.

She made several passes with the rake and then pulled the tractor beneath the shade trees to grab two bottles of water out of a cooler. Her throat was parched and she knew Harley was probably thirsty too. She drove up next to him and tossed him a bottle of water.

"Thanks, you must have been reading my mind," he said as he twisted the cap. "I feel like I could drink a dozen of these."

"I hear you. I feel like I've eaten a couple pounds of dust even through the bandana."

He took a long drink of water and looked across the field. "We sure could use some rain, but I hope we can get this round of hay in beforehand."

"Is there any chance for rain soon? I've given up watching the weather," she said.

"Possibly on Sunday, but who knows. That could change ten times before the weekend."

She became lost in her thoughts as memories of the heat and drought of the desert flooded back to her. She thought of Tessa and the guilt of her lover's death rode her hard. She felt a lump of emotion lodge in her throat. She realized she needed to move to get her mind focused on something other than Tessa.

Harley saw the pain in her eyes and his heart went out to the young warrior. "Let's get back to it and finish this field before the boss gets here with lunch."

Coal nodded, pulled the bandana over her mouth, and started the tractor. She waited for Harley to pull in front of her then split off a row ahead of him to continue the raking. As she made the turn at the end of the row, her eyes landed on Shadow. Tonight they would go for a ride. Both of them needed a run in the wide-open fields to stretch their muscles. It would help to clear her mind, or so she hoped.

She lost herself in the mundane task of raking the hay and when she looked up again, she saw Melissa driving the gator across the fields. She got Harley's attention, gestured eating to him, and raised her rake to drive back to the trees for lunch. Stormy and the boys had also entered the field they were working. Coal pointed toward the trees. Stormy turned to see Melissa approaching and sent her a thumb's-up sign. She watched as Stormy stopped the truck and told the crew to load up so she could drive them to lunch. She waved Harley past and turned back to retrieve Stan and the others for lunch.

✝

Melissa lowered the tailgate on the gator and started laying out lunch. A huge platter held egg salad sandwiches accompanied by several bags of chips and a large stack of fresh baked brownies.

Gene and the rest of the loaders had served themselves plates when she and Harley arrived. She cut off her tractor just as Gene let out a loud moan of pleasure.

"Tell me that's a brownie you are groaning about," Harley teased him.

"Oh my Lord, boss, these are the best brownies ever," Gene said, taking another bite.

"You better hurry before he starts on seconds," Melissa teased.

She walked in line behind Stormy. "How are you feeling?"

"I'm good. A little sore, but not bad."

"I brought your pills if you need one," Melissa said.

"No, thanks, I'm good," she assured Melissa.

"How long are you planning to work today?" Melissa asked Stan.

"Hopefully until we get the field they are working on done."

"I'll put on a roast for you guys then," she said.

"That's great, boss," Harley said. "Would it be too much to ask you to make a loaf of your homemade bread?"

Melissa chuckled. "I think that can be arranged, but it will probably take two for this crew."

"Two would be great," Harley said with a grin.

✝

After lunch, the crew picked up the pace and it took two more loads to finish off the field. When Stan called it a night, they rode back to the barn and worked together to get the last load into the loft. Shadow had followed them back to the barn and was grazing in the yard when they finished. She let out a whistle and he came rushing to her.

"He is just like a puppy," Stormy said.

259

"A big one," Coal said as she draped her arms around his neck. "Are you ready for a run, big boy?"

"I'll be glad when I can get back in the saddle," Stormy said.

"When can you ride?"

"Two more days," she answered.

"Just in time for us to do some breaking, if you're up to it."

"I'll do my best to be ready," she answered with a grin.

"Let's get you saddled," Coal said and walked to the front porch to retrieve her tack. Minutes later, she left the crew behind.

†

They cantered across a field and as he warmed up, she pushed him faster and faster until her hair was flying behind her in the wind. She had no particular destination in mind and allowed Shadow to pick the direction he wanted to run. He galloped west toward the sinking sun. When he reached a small patch of bluffs, he slowed to a walk, breathing hard from the exertion, his muscles twitching with adrenaline.

"That felt good, didn't it, big boy?" she asked as she patted his neck. He had worked into a lather of sweat in the heat, and when they reached the edge of a bluff, she dismounted and loosened the cinch on his saddle. Coal draped the reins over his neck and stood beside him as they watched the sky burst into a palette of brilliant color as the bright orb of the sun sank to the horizon as dusk approached.

With a deep sigh of contentment, she tightened the cinch and mounted Shadow for a slow ride home.

†

Mary Leah's car was in the drive as they entered the yard. Coal tended to Shadow and walked to the house.

260

"Hey, baby," Mary Leah said from the kitchen when she entered the house.

"Hey, doll, how was your day?"

"It was good, but better now that you're here," Mary Leah said as she spun around to kiss Coal. "Are you still up to grilling some chicken?"

"Yes, ma'am, just let me take a quick shower to wash this dust off me," she answered.

"Go ahead then and I'll start the grill."

Coal disappeared into the bathroom and enjoyed a hot shower to wash the dust and grime from her body. She loved the haying season, but the heat and dust was thick enough to choke a mule she thought as the water turned from dark tan back to clear as she rinsed her body. The scar from the shrapnel was starting to fade. She brushed her raven-black hair and walked to the bedroom.

She dressed in faded jeans and a worn tee before entering the kitchen. "I feel almost human again," she announced.

"Well, you certainly look and smell human," Mary Leah teased. "The grill is ready and the chicken is too. If you get started grilling, I'll finish up here and bring you a cold beer."

"That's the best offer I've had all day," she said with a wink.

"I plan to up that ante later," Mary Leah said with a grin as she handed her a pan filled with chicken and pushed her wildly grinning girlfriend to the door.

Mary Leah turned on the floodlights as Coal passed through the door into the slightly cooler Texas night. She placed the chicken on the grill and settled into a comfortable chair. Her eyes floated across the yard, following the flight of several fireflies as they danced through the air and in the distance she heard the howl and yips from several coyotes out on the hunt. She sent up a silent prayer that their hunt would be successful and they would not prey on any of the livestock. Melissa was willing to allow them on the property unless they became a nuisance and she hoped they wouldn't have to hunt them down any time soon. Coal loved all animals and would hate to have to be a party to eliminating the coyotes, but if necessary she would do her job.

She was lost in her thoughts when Mary Leah arrived at the deck carrying two cold beers. "A penny for your thoughts?" she asked.

She smiled up at her lover and took the offered beer. "I was just enjoying the night."

"I was listening to the radio on my way home and the weatherman said we had a teasing chance for some rain this weekend."

"We sure could use it and a break from this heat," she answered, and took a long drink. "Damn, this tastes good."

Mary Leah's head turned at the sound of the coyotes. "Are you worried they will become a nuisance?" She studied Coal's face as she waited for an answer.

"So far they have only been after wild game, but if they turn toward the livestock we will be forced to put them down."

"Let's just hope it doesn't come to that."

"Amen," Coal said as she stood and walked over to check the chicken. When she lifted the lid, the aroma of the cooking meat filled the air.

"That smells really good. Did you use your special sauce to marinate them?"

"Of course, the secret's in the sauce," she said, cracking a smile.

"I've got salads chilling and corn boiling, is there anything else you would like?"

"Do we still have some fresh Brussels sprouts?"

"Yes, we do."

"Excellent," she said and walked into the house. She located an aluminum pie plate and covered the bottom with olive oil and then cut the Brussels sprouts in half, dumping them into the oil. After coating them with the olive oil, she sprinkled brown sugar across the top and carried the pie plate out and placed it on the grill. "Tonight we are going to try something different," she told Mary Leah.

"I love your experiments."

†

The meal turned out fantastic, and after cleaning the kitchen together, Mary Leah announced she was going to take a shower. Coal undressed and climbed into the bed, listening to the sounds of the night as she waited for Mary Leah.

When she approached from the bathroom, Mary Leah asked, "Did you remember to take your medicine?"

"Not yet," she said with a smile as Mary Leah climbed onto the bed.

†

Wednesday morning passed quickly. At lunchtime, the crew looked up to see a semi turn into the drive to deliver the stock for training. Stan rode back on the gator with Melissa to see the stock settled in the corral. The crew was excited to begin the training and they finished the haying for the day and rushed back to get a look at the stock. Stormy pulled the truck into position at the barn to lift the hay into the loft, and they all piled out of the truck to walk to the corral.

"What a handsome bunch we have here," Coal said as they all climbed on the rails.

"I can hardly wait to get my hands on them," Gene said.

"Well, they have to wait another day until we finish bringing in the hay, and I see a full truck that still needs emptying," Stan said.

"Yes, sir," Harley said as he stepped down from the railing. "You heard the man, boys, let's get back to it."

The crew followed Harley back to the truck and quickly stored the freshly baled hay. When they finished, Coal rode for home to shower and prepare for her appointment with Del.

†

Mary Leah returned home just as she had finished dressing. "You look nice and refreshed," she said.

"Thanks, it was a good day," Coal answered.

"Mine too. I couldn't help thinking about last night," Mary Leah said with a blush.

"We were way overdue for some loving." She grinned. "I hope that made up for it."

Mary Leah sighed. "Last night was more than fantastic." Her gray eyes sparkled with excitement.

Coal reached forward to move a strand of Mary Leah's light brown hair behind her ear. "More to come soon, I promise," Coal said and they walked out to the car.

†

Del paced in her office after preparing for Coal's appointment. She planned to push her young friend as far as she could tonight and was anxious for the appointment. Coal had held up well to her previous therapy with the Virtual Iraq program and Del planned tonight's session to be the last for the week, giving her the weekend to process her thoughts.

She took a deep breath when she heard Coal arrive and went to open the front door. "Good evening," she said as she and Mary Leah entered. "How are you feeling? Did you experience any side effects from the last session?"

"Other than being incredibly thirsty and exhausted, I was good."

"That's a good sign. No nausea or lightheadedness?"

"Nope, all good, Doc, no motion sickness either."

264

"Okay then. Are you ready to get started?"

"Let's go, Doc," she said as Mary Leah settled into the waiting room.

†

Coal settled into the recliner and placed the helmet over her head, her heartbeat steady and breathing calm as she buckled it in place. She listened to Del's voice as she started the program. She placed a sensor on her finger and placed the controller in her hands, then took a seat across from her.

When the music stopped the video began and she soon found her body walking down the streets of Afghanistan once more. Her heart rate increased slightly as she reached the point where they had ended the previous session. She hesitated then continued her forward progress, moving deeper into the video series.

Del relaxed when she felt Coal move beyond her previous progress and sat back on the couch. She observed her closely but remained quiet, allowing Coal to move forward at her own pace.

The familiar sound of the helicopters overhead filled Coal's ears with the thumping rhythm and she tasted the hot dust of the desert in her nose and mouth. She reached for the bottle of water Del had placed next to the recliner and took a long drink. When she placed the bottle back on the table, the scene before her eyes had shifted. She was now in the mess hall, sharing a meal and laughing with Tessa and Mitch. She had her camera in her hand, snapping shots of them as they discussed plans for returning home in a few weeks. She knew one of those shots now rested in Melissa's den and a smile came to her face. This was a happy time for Coal. She remembered every detail of Tessa's face. She was beyond beautiful in her eyes. Her curls surrounded her cherubic face and the eyes that stared back into Coal burned into her heart. "I will love you forever," she whispered. They were the last words Tessa had spoken to her before they went on their final mission.

She reached out her hand to caress Tessa's cheek and the scene shifted before her eyes. Her hands clutched her sniper rifle as they walked in reconnaissance formation. Mitch and Tessa were behind the unit, geared up for a possible bomb detonation. Her eyes instinctively moved to the window where the terrorist had triggered the bomb that killed Mitch and Tessa, but there was no one there. Panic threatened to seize her as her eyes moved from window to window in search of the terrorist.

Del watched the monitor as Coal's heart rate and respirations increased dramatically. "Are you all right, Coal?"

"Yeah, I'm good, Doc," she said as her soldier walked to the car she knew in the past had held the bomb. She felt her eyes searching the trunk for the bomb only to find it missing. Her body broke out in a cold sweat, instantly soaking her T-shirt, and her hands felt suddenly clammy. "Where is it?" she groaned. She turned to see Mitch and Tessa approaching a different vehicle. "No, no, no," she yelled. Her eyes flashed to the window and she saw the curtain billowing in the wind. Still no sign of the terrorist. She trained her rifle on the window. Another chopper flew low overhead, filling the air with sounds that further confused Coal as her eyes moved from window to window. The sound of the chopper caused windows to fill as men and women peered out the windows. Panic seized her heart. "Where are you?" she growled between clenched teeth.

Coal's hands gripped the plastic controller so tightly Del feared it would shatter in her hands. Just a few more seconds and she would end the session, but she wanted her to see there were many options and there was no way she could cover all of them in preventing Tessa's death. She stood and killed the video, filling Coal's ears with soothing music. She took the controller from her death grip and replaced it with a bottle of water.

Coal sipped the cool liquid, soothing the ache in her throat from the dust and scorching heat. When the music ended she nestled the water between her thighs and removed the helmet, blinking her eyes from the light of Del's office.

"How do you feel?"

"Exhausted. Nothing was as I expected it to be. The bomb was different and there were multiple targets that could have been the terrorist."

"That is exactly what I wanted you to realize. You may have killed the right one, but he may not have been the one that actually triggered the bomb. There were so many variables at play; there is no way you could have saved them."

"But I should have, Doc. I was trained to pick the right one," Coal cried.

"You are only human, Coal. No one could have prevented what happened from occurring unless it never happened to begin with."

"That is something I could not control."

Del just smiled at her and let her own words sink in for a few seconds. When she saw a small lightbulb light in Coal's eyes, she changed gears. "When do you leave for Austin?"

"Next Friday morning."

"Good, let's take Friday off and we can do two sessions next week before you leave. Think about today's session and process it for yourself."

Coal stood and surprised Del by pulling her into an embrace. "Thanks for helping me."

"It's the least I can do," Del said. "You and others have given so much for us."

"Will you be coming to Austin?"

"Wild horses couldn't keep me away. I'm addicted."

She grinned. "Addicted to the adrenaline rush or the cute cowgirls?"

"Well, you got me there. I rather enjoy admiring Stormy's body in motion."

"Oh, do tell, Doc?"

Del blushed. "You can't deny she's a rather handsome woman."

"No, I can't. I don't think she's seeing anyone either," Coal hinted. "You should join us Friday night."

"What's happening Friday?"

"Friday is payday and the boys have talked Mary Leah and me into joining them at the Stockyards for a few drinks. Maybe you and Stormy could join us for dinner beforehand."

"Run it past her and see if she's game. Give me a call tomorrow night and let me know."

"I can already say yes for her. She's been asking questions about you," she answered.

"Oh wow," Del said. "Let's do it then. We could all use some fun."

"I'll call you with particulars tomorrow night then," she said as they walked to the door.

"Do I detect someone playing cupid?" Mary Leah asked as they entered the car.

Coal looked at her lover with the most innocent of looks, her dark eyes burning with excitement. "My dear, I have no idea what you're talking about. I simply invited Del to join us for dinner and drinks Friday night."

"Uh-huh," Mary Leah said. "You realize getting those two together could be very dangerous."

"How so?"

"The attraction between them is highly combustible and given the right circumstances a real romance may just be ignited."

"You talk like that's a bad thing," Coal teased. "Are you afraid Del can't handle someone like Stormy?"

Mary Leah chuckled. "Del can handle anything. I worry about Stormy. Have you noticed how Del's eyes light up whenever the talk is about her?"

"They do sparkle a bit."

"Sparkle hell, they absolutely glow."

"Well then, only time will tell," she said. "May I buy you an ice cream cone, sweetheart?"

"That depends. Do you have the energy to work all those extra calories off me tonight?"

"I think I can come up with something." Coal grinned and rolled down the window.

The cool air bathed her face as she relaxed and shelved the memories of the session for later review. Mary Leah reached across and took her hand, entwining their fingers.

"I may get a double scoop then."

Chapter Twenty

When Shadow and Coal arrived at work the following morning, she found Gene and Stormy looking over the newly delivered stock.

"They are a good-looking bunch aren't they?" she said when Gene turned toward her approach.

"Mostly colts with a few fillies mixed in, but a lively group on the whole. There's one big brute you are going to enjoy," Gene said as Shadow's ears twitched forward.

"Let me guess. The big paint at the end of the corral?" she asked.

"He definitely is the leader of this herd," Gene said.

"I'll take him first then," she said with a gleam of excitement in her dark eyes. "We should finish the haying today so maybe Stan will let us do some horse work tomorrow."

"I'm so ready," Gene said.

"Have you warned Stormy yet?" she asked.

"Warned her of what?" he asked, confused.

"Of how lily-white your legs are?" she teased.

"Well, at least I have more color than I did last year," he said.

"He darn near blinded me the first time I saw them." Coal chuckled.

Stormy looked at Gene and then back to her. "I'm confused. Why would I be seeing Gene's lily-white legs?"

"You will see tomorrow. Until then it's a mystery," Coal said.

"Would you like me to remove Shadow's tack for you?" Gene asked when she dismounted.

"Sure, you can drop it in the barn if you don't mind."

"Not at all," Gene said and walked Shadow into the barn.

"You have a date tomorrow night for dinner and drinks. I hope you clean up good," she teased.

Stormy chuckled. "Who's the lucky lady to get a date with me?"

Coal grinned at her new friend. "Del is joining the three of us for dinner and then we're meeting the boys at the Stockyard for a few beers."

Stormy swallowed hard and Coal could tell she was surprised. "If you're not interested I could ask someone else."

"Hell, yeah, I'm interested. I just didn't think Del would be interested in someone like me."

"I know, I wondered if maybe she had hit her head or something when she agreed so easily," Coal teased.

"Hush, smartass," Stormy said with a smile. "I better go to town for a haircut tonight then."

"I could use a trim too, if you want some company. Is after dinner good for you?"

"Yeah, that sounds great. I've got to check to see if I have some decent Wranglers to wear and polish up my boots," she said, already lost in planning. "I'll be right back," Stormy said and ran back to the house as Coal walked to the bunkhouse.

†

Stormy rushed into the house and nearly ran into Melissa. "Whoa, what's the rush?"

"I've got to put some clothes in the washer. I have a date with Del tomorrow night."

"So that's why you're wearing such a big grin. Start a load and I'll make sure they get in the dryer later," Melissa offered.

"Thanks, boss," she said and raced to her room.

Melissa shook her head and poured a fresh cup of coffee. "I sure hope Del knows what she's getting into," she said aloud with a smirk.

†

The crew worked hard to finish out the haying and had the last bales stacked and equipment stored by four. Coal was saddling Shadow for the ride home when Stormy joined her. "I should be done eating and showered by six. Do you want me to come get you?"

"Yes, that sounds great," she said as she climbed into the saddle. "See you at six."

†

Mary Leah was pulling into the drive as Coal emerged from the barn. "Welcome home."

"Hey, sweetheart, how are you?"

"Better now that you're home," she said as she held the door open for Mary Leah. "Stormy and I are going to town for haircuts at six," she announced.

"I take it she's a bit excited about her date then," she said.

"You could say that," she answered with a grin. "What would you like for dinner?"

"I'll whip up some pasta and a salad while you get cleaned up," Mary Leah offered.

"That sounds terrific," she said and kissed Mary Leah's lips. "I do need a shower."

272

"Yes, dear, you do. You are covered in dust from that hay."

"I'm on my way to the shower then," she said, kissing Mary Leah again before leaving the kitchen.

†

They were washing the last of the dishes when Stormy pulled up in her truck. Coal met her at the door and ushered her inside. "Let me run to the restroom and I'll be ready to go."

"Hey, Mary Leah," Stormy said when Coal left the room.

"I hear you are excited about our date night."

"Yes, ma'am, I'm looking forward to it," she said with a bashful grin. "A bit nervous too."

"Don't be. I've known Del for years and she's a lot of fun."

"I'm sure she is, ma'am," Stormy said as she shuffled her feet.

Coal returned to rescue Stormy before Mary Leah made her more nervous. "You ready to roll?"

"Just waiting on you," she answered with a grin.

"Let's go get handsome for our ladies then," she said, kissing Mary Leah before they left the house.

†

When they arrived at the barbershop, Stormy pulled off her ball cap and her unruly dark curls sprang to life. "Wow, I've never seen your hair this long," the stylist said.

"I never realized you had curls," Coal teased.

"The usual?" the woman asked.

"Yes, please. Tight on the back and sides and spiked up top," she answered.

"Coming right up," the woman answered.

273

Coal took a seat in the barber's chair next to them and watched as the stylist closely shaved Stormy's hair. When she had finished, she looked as clean-cut as ever. She swapped seats with Coal and the stylist turned to her.

"Tell me you don't want to go that extreme."

"Oh no, ma'am, not for me, just trim me back to my collar and over the ears."

"You have really nice hair. I wish I could convince Stormy to let hers grow out."

"Thanks," Coal said in appreciation of the compliment.

"No can do. The ladies like it short and sexy," Stormy said as she looked at her image in the mirror and played with the spikes.

"Some women enjoy grabbing a nice handful too," Coal said, causing Stormy to blush. "I'm beginning to like you in that shade of red," she teased.

"Oh stop, Coal, you're only going to make it worse."

"Yes, I know."

She and the stylist had a good chuckle at Stormy's expense, but she took it with good nature.

When Coal's cut was finished, they paid and tipped the stylist then walked back to Stormy's truck. "I reckon we are presentable enough now," she said.

"Where are we going to eat tomorrow night?"

"Mary Leah and I were thinking about the restaurant at the Stockyards. They have good steaks and the prices are reasonable. Are you all right with that?"

"Yes, that sounds good. Then we can just walk to the club to meet the boys."

"Are you feeling more comfortable about being with Del?"

"I'm not sure comfortable is the right word, but I will be on my best behavior."

"I think Del can handle anything you might throw at her."

"I'm not the best at nurturing a relationship. I rarely date the same woman twice," she admitted without shame.

"Just relax, be yourself, and let fate take it from there," Coal advised.

"Does Del live here in town?"

"No, she's about thirty minutes away, so she's staying with Mary Leah and I this weekend."

"That's cool," Stormy said as she cranked the truck and drove her home.

"I'll see you in the morning," she said when they arrived home. "Don't forget to dress in shorts and sneakers tomorrow."

"All right then," Stormy said. She watched her enter the house and then drove back to the MC2.

✝

"You are looking mighty fine, Ms. Bryan," Mary Leah said when Coal entered the den.

"Thanks, it feels good to get a cut. What are you doing?"

"I was getting ready to watch some television. Would you care to join me?"

"Will there be popcorn?" she teased.

"There can be," Mary Leah said.

"Pop some while I run through the shower to rinse the hair off and I will be right back."

"Sounds like a deal to me," Mary Leah said and walked to the kitchen.

✝

With the dawn came a cool crispness in the air that was virtually unheard of in Texas during summer. Coal saw Mary Leah off with a kiss and walked to the barn to saddle Shadow. "It looks like we are going to have a fine day, big boy," she said as she placed her saddle across his back. She

275

stroked his neck with a loving touch. "I reckon you will be right in the thick of things today as we train the new stock."

Shadow's soft brown eyes locked with hers as he listened to her speak. He caressed her cheek with his soft lips, tickling her and causing her to laugh and hug the dark horse's neck. "You know there are times I wish you could talk. I'd love to know what you're thinking."

Shadow answered by stomping his right foot. "I know what that means," she said as she slipped into the saddle. "You're ready to go and I'm holding you up," she said as they emerged from the barn and Shadow moved into a smooth canter. He was still a very young horse, but she admired the fine steed he had grown into and gave him his head allowing him to dictate the pace. Her newly cut hair lifted from her shoulders, blowing in the wind as Shadow accelerated into a full gallop, his powerful hooves sending dirt flying through the air. She leaned forward across his shoulders and the pair blurred into one as they raced across the pasture.

✝

Several of the crew sat on the railing, looking over the stock when she and Shadow arrived. Coal grinned when she saw Stormy, Gene, and Lucas in shorts and boots or sneakers. They looked like an unlikely bunch of ranch hands, but she knew they would be more comfortable dressed in that manner for the task of the day.

"Good morning," she said as she dismounted. "It looks like we are going to have a great day for training horses."

"Yes, it does." Lucas grinned.

"Will someone finally enlighten me as to why we are dressed like this to break horses?" Stormy asked.

"You fill her in while I take care of Shadow," Gene said, taking the reins from Coal.

"We do things a little differently around here. Instead of training in the traditional manner, we use the resistance of the water in the lake to help soften the blows and exhaust the horses while they acclimate to having a rider on their backs." She looked at her. "I assume you can swim."

"I'm no Olympic contender, but I can keep myself from drowning."

"Coal's method is much less painful for both horse and rider," Lucas added. "Hitting the water is much more comfortable than hitting this rock-hard ground."

"Well, this I've got to see," she said, disbelieving.

"Tom's already got a halter and lead on that big paint you wanted, Coal," Gene said.

"Have you boys got your horses picked out and ready?" she asked.

"Yes, ma'am, we're just waiting on you," Lucas answered.

"Okay then, step one is getting them down to the water. We begin by leading them in and allowing them to swim until they begin to tire and then we mount up bareback in the water. Just sit back and watch this round and Harley can explain the process."

Coal entered the corral and took the rope lead from Tom, who had been steadying the large painted horse. She moved slowly toward the horse and stroked down his face and neck while talking softly to him. The horse quivered with excitement under her touch and she could feel his muscles rippling under her hand. He was a magnificent specimen and she was certain he would prove very challenging. Coal placed her hand on the lead near the halter and urged him to walk beside her. The young horse immediately pulled away from her control, but she wisely used the advantage of leverage to bring him back to her. They walked together inside the corral for several minutes.

When Coal nodded to him, Roy opened the gate and she led the horse out of the corral. Once more, he attempted to break free of her control, but her speed and strength quickly turned his head preventing him from bolting away. She was excited to get the horse into the water, but Coal calmly led the horse to the lake and with gentle coaxing, walked him into the refreshing water. Coal snapped the other end of the rope lead onto the halter and slipped the makeshift reins over his head.

Stormy, Melissa, and Harley drove down on the gator with Coal's saddle and sat beneath the oak watching as Coal and the colt wandered into deeper water and the horse began to swim. Coal held onto the reins once she could no longer touch the bottom, allowing the horse to pull her along beside him as he swam.

"That actually looks like fun," Stormy said.

"It has proven a much better and safer technique in training," Melissa admitted as she turned to watch Gene and Lucas approach, each leading a horse to the water. "The first year Coal arrived, Gene and Lucas were hell-bent to do things the old-school way, but when they saw the results she had with Shadow without hitting the hard ground a dozen times they were convinced, and we have trained this way since."

"The most painful part is seeing those lily-white legs of the boys," Harley added with a grin.

"I heard that," Gene hollered as he and his horse entered the water.

Coal slowly slipped onto the horse's back as he continued to swim and allowed him to adjust to her weight. Stormy watched as she allowed the horse to return to shallower water, feeling the full weight of her body on his back. Each time the horse attempted to buck, she turned him back into deeper water, preventing him from the aggressive motion. For nearly an hour, Coal rode the horse in the water until she felt he was ready for a saddle. As they neared the shore, she slid from the horse's back and led him to the tree where Harley took the reins while Coal dried off with a towel.

"Now the fun part begins," Coal said as she wiped down the horse and placed the saddle on his back. She tightened the cinch then swatted the horse on his hindquarter with the soggy towel. The startled horse bolted away, the empty stirrups dangling against his sides as he bucked furiously trying to remove the foreign item from his body.

"What happens now?" Stormy asked, genuinely interested.

"Now, I go change into riding clothes while he wears himself out trying to buck the saddle off. When I return, I'll ride him until he's too tired to fight."

"Can I give you a ride back up to the house?" Melissa asked. "I can start on lunch while you change and put your wet clothes in the dryer."

"That sounds good to me, boss," she answered.

†

Coal rinsed off in the shower before dressing. When she emerged in jeans, boots, and a clean shirt, towel drying her hair, she found Melissa in the kitchen.

She looked up to see Coal enter and smiled. "I was thinking about some fried pork chops, green beans, and scalloped potatoes."

"My mouth is already watering."

"Would you mind taking a cooler back with you, I've made fresh lemonade."

"I don't mind at all," she said as she left the room to toss the towel in the dryer.

"Is everyone ready for the big date night tonight?"

"To be honest it's hard to tell who is more excited, Del or Mary Leah."

"What about Stormy?" she asked.

"I think she's too nervous to be excited." Coal grinned. "I think our cocky, young cowgirl is a bit intimidated by the good doctor."

"Don't worry, I'm sure she'll settle down and you'll have a great time out."

"Will you reconsider joining us?"

"Thanks, but I'll have the place all to myself tonight and plan to have a nice quiet evening."

"I can understand that. Are we all set for Austin next weekend?"

"Yes, I got our confirmation for the rooms yesterday so we should be good to go."

"Awesome. Well that paint isn't going to train himself so I better get back at it," Coal said as she picked up the cooler. "Lunch at noon?" she asked.

"I'll have everything ready, so bring the crew back with you."

"Yes, ma'am," she said and left the house.

†

Shadow waited for her beside the gator. "Are you going to help me chase down that paint?"

Shadow pawed the ground with his front hoof to answer her question and she laughed as she put the cooler in the back. "Let's get to it then."

She drove back to the pond and poured cool drinks from the cooler. Lucas and Gene were still in the water with their mounts. "Does it look like they are about ready to come out of the lake?" she asked Harley.

"I would think any minute now, especially since you're back." He chuckled.

She handed him a drink and looked off in the distance to find the paint grazing quietly. "How long did he fight the saddle?"

"He just stopped a few minutes ago," Stormy said.

"He should be good and tired by now then," Coal said as she slipped a bridle over Shadow's head and swung her body onto his bare back. She looked at Stormy and asked, "Are you ready to give it a go?"

"Yeah, I think I am."

"Roy and Tom have a few more of the colts haltered in the corral if you want to go pick out one."

"Come along then and I'll give you a ride in the gator," Harley said as Coal and Shadow turned away.

†

It had been a long time since she had ridden Shadow bareback. She enjoyed a leisurely walk toward the paint that had stopped grazing and was staring at them with his blue glass eyes as they approached. He was a handsome bit of horseflesh and would make someone a great cow pony soon, but first she had to establish the rider as dominant. When Shadow was within ten feet of the horse, she pulled him to a stop and she stared into the horse's bright eyes. Curiosity soon got the better of him and he took several tentative steps toward Shadow.

She tied the reins together so they would not drag the ground once she dismounted Shadow. She sat patiently until the paint had walked closer then slowly dropped from Shadow's back and walked to his head. She stroked Shadow's face as the horse looked on, demonstrating to him that she and Shadow had a special bond. Shadow's ears flickered back and forth as the young horse carefully approached. Coal slipped a concealed carrot from her back pocket and broke it in half, offering the first half to Shadow. His soft lips took the offering from her palm and he crunched on the special treat.

The paint looked on curious. She reached out her hand offering the remaining half to him and stood her ground. He would have to close the distance between them and she hoped the crunchy carrot would be a suitable bribe. She held back a chuckle when she saw his tongue flick out to lick his muzzle. He took a step toward her.

A few steps closer and he stretched his neck to take the carrot from her open palm. She stepped forward to stroke his face and her right hand held onto the halter as the horse devoured her bribe. "Are you ready to be ridden?" she asked softly as her hand calmly stroked the horse. His muscles quivered beneath her hand as much from exhaustion as excitement as she spoke to him. Slowly she moved down his side and took the rope lead in her left hand as her foot found the stirrup. She swung into the saddle. Coal could feel his body tense beneath her in preparation to buck and she pulled his head to the side. She controlled his movements and as long as she kept him off balance, he could not buck. She turned the young horse in circles for several minutes until he realized she was in control. She stopped his movement, allowing him to make a choice to either stand quietly or begin turning circles again. When the horse remained calm, she reached down patting his neck and giving him praise. "Now we will ride," she said.

Shadow walked along beside them as she gave the horse his head and used her heels to urge him forward. She taught him the pressure of the reins along his neck would determine his direction and when she pulled back on the reins, he quickly learned the art of backing. He was a smart pony, and a spirited one. When the crow hop that she was expecting finally came Coal spun him around in a tight circle. When she determined the time was right, she pushed him forward into a smooth canter, then further into a gallop across the field, Shadow easily keeping pace beside them. Twenty minutes later, the horse's nostrils flared from exhaustion, his coat slicked with sweat as she pulled him to a halt and dismounted. She lifted the rope reins over his head and led him to the lake for a drink of water. When his thirst was satisfied, she walked beside the horse back to the tree where the others were gathered.

Gene and Lucas had finally emerged from the water and had saddled their mounts. Coal held the reins tight as they startled the horses and watched them bolt across the field, bucking wildly in an attempt to dislodge the saddles. She was very pleased, the young paint did not startle. "He's going to be a good cow pony," she said as she stroked his neck.

"Would you like me to unsaddle him and walk him back to the corral for you?" Gene asked.

"No, I'd like you to ride him back to the corral. I'll get my saddle later. You can bring me down another colt when you return in dry clothing."

Gene grinned and carefully mounted the paint.

Coal could tell he was waiting for the colt to buck and was surprised when the horse calmly stepped forward. She watched as they walked back toward the corral then turned to see Stormy in the lake swimming with a black horse.

"How are the others coming along?" she asked Harley.

"Y'all are doing well. If you can do two each today, we will be ahead of schedule."

"That shouldn't be difficult for us," she answered.

Her eyes followed Stormy across the water. The wet clothing clung to her skin and she realized why Del was so physically attracted to her. She had a very physically fit body, and the smile of contentment she wore while swimming with the horse made her extremely handsome. "She seems to be getting along well."

"She's not you, but she'll do in a pinch," Harley teased.

✝

After a hearty lunch, the crew each worked another mount and when the last of the horses returned to the corral, Harley announced the end of the workday.

"I reckon we'll see you later tonight," Gene said as he saddled Shadow for her ride home.

"You certainly will. I think we all deserve a night out after the last few weeks."

"Amen to that," Gene said. "I'm looking forward to it."

"I'll see you later then," she said.

When she got Shadow settled in the barn, she walked to the house and stripped out of her dusty clothes. She was leaving the shower when she heard Mary Leah arrive home. "Hey, baby," she called from the bathroom.

"Hey, darling, I'm glad to see you home already."

"We finished up early. I think everybody is ready for a night on the town, including Harley."

"I don't know about you, but I'm ready for a steak. I'm starving."

"Melissa cooked a hearty meal for lunch, but I've already burned through that. I wish we could convince her to go with us."

"I think she'd feel like a fifth wheel. I called her this afternoon and asked again, but she declined saying she just wanted a relaxing night at home."

Coal wrapped the towel around her waist and took Mary Leah in her arms for a kiss. "Do you think Melissa will ever fall in love again?"

"I don't think so. What she and Mitch had was so special. She told me she feels she's had the love of her life. She seems content with her memories and life on the ranch."

She felt the deep sigh escape her lover's body and knew Mary Leah also wished happiness for her sister. "You better get a move on if you're going to get a shower in. Del will be here any minute, and I bet Stormy is already pacing the floor."

Mary Leah chuckled and headed for the bathroom as Coal started to dress.

<h1 style="text-align:center">Chapter Twenty-one</h1>

When Del arrived, Coal carried her overnight bag inside into the guest room. She offered her a beer and they sat in the den chatting while Mary Leah got dressed.

"We'll swing by and collect Stormy on our way out," she was telling Del when Mary Leah entered the room.

"You look fantastic, my dear," Coal said when she looked up to Mary Leah.

"Thanks, sweetheart. Good to see you, Del, are you ready for a relaxing weekend?"

"I am beyond ready," Del said as she walked over to hug Mary Leah and kiss her cheek.

"Let's roll, ladies," Coal said. She grabbed the keys to Mary Leah's car and ushered the others out the door.

†

Stormy heard the rumbling of Del's car as she drove up the driveway to Coal and Mary Leah's home and she began pacing again.

"Relax or you're going to wear out my flooring," Melissa teased.

She dried her sweaty hands on the legs of her black jeans. "Should I change?" she implored of Melissa.

"Heaven's no, you look good enough to eat," Melissa said, causing Stormy to turn scarlet. "You clean up very nicely, and I'm sure Del will be impressed."

She kept pacing despite Melissa's pleas. The black jeans and form-fitting shirt accented her body nicely, but she worried she was too casual for Del.

"Do I need to pour you a shot of something to get you to relax?"

Stormy smiled and was about to say yes, but reconsidered when she thought of smelling like alcohol.

"Come, have a shot of Jack with me. You can go brush your teeth again," Melissa said, apparently reading the concern on her face. "At least you'll give this carpet a few minutes of rest."

She compliantly followed Melissa into the den and accepted a shot of the strong whiskey.

"To tonight," Melissa said, touching her glass to Stormy's. "Now bottoms up, for heaven's sake."

Stormy downed the shot, wincing as she swallowed the fiery liquid. "Damn, that's good stuff."

"Only the best in this house," Melissa said. "Now go brush your teeth and check your hair one more time. The girls will be here soon."

Stormy handed the shot glass to Melissa and spun on her heel to cross over to her bedroom. She looked into the mirror and smiled. "I do clean up good," she said and reached for the toothbrush as the strong whiskey performed its magic and calmed her nerves.

When she walked into the living room, the sun had set and she could see the glow of headlights as Mary Leah's car turned into the drive.

"I was wondering if you would do me a favor," Melissa said.

"Sure, boss, what can I do?"

Melissa handed her a fifty-dollar bill. "Buy a round of drinks for the crew for me tonight and give them my thanks for a hard week."

"Consider it done," Stormy said, tucking the bill in her pocket. "Are you certain you won't join us for dinner?"

"I'm positive, but thanks for asking."

The car arrived and she looked back at Melissa with a smile. "Here we go."

"Have fun," Melissa called after her as she pushed through the screened door.

†

"Wow," Del said as Stormy stepped beneath the porch light.

"Are you sure you can handle Stormy?" Coal teased.

"Well, I'm sure going to die trying," she answered as Mary Leah punched Coal's shoulder.

"Be nice, Coal," Mary Leah warned.

"I was being nice," Coal said with a wink to her lover.

They watched as Stormy walked across the yard, opened the door, and climbed inside the car.

"Good evening, ladies," she said as they all looked at her.

"You clean up good, girl," Coal said, then put the car in gear.

"Thanks," she said, the heat rising slowly up her neck.

"You look very handsome," Del said.

"So do you," Stormy answered. "I hope I'm not underdressed."

"Not at all, you look really great," Mary Leah added. "I hope you're hungry because the rest of us are starving."

"I feel like I could eat a steer by myself," Stormy said.

"Now we're talking," Coal said as she drove to the paved road and turned toward town.

†

The restaurant turned out better than Stormy had anticipated. Once they had finished their meals, the group decided to walk over to the club. Coal's eyes searched the parking lot and she smiled when she saw Harley's truck.

"The boys have already made it. Hopefully they have gotten us a table," she said.

"The place looks packed already," Mary Leah said.

"Well, it is Friday night ladies," Del said as she led the way to the club's entrance.

"That it is," Coal said. She walked through the door and pulled out her wallet to pay the cover charge.

"Come on in, ladies," the bouncer said.

Coal lifted her hand to pass him a twenty-dollar bill and he waved her off. "Your cover has already been paid by a group of thirsty-looking cowboys." He grinned. "Harley and the boys are at a table on the right of the dance floor, by the pool tables. Have a great night."

"Thanks," she said and led the others inside.

Gene was the first to see them enter and he let out a loud whoop, waving his hat in the air for Coal to see. "What are we drinking\?"

"Coors Light all around?" she asked.

"Sounds great," Del, answered.

"What do the boys drink?" Stormy asked.

"Three Bud Lights and a PBR," Coal answered.

"Would you help me for a second?" she asked Del.

"Sure."

"We'll join you in a minute," Stormy told Coal.

She and Del walked to the bar and ordered the drinks. Del carried the Coors Light while she delivered the boys' drinks. "Compliments of the boss lady for a hard week's work," she said as she placed the cold bottles on the table.

"Welcome, Doc," Harley said. "Glad you could join us tonight."

"Thanks, Harley, I'm glad to be here."

"So what's shaking tonight? Is there anything special going on?" Coal asked Gene.

"Do you mean is there anyone you can fleece out of their money at the pool tables?" Gene teased.

"Well, yeah, that too." She grinned.

"I already have us signed up. I hope you don't mind being my partner again," Harley said.

"I couldn't ask for a better partner," Coal answered. "We are behaving tonight aren't we?" she asked, shooting a look to Lucas.

"We always behave well," Lucas said.

"You know what I mean," Coal chided him.

"Billy Ray's no longer here to mistreat women," Lucas reminded her.

"No he's not, but there seems to always be plenty of others just as mean."

"I'm here to get a good buzz on while I watch you and Harley kick some ass on the pool tables," Lucas said and crossed his heart.

"What are we missing here?" Stormy asked.

"Lucas and I got into a scrape with a couple of ornery cowboys the first time we were here."

"That was a long time ago," Gene said. "They kicked some redneck ass that night though."

"Coal did at least. I remember getting my ass kicked pretty well," Lucas admitted.

"You survived," she said and slapped him on the back. "Let's not have a repeat performance tonight, though."

She looked at Harley. "What's the competition look like?"

"We got this," he said with a wink. "We start playing in fifteen minutes. Just a few teams so it shouldn't take all night."

Gene took a long drink of his beer and returned it to the table. "Who's going to be the first lucky lady to dance with me tonight?"

Stormy surprised them by volunteering. "Come on, big boy, and I'll show you how to two-step," she teased.

Gene laughed and followed her onto the dance floor as the group looked on.

"I hope she can keep up with him. He's pumped up tonight," Lucas said.

"I have a feeling Stormy will hang right with him," she said.

✝

After watching them dance two songs, Harley and Coal walked over to the pool tables to take on their first opponents. As they selected their cues, Harley leaned into Coal's shoulder and whispered, "Those two at the next table will probably be our biggest competition. Ronnie and his sidekick Don ride for Big Bob. Not as mean as Billy Ray, but too close for my taste."

Coal whispered back to him, "Let's kick their butts on the pool table, and hopefully that will be enough for them." She winked and picked out a cue.

The first pair they faced turned out to be mediocre players and it didn't take long for Coal and Harley to defeat them. Ronnie and Don played on the table next to them, which gave her an opportunity to watch while they waited for their next opponents. Don was the better of the pair, with a soft touch for the delicate shots. Ronnie was a brute, who thought his power should sink every ball on the table. She felt a smirk growing on her face as she watched him blast a ball down the table, easily missing the pocket.

"Great game," Stormy said as she brought her a fresh beer. She stood beside her as they watched the game in progress.

"Thanks," she said and turned back to see Ronnie glaring at them.

"He's a mean one," Stormy said and blew him a kiss.

"Don't agitate him then. I don't wish to have to fight my way out of here again."

"Relax, he's a blowhard. He thinks his size intimidates everyone else."

"Well, he is a big boy," Coal said as she turned her back to him to look for Mary Leah and Del. "How are things going with Del?"

"She's an incredible woman. I'd love to ask her to dance, but I don't think that would go over well in here."

"Probably not. Maybe we can find a gay bar in Austin next weekend, so you can ask her to dance," she teased.

"That could be fun," Stormy said. "So she's going for sure?"

"Del said she wouldn't miss it for anything. I think she's now a rodeo junkie." Coal chuckled.

"We're up again," Harley said.

"Good luck," Stormy said and returned to the table.

"Your turn to break," Coal said as she handed Harley his cue.

†

They next round passed quickly. She and Harley were playing well and finished them off easily. As Harley had predicted, they would play Ronnie and Don in the final match. Harley and Don rolled to see who would break first and Don won the roll.

Coal caught a glimpse of Gene dancing with a gorgeous Latina woman and then turned back to watch the break with a smile.

Don broke well and then proceeded to miss his second. "Go get them, tiger," Coal said, as Harley took his cue and walked to the table.

Harley took his time to line up each shot with precision and ran the table sinking the rest of the balls to take game one.

"Great job," she told him, delivering a high five while the losers racked the balls for the next game.

"Thanks," Harley said as he drained his PBR.

"You ready for a fresh one?"

"Not just yet, maybe after this game," he said.

Coal broke the next rack and sank two balls before missing a cut shot. As she walked back to Harley, she noted the song had ended and Gene and the woman were walking back to the table. But instead of following Gene, the woman dropped down in Stormy's lap. "Could be trouble brewing," she whispered to Harley.

†

"Welcome back," Mary Leah said.

"This is Lana," Gene said as he took his seat.

"Is everyone ready for a fresh round?" Lucas asked.

"Sure," Del said. "Come on I'll help you."

"What do you drink, Lana?" Lucas asked.

"I'll take a shot of Patrón," she said with a wink, and then turned back to Stormy, playing in her hair. "So why haven't you called me?" she said in a pouty voice.

"Lana, you knew ahead of time that I wouldn't call you."

"I know you're only a one-night stand woman, but I hoped you'd be different with me," she said, placing a kiss on Stormy's cheek.

She grasped Lana's hands, removing them from her hair. "If you'd like a chair to join us, I'm sure Gene can find one," she said rather coolly, embarrassed by Lana's flirtations in front of Del. She had finally found someone special and she'd be damned if she'd screw it up tonight.

Lana stepped off her lap and followed Stormy's eyes to the bar where Lucas and Del were ordering their drinks. "So is that your newest woman?" Lana purred.

"I hope she will be," Stormy answered honestly.

"I've never seen her before. Have you already slept through the rest of the women in town?"

Mary Leah could see the anger rise in Stormy. "What is it you do in town, Lana?" she asked.

Lana barely glanced at Mary Leah, refusing to take her attention from Stormy. Stormy had been the best romp in bed she'd had since she hit town almost a year ago. "I work at the bank as a teller."

"That must be interesting work," Mary Leah said.

"Not near as interesting as Stormy," she said as she reached over to play in her hair.

Stormy again caught her hands. "You can stop now, Lana, I'm not interested," she said as Del returned to witness the exchange.

✝

Coal wasn't the only one watching the exchange between Stormy and the Latina woman. Ronnie was also playing close attention, his knuckles turning white from the grip on his cue. He was due to follow Coal, and when she missed her shot, his anger was evident in his shot. He struck the cue ball so strong it flew off the table, further infuriating him.

Harley quickly moved in to run the table and end the game, giving them the win in the tournament. Harley reached out to offer his hand to Ronnie, but his focus was on Lana flirting with Stormy. He stormed past them to rush to the table with Don, Coal, and Harley hot on his heels.

✝

Stormy looked up to see Ronnie barreling through the room toward them and her heart caught in her throat. She had worked with the big man and he could be a brute when angered. He surely looked very angry now.

Lana also looked up to see Ronnie rushing toward them. She blanched and leaned closer to Stormy. "Oh shit, this isn't going to end well," she said.

When Ronnie reached the table, he looked at Lana then turned his glare toward Stormy. "What the hell are you doing with my woman?" he sneered between clenched teeth.

"Nothing, she joined our table on her own," she growled back. "She was not invited."

Lana made the worst possible comment she could have made. "Well, you didn't turn me away last time."

The realization of Lana's words struck deep into Ronnie's brain. "You slept with this trailer trash?" he yelled.

Stupidly Lana looked up at him and smiled. "She's more of a man than you are."

"Oh, dear Lord," Coal said as she caught up to Ronnie. She saw the panicked look on Stormy's face as Lana incited Ronnie to attack.

"I think that's enough," Coal said as she stood beside Ronnie. "Will you take your woman and leave our party?"

Ronnie tore his eyes away from Lana and whipped his head around to glare at Coal. "Who the fuck are you to tell me what to do?"

"Someone who just wants to drink a few beers with her friends without any trouble," she answered.

"Aren't you the dyke who kicked out Bubba Brewster's teeth?"

"Yeah, Bubba was being stupid, and he met my boot heel up close and personal, but we've worked through that incident."

"Well, I ain't Bubba, and I can't stand carpet munchers who prey on the women of this town, especially this piece of trash. It's not surprising she ended up with the likes of y'all."

"Wait just a damned minute," Gene said as he jumped out of his seat.

"Relax, Gene, I've got this," she said. "Please just take the woman and be off."

"There's no way in hell you are telling me what to do," Ronnie said, taking a swing at Coal.

She easily dodged the strike and caught Ronnie's arm, wrenching it behind his back.

"Take it outside," the bouncer yelled from the door.

"Do you really want to continue this?" she asked through gritted teeth. Her patience was gone and if the brute wanted an ass kicking, she would gladly deliver.

Ronnie saw the glare of anger in her dark eyes and for a second a flash of fear crossed his face. He was doomed. A woman had called him out. Ridicule and humiliation would haunt him forever if he didn't rise to her challenge.

"Yeah, bitch, I do. This one obviously is used goods, but I'd love to see you groveling at my feet," he sneered.

"That'll never happen, but let's go," she said and pushed him toward the door, finally releasing her hold on his arm.

"You don't have to do this," Stormy said as she rose to stand beside her.

"Yes, Stormy, I do. No one treats my family like that."

"Let me fight him then," Gene said.

She smiled at Gene. He had beefed up, but strength to strength, Ronnie still had him by an easy fifty pounds. "I got this, but keep an eye on his buddy Don for me."

"Will do," Gene said as his chest swelled with pride.

Her eyes fell on Mary Leah. "I'm sorry for spoiling your night out."

Mary Leah smiled. "I'm getting used to your brawling, but please be careful."

"Always." Coal grinned and stalked toward the door, Gene hot on her heels.

"Drink up, folks, this night is over," Harley said.

The group pushed back from the table and headed for the door with a small group of onlookers.

"I hope you're pleased with yourself," Stormy growled at Lana.

"You really should have called me," Lana said.

"You can forget that ever happening," she said. She took Del's arm and left the bar.

☦

The cooling night air enveloped Coal as she stepped from the bar and the pounding beat of country music faded, replaced by the sound of crickets. She looked to her left to see Ronnie standing in an open area of the parking lot, Don right beside him. She stepped off the sidewalk and the gravel crunched under her boots.

"You sure about this," Gene whispered.

"Have some faith," she said.

The crowd gathered in a circle around them as Coal stepped onto the gravel and approached Ronnie. Stormy placed her hand on Mary Leah's shoulder. "I'm really sorry about this."

Mary Leah turned to face her. "This isn't your fault. You didn't invite her to join us. Coal can handle herself, so don't worry."

"I just hope she doesn't hurt him too bad," Harley said as he rocked on his heels.

"I'm beginning to wonder if I should change fields and go into dentistry," Del surprised them.

"Oh, that's priceless," Mary Leah said with a chuckle.

☦

She blocked out all sound and focused on Ronnie as he approached her, fire burning in his eyes.

The crowd watched as Ronnie growled and rushed at Coal. She sidestepped his path. His momentum prevented him from changing direction and her knee drove into his midsection. Her elbow slammed between his shoulder blades as he bent over attempting to regain his breath. Ronnie dropped to his knees in the gravel, gasping for air.

She spun to face him, bouncing on the balls of her feet as she watched him slowly regain his feet. Ronnie shook his head and approached her, slowly this time, as he measured Coal's strength. He expected a punch from her, surprised when her boot landed a kick to his left jaw. He staggered to the side barely keeping his footing in the shifting gravel.

"Enough?" she asked.

His answer came in the form of a roar as he punched wildly, failing to make contact with Coal. Her quickness allowed her to nimbly step out of his reach, further infuriating Ronnie who crashed into a parked truck.

He wheeled again with surprising speed and finally landed a glancing blow to her left eye. She grinned at him and landed a punch to his jaw, her knuckles raking painfully against his bared teeth. She followed the punch with a powerful kick to the side of his head and Ronnie went down to the ground. He clawed his way back to his feet and rushed directly into the path of another kick. Ronnie went down for the final time.

Coal turned to Mary Leah. "Take us home, please," she said and walked away from Ronnie. Don had rushed to his side and was attempting to rouse his friend.

Don looked up at her with vengeance in his glare.

"Don't even think about it," Gene said as he filled the path between Don and Coal.

"This ain't over," Don snarled.

"Oh, I think it's plenty over for now," Gene said and turned to join his family.

†

Once in the car and on their way back home, Del turned to Coal. "How's your hand?"

"It'll be fine, just some skinned knuckles."

"The boys are making a stop for beer and wanted to know if we'll join them for a party of our own back home," Mary Leah said.

"I hope you told them yes," Coal said with a grin. "We didn't get our buzz on."

"I am so sorry about that drama," Stormy said.

"Will you stop? What happened was not your fault," Coal said.

"Coal's right. Ronnie was begging to have his butt kicked," Del added.

"I think I'm done with the Stockyard," Coal said. "It's too easy to get into a brawl."

"Coal mentioned finding a gay bar in Austin next weekend. Would you enjoy that?" Stormy asked Del.

"That sounds like fun. Maybe we could have a good time without being harassed."

"Let's do it then," Mary Leah said.

Coal checked the time. "I wonder if Melissa is still awake."

"If not, she will be soon." Mary Leah chuckled as she turned onto the long drive. "Lights are still on."

†

Melissa heard car doors slam and turned to look at the clock. It wasn't even ten yet, so it couldn't be the crew home this early. She walked to the back door to find Coal, Mary Leah, Del, and Stormy walking across the yard.

"Is everything okay? I wasn't expecting anyone home this early."

"The brawler here got us kicked out again," Mary Leah said with a nod toward Coal.

"Again? Good Lord, Coal, what are we going to do with you?"

"It wasn't my fault. Some big redneck was harassing the family and needed to be put in his place," she said in her defense.

"And you were just the woman to do that. Do you have any injuries we need to take a look at?"

"Just some scraped knuckles," Del said. "She may have a shiner too."

"Someone actually landed a blow?"

"Just a glancing one, he barely got me," she said.

"You must be slowing down in your old age," Melissa teased.

"Speaking of old age, I hope you weren't planning to go to bed anytime soon," Mary Leah said. "After the excitement at the bar, the boys decided we would bring the party here. They should be home any minute."

"Let's get you cleaned up then before they arrive," Melissa said and guided Coal to the bathroom for first aid.

"Let's get some chairs and tables set up out in the yard while we wait for the boys," Mary Leah suggested.

Mary Leah, Stormy, and Del walked out to the barn to collect tables and chairs.

"So what really happened?" Melissa asked when the others had left.

"Some woman was hitting on Stormy and her boyfriend didn't like it," she explained.

"I asked him nicely to leave us be, but he insisted on being an ass, so we went outside to settle our problem."

"Did you leave him standing?"

"No, ma'am. I do believe he will have a heck of a headache tomorrow and several painful bruises."

"Good then. Who was it?"

"A monster named Ronnie from over at Big Bob's place. I think he and Stormy had some history too from the nasty slurs he was making."

"I'm so glad she got away from there," Melissa said.

"Yeah, I am too."

"I think the boys have returned," Melissa said.

"I'm sorry if we ruined your plans for a quiet night."

"No need to be sorry. I'd gladly have a few drinks with y'all."

"Let's go then," she said and offered Melissa her arm.

†

The crew drank cold beer and danced to country tunes on the radio for several hours. Melissa and Harley were the first to call it a night. As the night wound down, Stormy and Del walked over toward the corral to have a private conversation.

"I'm sorry about what happened tonight, I hope you'll let me make it up to you."

"There is nothing to apologize for, and besides, I've had more fun with you here tonight than at the bar," Del said.

Stormy breathed a sigh of relief. "What plans do you have for tomorrow?"

"I plan to sleep in, and then Mary Leah has promised to bring me over to watch y'all train the horses."

"May I cook for you tomorrow night then, just for the two of us?"

"That sounds promising," Del said.

"Thank you."

"For what?"

She shot her a grin, "For allowing me to spend this time with you."

"That is very sweet of you to say. I enjoy being around you too."

"Good," she said and leaned down to kiss Del's lips. "I think the ladies are ready to head home, so I guess I'll see you later today."

"I'll look forward to it," Del said and took Stormy's hand to walk back to the group.

†

"Are you guys ready to wrap this up?" Stormy said.

"We probably should since we have horses to ride tomorrow," Lucas said. "Come on Gene let's put this furniture back in the barn."

"I can help," Stormy said.

"Y'all got it set up, so we can break it down. Go ahead and see the ladies off and we'll take care of this and see you in the morning," Lucas said.

"Thanks," Coal said and they walked back to Mary Leah's car.

"This was an enjoyable evening," Mary Leah said as she opened a door and slipped inside.

"Yes, it was," Del said. "Sleep well and we'll see you tomorrow," she said, stretching up to kiss Stormy.

"Sweet dreams," she said and closed the door behind Del. Coal grinned at Stormy. "I'm glad the night ended well."

"Me too, I'll see you in the morning."

"Count on it," she said and slipped in behind the wheel.

Stormy watched them drive home and when the porch light went off at their house, she climbed the steps onto Melissa's porch and slipped inside.

†

Stormy joined Melissa in the kitchen the next morning for coffee. "Could I talk you into helping me with something today?"

301

"Well, that depends, but I'm feeling pretty generous. What's up?"

"I want to cook for Del tonight to make up for last night. I thought I'd go to the store this morning and pick up steaks and some vegetables for a cookout, but I was wondering if you would steam the veggies for me and wrap them in some aluminum foil so I can throw them on the grill to reheat them."

"That sounds very interesting and easy to do, but I have veggies and steaks here unless you just want to grocery shop. I can lay out two steaks and place them in some marinade for you this afternoon."

Stormy grinned and leaned over to kiss Melissa's cheek. "You're the best. Just let me know how much and I'll reimburse you."

"Don't be silly. You and Del are part of the family. I am curious, though, where are you planning to cook out?"

"I thought I'd set up a spot out on the bluffs so we can watch the sunset. I can grill some steaks and then we can star gaze and have a nice private place to talk."

"Oh my, that sounds romantic."

She blushed profusely. "I really like Del and I don't want to screw things up with her."

"Don't stress over things so much. Just relax and be yourself, that's what attracted her in the first place," Melissa said. "Would you mind if I made some fresh bread to go with your meal?"

"That would be perfect. May I ask for a recommendation for a wine though, I haven't a clue."

"Just leave it to me and finish work today. I'll get a picnic basket put together with what you'll need. I bet you can find a small grill to take out with you in the barn and some lounge chairs too."

"Thanks, boss," she said and left the kitchen to check in the barn for the supplies she mentioned.

She was loading the chairs and a small grill into the back of her truck when Coal rode up.

"Looks like you are planning to be busy later. I was going to ask you to dinner."

"I'm going to be cooking for Del tonight."

She told Coal of her plans to cook dinner and have a quiet evening with Del, but made her promise not to tell Del or Mary Leah of her plans.

"I think you'll both have a wonderful time. Now let's get to work so you can get ready to wine and dine," she teased.

†

Mary Leah, Del, and Melissa joined them midmorning as they worked the stock. They stretched out comfortably under the oak to watch as the four ranch hands swam with their mounts in the pond.

"That looks like fun," Del said.

"It's so much less painful on the horse and rider than the traditional way of training horses," Melissa said. "After watching Coal with Shadow, Gene and Lucas jumped on board with her method of training."

"Speak of the devil," Mary Leah said, nodding toward an approaching Shadow. "He can't stand to be far away from her for long."

Melissa and Del laughed. "They do make a handsome pair," Melissa said.

"Speaking of a handsome pair, did you see Del and Stormy two-stepping last night?" Mary Leah said.

"As a matter of fact I did. You two move well together," she said to Del.

"She is a very good dancer."

"I hope you won't let what happened at the bar last night taint your impression of her," Melissa said. "I think our young friend has had a very difficult time in her life and she deserves our support."

"I wouldn't dream of it," Del said.

"What do you know of Stormy's past?" Mary Leah asked Melissa.

"Not much really. She's originally from Montana, worked for Big Bob for a year before joining us. I can say she's a good worker and gets along well with everybody. I think the girl's got a good heart that needs to be treated with kid gloves."

"You seem fond of her," Del noted.

"I am. She grows on you quickly," Melissa said with a grin. She stood and stretched. "I'm off to the house to finish lunch. Do y'all need anything?"

"Is there anything we can do to help?" Del asked.

"Nope, I've got this in hand. I'm used to feeding this bunch."

"We'll stay and watch, but holler if you need help," Mary Leah said.

"Will do," she answered and drove back to the house.

†

Melissa served Coal's favorite for lunch, egg salad sandwiches, beneath the shade of the oaks.

"I swear this tastes better every time you make it," she said as she picked up a sandwich.

"You are so easy to please," Melissa teased.

Stormy and Del had finished eating and walked over to the lake where the horses were taking a drink.

"I'll pick you up at five if that's good for you," Stormy said.

"Five will be great, but can you tell me how to dress since I have no idea what you've planned."

"Something that's comfortable. We'll be outside, so maybe wear a long-sleeved shirt, or bring a light sweater if you have one."

"I can manage that. Is there anything I can do to help out?"

"No, ma'am, I think I have everything under control."

"I'll look forward to tonight then," Del said as Harley called an end to lunch.

✝

By midafternoon, Stormy was racing her mount across the field in a steady gallop, and when she turned back toward the lake, she saw Mary Leah and Del walking back to the house. She smiled eager to finish her task and prepare for her night with Del. Her mount sensed her lack of concentration and took the opportunity to buck, sending her flying through the air. She hit the ground hard, cursing the horse that was now galloping away.

"Did someone get distracted?" Coal teased as she pulled her horse up next to her.

"Something like that." She grinned as she reached for the arm Coal offered.

"Come on then. Let's go catch your horse so you can finish your job," she said, pulling Stormy onto the back of her horse. The horse grunted feeling the extra weight on his back, but responded to Coal's urgings to race to catch up with Stormy's rogue mount.

✝

An hour later, they unsaddled the newly trained stock and placed them back into the corral with the rest of the horses.

"Will I see you later?" Coal asked Stormy.

"I'll be around at five to pick up Del."

"Great. Have fun tonight," she said as she mounted Shadow for the ride home.

305

"We will," Stormy said and turned to walk into the house to shower.

Melissa was in the kitchen finishing her picnic basket when she walked inside. She looked at the work Melissa had accomplished.

"This looks great. Thanks, boss."

"You're welcome. Now go get showered, and get your picnic site set up before it's time to go collect Del."

"Yes, ma'am."

†

Stormy laid a fire in the grill and soaked the charcoal with lighter fluid. She repositioned the lounge chairs, placed a cooler with the chilled wine between them, and when satisfied she was ready she went to pick up Del.

Coal met her at the front door when she arrived. Del and Mary Leah were in the kitchen cooking their dinner.

"Be sure to have her home before midnight," Coal teased as Del walked over to greet her.

"Don't listen to a word she says," Del told her as she punched Coal's shoulder. "Don't wait up, dad."

"You two have a good time," Mary Leah called from the kitchen.

"Thanks," Stormy called. "Are you ready?" she asked Del.

"Yes, let's go."

"See you later," Stormy said to Coal.

"That's doubtful if you don't bring her home before midnight," she answered.

"Later then," she said and offered her hand to Del as they walked out to her truck.

Mary Leah slipped her arm around Coal's waist as she stood at the door watching the truck disappear down the drive. "Do you think they will make it together?" she asked.

"Only time will tell what fate has in store for them," she said, turning to kiss Mary Leah.

†

Del turned to look at Stormy as she drove past the house into the open field they had been in earlier in the day, but remained silent as she drove toward the setting sun. When she finally stopped the truck at the edge of the bluffs, Del's eyes locked on the beauty of the landscape.

She raced around to open the passenger door and assisted Del out of the truck. "Welcome to my restaurant," she said with a smile as she led Del to a lounge chair. "Let me light the fire, and I'll be back to pour us wine."

"This view is stunning," Del said as she looked across the open plains.

"One of the most beautiful spots on the ranch," Stormy said as she lit the fire. She took the chair next to Del and opened the cooler. Taking two wineglasses, she handed them to Del and poured the wine.

Del handed her a glass and then offered a toast. "Here's to a beautiful sunset and a terrific night."

"Agreed," she said and touched her glass to Del's.

The sun was rapidly sinking into the horizon, painting the sky with brilliant reds and oranges. Del and Stormy rested back on the chairs to watch the night sky while the coals burned brightly.

When the sun had disappeared, she turned on several lanterns to give them light.

"So tell me about you," Del said as she poured them both another glass of wine.

Stormy hesitated and then sat up in her chair. "I've got flaws, but I hope they won't be such to turn you away from me," she said, her voice cracking with emotion.

"We all have flaws, Stormy," Del said, placing her hand on her arm. "Tell me what you fear will drive me away."

"I lived in Montana before coming to Texas. My parents kicked me out at seventeen when they found out I was gay, and I lived with my grandmother until I finished high school a year later." She took a sip of wine to wet her throat that suddenly felt parched. "After graduating, I took a job at a ranch on the border of Yellowstone, and I worked there for two years. I loved the job and fell in love with a woman in town. We shared a small home for over a year and I believed I had found true love."

Stormy paused again as she relived the memories. Several minutes passed before she realized she had fallen silent and Del was patiently waiting for her to continue. The coals were ready, so Stormy stood to place the meat on the grill and the foil-covered vegetables on to warm.

"Terri was beautiful and stole my heart from the first time we met. We moved in together right away, and I thought I was her heart and soul, or so she told me." She paused again to pour more wine. "Every year the ranch had a big roundup, where they moved the large herd down into greener pastures, which took the hands away for several days. Terri must have lost track of the days because when I came home, covered in dirt and exhausted from days in the saddle, I found her in bed with the rancher's son."

"Oh my," Del said, truly shocked.

Stormy jumped up to turn the meat, and then walked back to the chairs.

"What happened then?" Del asked.

"We rode the trails armed due to the wildness of the area. I had a pistol strapped to my side and when I saw the rancher's son gloating, naked in my bed, I snapped. I pulled the pistol, placed the barrel on his forehead and cocked the gun. I could feel the tremors running through his body from his terror. I looked over at Terri and she looked on in shock, hiding her nakedness with a sheet, like I was the intruder." She took another sip and sat the glass down. "I could feel my finger as it slowly pulled on the trigger. I wanted nothing more than to end his miserable life right then. He must have seen the rage burning in my eyes and his bladder released. The scent of his urine filled my nose and I started to laugh. Just a chuckle at first, but then the laughter overcame me, and I couldn't stop. I removed the barrel from his head and safely holstered the gun."

She stood and walked to the grill to check the meat, finding it nearly done to perfection. "Come," she said and motioned Del to join her at the tailgate of the truck. "The meat is almost ready."

Del stood and walked over to her.

"When my laughter finally died, I looked at Terri. I hope he makes you happy, I said, and left the house. I knew my job was screwed, so I stopped at an ATM, cleaned out my account, drove to the ranch and loaded my horse in my trailer and started driving south."

"That's when you came to Texas?"

"Yes, after a brief stop in Oklahoma. I heard about the opening at Big Bob's and got the job right away. The foreman in Oklahoma put in a good word for me and I got the job at the Brewster's."

Del carried their plates to the grill and waited until Stormy served the steaks and the steamy vegetables. She carried them back to the tailgate that would be their table for the meal. "Is this the point where I'm supposed to run screaming into the night?" she asked.

"I've never told anyone else. I just assumed most people would be scared I'd snap again."

"Darling, your reaction was very normal given the circumstances. Trust me when I tell you I've heard much deeper flaws than what you have described to me tonight."

Stormy felt a huge weight lift from her shoulders. Relief flooded through her after hearing Del's comments to the story she was worried would end their relationship before it had a chance to blossom.

"I have to be honest though," Del said as she sat in a chair Stormy placed at the tailgate for them. "I'm more concerned with your promiscuity, if what that horrid woman said last night was true. I'm not a one-night stand type of woman."

The relief she felt melted away. She hung her head, shameful of her irresponsible behavior. "I cannot deny what Lana said. Since my experience with Terri, I've not cared to have a lasting relationship with anyone. Until now," she added.

Del placed her hands under Stormy's chin and lifted her face to meet her eyes. They sparkled in the lantern light and glistened with what Del worried were tears of disappointment. She smiled softly. "I'm an old-fashioned girl and expect to be properly courted. Don't expect me to fall into your bed just because I think you're incredibly sexy."

Tears slipped from her eyes. Del brushed them away with her thumbs, stroking Stormy's cheeks. She was touched, and surprised, by the depth of emotion she was displaying. "We will take things one step at a time," she said and Stormy nodded her acknowledgment. "Right now, I've got to have a bite of this steak. It smells heavenly."

Stormy released a nervous laugh. "I hope you enjoy it. We have fresh bread to go with it as well," she said and opened the warmed bread. "Would you like more wine?"

"I'd love some," Del said then moaned loudly as the flavor of the steak reached her taste buds. "This is fantastic. Your selection of locations is better than any restaurant could be. The view is spectacular, and the company's not bad either."

"I'm happy you approve," she said as she portioned out vegetables.

After the meal was finished, Stormy placed the dishes into the picnic basket and then joined Del on the lounge chair. The glow on the horizon had faded into the darkness of night, and the sky filled with a blanket of stars.

Stormy let out a deep sigh as her eyes scanned the sky.

"What's with the sigh?"

"The night sky reminds me of Montana. The lack of artificial light makes the stars shine so brilliantly."

"It's peaceful out here," Del admitted. "Do you miss Montana?"

"Only during winter, I miss the snow, and the mountains."

"Well, maybe we can visit. I've never seen more than a few inches of snow. I'd like to see real mountains too," Del said.

"I would love to show you Montana. I don't care much for skiing, but snowmobiling is a blast."

"That sounds like fun," Del said as she reached over to place her hand on Stormy's arm.

Enjoying the warmth of Del's touch Stormy placed her hand on top to hold it in place. "Tell me about you," Stormy said. "You know most of my story, but I don't know anything about you."

†

Hours later, Del shivered. The night air had significantly cooled and they both felt the chill against their skin. "Are you ready to head home?"

"Not really," Del said. "It's so beautiful out here, but it's cooler than I thought it would be."

"Go get into the truck and turn some heat on while I pack up here real quick."

"Is there anything I can help with?"

"No, I've got this," Stormy said with a smile. She worked quickly to load the chairs and picnic basket in the back of the truck then poured the water from the melted ice in the cooler on the coals to ensure the embers fully

311

extinguished. As hot and dry as it had been lately, the last thing they needed was a wildfire from a careless fire. She closed the lid and walked to the truck to climb inside.

"All set," she said as she put the truck in gear and slowly crawled across the open field. Red eyes glittered at the edge of the headlights as a pair of coyotes roamed the night. "I've really enjoyed being with you tonight."

"Dinner was fantastic, and it was nice having you alone for a change," Del said.

"When may I see you again?" she asked as they pulled into Coal and Mary Leah's drive.

"How about lunch tomorrow, with the girls? I was supposed to ask you earlier, but I forgot."

"That sounds great. Do you ride?" she asked.

"As in horses?"

"Yes, as in horses. Would you like to take a ride with me in the morning?"

Del thought for a second. "I'd like that. What time do I need to be ready?"

"Ten, so we can be back to help with lunch," Stormy answered as she opened her door. She helped Del out of the truck and walked her to the door. "Thanks for a great night," she said as she shuffled her boots.

"I had a great time too," Del said and leaned toward Stormy.

Stormy smiled a nervous smile and leaned in to kiss Del softly on the lips. She desperately wanted to deepen the kiss, but would honor Del's request to take things slowly and court her like a proper woman. She ended the kiss and stepped back. "I'll see you tomorrow."

"Goodnight, Stormy," Del said and stepped inside the door.

Stormy's feet barely touched the ground as she made her way back to the truck and drove to the ranch. Melissa had left the porch light on for her, making her smile. She pulled the truck to a halt and hurriedly placed the chairs back in the barn and carried the basket inside.

She was busy washing the dishes when Melissa walked into the kitchen.

"I hope I didn't wake you," she said.

"Nope, I got thirsty so I thought I'd get some water. How did tonight go?"

"Fantastic, thanks to you. I appreciate all you did for us."

"It was my pleasure," Melissa said. "What's the next step?"

"We are going for a ride tomorrow morning and then have lunch with Coal and Mary Leah before Del goes back home."

"That sounds like fun," Melissa said as she picked up a dishtowel and dried the dishes as Stormy washed them.

When they had finished, Melissa walked down the hall with her. "Sweet dreams," she said.

"You too, boss, see you in the morning." She entered her room and slipped out of her clothes and into shorts and a T-shirt before crashing onto the bed. It had been a long day, but the ending had turned out superbly. Stormy fell asleep, a smile gracing her face.

Chapter Twenty-two

Coal was at the kitchen table sipping coffee when Del entered the room. "Good morning, mind if I join you?"

"Please do. How do you like your coffee?" she said as she moved to stand.

"Sit tight, I believe I can manage. Do you need a refill?"

"Thanks, but I'm good for now. Did you sleep well?"

"Like a log. How have you been sleeping?"

"So well I didn't even hear you come in last night. You did come home, right?" she teased.

Del chuckled. "Yes, and it was even before midnight."

She smiled as Del took a seat across from her. "Did your night go well?"

"Very well. I had a really nice time. I'm going riding with Stormy this morning at ten."

"That sounds very promising."

Del took a sip of her coffee. "We had a very candid talk and agreed to proceed slowly."

"How long do you think that will last?" Coal asked with a grin.

"At least until the first few dates, but damn that woman is hot." Del chuckled.

"I thought I heard someone talking," Mary Leah said as she entered the room, scratching her head.

"Good morning, sunshine, join us and I'll get you some coffee," Coal said. "Love the hairdo, babe," she added with a wink to Del.

"I bet I have a great case of bed head," she said.

"I don't think we could argue with you over that," Del said, smiling at her friend.

"How was your date?"

"Dinner was fantastic, very romantic actually, and she is very interesting," Del said.

"Oh, do tell," Mary Leah said as she settled into a chair.

"She cooked an excellent steak dinner. The sunset was gorgeous and the stars were spectacular. Once it started to cool down, we came home."

"Did she at least kiss you goodnight?"

"As a matter of fact, she did," Del said.

"Is she coming for lunch?"

"Yes, we're going for a ride this morning, but we'll be back in time for lunch."

Coal placed a mug of coffee in front of her lover and kissed the top of her head. "Am I cooking burgers today? Is that the plan?"

"If you'll grill the burgers and onions, I'll fry up some potatoes and whip up a salad."

"That sounds delicious," Del said. "Is there anything I can do?"

"You can have fun with Stormy," Mary Leah answered, grinning.

"I thought I'd cook some omelets for breakfast," Coal said as she stood and walked to the refrigerator. "Are you two hungry?"

"I am now that you mentioned omelets," Del said.

"If you don't mind, I'm going to shower and get this hair under control."

"Go ahead, darling, I'll cook yours fresh when you get back."

"I'll see you soon then," Mary Leah said, taking her coffee and leaving the kitchen.

Coal pulled out ingredients for breakfast and placed a bowl on the counter.

"What can I help with?"

"You can slice some ham for me. Do you like fresh green onions?"

"Oh yes, I love them."

"I was thinking ham, cheese, and some green onions."

"Let me get to slicing then," Del said as she picked up a knife.

Del had finished slicing the ham. "You can drop a handful in the bowl if you would, please."

Del added the ham as Coal poured green onions in and continued to whip the eggs. "Would you like toast?"

"That sounds good and some juice."

"You'll find apple and orange juice in the fridge, and wheat bread in the pantry. You can go ahead and drop your toast."

Coal slid the first omelet onto Del's plate and moments later had her breakfast ready too. She joined Del at the table.

"Mary Leah is a very lucky woman," Del said after a moan. "This is delicious."

"Thanks, I'm glad you approve, but I think I'm the lucky one to have met Mary Leah."

"You certainly seem to be good for each other."

"Yeah, she's a terrible breakfast cook," Coal said with a wink as Mary Leah entered the kitchen.

"Hey, I heard that, but she's absolutely right. My idea of breakfast is something you can cook in a toaster."

"Well, there is something to be said for Pop Tarts," Del teased. "Though seems like I remember you burning some of those in college."

"I have mastered the art of toasting finally," Mary Leah said as she poured a glass of apple juice.

"Hang on a sec and I'll cook your omelet."

"Take your time, sweetie, I'm in no hurry. You know, Del, when she first arrived two years ago she couldn't cook an egg to save her life and now look at these great omelets."

"I've had lots of opportunities to practice. Besides, Harley's a great teacher."

"So when is everyone headed to Austin for the rodeo?" Del asked.

"We are rolling out early Friday morning," Coal said. "Can you drive out Thursday night and ride with us?"

Del looked at Mary Leah as Coal returned to the stove to cook. "That's not a bad idea. Will you have room for me?"

"Plenty, Melissa's cowboy Cadillac seats six comfortably," Mary Leah said.

Del chuckled. "Her what?"

"Melissa's truck is a dually and we call it her cowboy Cadillac," Coal explained. "Do you need seconds?" she asked, seeing Del's empty plate.

"Heaven's no, I'm stuffed, but thanks."

✝

They were finishing their coffee when Coal looked up to see Stormy's truck bouncing up the drive. "It looks like your date is early," she teased.

"Holy cow, what time is it?" Del asked.

"Nine forty-five," Coal said. "Stormy must be excited."

"Let me finish getting ready then," she said, nearly knocking the chair over when she stood up quickly.

Mary Leah and Coal looked at one another and chuckled. "I think it's hard to tell which of them is more excited," she said as she stood to meet her at the door.

"Good morning," Stormy said, wearing a grin.

"Yes, it is. How are you?"

"I'm great, thanks. Del and I are going for a ride this morning."

"So we heard. Come on in, she's getting ready. We just finished breakfast. Do you want something?"

"Thanks, but I'm good. Hey, Mary Leah," Stormy said as they walked into the kitchen.

"You're looking bright and shiny this morning," Mary Leah said. "Del will be ready in just a few minutes."

"That's fine. I know I'm early but Melissa kicked me out, said I was wearing out her floor."

"That sounds like Melissa," Coal said. "Where are you riding this morning?"

"I thought we would ride down by the creek," Stormy said. "It's going to be hot again today, so we won't go far."

Coal sat next to her. "I'll fire up the grill about noon then."

Del walked into the room and Stormy stood up. "You look great, Del."

"Thanks," Del said. "Are you ready to ride?"

"Just waiting on you, ma'am," Stormy said.

"I guess we'll see you two later," Mary Leah said as they walked to the door.

"Have fun," Coal said.

"We will," she answered on her way out the door.

"They are just too cute together," Mary Leah said. "I've never seen Del this excited before."

"Maybe she just needed a handsome cowgirl to toss a rope around her heart," Coal stated, shocking Mary Leah.

"Maybe so, I know I sure love mine."

"I love you too. So what do you want to do until lunch?"

"I know you want to go care for Shadow, so I'll put our salad together and patty the hamburgers while you're in the barn."

"I'll be back soon then," she said and kissed her lover.

†

She squinted in the bright sunshine as she left the covered porch and headed to the barn. Shadow had been grazing and rushed to the barn when he saw her approaching. "Hey, big boy," she said as he stepped into his stall. She filled his feed bin and refreshed his water then grabbed a shovel to muck his stall.

She carried the manure to the compost pile and then scattered fresh shavings in his stall. Shadow was still eating while she brushed his coat and checked his hooves. "I need to get the farrier out this week before we head out to Austin," she said as her hand stroked down his back. "We should probably get some practice in this week."

Coal finished her chores and walked back into the house as Mary Leah finished the salad. "You know I was thinking we might put in a garden in the spring. Our compost pile is getting big and would be great to fertilize the soil."

"Fresh vegetables would be nice, but don't you think you work hard enough already?"

"Growing your own isn't like work."

"Well, I bet I know a few ranch hands that would be more than willing to help out."

She smiled. "I would definitely use Gene's muscle on the tiller."

"I swear that young man would do anything for you," Mary Leah said.

Coal swiped a carrot and munched on it as she leaned against the counter. "Probably so," she agreed.

✝

After lunch, the group relaxed in the living room. "What plans do you have for the afternoon?" Coal asked Stormy.

"Nothing that I'm aware of why do you ask?"

"I thought about getting some rodeo practice in this afternoon if Gene's up for it," Coal answered.

"Did the sun come up in the east?" she chuckled. "I guarantee he could be saddled and ready to go in five minutes. Do you want me to give him a call?"

Coal looked at Del. "What are your plans this afternoon, Doc?"

"I could watch for a while then head home around four to get ready for next week."

"Let's eat some dirt then," Coal told Stormy.

"Let me go call the boys," she said and stepped outside to use her cell. "We're all set for two," she said when she returned.

"Just enough time for lunch to settle," Mary Leah said.

"What events are you competing in?" Del asked Stormy.

"Bareback and saddle bronc riding, and barrel racing."

"Is your shoulder healed enough for all that?"

"I feel fine. I'm sure I'll be sore afterward, but I'm cleared to ride."

"We'll be sure to have some ice packs ready," Coal said.

†

Del, Mary Leah, Melissa, and Harley sat under the shade tree to watch the practice session. Coal and Stormy had dismounted and were walking toward them across the corral, leading their horses. Their movements sent dust swirling around them in a shroud. "Cowgirls do it in the dirt," Melissa said.

"What was that?" Mary Leah asked.

"A bumper sticker I saw the other day in town. It said cowgirls do it in the dirt. Watching Coal and Stormy walk across the corral reminded me of that."

"It is rather fitting, isn't it?" Del asked.

"A Kodak moment," Mary Leah said as she picked up her phone and snapped off several photos. She lowered the phone to preview the shots and Del whistled.

"I have got to get a copy of that blown up," Stormy said. "That's a fantastic shot."

"Wow, that is really good. Better get two, one for me," Melissa said.

"I can do that," Mary Leah said as Coal and Stormy approached. "Are you two done for the day?"

"I am," she said, "but Coal and Gene are going to rope a few steers."

"I hate to break up this party, but I do need to start for home," Del said.

"Hang on and I'll give you a ride back to your car," Stormy said as she tied off her horse.

"I'll see you tomorrow night then," she said to Mary Leah. "Thanks for allowing me to ride with you to Austin," she told Melissa.

"The more the merrier," Melissa said. "See you later this week."

Stormy ran ahead to open her truck door for Del and got her seated safely inside.

"I think someone is truly smitten," Melissa said as she watched Stormy rush around to the driver's side.

"Which one are you referring to?" Mary Leah asked.

"Good point," Melissa said. "I'm glad to see they are hitting it off well."

"Me too, but I admit I'm very surprised. They are so different from one another," she said.

"Just like another happy couple I know," Melissa said with a smile.

"Point well made," Coal said.

Gene yelled across the corral. "Coal, are you ready?"

"Be right there," she hollered back. "I'll see you soon."

†

The week passed quickly and after Coal's Wednesday night appointment, Del said, "I'm very impressed by the

321

progress you have been making in therapy. Are your dreams still interfering with your sleep?"

"Knock on wood, I haven't had a nightmare for weeks."

"That's good. Your vital signs during the video sessions have drastically reduced, and you've made it all the way through the scenarios twice now. Do you feel you're ready to go back to traditional therapy?"

"Yes, I think so, I'm not as anxious about Tessa's death as I have been."

"I think you have progressed remarkably. I can't promise you that you'll ever be cured of the PTSD, but at least you will have learned how to minimize its control on you before we're done with therapy."

"I can't thank you enough for helping me. I feel so much better since I started seeing you."

"We still have battles to face, but I think it's safe to say the worst is over for you. I still recommend going to visit Tessa's grave. I think you have the right words to say to her now."

Coal nodded her agreement as she felt her eyes filling with tears.

Del pulled Coal into a hug. "Don't forget that it's okay to cry when you need to."

Coal stepped back and wiped the tears from her cheeks. "Thanks, Doc."

When Coal regained her composure, they left the office and Del walked them out to the car. "Why don't I bring some pizza with me tomorrow night?" she asked.

"We have beer," Mary Leah said.

"Will you let Stormy know? I hear you talk for hours every night," Coal teased.

Del grinned at Coal's comment. "Yes, I'll be sure to let her know. Be careful and I'll see you tomorrow night."

"You too, Doc," she said as she climbed inside the car.

Coal and Stormy were helping the men load the horses and gear Friday morning when Melissa pulled Coal off to the side. "I just thought of something I need your opinion on."

"What's up, boss?"

"When I booked rooms I didn't get separate rooms for Del and Stormy. Do you think they are ready to share a room, or should I ask Del if she wants me to get another room?"

"I think they are more than ready to take the next step, but be safe and ask Del. I know Stormy won't mind."

"I didn't think she would." Melissa grinned. "I'll ask Del before we leave."

Harley and the boys were set to pull the large trailer with the horses and when they were loaded, Melissa drove the cowboy Cadillac to pick up Del and Mary Leah. While Stormy and Coal loaded their luggage, Melissa pulled Del to the side to inquire about room arrangements.

Coal watched carefully to gauge Del's reaction. After a quick blush, Del nodded her head and hugged Melissa. Then they walked over to the truck and Melissa gave Coal a nod.

"Hang on a sec," she told Mary Leah. She took Stormy by the arm and walked toward the barn. "I hope you packed pajamas."

"The usual, shorts and tee, why?" Stormy asked.

"Because, unless you have a major objection, you are sharing a room with Del this weekend," she said.

"What?"

"Melissa only booked one room for the two of you. She can correct that if needed, though."

"No, I can handle this arrangement," she said.

"Good, that's what Del said too, so maybe it's time to take the next step."

She shuffled her feet. "That will be up to Del. I promised to be on my best behavior."

"I think you have done so impressively. So relax and enjoy your time together."

"I will," she said.

"Let's go then," she said and slipped her arm around Stormy's shoulder.

†

The trip to Austin passed quickly. The group located the Travis County Expo Center, where the rodeo would take place, got registered and the horses settled into stalls. Gene would again be staying in the sleeper compartment in the trailer to look over the stock and spend time with other cowboys. He loved hearing the stories the older riders were eager to share with the younger generation.

"I don't know about the rest of you, but I'm ready for some lunch," Melissa announced.

Mary Leah surprised them all when she stated, "I could eat a bear."

"Well, let's feed that beast of yours then check into the hotel," Melissa said with a chuckle.

"What time does your first event start tomorrow?" Mary Leah asked.

Coal looked at the schedule. "The barrel racing starts at ten. What do you have in mind?"

"I thought we might check out one of the local ladies clubs if you all would like to," Mary Leah said. "Have a few drinks, and maybe a dance or two."

"Do you think you can keep these two out of trouble?" Melissa asked.

"With your help, I'm sure I can."

"Okay, so what do you think, ladies?" Melissa asked.

"I'm game, but we need to get a good night's rest. Tomorrow will be a long day for us," Coal said.

"Agreed," Stormy chimed in.

"All right, so after dinner we find a good spot and plan to be back at the hotel no later than eleven. Is that good?" Mary Leah asked.

Coal looked at Stormy, who nodded and answered, "I think we can handle that."

"Okay, so you're in charge of researching the clubs while the rest of us get settled into the rooms," Melissa instructed Mary Leah as they pulled into a diner for lunch.

"Sounds like a plan to me," Mary Leah said, wearing a huge smile.

†

The hotel was close to the Expo and they settled into the rooms as Mary Leah did her research on a laptop. Coal stretched out on the bed. She was seriously considering a nap when Mary Leah snapped the laptop closed and swiveled around in the desk chair.

"There's a women's bar two miles from here that looks promising," she told Coal.

"That sounds good to me."

"You do promise to be good tonight, don't you? No brawling."

"Darling, it's not like I go out looking for a fight," she answered defensively. "They just seem to find me, especially when alcohol is involved, but I promise to do my best."

"Thanks, honey. I hope we can escape a visit to the emergency room for everyone this weekend and just have a good time."

She couldn't hide the fact that Mary Leah's comment had left her feeling a bit bruised. Instead of answering with a cheeky remark, she stood and stretched. "I'm going over to Melissa's room to get a drink, would you care for anything?"

"A Coke would be nice," she answered.

"I'll be back," she said.

She walked over to Melissa's room and knocked on the door. A few seconds later, Melissa opened the door and welcomed her inside. When she saw the look on Coal's face, she couldn't help but ask, "Is there something wrong? You look a bit perturbed."

Coal took a Coke from the cooler in Melissa's room and flopped down in a chair. "I guess I'm wearing my feelings on my sleeve today. I let an innocent comment Mary Leah made fly all over me."

"What did my sometimes obtuse sister say to upset you?" she teased.

"She sort of implied I go out looking for fights."

"Good grief. She doesn't realize that's the last thing you want to do on a night out?"

Coal shrugged. "I guess not, but a few times we have been in a bar, I did end up in a fight."

"If my memory hasn't totally abandoned me, you fought to defend your family. First it was Lucas and this last time Stormy."

"Yeah, that's right, and I would do it again."

Melissa took a seat next to her. "I have no doubt that you would, and I think it is very honorable. Mary Leah is just wired a little differently than we are, so be patient with her."

"I know she didn't say it to offend me, but it stung coming from her."

"I know it did, honey. I will take the opportunity to educate my sister this weekend, so try not to dwell on it and just have fun."

"I will," Coal said. "Will you save me a dance tonight?"

"Did you bring your steel-toed boots?"

"Nope, but I've been told I'm pretty quick on me feet," she smirked.

"Very well, just don't claim I didn't warn you."

She downed the rest of her drink. "I reckon I should take her drink to her. Thanks, boss."

"Go ahead and take several and put them in your mini fridge," Melissa suggested. "You can still come over if you need a break," she added with a wink.

Taking four cans of Coke, she returned to the room, handing one to Mary Leah and placing the rest in the refrigerator. Mary Leah was sitting in the recliner watching television.

"I think I'll catch a quick nap if that's okay with you?"

"Sure, go ahead. I'll go over to Melissa's so I don't bother you."

"You wouldn't be a bother, but I'm sure she would like some time with you."

"I'll be back to wake you in time to prepare for dinner then," Mary Leah said and kissed Coal before leaving the room.

Coal watched her leave and then dropped the temperature on the air-conditioning unit before stripping down to her underwear and crawling under the covers. The coolness of the crisp sheets against her skin felt wonderful as she snuggled deeper for a nap.

†

Dinner was another great steak dinner, and when they hit the nightclub the crowd was still light. After a few rounds of beer and several dances, the Friday night crowd began to filter in. The all-female crowd was much less rambunctious than the normal crowd at the Stockyard, and much to Mary Leah's delight there wasn't even a threat of a brawl. At ten, they decided to call it a night and go back to the hotel.

Coal noticed that Stormy seemed nervous at the club, and as they walked back into the hotel, she told the others, "Go on up. Stormy and I will be there in a few minutes."

"What's up?" Stormy asked when the elevator doors closed and their friends disappeared.

"I was wondering if the great Stormy Braxton was scared about sleeping with Del for the first time. You seem nervous as a cat on a hot tin roof."

"I just don't want to disappoint Del," she admitted.

"Relax, be gentle, but passionate, and do what you know best. I know you won't disappoint Del."

"I sure hope you're right. I really like Del."

"I think it's pretty obvious she really likes you too. Have fun together and take things as they come."

She looked up at Coal. "Thank you for being such a good friend."

"That works both ways, my friend," Coal said. "Now, let's go see our women."

Stormy pushed the button for the elevator and they rode up to their rooms. "See you in the morning for breakfast," she said as they approached her room.

"If you're not having breakfast in bed," Coal teased, causing her to blush profusely. "Goodnight, Stormy," she said and walked to her room. She slipped the electronic card into the slot and gave Stormy a thumbs-up sign before disappearing into her room.

"What was that all about?" Mary Leah asked.

"Just giving her a little pep talk," Coal said as she began undressing.

"I think Del is really excited to be with her."

"I think they'll both be fine once they relax a bit."

"Yes, I'm sure they will. Are you ready for sleep?"

"Not really," Coal answered.

"Good, come warm me up then."

She smiled and crept between the covers next to her lover.

Chapter Twenty-three

Coal was finishing off her second waffle, covered with peanut butter and syrup, when Stormy and Del entered the breakfast area. A smile plastered on Stormy's face told her that their first night together had gone very well. Del also wearing the same pleased look on her face made her smile as they approached.

"Good morning, ladies," she said as they took seats across from her. "I trust you slept well," she said, failing to resist teasing them just a bit.

"You could say that," Del said as color flared on her cheeks.

"Fantastic. Eat a hearty breakfast. It's going to be a long day. They will cook to order breakfasts for you if you don't want continental."

"I bet their omelets don't hold a candle to yours," Del said.

"Sadly, I can confirm that," Mary Leah spoke up. "It was good, but nothing like Coal's."

Coal smiled at her lover. "Thanks, babe."

"Let's go check their hot bar," Del told Stormy, who stood and followed her like a puppy.

"They seem happy this morning," Melissa said with a grin.

"I'd say love is in the air," Mary Leah said.

"Or at least a strong case of lust," Coal said and was punched in the shoulder by Mary Leah for the crudeness of her comment. "Ouch. Easy there, brute, I'm just being honest, love takes time to grow," she said as she rubbed her shoulder.

"You are such a cupcake," Melissa teased.

"Cupcake, I didn't see any cupcakes up there," she shot back. "I do think I'll have a bacon filled bagel. Can I get you ladies anything?"

"No, I think we are good here," Melissa said.

Del and Stormy had filled their plates and returned to the table when Coal came back. "Oh, those grits look good," she said, setting her bagel on the table and returning for a bowl of grits.

"She did eat supper with us last night, right?" Del asked.

"Yeah, but she worked up an appetite last night," Mary Leah said.

"She's not the only one," Stormy said as she bit into her toast. "I'm starving."

Melissa chuckled. "Should we pack a goody bag for you two for later?"

"That might not be a bad idea," she said with a wink.

✝

When they had finished eating and poured themselves a coffee to go, the group was ready to head out to the Expo Center. Harley, who had been up for hours, was sitting on the tailgate enjoying the early morning when they approached the truck.

"Are we ready to roll?" he asked.

"I think they finally ate their fill," Melissa teased as she tossed him the keys.

"Got to get your money's worth, boss," he teased back.

"I may owe the hotel more after that breakfast," she said as Coal held the door open for her.

"Lucas took the truck to get the horses fed and ready to saddle when we get there," Harley told them.

"I wonder if Gene slept at all last night," Coal said as she climbed in beside Melissa.

"That's doubtful," Harley said. "You know how he is at rodeos. He likes to soak up every story he can from the older riders."

"He's like a kid in a candy shop," Melissa said.

†

It was obvious that Gene wasn't the only one that was excited. When they reached the Expo Center, Coal and Stormy bailed out of the truck quickly to head into the stables. "Let's hang around long enough to wish the girls good luck and then we can go find a seat," Melissa said as they walked to the stables in pursuit of the crew.

Coal and Stormy stopped at the trailer to get their chaps, hats, and tack before walking to the stable to begin saddling up. The barrel-racing event would be the opening event, and both she and Stormy would be competing along with Shelly Brewster.

Coal would also compete in the pole bending competition and then be done until the roping began on Sunday morning. Stormy and the boys would compete in bronc riding and steer wrestling later in the day, after the first rounds of bull riding were complete.

Gene was brushing down his horse when Coal walked into their section of the stables. "Good morning," he said as he rushed out of the stall. "Can I help you get Shadow ready?"

"Sure thing," she answered. "Did you have fun last night?"

"Yeah, I did. Some of these guys have rodeo experience that goes back fifteen years," he said, obviously excited.

"I bet you heard lots of good stories."

Gene took a brush and stroked it across Shadow's back before placing the saddle blanket on his body. "Some of the guys were talking about injuries, and I no longer have any desire to try my hand at bull riding after hearing about the injuries some of them have suffered."

Coal bent down to attach her chaps when she heard Shelly Brewster's high-pitched voice down the aisle. "The wicked witch has arrived," she whispered to Gene, who broke out laughing. "I was hoping she would stay at home since she only qualified for barrels."

"She would never miss an opportunity to perform her beauty queen routine," Gene said with a snicker.

"I know that's right," she said as she placed the bridle over Shadow's head.

"I hope you and Stormy both kick her ass," he said. "Have you drawn for positions yet?"

"No, we decided to saddle up first and then go before warming up."

"Y'all go ahead. Lucas and I will finish up here and meet you at the warm-up ring."

"Thanks." Coal went in search of Stormy. "Let's go pull positions," she said when she found Lucas helping Stormy. "We'll meet the guys at the warm-up ring after."

†

"We're going to pull our positions," Coal told the others. "Then we'll get warmed up and ready to go."

"I think we'll head into the stands then to find some seats. Good luck you two," Melissa said.

"Knock them dead," Harley said and stepped aside with Melissa.

"Good luck, sweetheart," Mary Leah said. "Be safe, ride hard, and win this thing."

"I'll do my best, baby," Coal said. "Ready?" she asked Stormy.

"Just waiting on you," she answered. "See you soon, ladies."

"You can bet on that. Good luck," Del said with a wink to Stormy.

†

Stormy and Coal located the officials' tent and fell in line behind the other competitors for the barrel racing. There were twelve total for the barrel racing, and Shelly was at the head of the line.

"She drives me nuts with her fake personality," Stormy whispered to her.

"I know exactly how you feel," she answered.

They watched as Shelly stepped forward, drew a piece of paper, and then giggled with excitement as she handed the slip to the official. When she turned away, she walked toward Coal and Stormy and stopped in front of them.

"Of course I would draw the first run," she said excitedly.

"Set the bar high for the rest of us then," Stormy said.

"Good luck," Coal added.

"Thanks, you too," Shelly said and sashayed away from the tent.

"Good grief," a rider in front of them said. "She actually made the cut for the competition?"

"She's got a fast horse, but she's a terrible rider," Coal said.

"Gotcha," the woman said and stepped forward in the line.

When they finally reached the table, Stormy pulled the eighth slot and Coal was dead last at twelve. "Well, at least you'll know exactly what you have to run to win," she said.

"That's true," Coal said. "I hate waiting until last though."

Stormy slapped her friend on the back as they began the walk to the warm-up ring, "Patience, my friend."

✝

"What's the verdict?" Gene asked as he handed Coal her reins.

"Stormy is eighth and I pulled twelve, dead last."

"That's good," Gene said. "What did the princess pull?"

Coal chuckled at his reference to Shelly. "The princess runs first, just as she imagined she would."

Lucas laughed and said, "I saw Bubba a few minutes ago. It looks like you did him a real favor. His new teeth look much better."

She flinched at his comment and swung into her saddle. "You are so not right, Lucas," she teased.

"Yeah, I know, but you still love me."

"Yes, I do," she said. "Thanks for getting the horses ready for us."

"You're welcome," they both answered.

"We'll see you at the arena in a few minutes," she said and turned Shadow toward the ring to warm up.

✝

When the overhead speaker announced the start of the barrel racing competition, Stormy pulled up beside Coal. "Let's do this," she said and offered a gloved fist to Coal.

She bumped fists with Stormy. "You better have a fast run today. Shadow's feeling ready to run."

"I could handle placing second to you," she said with a wink. "But only you, so don't let me down," she said as they rode over to the arena.

334

Shelly was doing her normal beauty queen act, smiling and waving at the crowd as the announcer called her name as the first competitor. "She makes me want to gag," she overheard Gene say as they rode next to him and Lucas.

"Be nice, boys," Coal said.

"She makes it hard to be nice with all that fake niceness," Gene said with a growl.

"Let's see if she's finally learned to ride that horse of hers," Coal said as she leaned forward to watch Shelly's performance.

They watched as her horse bolted across the start line toward the first barrel. Coal found herself holding her breath as Shelly's boot hit the barrel, and it tilted precariously, threatening to tumble over. Lucky for her the barrel rocked back into place in the thick sand. She rounded the second barrel wide after rocking the first, losing precious time and raced to the final barrel to complete the cloverleaf. Turning for home, she held tight to the reins and whipped her horse's flanks with a riding crop. The horse would have run much faster if Shelly had given her the chance to lower her head and run naturally. Her time was decent, but she and Stormy both knew it wouldn't hold up as a winning time.

"I hope Shelly's ready to go home," Stormy growled.

The next few riders made their runs and Shelly's time dropped to second and then third before Stormy rode into the arena for her run. They held their breath as they watched her put in a nearly perfect run, a full second ahead of the current leader, dropping Shelly out of the competition.

"Damn, that was a great run," Lucas said as she rode toward them.

"Great job," Coal said. "That was a beautiful run and will be hard to beat."

"You can do it," Gene said with confidence.

"I've seen you two run faster," Stormy said. "Don't leave anything out there in the dirt."

She nodded and rode Shadow toward the arena to wait for their run. "It's up to us, big boy, to show everyone how it's done," she whispered to him as she leaned forward to stroke his neck. Shadow's ears twitched forward at the sound of her voice and his feet danced. He was ready to run.

Coal's heart rate increased as the announcer called her name. "Let's do it," she told Shadow, and they blasted into the arena. The roar of the crowd was lost to Coal as her focus was only on the barrel they were rushing toward. By the time they reached the final barrel, she knew they had a good run going. All they needed to do was make a hard run home. Her left hand reached forward onto Shadow's neck, giving him a free head to run, and run he did. When they crossed the finish line, the crowd noise returned to her ears as they roared at the time Shadow had run. She watched with great pride as her name moved to the top of the list, replacing Stormy's by several hundredths of a second.

Gene, Lucas, and Stormy were hollering as she approached, but her eyes roamed the stands until they fell on Mary Leah's smiling face. One event down, and several to go, but the crew of MC2 had made a terrific start.

"Damn girl, that was fast," Stormy said when she rode up to the crew.

"Thanks. You set the bar high, so it had to be a best run ever to beat you," she said.

"Well done," Stormy said. "Are you going to pull for the pole bending?"

"Yes, that will be coming up soon."

"Go ahead and I'll keep an eye out for Shadow," Gene said.

Stormy joined Coal and they walked to the officials' tent for the second time that morning. "Let's hope I pull an earlier run this time," she said.

She watched as Coal reached into a jar and pulled out a slip of paper.

"Third," she said when she opened the slip.

"That's a good spot. When you finish, you can get Shadow settled in, and we can grab some lunch before the afternoon events start."

"Are you hungry again already?" Coal teased.

"I can always eat," Stormy said.

Coal grinned at her as they walked back to the arena. "I take it last night went well."

Stormy blushed. "Del was fantastic," she said. "I was worried I wouldn't sleep last night, but she wore my ass out."

Coal broke out in a fit of laughter. "I'm so happy for both of you."

"She's a special woman," Stormy said rather dreamily.

"You make a good couple."

"Yeah, I think we do too."

"Treat her right, or I'll kick your butt," she warned.

Stormy chuckled. "I don't think you'd have to. I think Del could do that quite well on her own, but I promise to do my best by her."

"Good," Coal said and wrapped her arm around Stormy's shoulder as they walked.

Melissa looked up first to see their approach, and her smile made Del and Mary Leah turn to see what brought the smile to her face. "There is another Kodak moment," she said as she lifted her camera and snapped off several shots.

"That is a sight for sore eyes. Two handsome women having the time of their lives," Del said.

"We are lucky women indeed," Mary Leah added.

"That we are," Del agreed with a smile.

†

"Welcome back," Melissa said.

"Thanks, boss," Coal said. "I pulled third this go around, and we were just discussing lunch. What do you have in mind?"

337

"My nose has been tempted all morning by the smoker at the end of the arena," Melissa said. "Harley says they are cooking brisket, ribs, and pork shoulders. Are we up for some BBQ?"

"Oh, heck yeah," Stormy said.

"After the pole bending we are free until one, when the steer wrestling starts," she said. "I'll get Shadow settled in after our run, and we can get a head start on the crowd."

"My mouth is watering already," Gene said.

✝

After another flawless run, Coal was in the top spot. Stormy had waited to care for her horse until Coal had finished. Gene and Lucas volunteered to help them out.

"Let's go find a table and order some food," Melissa said. "I thought we would order some of everything."

"Sounds great, we'll be there shortly," Gene said.

Six more riders competed while they were getting the horses settled, and Coal's time was still holding in first place. "Only three more riders to go," Gene said as they stored the tack and walked out of the stables.

"It's looking good that you'll be in the money somewhere," Stormy said as the current rider missed a turn, eliminating her from the competition.

The next rider finished the run, but at a slower time than the top three scores. The last rider entered the arena. Coal held her breath as the horse and rider lurched into action, weaving smoothly between the poles as they walked along the arena toward the food vendors. On the last turn, the horse made a misstep and it slowed him just enough to give them the second-place time.

"It's official, you're two for two," Gene said, giving Coal a high five. "Way to go!"

"Thanks," she said. "It will be your turn this afternoon while I kick back to watch."

†

"Congratulations," Harley said with a slap to Coal's back when they reached a picnic table filled with food and drinks.

"Thanks," she said. "Holy cow, this looks good."

"I don't think anyone will go hungry," Melissa said.

They feasted in the shade of a large oak, finishing off the entire bounty of food. Unbelievably, Gene went in search of the funnel cake vendor for a sweet finish to the meal. When he returned with a mound of fried batter covered in confectioner's sugar, he offered the group a taste.

"I couldn't dream of another bite of anything," Coal said.

"Me either," Stormy chimed in.

"I'll give it a go," Melissa said, and pulled off a small section. "Dear me, this is sweet," she cried when the sugar hit her taste buds.

"I hope we don't see that again after you bronc ride," Harley teased.

"Aw man, Harley, that's disgusting," Gene said and pushed the remainder of the heavenly sweet treat over to him.

"Maybe so, but that worked out quite well for me," Harley teased and took a large bite.

Gene broke out laughing. "I'll get another after I ride."

†

The crew of the MC2 performed well that day, taking first and third place in steer wrestling and saddle bronc, and first and second in bareback.

After the horses were cared for and tack stored for the night Melissa announced she was treating everyone to dinner at the steakhouse they had visited the night before. "We'll be back to pick you up at seven unless you want to go with us now?" she told Gene.

"I could probably use a good shower," he said.

"Come on then, you can use ours," Harley said.

✝

After another hearty meal, the crew retired early. The competition would start early the next morning, and they would check out of the hotel to be ready to head home when the awards ceremony ended.

Coal pulled out her clothes for the next day and packed the rest of her bag before climbing into the bed with Mary Leah. "Today was a great day, thanks for sharing it with me."

"I've had a blast," Mary Leah said. "I had forgotten how fun rodeos can be."

Mary Leah turned on the television to find a movie and when she turned back to ask Coal if the movie was good for her, she found her softly snoring as she slept. Mary Leah kissed the top of her head and snuggled under the covers next to Coal.

✝

Sunday dawned cooler than normal and with ominous clouds growing in the west. After a quick breakfast, they carried their bags out to the truck to head to the Expo. Harley glanced up at the clouds and said, "I sure hope that rain holds off until the rodeo finishes."

"Me too, at least through the roping competition," she said with a grin.

Raindrops pelted the windshield as they pulled out of the hotel. "Will they cancel the events?" Del asked.

340

"Not unless it starts lightning or we go under a tornado warning," Harley said. "It's a good thing the Expo is a covered arena."

"Let's pray that doesn't happen," Coal said. "We need the rain, but not a twister."

"Hopefully you and Gene will pull an early run so we can get packed up and ready to roll."

"I hope so," Coal said as she slumped back on the seat and watched the rain trickle down the glass.

†

Gene met them at the stables. "I've already pulled our run. We have second spot. I hope you don't mind."

"Heaven's no. You did well for us," she said. "How is the arena looking?"

"Dry, thank goodness. If we don't get drowned riding to the entrance, we'll be in good shape."

"We're going to make a dash before it rains any harder and get our seats," Melissa said. "Good luck you two."

"Thanks," Coal and Gene said in unison. "Be careful getting to your seats," Coal added.

"We will," Mary Leah answered.

Lucas and Stormy stayed behind to help them gear up. Gene and Coal pulled on their chaps while Lucas and Stormy got their mounts saddled and ropes attached to their saddles. They stretched and then mounted up. "We still have a few minutes before the event. Let's warm the horses up a bit," she suggested.

Several other teams were also in the arena getting their mounts ready for the competition. When the announcer cleared the arena to start the event, Lucas and Stormy wished them luck and went in search of the rest of the crew.

She sat next to Gene and slipped on her gloves. "You ready to kick up some dirt?" she asked.

"More than ready," he answered. "Why do rodeo weekends always fly by?"

"Because we are having so much fun," she said. "It gives us something to look forward to all summer long while we're sweating our asses off baling hay."

"I know that's right," he agreed. "Honestly, though, Coal, I don't think there's anything else I'd rather do."

"Me either," she said as the announcer called the first team into the arena. "Let's go, we're next."

They rode to the entrance of the arena and double-checked their gear. They watched as the team backed into position and nodded for the steer to release from the chute. They made a good clean run, but the time was not impressive.

"Just like practice," she said to Gene, who shot her a grin.

"Let's do this," he said and led them into the arena.

Coal backed Shadow into position and she could feel his muscles quivering with excitement beneath her as they waited. "Steady, big boy," she soothed as she made her loop and watched as the steer loaded into the chute. She was ready and nodded to Gene.

Gene nodded to the starter and the chute man used a hot rod to send the steer flying out of the chute. The rope barrier released from the steer and they were off in pursuit. Gene's rope landed squarely over the steer's neck and he quickly turned him in position for Coal. She took a slow breath and threw her rope. It landed perfectly, but for a split second, she feared the steer would kick out of her loop before she could snap it tight. Fortunately, her rope snapped around the steer's legs, and she backed Shadow quickly to stretch the steer to end their run.

They looked up at the clock at the same time then rode toward the steer to release the tension and gather their ropes.

It was a good run, but only time would tell if the time would hold up in a money slot.

Gene grinned at her. "Not a bad run," he said as they cantered to the end of the arena.

Melissa watched her crew leave the stands and turned back to see Del watching her. She smiled. "What?"

"You're very proud of them, aren't you?"

"Yes, all of them. Especially Gene and Coal, they've worked really hard on improving this year."

"That seemed like a good run," Del said. "Do you think the time will hold up?"

"We can only hope," Melissa answered. "It was a clean run, so cross your fingers."

✝

Gene and Coal raced across the open field back to the stables, mud splattering them as they rode. They laughed like children playing in a mud puddle, and for a moment, she contemplated making a circuit around the stables just for fun. A loud clap of thunder booming in the distance put a quick halt to that idea and she slipped from Shadow's back as soon as they entered the stables.

Stormy and Lucas entered the stables moments later. "Harley's going to pull the trailer as close as he can so we can get loaded without getting soaked," Lucas told them. "Horses first and then we can get the tack stored away," he said.

Stormy started to remove the saddle from Shadow's back, slipping his bridle off and replacing it with his halter and lead. "You did good, big boy," she said as she stroked down his face. "Has anyone heard anything on this weather?"

"Harley said it was going to be mostly heavy rains and some winds, but no tornado cells are in the area yet," she told her. "I think he's anxious to get the horses on the road before it worsens."

"That's not a bad idea, I'll see if he wants me to ride with him," Coal said.

"You stay and I'll go with him," Stormy said.

"You and Gene can collect our winnings," Lucas added. "Stormy and I can help Harley."

"Are you sure that's what you want to do?" Coal asked.

"Yes, just tell Del what's going on, and I'll see her when y'all get home."

"Are we ready to load up?" Harley said, wiping the rain from his arms.

"Yes, we are. Lucas and Stormy are going to ride with you back to the MC2," she said.

"Good, you can drive in this mess. Your eyes have to be better than mine," Harley said and tossed the keys to Lucas.

Lucas snatched the keys out of the air. "No problem," he said and led his horse to the open trailer.

Several minutes later, they were soaked to the bone, but the horses and tack were safely stored. "Hop in and we'll drop you as close to the arena as we can," Harley said.

When they arrived at the entrance to the arena, Lucas pulled the truck to a stop. "Hopefully we won't be too far behind you," Coal said. "I'm hoping they will skip the closing ceremonies to allow everyone to get a start for home."

"I hope you're right. Some of these folks have a long way to travel today," Harley said.

"Drive safe, and we'll see you soon," Coal said. Then she and Gene made a dash for cover.

They turned to watch Lucas pull away then stepped inside to find the others.

✝

Melissa saw Gene and Coal enter and waved to them. "I wonder where the others are?" she asked aloud.

Gene followed Coal into the stands. Del frowned as they approached, but refrained from saying anything. "Harley, Lucas, and Stormy are driving the horses back to beat the worst of the weather, or at least they are hoping," she explained. She took a seat next to Del. "Stormy said she would she see you when we return."

"That's fine," she answered, but it was obvious she was disappointed.

When the roping events concluded, the officials announced their decision to cancel the closing ceremonies to allow the crowd to travel home safely. They requested winners visit the official tent to pick up their winnings and trophies.

"Now we're talking," Gene said. "Let's grab the goodies and go home."

When they reached the tent, she and Gene picked up their winnings and Del collected for Stormy. Melissa was surprised when an official tapped her on the shoulder and handed her a large trophy.

"Congratulations, Mrs. Conway, your team won Top Cowboy honors," he said and handed her a check for five hundred dollars.

"Oh, my goodness," Melissa said as she hefted the trophy. "I had no idea."

"This will look great in your den," Mary Leah said.

"Yes, it will," she said with a smile. "Let's go home." She handed the trophy to Gene.

Chapter Twenty-four

The heavy rains had followed them home. When they pulled up to the house, Harley sent Lucas and Stormy out to greet them with umbrellas and bring them to the bunkhouse. They had been busy preparing a meal after they had the stock settled.

"Something smells wonderful," Melissa said as they stepped inside.

"Pot roast and biscuits, but it's hot and hearty," Harley said.

"Sounds wonderful," Melissa said.

Del handed Stormy the checks from her winnings and Coal passed checks to Lucas.

"We also had a pleasant surprise," Melissa said. "We won Top Cowboy, a large trophy, and a five-hundred-dollar check."

"All right!" Lucas and Stormy shouted.

"Congratulations everyone," Harley said.

"This is a team win and you are all a part of it," Melissa said. "I'll deposit the check, but it will be up to you to decide how to spend it."

"I think that's an easy decision," Coal said. "Put it toward next year's rodeo expenses. It can't be easy paying for the travel expenses."

"No, but you guys deserve it for the hard work you do all year," Melissa said. "It's the least I can do for you."

"We all have our winnings," Coal was quick to remind her.

"She's right. Please save this for next year," Gene said.

Melissa smiled. "Consider it done then. Now let's eat, I'm hungry."

†

The rain finally let up and the women took advantage of the break to make a dash for the house. Gene carried the trophy and placed it in the den for Melissa.

"Will you do me a favor before you head back?" Mary Leah asked him.

"Sure thing, what can I do for you?"

"Bring in the two packages I have in my backseat, please."

"I'll be right back," Gene said and sprinted out of the house.

"What are you up to?" Melissa asked.

"You'll see in just a minute," Mary Leah said as Gene returned with the packages.

"Here you go," he said and placed them next to Mary Leah.

"Hand one to Del and the other is for Melissa," she said.

Gene delivered the packages as requested and sat beside Coal.

"I bet you two thought I forgot," Mary Leah said. "Go ahead and open them."

Coal looked at Stormy, who was just as confused, and shrugged her shoulders.

Melissa and Del took their packages and took a seat on the sofa as the others looked on. Melissa unwrapped hers first, revealing a framed photograph.

"Would you look at that," she said, amazed. "It came out great." She turned the frame around to show Coal and Stormy.

The photograph was of her and Stormy as they walked together leading the horses behind them with the caption at the bottom, which read, 'Cowgirls Do It in the Dirt.'

"When did you take this?" she asked Mary Leah.

"They last time y'all practiced," she answered. "Before you ask, we have a copy also."

"That is really something," Stormy said as she looked at Del's copy.

"Thank you, my love," Coal said as she bent down and kissed Mary Leah.

"Cowgirls do it in the dirt," Stormy said. "Hell yeah, we do."

This is only the beginning.

About the Author

Ali Spooner

Ali Spooner is a native of Florida, currently living and working in Memphis, TN. Home for Ali is Pensacola, Florida where she has a partner of twenty years, one son and a grandchild that has her wrapped completely around her little finger. Her other children are all four legged, three dogs and two cats, and her dearest companion in Memphis, Rascal, a rescued tiger kitten named after her favorite country group.

A true daughter of the South, Ali enjoys spinning stories about the South, the strong, but gentle women and creatures that make it a wondrous place to live.

As an "Indie" author, Ali has been writing for many years as a hobby, and after a cancer diagnosis in 2010, she decided to take a leap and start self-publishing and has published over a dozen stories. Ali's characters range from cowgirls and psychics, to a healthy dose of supernatural beings. She has written stand-alone titles and series. Ali frequently writes several stories at a time, depending on which characters are bouncing around loudest in her head.

Ali is an avid reader and her other hobbies include photography, outdoor activities and watching college sports.

Other Books from Affinity eBook Press

The Chronicles of Ratha: Book 1 Children of the Noorthi— Erica Lawson Jordana Laren is a hard-drinking, hard-fighting womanizer, who works as a freighter pilot in her spare time. Her latest customer drugs her, steals her ship, and abandons her on a desert hellhole called Rigeus, infamous penal planet for the worst women criminals. Her chances of survival aren't looking good. She has no food, water, or weapons, and the nearest bar is a million miles away. Just when she's ready to write her last will and testament, Jordana is rescued by a group of barely-clad women. Has she found nirvana? Her own personal harem seems like a possibility, until the intercession of their enemy, the Velkren. Their leader, Vel, remembers Jordana well, and not fondly. But why is Vel on this planet, surrounded by murderers, thieves, and bad-tempered bitches? Jordana knows Vel isn't a prisoner, so why is her nemesis on Rigeus mining mud, of all things? Jordana knows only one thing. She has to get off the planet before Vel kills her. Unfortunately, the women who saved her reveal themselves to be holy. They are the Noorthi, and Jordana's dream of endless debauchery becomes a nightmare of eternal servitude. The Noorthi make her one of them, marking her with a wrist tattoo, and leaving her no choice but to protect them with her life. The last thing Jordana wants is to become involved in galactic politics or heroic actions. But the tattoo ochre in her body is suddenly giving her morals and scruples, not to mention a better vocabulary! And she really can't pass up a chance to outwit Vel, whose megalomaniac plans are endangering not only the Noorthi, but the civilized galaxy itself. But Jordana is torn. Does she stop Vel at all costs, or does she get out from under the thumb of the Noorthi while she can? Some things were never meant to be easy…

If I Were a Boy—Erin O'Reilly Katie McGuire appears to have it all. A devoted husband, a job she loved, and a comfortable lifestyle. Helen Swenson is a successful financial director of a prominent investment firm, with an unfaithful husband, and few friends. Their husband's annual trip to Padre Island National Seashore to reunite with their air force pilot squad becomes a pivotal point for the two women. Their lives take on a completely new meaning when an undeniable magnetism between them draws them together. Passion and secrecy becomes the norm, as they have no choice but to succumb to their attraction. Can the vacation love affair continue? When they leave for their respective homes, will they regret what happened? Life is not that easy to change and the people around them are the hardest to convince. There is no more powerful motivation than love. Except hate and there are plenty of people who want to see their relationship destroyed. Will Katie and Helen be able to make a life together work or succumb to doubts and the pressures of family? This story will fill you with the thrill of passion and the tenderness of love.

Nesting—Renee MacKenzie Macy Stokes, a divorced mother who is struggling with her sexual identity, jumps at a once-in-a-lifetime opportunity to help her friends. She doesn't foresee it will put her in jeopardy of losing her son, Jeremiah. Fresh out of high school, Cam Webber travels to Augusta, Georgia, to reconcile with her aunt. When she learns that's impossible, she determines to gain acceptance from her aunt's partner, Sharon. Meanwhile, Cam sets her sights on Macy, but Macy has other ideas. Kenny Brewer is a good old boy who loves his wife, Dorianne, even when he thinks she's gone totally off her rocker. Dorianne gets it in her head that a local woman is her long-lost half-sister. But soon, her obsession with that is eclipsed by medical problems that involve them all. Set in Augusta, Georgia, *Nesting* explores the age-old issues of guilt, regret, and redemption, and the part they play in driving people to create and protect family-at any cost.

Reece's Faith—TJ Vertigo In the return of the main characters from the bestselling novel *Private Dancer*, we see the blossoming relationship of bar owner, Reece Corbett and actress, Faith Ashford. The two women explore new, uncertain territory together, using sexual intimacy as a glue of comfort, helping them become strong and whole. A trusting Reece shares with Faith the sordid tale of how she became *The Animal* and Faith finds herself newly empowered by Reece's ongoing trust and support. Jealousy arises when Faith has to kiss a man on her TV show and two amorous women stalk Reece. When Faith is outed on her television show, things get crazy. With the arrival of her parents on the scene, the craziness escalates. As Faith tries to justify her lifestyle and defend her love for Reece, she discovers that nothing about her parents is as she once believed. This, not to be missed passionate and erotic romance, will have you begging for more.

Starting Over—Jen Silver Ellie Winters, a successful potter, is living on a remote hilltop farm inherited from her parents. Her well-ordered life is shaken apart when her past meets her present. Robin Fanshawe, Ellie's philandering long-term lover, has a fragile truce with Ellie. The arrival of women from Robin's present threatens to break that tentative pact. Charming Dr. Kathryn Moss, an archaeologist and an old lover of Ellie's, arrives on the farm searching for a new site to dig. When she discovers a previously unknown Roman settlement and ancient burial site on Ellie's farm, Ellie allows her to start an archaeological dig of the area. Will Ellie also allow the rekindling of an old romance or will she stay with Robin? Can that long term relationship, albeit tentative, recover from this collision or will an old romance trump everything she knows? Will Robin, seeing the interaction between Ellie and Kathryn, leave her womanising ways behind? Will she take a chance on giving herself wholly to the woman she loves? These questions and the mystery of whose royal resting place is disturbed at Starling Hill are answered in this classic romance of simmering passions, anguished loss, and the wonder of love.

Twisted Lives—Ali Spooner A twist of fate leaves Bet and her daughter Kylie stranded at the entrance of the home of Alex Graves, as she flees the control of an abusive husband. When custom–homebuilder Alex arrives to find steam boiling from Bet's car and a beautiful child asleep in the passenger seat, her heart goes out to them. Alex offers shelter to the pair setting off a chain of events that bring both mother and daughter close to her heart and danger to her door. A heartwarming story of true love that will keep you smiling long after you've finished the book.

Malodorous—Del Robertson Sequel to My Fair Maiden Something in Fairhaven stinks. Other than the mutton stew, that is. Gwen thought life after being a virgin sacrifice would be a bed of roses. Bodhi was just looking for a wench to bed. Neither less-than-dashing hero nor not-quite-so-pure maiden imagined they would meet again, much less be trapped together in a city the likes of the ill-named Fairhaven. There's a killer on the loose. Fairhaven's on lockdown, its citizens fearful for their lives. The local guards are corrupt. And, Bodhi's been accused of murder…

Desert Blooms—Dannie Marsden Luce's story continues in DESERT BLOOMS… When we last met Luce Velazquez in Desert Heat, she went through hell and back to salvage her soul and reputation. Hoping to get her life back on track with lover Beth Ryan, a woman who understands her pain and can relate on every level. Instead, Luce is in the hospital, and Beth in protective custody. Jessica Sullivan, Luce's friend and ex, has big doubts about the sincerity of Beth's love, and is in no hurry to release her from custody. Can Luce's new found happiness last, or is Jessica correct in her doubts? A heart stopping romance that will fill you with the wonder of friendship, anger of betrayal, and the everlasting vision of love.

Finding Her Way—Riley Jefferson Is it love or just great sex? After ending an abusive marriage, Jerrica Kerrison is finally alive and she's apologizing for nothing! She has a job with a financial firm in Boston, a townhouse in Newburyport, and a sports car she drives way too fast. Jerrica has everything except that indefinable emotion called love. Madison Jeffrey is a lost soul. A PR job in the south has always protected Madison from the pressures of her family. But one day, fate brings her back to New England, forcing Madison to face her long buried demons, and a sister who despises her. When a chance meeting brings Jerrica and Madison's separate worlds crashing together, the attraction is instantaneous. After one passionate night together, Jerrica retreats into the safety of her world, leaving Madison to figure out what happened. Will Jerrica open up her heart to the idea of love? Can Madison finally believe that she is worthy of unconditional love? Or will a devil hiding in the shadows tear them apart?

HER—Lisa Ron Fox has been looking for that one person who will make her feel complete-her perfect match. Together with her friends, Megan and Tree, Fox continues her quest while dodging exes and clingers, laughing a lot along the way. When she meets Madeline, she instantly knows that she has found HER. Madeline has her own problems-notably a domineering husband. Can Fox win her heart? Can they make a life together? This story will make you laugh, cry, and hold your breath as the story unfolds. With the right person love can conquer all.

Bayou Justice—Ali Spooner Hell hath no fury like a woman scorned. When Kara, Sasha's new lover is taken hostage as a diversionary tactic to allow the drug dealing Bellfontaine brothers to escape justice, Sasha springs into action. Kara is released physically unharmed, however her emotions and budding career in the District Attorney's office are left in shambles when she is held to blame for their release, Appalled by the failure of the criminal justice system, Sasha exacts her own brand of justice for the acts committed against her lover. From the Bayous of Louisiana to the jungles of South America, Sasha plots her revenge.

Out of Retirement—Erica Lawson Melanie Stokes was a doctor—a very good one, or so she hoped. She was calm and cool under pressure, and very little fazed her. Until…Caitlin Joseph ran a small retirement home for older women in need. The fact that everyone in the house was gay was a coincidence, although it did cut down the number of women agreeing to live there. Mel took up an offer to do some relief work for a local community center when their regular doctor was away on holidays. As soon as she arrived at the home she knew something was different about the place. Was it the little old lady chasing the paper boy down the street or the sign saying "Dykes Retirement Home"? But there was something about the place that also appealed to her. Sure, Caitlin was cute as a button, but it was more the fact that she took very good care of her charges despite their rather bizarre behavior. The older women seized the opportunity to introduce a woman into Caitlin's lonely life, using any means possible to keep Mel coming back. Their plans were boosted by the introduction of another woman into the house, who set hearts a fluttering and blood pressure rising. Now if she was a lesbian it would have been perfect...

Letting Go—JM Dragon   A failed relationship puts Stella Hawke's life on the brink of chaos. When her grandmother falls gravely ill in Ashville, Stella ends her army career to take care of the woman during her last weeks. Little does she know that an old army comrade, socialite Reggie Stockton, whose family owns the local newspaper, also lives in Ashville. Will she allow herself to accept Reggie's help to turn her life around and let go of the past? This is a journey where both women re-evaluate what they want out of life. Will that path lead to happiness or to a parting of the ways?

Through the Darkness—Erin O'Reilly   Becca Cameron is a loner—by choice. She lives in a hundred year old farmhouse built by her great grandfather. A tragic accident in her home a year earlier drove away her lover, and Becca tries to accept what she cannot change and hang on to the belief that love can conquer all. Chase Hunter had a meteoric rise in the Eastman Corporation and was, at thirty-four, the youngest vice-president. To Chase, her work was all consuming leaving little time for friends or lovers. There was simply no place in her life for anything but her job.

When Becca and Chase meet at their work place, the attraction is spontaneous. Life begins to look brighter for both women as work takes a second seat to romance. Unknown to either woman, someone is watching their every move… Will passion outweigh doubt? Can love conqueror fear?

Beginning of the End—Alane Hotchkin What happens when life doesn't go exactly as you planned and you must protect others from your own fate? Escaping a horrific childhood, Nikki longed to find happily ever after in adulthood. What she found was Hell. Or did it find her? Finding the courage to break the cycle of betrayal, she opens her heart one last time. Alex lived a childhood others dreamed of. Her father never once denied the young rebel a thing. All her life she dreamed of protecting others; to follow in her father's footsteps. Soon though she learned sex and fists made the most powerful of weapons. Alex controls the women in her life through fear and sex, will breaking the cycle be too much to overcome? Will loving Nikki be enough to change her, or is Alex beyond help? Alex would give Nikki the world, but at what price? When a person's tightly controlled reality snaps, what then…? This is the Beginning of the End for one of them and the ultimate sacrifice for the other. But who is who in this game of life?

Galveston 1900: Swept Away—Linda Crist On September 7-8, 1900, the island of Galveston, Texas, was destroyed by a hurricane, or 'tropical cyclone' as it was called in those days. This story is a fictional account of Mattie and Rachel, two women who lived there, and their lives during the time of the 'great storm'. Forced to flee from her family at a young age, Rachel Travis finds a home and livelihood on the island of Galveston. Independent, friendly, and yet often lonely, only one other person knows the dark secret that haunts her. Madeline "Mattie" Crockett is trapped in a loveless marriage, convinced that her fate is sealed. She never dares to dream of true happiness, until Rachel Travis comes walking into her life. As emotions come to light, the storm of Mattie's marriage converges with the very real hurricane. Can they survive, and build the life they both dream of? This second edition of one of Linda Crist's best-loved novels maintains the original story, while incorporating some reader-pleasing passages that were cut from the first edition. As an added bonus, the short story "Something to Celebrate" is included at the end of the novel, detailing further adventures of Rachel and Mattie.

Rapture: Sins of the Sinners—A. C. Henley & Fran Heckrotte A serial killer is targeting young lesbians throughout the state of Texas. Texas Ranger Cochetta Lovejoy is assigned to the case. Convinced she knows who is committing the murders, Ranger Lovejoy is willing to do whatever it takes to put the perpetrator behind bars--even if it means stretching the limits of the law by manipulating the judicial system. Detective Agnes Kelly-Elliott is one of Ft. Worth Police Department's finest investigators. When Ranger Lovejoy appears on the crime scene of a recent murder, Agnes fears a dark secret that, if revealed, could destroy her family ties and end her career. This is a dark, gritty, graphic tale of desire gone awry, and flawed characters looking for redemption in all the wrong places.

Absolution—S. Anne Gardner Games of the rich and famous, love, lust, and forbidden passions weave this tale that play out through decades and the world. The close ties the Alcalas have to the royal house of Spain provide them with an unspoken untouchable policy. Their passions and their secrets are about to come to light with a force that cannot be stopped. In this whirlwind is Cristina Uraca Alacala who is searching for a truth that has been denied to her most of her life and she must find. She is not unlike her family; Cristina does not stop until she gets what she wants. In the fog lies the truth that she must travel through to find. In this tale wealthy socialite Annais Francesca D'Autremond is a pivotal person of interest in Cristina's search for the truth. When these two women meet they find themselves drawn together by something greater than themselves. As the truth of a hidden past becomes clearer their passions grow beyond the realm of the no return instead of a status quo. Both tied together by destiny; will both survive the onslaught of past and present passions?

Denial—Jackie Kennedy   Time spent in Somalia has Doctor Celeste Cameron accustomed to living and working in a war zone. Coming back home to America, Celeste is glad to see the end of the peril she has been in—or so she thinks. Danger seems to follow Celeste and she finds it in the shape of Amy. What Celeste feels for Amy scares her more than anything she has faced in war zones. Amy has the same feelings, but is in denial and vows to marry Josh, Celeste's twin brother, no matter what. When fate brings them together again, will they give in to their mutual attraction or will they once again deny what they feel?

Taming the Wolff—Del Robertson   ONLY ONE WOMAN... As devastatingly beautiful as she is headstrong, noble-born Alexis DeVale abruptly finds her preordained life in upheaval. Abducted at sword-point, held for ransom, thrust into a maelstrom of lawlessness and piracy... HAS THE POWER... The strength of her passion, the depth of her love... TO TAME THE WOLFF... Mayhem. Brutality. Murder. These are the tools of the trade - and Kris Wolff is the master of her profession. Captain of the high seas, a roguish pirate, her heart hardened by life, her passion tightly controlled by the secret she's forced to keep. Faced with a new danger, The Wolff finds herself unable to guard her heart from the tumultuous desires that Alexis DeVale has awakened.

Private Dancer—TJ Vertigo   Reece Corbett grew up on the mean streets on New York City, abused, used and in trouble with the law. Faith Ashford grew up wealthy, with all the creature comforts that money provides. When they meet fireworks begin.

Miriam and Esther—Sherry Barker   Miriam thought her life would play out in the bustling metropolis of Dallas, but after a life-changing accident, she moves to the small town of Cool Lake, Texas to get her head on straight and regain her senses.

E-Books, Print, Free e-books

Visit our website for more publications available online.

www.affinityebooks.com

Published by Affinity E-Book Press NZ LTD
Canterbury, New Zealand

Registered Company 2517228